BROODING REBEL TO BABY DADDY

ALLY BLAKE

HIS PLAN FOR THE QUINTUPLETS

CATHY GILLEN THACKER

MILLS & BOON

First Published in Great Britain 2020
by Mills & Boon, an imprint of HarperCollinsPublishers,
1 London Bridge Street, London, SE1 9GF

Brooding Rebel to Baby Daddy © 2020 Ally Blake
His Plan for the Quintuplets © 2020 Cathy Gillen Thacker

ISBN: 978-0-263-27888-0

0720

Printed and bound in Spain
by CPI, Barcelona

BROODING
REBEL TO
BABY DADDY

ALLY BLAKE

To my bright, beautiful, bumptious babies
and *their* baby daddy, for living with my distracted
brain, boxes of books and weird working hours,
and accepting that that's just me.

Australian author **Ally Blake** loves reading and strong coffee, porch swings and dappled sunshine, beautiful notebooks and soft, dark pencils. Her inquisitive, rambunctious, spectacular children are an exquisite delight, and she adores writing love stories so much she'd write them even if nobody read them. No wonder, then, having sold over four million copies of her romance novels worldwide, Ally is living her bliss. Find out more about Ally's books at allyblake.com

Cathy Gillen Thacker is a married mother of three. She and her husband reside in North Carolina. Her stories have made numerous appearances on bestseller lists, but her best reward is knowing one of her books made someone's day a little brighter. A popular Mills & Boon author, she loves telling passionate stories with happy endings and thinks nothing beats a good romance and a hot cup of tea! Visit her at cathygillenthacker.com for information on her books, recipes and a list of her favourite things.

Discover more at millsandboon.co.uk

CHAPTER ONE

IT WAS CHILLY in the high-country town of Radiance, Victoria, the day Sable Sutton returned. A damp, grey wash coated the countryside like a filter, but the air was as sweet and sharp as a green apple on the verge of ripening.

It was about as different as it could be from the squinty Los Angeles sunshine and bone-dry Santa Ana winds Sable had left behind.

She shivered as she stood by the wonky front gate. Vintage men's jacket rolled at the cuffs, light silk shirt and ripped jeans doing little to keep out the icy air, as her gaze skipped over the veil of sodden autumn leaves covering the overgrown path leading to the shrouded house beyond.

The trees had grown in since she'd been away, crowding the pitched roof, the dark gables, the arched windows, making it look even more like the Gingerbread House the local kids had called it. Not only because of its fairy-tale appearance, but due to the witch they believed lived inside.

The witch being Mercy Sutton, Sable's own mother. Drier of herbs. Maker of potions. Scowler at children. Spurner of public displays of affection. Private ones too.

Sable flinched as her left butt cheek twitched, but it was *not* her mother, poking her with a metaphorical stick through the bars of her cage, demanding to know why she'd come back.

It was her phone buzzing in her jeans pocket. A long message from her agent, Nancy, promising work, soon. Photography jobs on the horizon after no doubt calling in every favour owed to give her pariah of a client a way back in. Only then did she ask where on earth Sable was. Though

Nancy barely acknowledged there was a world outside New York, so Sable had no clue how to explain Radiance.

The stiletto heel of Sable's ankle boot scuffed the ground, the scrape unsettling a crow who lifted into the air with an offended *Ark!* and a flapping of wings. She watched it fly over the trees towards the neighbour's place.

The Thorne place.

Rafe Thorne.

Her heart twinged, the way it always had when the boy next door winked into her subconscious. Though for someone whose emotions had always run close to the surface, she'd done a pretty fair job of shutting all that down over the years, the twinges *and* the winks.

No use musing over brooding eyes the colour of scorched earth, when they were on the other side of the planet. Same went for wild dark curls. Fingernails permanently stained from the hours spent under the bonnet of some broken-down car or another. Body tough, lean and wiry. Yellowed leaves shifting beneath heavy boots as he chopped wood. Sweat glistening on his strong arms. Brow furrowed in endearing concentration…

Sable blinked herself back to the present to find her heart not only twinging, but now skittering, and performing some pretty spectacular thumpity thumps.

For the wood chopping was the last true memory she had of Rafe—nineteen years old and smouldering—the day before she'd skipped town without saying goodbye.

She let out a hard, fast breath, and gave herself an all over body shake.

Her heart had been through the wringer of late and was not in any shape to twinge. Or skitter. And *especially* thump. Besides, that was not why she'd come back to Radiance.

When a person's life unravelled, as swiftly, relentlessly,

and mortifyingly publicly as Sable's had just done, once the dust settled it brought with it a sense of clarity.

Her epiphany? Her meteoric success as a photographer, the notoriety that came from dating someone even more well known than she, and the creature comforts that had come with all that had clouded things for a good while.

When it had all been stripped away, she'd been left to figure out who she was without those safety nets. What she wanted.

And what she wanted most hadn't changed. Not since she was a teenager, traipsing barefoot through the forest surrounding this small town, ancient camera in hand, mooning after the local bad boy, imagining a softly filtered version of what her life might one day look like.

Deep down, she wanted nothing more than to be someone's mother.

So here she was. Back in Radiance. The place she now saw as the crossroads of her life. Where, if she'd taken a left, instead of a right, things might have turned out very differently.

Too jet-lagged to face her mother, Sable turned away from the Gingerbread House, and gripped the handle of her suitcase, dragging it over the bumpy cracks in the footpath, and made her way next door.

Only once the overgrown forest came to an abrupt end at her mother's fence line, she stopped so suddenly her suitcase bumped against the back of her boots.

"What on earth—?" The mist in the air all but swallowed her words.

For instead of overgrown grass, sad patches of dirt, tangles of blackberry bushes, husks of old cars and farm machinery, there lay acres of lush green grass, a few goats, a cow or two, and a plethora of happy chickens. For a second she wondered if her terrible sense of direction had failed her yet again, and the Thorne place had been over the other fence.

But no. There was the tree that had once shaded a darkly foreboding pile of wood in the shape of a house. Only now it draped over a gleaming Airstream caravan, shining like a silver dollar against the distant backdrop of the fiery poplar, maple, and liquid-amber-covered foothills leading up to the peak of Mount Splendour—more of a big hill, really—that overlooked the whole of Radiance.

She'd not expected life to have been put on hold when she'd left, but how had *this* not come up during one of Mercy's rare, uncomfortable phone calls? Something along the lines of, *Oh, and by the way, the Thorne house burned down/fell down/was taken up by aliens.*

Then Sable spotted a window slowly closing at the side of the van. Meaning someone was home.

Twinge.

Was it Rafe's father, the fearsome Mr Thorne? Or could it be Rafe himself?

Skitter. Thump.

Was Rafe even *in* Radiance any more? Her mother's news reports were clearly lacking.

Only one way to find out.

Luggage bumping along behind her, Sable strode down the compacted dirt driveway, around the dam—its golden-brown water a reflection of the cloudy autumn sky—and up to the front door of the shiny Airstream.

She lifted a hand and knocked. Her heart thumping so hard she could now feel it in her throat.

After a few long moments, the door swung open, nearly hitting Sable in the nose. And a lanky dark-haired young woman blinked back at her.

For a snapshot in time Sable imagined it might be Rafe's girlfriend. Or wife. Even while her stomach rolled at the thought, like a ball of wool tumbling over the edge of a cliff, she reminded herself she'd been prepared for the possibility.

And that it didn't change anything. Not for her.

For it wasn't Rafe's heart she was after. Not that he'd ever look at her that way again after the way she'd left. As for her heart? Bruised, shaken, and shamed by recent events, it was in recovery and would be for some time.

The young woman's eyes rounded comically. "Sable Sutton? Oh, my gosh! It's you! It's really you!"

A heartbeat later, Sable's synapses came back online and she realised it was—

"Janie?"

Rafe's younger sister had been a little kid when Sable had left. Not even ten. Now a grown woman, she threw herself at Sable, wiry arms wrapping her up tight. Tighter than she'd been hugged in years. Which made her bruised and shaken heart cough and splutter, like an old engine trying—and failing—to catch.

Sable gently extricated herself from the hug.

"Look at *you*," said Janie, eyes skipping over Sable as if she thought she might disappear in a puff of smoke at any second. "Still the wild-haired wood elf I always thought you were, but with an edge. Yep, it's official. You're even more ridiculously cool in person than you are in your feeds!"

Sable somehow kept her next breaths even.

She'd prepared herself for the possibility that some locals might have found her online. It wouldn't have been all that hard. The photography contest she'd won, and the prize—a year in New York with a place to live, a guaranteed gallery show and a top agent—had been a big deal. But it was her move to LA after that was all said and done, her connection with a certain well-known TV chef, and the recent blistering disintegration of said connection that had made her life the stuff of social media heaven.

"Thank you," Sable managed. "But I've never been close to cool my entire life. And the social media stuff? My publicist—" *well, not hers, her ex's* "—put most of that together. Ninety-nine per cent of it isn't *really* real."

Ha! laughed her subconscious. If only *she'd* figured that out years ago.

"Do not deny me my fervour," said Janie. "You're the most famous thing ever to have come from this place. Apart from Carleen McGlinty, of course. But she's locally famous. And only during the Pumpkin Festival."

"Carleen. Isn't she the one who—?"

"Runs naked through town after imbibing too much pumpkin spice wine? The very one."

So, some things hadn't changed.

Janie followed Sable's not so surreptitious glance over her shoulder into the belly of the caravan, then gave her a look—direct and calculating—that was so very Rafe, Sable's heart tripped and tumbled so hard she winced.

Janie said, "So, it's *not* me you've come to see after all these years, fancy suitcase in hand. Big shock."

Sable glanced down at the hand now white-knuckling her luggage handle and released her fingers one by one. "Is he... *Is* Rafe around?"

Janie shook her head and Sable's heart dropped.

Till Janie seemed to soften, just a smidge, before saying, "He's in town, I think."

Sable's heart jumped. If she didn't get control over the thing, and soon, she was going to do herself a damage.

"I can call him," said Janie. "Let him know you've arrived—"

Sable reached out a staying hand. "Don't. Please."

"No? Then I take it my big brother has no clue you're back. How interesting. Do you think he'll be delighted? Or will he cut and run?" Janie clicked her fingers. "Right, no, that's your move."

Sable flinched.

She hadn't expected her return to be easy. But then neither should it be. The things that had come her way without effort had disintegrated just as swiftly.

Janie flapped a hand her way. "I'm just messing with you. I honestly have no clue how he'll react. But, oh, to be a fly on the wall!"

No flies would suit Sable best. Or witnesses of any kind.

Being a person of interest in LA was bizarre. Strangers butted into her conversations at lunch. Posted pictures of her walking, talking, eating. They direct messaged from the safety of their phones with questions, suggestions, professions of love and outright vitriol because to them she was a construct.

But being a person of interest in a small town was a different kind of hell. They talked about her right in front of her. About her mother, about Sable's ragged clothes, about her connection with the Thorne boy. It had been harder because they *did* know her.

Which was why—when all this was said and done—she'd find a place big enough to disappear, where nobody knew her name. Nobody knew her business. A place she could live freely, where any decisions she made would be hers alone.

"I'd better head home," Sable said.

After a beat, Janie looked at her suitcase and said, "So this was your first stop? Interesting. Very interesting. Don't be a stranger!" With that Janie gave her a wave before heading back indoors.

Leaving Sable to stare at the closed door.

Well, she'd just jumped the first hurdle of her return to Radiance without tripping and falling on her face, which after the past few months was a huge win.

Sable headed back up the dirt path. Her stiletto heels

sinking into the packed dirt of the driveway. And for the first time since she'd stepped off the plane, Sable felt herself fully breathe out.

Rafe's backside hadn't even hit the stool at the counter when Bear—owner of The Coffee Shop on Laurel Avenue, Radiance's main street—said, "Did you hear the news around town?"

Rafe sat. Grabbed a napkin to wipe his already clean hands, a habit built on years of living beneath the bonnet of a car. Ordered coffee. And waited for Bear to go on.

For there was no stopping the spread of news in Radiance, whether you wanted to or not.

Bear was big, bearded and gruff, like a Hollywood biker. His eyes gleamed as he slid a glossy long black and a small jug of milk over the counter and, in his rusty baritone, announced, "She's back."

Napkin balled up ready to toss into the bin behind the counter, Rafe's hand stilled mid-air. Only one person he knew of from around these parts who would garner that level of ominous expectation.

Rafe tossed the napkin into the bin, damned delighted it didn't miss. As if not appearing jarred meant he wasn't. To push the point home, he lifted off his seat, pilfered a doughnut from the glass case on the bench, put the lid back into place. Took a bite. Chewed slowly.

And said nothing.

Bear, looking fit to burst, boomed, "It's Sable freaking Sutton! You know—the Aussie photographer. Used to live around these parts, before my time. Dates what's-his-name—the ice-cool chef from that TV show. Though, hang on, that all went kaboom a couple of months back. Affairs…plural. Can't remember who strayed. Scandalous stuff though."

Rafe didn't as much as blink.

"Come on," Bear protested. "You know who I mean, right? Even if you're not a photography buff. Blonde? Wild-eyed? Bohemian beauty?"

Rafe poured in a dash of milk, cupped the black glass in his palms, took a long leisurely sip of the steaming hot brew and gave the guy nothing.

Bear muttered about the sincere lack of pop culture knowledge from the straight men in this town.

Leaving Rafe to brood over the fact he hadn't known she was back. A scent on the wind, a rustle of leaves, a ripple in the space-time continuum—surely something ought to have alerted him.

Unless enough time had passed that ripples, where she was concerned, were no longer his to feel.

Bear cleaned the froth spout on his big coffee maker as he said, "Trudy saw her get off the bus from Melbourne not two hours ago, dragging a big fancy suitcase behind her. Story goes, she was heading towards your place."

That had Rafe off the stool.

Janie was home.

Bear shot him a look that said, *Got ya.*

Rafe threw a ten-dollar note on the counter and gave in. "Towards her mother's place, you mean."

"Her mother?"

"Mercy."

Bear's eyebrows leapt. "You're kidding." He scratched his bearded chin. "So, is that how you and the younger Ms Sutton became a thing back in the day? 'Cause you lived next door?"

Rafe let a beat slink by. "Held onto that question pretty tight."

Bear had the grace to blush. "Wanted to give you the chance to tell your side of the story before believing everyone else's."

Rafe breathed. And reminded himself that he liked Bear.

And the guy was relatively new in town. So, while Rafe's part in the Sable Sutton story was ancient history, to Bear—his friend—it was news.

Rafe ran a hand over the back of his neck. Then again. Harder. As if warming himself up for what he was about to say out loud. "Yes, she lived next door. Yes, we were a thing. She was seventeen when her photos got her a shot at an agent and a gallery show in New York. She went. The end."

Bear lifted his chin towards Rafe, mouth down-turned: the manly man's international sign for respect. "My ex was obsessed with her Broken Botanicals series—had these huge amazing prints of fallen trees, snapped stems, shredded leaves. Couldn't afford the originals. He'd die to know she was here."

Rafe wondered if Bear knew he was grinning at the vision of his ex dying.

Then Bear swished his black-and-white-checked apron aside and pulled his phone from the back pocket of his black jeans and held it out to Rafe. "Do you follow her?"

"Do I—?"

"Online. She's got quite the following for someone who doesn't post pictures of herself in a bikini. Or isn't a reality TV star."

Rafe kept his gaze on Bear's face, refusing to look. Until Bear's mouth kicked up in a knowing smile.

Fine, he'd look, then they could change the subject.

Rafe dropped his gaze to the phone.

And there she was. Sable Sutton. Staring right back at him.

Chin lifted, mouth slightly open, long hair, a hundred shades of blonde, a windswept halo around her face. The pose said, *Take one step closer and I'll burn you alive.*

Notions Rafe believed he'd long since buried, began to simmer and shift. Ripples, after all. He shut them down fast. Well practised. From a time when reacting had meant the difference between dinner or a beating.

"You okay?" said Bear.

"Course I'm okay," Rafe grumbled. "Just leave me out of the story the next time you tell it, okay?"

"Done," Bear promised, his voice deep, and deadly serious. A good guy. A good friend. And there had been a time, in this town, when Rafe hadn't had all that many of those. Having the last name Thorne meant having a target on your back. Not that Sable had ever cared about that. She'd only cared about him.

And then she was gone.

And now she was back.

And his head hurt.

Rafe rapped his knuckles on the counter as goodbye, then strolled out of the warm, hipster haven and into the chilly autumn day outside.

Sable. Despite his best efforts not to listen, her name whispered on the breeze. *Sable Sutton.*

Rafe glanced down Laurel Avenue, towards the outskirts of town. Not the showy bit, with the quaint shops, the faux vintage street lamps, the autumnal trees overhanging the neat footpaths, but the old section. Not that long ago—before the beautification tourist money had poured into the outskirts of the snow fields—people had been hanging on by their fingernails.

His phone chirped. A message from Janie, reading,

Hey bro, you'll never guess who's back!

He put his phone away. And when he next breathed in, he could taste it.

Change. A change was coming. And it had nothing to do with the weather.

He shoved his hands deep into the fleece-lined pockets of his coat, turned, and walked the opposite way.

Sable didn't bother to knock, for her mother's front door was open, letting the cold air seep inside. There was also no doorknob, just a hole where a doorknob should be.

Her place in LA—her *ex's* place—had deadbolts, security cameras and an alarm. Not much help when the person doing you wrong was on the inside.

Sable lifted her heavy suitcase over the threshold and trundled down the dark hall.

She followed the sound of Bob Dylan to find her mother in the sunroom at the far end of the house, standing on an ancient wooden step stool, hanging bunches of vibrant, dried chillies upside-down by hooks on the ceiling.

"Mercy?"

Her mother's hands paused, before she looked over her shoulder. "Sable," Mercy drawled. "What on nature's green earth are you doing here?"

Missed you too, Mum.

"I'm back. For a visit," she added quickly, when her mother's eyes narrowed, making her crow's feet pop.

"Why?"

"You could at least try to look happy to see me."

"Of course, I am. I'm just surprised."

Right.

Mercy exhaled hard, wiping her hands in the length of her flowing skirt as she jumped down from the stool. Then she padded up to Sable, feet bare, ankle bracelets jangling, long auburn hair streaked with silver floating behind her like a fiery cloud.

She stopped a good metre away from her daughter. No hugs. Not even a pat on the arm. "Have you been next door?"

Round one, here we go. Sable nodded.

"Didn't take you long to go sniffing around that place again."

The urge to duck her head was potent. It took every bit of courage she had left to fight it. To look her mother in the eye.

Sensitive as a kid, Sable had always tended towards conciliation. Avoiding eye contact, making herself appear smaller than she was, in the effort not to make her mother sad. For she loved her mum, as hard as Mercy made it to do so.

But when it had hit her, a few months back, that she had fallen into the *exact* same pattern in her relationship with her ex—not rocking the boat, putting his needs, his career first—that had been the real beginning of the end.

First time she'd stood up for herself, in a real way, he'd acted swiftly, brutally unburdening himself of all the secrets and lies she'd allowed herself to simply not see in order to keep the peace.

She was not going to make her own needs appear smaller for someone else's sake ever again.

Sable lifted her chin a fraction. "I caught up with Janie. And kept any sniffing to a minimum."

Mercy snorted her response, then slanted her daughter a rare look of respect. Maybe this "standing her ground" thing would work on more levels than she'd imagined.

On that score... "What on earth happened to the old Thorne shack?"

Mercy's inner battle was written all over her face before she admitted, "He knocked it down."

"Mr Thorne?"

Mercy shook her head.

"Then who?" S*ay it,* Sable thought. *Say his name.*

"Rafe Thorne."

Never one name, always both. Like a serial killer.

"The father finally drank himself to death a few years

back. Day after the funeral I woke up to a god-awful racket. Found your boy tearing the place apart. He carried every single piece of the place away until there was nothing left but the footprint. Then he dug that up with an excavator and grassed the lot over."

Oh. She hadn't even known Rafe's father had died, much less the rest. If she had, she *would* have sent word. Though which words? Sorry didn't seem quite right. Neither did good riddance.

"Why didn't you tell me?" Sable asked. "You know… when I rang and said, 'Anything exciting happen in town?'"

"It mustn't have seemed relevant at the time."

Relevant? Hang on… "Did you think I'd come running home if I knew?"

The glint in her mother's eyes said it all.

"I wouldn't have." *Probably.* "Just so you know. I wouldn't have run back. I had a life over there. Just like you always wanted for me."

Only, in the end, that life hadn't been for *her.* And Sable was more than ready to curate one that was.

"Anyway, it's been a very long couple of days. I'd love to crash, if it's okay."

Mercy waved a hand in the direction of the bedrooms. "There's a couch in one of the rooms. You might have to move a few things."

Super. Sable spun her suitcase over a knot in the floor before heading back down the hall.

One room was full of nothing but dust motes. Her mother was not a collector of things. Too hard to cut and run. In the front room her mother's unmade bed with its slew of hand-woven blankets showed through the wide-open door.

The only room left was Sable's old bedroom.

It was the first room she'd stayed in long enough to tack things on the walls: pictures torn from magazines, drawings, photos she'd shot as her interest in photography had taken off.

That room was why Radiance was the first place that had ever felt like home.

That room *and* the boy next door.

It took a nudge with her boot to encourage the door open as it caught on a rug that had not been there when she'd left. The desk under the window was a new addition too. And the faux suede couch with bottom-shaped dips in the seat cushions and an escaped spring in the back. In fact, not a single reminder of her had remained.

That was Mercy in a nutshell. Seeing sentimentality as a weakness. Leaving her daughter to feel as if she left pieces of herself behind every place they lived.

Sable sank into the couch with a groan and stared blankly at the bare walls long enough to make out the sun-stained echoes of the pictures that had been stuck there years before.

She imagined she knew how they felt.

CHAPTER TWO

SABLE WOKE WITH light burning into the backs of her eyelids. She didn't even remember falling asleep.

Opening one eye, she found warm afternoon light streaming into the room, sharp, square and split into shades of white and gold, like something out of a Rembrandt painting.

Instinct had her reaching for her camera only to remember how long it had been since she'd held the thing. Long enough she hadn't been able to find it when she'd madly packed everything she could fit into a single suitcase and moved into a hotel.

The impulse to capture the view dissolved away.

She checked her phone to see the time, only to find another message from Nancy in New York.

When do I get you back? Soon, I hope! I've a jaunty little Greek magazine super-keen to hire you. Summer spread. Rugged location.

In Nancy language, "keen" meant Nancy was hounding them. As for "jaunty little Greek magazine", that was no doubt a far cry from her last gig with Italian *Vogue*. And light years from a show of her own.

She sent a quick message back.

Hey Nance. I'm alive. I'm fine. Off the grid for a bit. Taking a break from work. Talk soon.

Her phone rang immediately. She turned it on silent and slid it back onto the desk.

She listened to the sounds of the house. No music, meaning her mother was no longer home. And realised she was starving. Meaning she'd have to head into town. For her mother's fridge would contain little in the way of edible food.

She slid her boots back onto her feet and swapped her man's jacket for a faux fur coat. A *tad* over the top for downtown Radiance, but it had been a long time since she'd owned Ugg boots and flannel.

She checked the cupboard for a hat or scarf to cover the mess that was her hair only to find something else instead.

A vintage Kodak box Brownie—the first camera Sable had ever owned. Picked up at a yard sale when she was fourteen years old. A week before they'd arrived in Radiance.

She turned the camera over, ran fingertips over the leather casing.

She'd not taken photos of people back then, so much as old leaves piled up in their backyard, jasmine trailing over their broken fence, a flat tyre dumped in the pristine creek that ran behind their place.

Chaos and harmony. Death and rebirth. Themes that had helped her make sense of her nomadic reality had resonated with people far beyond the boundaries of their small town after entering a few online contests had brought her attention. Prizes. Money. Opportunities. Notoriety. And, ironically, a way out of the nomadic existence that had led to her interest in the first place.

She tilted the thing towards the window, around waist height, and looked down into the small viewfinder.

The first time she'd seen Rafe had been through that lens.

She'd been lying on the bank of the river, the camera to her eye, stones digging into her back, a hank of her long tatty hair floating in the water, trying to get the best angle on the crooked branches hanging overhead, when a face had suddenly blocked her view.

And a deep, male, teenaged voice had said, "What you lookin' at?"

Sable moved the camera a fraction, until the angles were sharp. She held her breath as she waited for the waft of the gauzy white curtain hanging from her old bedroom window to hit the right spot and…

Click.

She blinked, pulled the camera away from her eye. A quick check of the gauge showed her a small black number eight. She turned the crank over, watched the word *Kodak* appear, then the number nine.

"Huh." Would the film still be viable? Unlikely. Nevertheless, Sable slid the frayed rope attached to the camera around her neck, popped her phone case in her pocket, then headed out into the fray.

It must have rained while she dozed, the sky now a dome of pale grey cloud that refracted the weak light in such a way it made a person squint. Still, surrounded by towns with names such as Bright and Mount Beauty, it really was a pretty part of the world. And at its prettiest now, bolstered by the array of rich autumn colours.

Sable tucked her hands as deep as she could in the satin pockets of her coat. Her breath made white clouds in front of her as she walked. Her feet turned numb in boots made for form over function. Her belly rumbled.

When she spotted a sign that read The Coffee Shop she could have wept with relief.

She ducked inside, a small brass bell tinkling as the door sprang shut behind her. The place was warm and lovely. Retro black-and-white-tiled floor, recycled wooden bar, huge shiny coffee machine, ironic quotes hung in mismatched frames on the matt black walls—Radiance had gone hipster.

"Sable Sutton."

Sable spun to find a huge, bearded man grinning at her from behind the counter.

"I'm Bear," he said, banging a meaty paw against his puffed-out chest. "You don't know me. New in town. But I know who you are."

For a beat Sable felt that slight lift in her chest that came when people recognised her. Once upon a time it had felt like validation. For her work. Her tenacity. For the hard choices she'd made in order to make something of herself.

But nowadays she was far better known for being "that famous chef's ex-girlfriend, the one he cheated on".

She looked to the door, regretting the fact she'd have to head back out into the cold, her stomach still empty.

When Bear called, "Sorry. That sounded creepy. Please stay. I make great coffee."

Sable turned to see a face screwed up with chagrin, and beyond the gruff exterior a pair of kind eyes.

She moved to the counter. Sat. Unhooked the strap of her old camera from around her neck to lay it on the bench.

"There we go. What'll it be?" asked Bear.

She glanced at the chalkboard, an order for cool, weak, green tea on the tip of her tongue. But the thing was, she didn't much like tea, green or otherwise. The chef had his own line of them, so that was what they'd drunk in public. Like so much of her life, it had been easier to go with the flow.

No more.

"Double espresso, please," she said. "Strong. Scorching hot."

"Dark, strong, hot," he repeated. "Just how I like my men."

He held out a fist, she gave it a bump in solidarity.

Bear grinned. "When I moved here, I imagined I'd find

hordes of them. Strong silent types. All scarred and muscled from chopping wood all the time."

They both paused, as the coffee machine hissed and steamed, imaginations whirring.

"No luck?" Sable asked when all was quiet.

Bear slid her drink across the counter. "Well, I won't say I've had *no* luck…"

Sable smiled and found herself wondering if Rafe still fitted that bill. Or he might have a beer belly. Thinning hair.

She hoped he was content. Had tearing down his father's house exorcised the demons he'd carried with him as a kid? Or had the fire in his belly morphed into something darker?

Was he single? What if he had kids?

No. *No kids.* That she was sure of. It had been their one sticking point, the one thing they'd ever truly argued about. For him children would never be on the cards. Growing up the way he had—his mother deserting them, his father an angry drunk—having all but raised Janie on his own had devoured any desire on that score.

She'd cried into her pillow more than once, knowing that choosing him would mean giving up her own dream to have a family. A very different family from the way she grew up.

Before she'd taken the decision off the table entirely by leaving.

Only now, with her newfound clarity, she'd figured out a way for them both to get what they wanted.

Bear leant his elbows on the counter, bringing his face near level with hers. "Fair warning," he said. "Now that we're proper friends I feel like I should tell you—people like to tell me things. As if I'm a hairdresser, taxi driver and priest combined. And you're the talk of the town."

Sable shifted on the stool. "And now that you've met me what will you tell them?"

"That my doughnuts are fresh and my coffee is the best in town."

"Thank you," she said, and meant it. For she believed him. And it had been some time since she'd felt as if she had someone on her side.

Then, right as she began to feel better about things, there came a rush of cold air from outside, right as the brass bell rang over the door.

Bear looked up, his smile appreciative. Flirtatious.

And by the way the hair on the back of her neck stood on end Sable knew—someone dark, strong and hot had just walked through his door.

"Hey, Bear," an all too familiar voice rumbled behind her. "What's the big emerg—?"

Like a subtle shift in the air, a vibration that sang through her bones, Sable felt the moment Rafe saw her. Recognised her. Even before his words slammed to a halt.

Had *he* heard she was back? Or did he simply know the shape of her, the way she'd have recognised the shape of him anywhere?

Bear cleared his throat. Motioned to her with his eyes. Reminding her that wanting to be invisible and actually achieving it were two very different things.

Sable turned slowly on her stool. Her cheeks burning. Blood roaring behind her ears.

And she looked up to see Rafe Thorne—the boy next door, her first love, the man who held her future dreams in a simple yes—standing right in front of her for the first time in nearly a decade.

She'd prepared herself for this moment. Practising conversations with herself in the mirror in the bathroom on the plane. But seeing him, in the flesh, it all went out of the window.

For the boy she'd known was no more as he'd been honed into a man with fierce abandon.

She was powerless to stop herself—her eyes roved. Taking in the curl of his cowlick. The bumps of his knuckles.

The solid strength of his throat. Hair still thick, still curled, still wild. Stubble covering a hard, tight jaw. Lips that had always made her knees go weak.

Dark chambray shirt, sleeves rolled to the elbows showcasing forearms laced with the kind of roping veins that made a girl swoon. Collar unironed, top button undone—no, missing, having fallen from its length of unspooled cotton. Jeans softened in places where they'd been made to work hardest—knees, pockets, zipper. Rugged brown boots with the toes scuffed, the laces fraying.

Twinge, skitter, thump.

Now that there was no longer a planet between them her heart went on a rampage behind her ribs.

In both hands he held a piece of…something. She couldn't tell what. But it was a habit he'd had, even as a kid. Picking flowers, or grass stalks, as he'd passed, knotting them, stripping them, folding them… Those ingenious hands of his always needed to be occupied.

The flash of familiar brought her consciousness back into her body. Until she could feel the stool beneath her backside. The uncomfortable heat in her cheeks. The tremble in her legs.

For this was why she'd come home.

Not to flee the disintegration of her old life. Not even to see Mercy.

She'd come home for Rafe.

To ask a favour of him she'd *never* consider asking of anyone else. A favour that would change her life.

For she planned to ask him to father her child.

Not to help her raise it, or even know it for that matter. She wanted nothing from him bar his DNA. Then he'd never have to see her again.

She slid from the stool, the clack of her heels on the tiled floor jarring in the heavy silence. "Rafe," she said. "Hello."

Rafe, on the other hand, didn't say a word. His eyes cavernous, the deep dark depths giving nothing away.

She hungrily searched his face for a way in. For anger. Hurt. Surprise. For pleasure. Something.

Anything but ambivalence. It was the one emotion she'd never been able to match.

Then Rafe's gaze lifted away from hers, caught on the big man behind him, and he said, "You, I'll talk to later."

Then he turned on his boot and walked out of the door. The brass bell singing prettily before the door shut with a decisive snick.

What? Wait! No!

Words spluttered and puffed inside Sable's head.

Until Bear said, "Go! Go after him."

And as if she'd received a metaphorical shove in the back, Sable rushed forward, dragged the door open and hastened after Rafe.

Past the trees growing out of little garden squares in the concrete, and out onto the road, her boots slipping on the rain-slicked bitumen. Her coat swung heavily as she spun in a full circle. The avenue was vacant in both directions. Unless he was hiding behind one of the cars parked at an angle towards the shopfronts, he'd vanished.

She let her arms drop to her sides and sighed.

What did she expect, showing up out of nowhere the way she had? That there'd be enough water under the bridge. That time would have healed all wounds. And whatever other naff sayings she could pull out.

She should have planned this better. Worked harder on the first words she'd say when she saw the guy again. Something more persuasive than a breathy, *Rafe. Hello.*

"Ugh!" Sable went to make the long walk home, to make a plan for a proper ambush, before she remembered she'd left her camera in The Coffee Shop.

She turned to head back inside only to catch a glimpse of blue out of the corner of her eye.

Rafe sat on a set of rusty stairs tucked into the alleyway between the café and Mike's Bikes next door. One boot on the ground, another on a step, head down as he toyed with whatever was in his hands.

Heart thumping like crazy, Sable headed down the alley. Her shoes scraped on the wet concrete and Rafe stilled, his nostrils flaring, before he tore the piece of grass he'd been playing with in half and tossed both pieces onto the ground.

Laying hands on his knees, he pressed himself to standing.

When his eyes met hers, there was no ambivalence, which was a relief. But he did *not* look happy to see her. He looked ready to walk. Again.

She swallowed, licked her dry lips, readying to stop him. But his gaze followed the movement. Locking onto her mouth.

She'd been sure time would have numbed any latent attraction. Instead she felt sharp. Achy. Overly bright. As if she were standing barefoot on an iceberg, while looking into the sun.

Then his gaze lifted, his liquid dark eyes staring into hers.

Time seemed to stop, and stretch and dissolve, until she was simply Sable and he was simply Rafe.

For one brief, crisp moment she imagined just leaping right in.

Rafe, she saw herself saying, *I want a baby, and I want you to be the father.*

Then a muscle flickered beneath his eye, and she saw past the unblinking facade to the heaviness in his eyes. Yes, there was curiosity, but only on the other side of a great gaping crevasse of trauma.

Leaping in was not an option. There was too big a distance to bridge.

Unfortunately, time was not on her side. Not only did she plan to stay in Radiance for as short a time as humanly possible, her own body was against her. For it had decided to make baby-making a challenge. Which meant she had to get building that bridge and quick.

Sable levelled Rafe with a look. "*You*, I'll talk to later."

"Excuse me?"

He'd responded! Sure, it was gruff, but that was better than *not* responding.

"Back there, to Bear, you said, 'You, I'll talk to.' Making it clear you didn't want to talk to me. I know a diss when I hear one."

Rafe's dark eyes narrowed and Sable felt her heart thunder, hoping the risk of playing things loose and familiar would pay off. Would rekindle their old rapport quicker than not.

And *there*. A flicker behind the wall. A gleam.

Rafe slowly moved to lean against the brick wall, folding his arms across his broad chest and staring her down. "This is how you choose to go about the first conversation we have in years. By quibbling?"

"I did say hello, back there in the café, but you must not have heard me."

A twitch. At the corner of his eye. Good twitch? Or bad?

"Unbelievable," he mumbled, glancing away as he rubbed a hand over his mouth. But not before she caught the quiver of a smile.

Trying to ignore the way the drop in his voice sang through her bloodstream, Sable cocked her head. "Would you like me to start again? Talk about the weather perhaps? Like normal people?"

Normal people. It was a line they'd used often. A way of coping with how the locals looked sideways at their less than typical families—her "alternative" mother and his volatile father. One of the many threads that had connected them.

She saw the moment he remembered. The tightening at the corners of his eyes. The way his fingers gripped his forearms.

But then he seemed to let it go. To *decide* not to care.

He'd been good at that. While she wore her heart on her sleeve, every emotion written on her face, he was better at hiding his thoughts than anyone she'd ever known.

A tactic to survive his father.

Just as making herself smaller had been her way of surviving her mother. *Had.* Past tense.

She lifted her chest, and her chin. Ready to show him just how big she could now be.

When he surprised her, saying, "I'd like to see you try to be normal."

And before she even felt it coming, she coughed out a laugh. Then gave him a look that said, *Really*. Felt a little tingly in the belly region when he gave her a slow nod.

Riding the rapport, she wiggled her fingers, shook her head, took a deep breath, plastered a big fake smile on her face and said, "Rafe! Oh, my gosh. It's been years. It's *so* good to see you. How have you been? Great, I hope! You look…" *Hot. Savage. Mouth-watering.* "Well."

Her words, full of faux cheer, seemed to bounce around the alley before dissipating in a hiss of steam as they reached his dark, still self.

Then the edge of his mouth kicked up at one side. She felt it deep inside. Attraction. History. Heat. Pulsing through her like a fresh current.

"I've been just…fine. Thanks." Infinitesimal pause before the "fine". Then he said, "You also look…well." The pause before the "well" was longer still.

Now what? Small talk? Big talk? Hard talk? Dirty talk? *The* talk?

Slow down, kiddo. Bridge-building, she told herself. *This here is all about building that big old bridge that is going to get you what you want most in the world.*

She took a small step towards him. "Bear told you to come to the café, didn't he? Just now."

After a beat he nodded.

"Because I was there," she said.

Another nod.

"And I thought he and I were friends."

A small frown, then, "Why are you here, Sable?"

Ah, the sixty-four-thousand-dollar question. One she absolutely planned to answer but not while there was so much tension in the air she felt as if she could levitate. "Look, can we go somewhere? Grab a coffee?"

No. Not a coffee. Other than The Coffee Shop, every other place in town would be filled with people who would gawp and gossip and she'd be in less of a position to talk, to *really* talk, than she was in this alley. And while Bear might promise to keep his lips zipped, she really didn't know the guy at all.

Before she could press again, the rumble of an engine—big, meaty, eight-cylinder—heralded a muscle car cruising up the main street. Neither of them said a word until it was gone.

"I have to get to work," said Rafe, lifting away from the wall, his arms unfolding, hands moving to slide thumbs into the front pockets of his jeans.

It was so reminiscent of the old Rafe, her Rafe, her chest ached.

"Right," she said, shaking her head. "Of course."

What kind of work? Should she ask? Or save it? For next time. For she'd make sure there was a next time. As many next times as it took till the right moment arose.

To ask him to father her baby. Then watch her walk away again.

It started to drizzle. Sable pulled the collar of her coat together.

Rafe stepped down onto the concrete and slowly walked past her. She had to look up to watch him pass. Catching his scent over that of the smattering of fine rain. Soap, diesel, and clean warm male.

Before she even knew what she was doing she closed her eyes and drank it in.

"You in town long?" he asked.

She opened her eyes to find him beside her. Close enough to touch.

"For now."

He gave her one last look, so dark and deep she had no hope of discerning what it held. And he said, "Then I guess I'll see you 'round."

She nodded. Then watched him amble down the alley and out onto the street.

The drizzle created a halo around the solar-powered street lights as they flickered to life as the afternoon gloom set in. Sparking off Rafe's dark hair, his strong shoulders, the water flicking off his boots.

"Hot damn," Sable swore beneath her breath.

"You said it, honey."

Sable spun towards the voice, hands raised, as her mother had taught her. *"Men are dangerous. To body and soul. Protect yourself."* Only to find Bear coming out of the door by the steps on which Rafe had been sitting.

He had her camera and a huge rainbow-coloured umbrella, which he tipped over her head.

She tucked herself in beside him, even as she shot him a glare. "Were you listening that whole time?"

"Not the whole time." His expression was so innocent Sable had no choice but to laugh.

Then, "So how long *are* you sticking around? This time?"

Sable gave Bear a look. "Whose side are you on here?"

"No sides. All sides." He put big hands up in surrender before he slipped back inside his shop, leaving her with the umbrella.

When she looked back Rafe was leaning in the window of what looked like Old Man Phillips' rusty old Oldsmobile—only in the intervening years it seemed to have been given the fairy-godmother treatment, painted sparkling blue with silver wings down the side.

Once Old Man Phillips drove off, Sable watched for another minute or two as the traders of Laurel Avenue each popped their heads out of their shops to wave to Rafe. Back in her day they used to lock their doors when they saw him coming.

No pot belly, no bald patch. And he'd clearly made good. It was as bewildering as it was mesmerising.

Sure, to the very marrow of her bones, she would not get the same felicitous reaction, Sable pulled her collar up around her ears and began the long walk back home.

CHAPTER THREE

AFTER A LONG afternoon spent working beneath a Stingray at the Radiance Restorations workshop, Rafe opened the front door to the Airstream to find his sister in the small kitchen, headphones clamped over her ears, dancing as she stirred some kind of horrid-smelling goop.

He snuck up on her and jabbed her in the side.

Janie screamed, and spun on him with her ladle, painting the ceiling with an arc of homemade vegetable stock.

"What the heck, Rafe?" she said, tugging out her earbuds. "If that had been a knife—"

She stopped before another word came out. Her eyes widening. The colour leaving her cheeks. Not the first time a knife would have been brandished in threat by a Thorne. Though, thankfully, not by either of them.

And not in this space. This pristine, fully modernised, impossibly expensive tiny house of Janie's.

He'd had every intention of walking away from Radiance himself after knocking down his father's house. Letting the blackberries eat the lot alive. Till Janie—eleven years old, all knees and elbows—had looked at him and said, "But it's our home."

Next day he'd made a deal with Old Man Phillips to take the dilapidated Airstream off his hands, pimping the older man's Oldsmobile for free in exchange.

For Janie it had been therapy. Scrubbing, panel beating, building, surrounding herself with warm colours, soft fabrics. Comfort. A true home.

Leaving Rafe no choice but to make peace with the town. To stop slouching in the hopes no one would notice him, stop scowling the way they expected a kid of Ron Thorne's to scowl, stop refusing to make eye contact lest he see abhorrence in their eyes. To stop pining for the girl who'd left him in her dust. To become his own man.

Unthinkingly, Rafe took the ladle from Janie's hand and tasted the cooling mixture. He coughed as the tart taste hit the back of his throat.

"Give it." Janie grabbed the ladle right on back. "It's super healthy. And a work in progress. Besides, I had no idea you'd be back here for dinner."

Even while several years down the track, Rafe had built himself his own little sleepaway spot on the property, he often slept on the couch in Janie's van when he was in town. She liked playing hostess. Liked looking after him for a change.

And he let her. For while she was an adult now, which she was at pains to constantly remind him, the way she still bit her fingernails to the quick, and preferred staying in her little cave than being anywhere else, reminded him of all she'd had to overcome.

No matter how grown up she was, he'd always be her big brother.

"I thought you were flying to Sydney this arvo to give the final okay on the Pontiac," said Janie.

Rafe leaned his backside against the edge of the kitchen bench. "I was."

Janie glanced through the small window facing the overgrown forest blocking any view of the neighbour's house. "But you just had a sudden urge to stick around, hey? Did news get around I was making soup, or—"

"So you had a visitor," said Rafe, not bothering to pretend a certain someone wasn't forefront on both of their minds.

"I did! For about three minutes before she scuttled away. I recognised her in a second. All that ridiculously fabulous hair. And those eyes—like she could see straight through to my soul." Janie sighed. "I was smitten with her back then. Total girl crush."

"That so?"

"It was the way she moved, all slow blinks and liquid limbs. Like she was floating through life."

Floating through life. That was Sable. Like flotsam. Tossed about on her formidable mother's whims. Tossed to New York by a rare chance. To LA by some famous chef…

Now back again.

Rafe had no doubt she'd be tossed somewhere new soon enough.

As if she'd read his mind, Janie added, "She's different now, don't you think? Grittier, somehow. Grounded. Dare I say, more interesting?"

More interesting? Even as a teenager she'd been more interesting than he'd known what to do with. Sensitive, emotional, beguiling, and ingenuous, with those strange dreamy eyes, the kind you couldn't look at long for fear of falling in…

But that was then. And if she was "different" now, he was a new person entirely.

Rafe looked down at his hands. At the oil tattooed into the grooves. The bruises under half his nails. The stubby ends of his fingers. The swollen knuckles. Okay, so not entirely.

He felt the frown pulling at his forehead. He might still be found beneath the bonnet of a car, more often than not, but he was also a successful businessman. A well-regarded collector. Renowned the world over for his ability to spot a gem, to restore the unrestorable.

Not that she needed to know any of that. He did not owe her a thing. Not a conversation, not a coffee. Not any more.

Rafe tipped his chin. "You got all that in the three minutes in which you spoke?"

"Yep," said Janie with a grin. Then her eyes narrowed.

"Hang on a second. She found you, didn't she? I can tell by the mulish look on your face. How was it? All hearts and flowers and swelling string section? Or did you pull a you and answer in monosyllables?"

Rafe shot Janie a flat stare, only to find she wasn't laughing at him. She looked concerned. But Janie had nothing to worry about. He leaned over, wrapped an arm about her neck and ruffled her messy hair.

"Hey! This do takes effort." She ducked out from under his loose grip. "Come on, I want to know how it all went down."

"While I want dinner. So, I'm gonna head back into town for a real meal."

Janie threw her ladle into the sink with a clang. "This is barely good enough for the chooks. Give me five minutes to wash up. I'll drive."

Rafe laughed before he even felt it coming. Janie, a Thorne and therefore a rebel, drove a tiny battery-operated tin can on wheels when he could have sourced her the coolest muscle car on the planet if she'd let him. "Funny girl."

"I know right. Don't leave without me."

Rafe smiled. "Never."

For Janie had been right. Radiance was home.

And though Sable Sutton was out there somewhere, and they might yet cross paths again, she would leave, and he'd stay, and that really was all that there was to say about that.

Rafe stood outside the front door of the Airstream, stretching his arms over his head as the weak wintry morning light poured over his bare arms and a sliver of belly beneath the lift of his old T-shirt, the crisp mountain air sending goosebumps in its wake.

The roar of a quad bike had woken him. Janie was out in the paddocks, zooming around checking on her animals.

Smiling, he turned to make his way back inside when he saw someone at the front gate.

Not just any someone. Sable Sutton. Sitting on a post. Boots kicking against the fence palings. What looked like her old camera swinging around her neck.

She must have seen him watching her, as the fence kicking stopped. She lifted her hand in a wave, hit the ground with both feet then started down the drive.

Equal parts disquieted and curious, he made to meet her halfway.

They came to a stop around two metres apart. Minimum safe distance.

She was carrying a tray from Bear's in one hand, the other she held up to her forehead as she squinted against the morning sun. Her shadowed gaze giving him a quick once-over. He figured he was decent enough in pyjama bottoms and a ragged T-shirt. Till he glanced up in time to see her swallow.

"What can I do for you, Sutton?" he asked, his voice a little rough.

"Me? I'm…" Her gaze dropped to his chest. "Aren't you frozen solid?"

"I run hot. Remember?"

With that one word, she stilled. Her gaze lifting to meet with his. The years stripping away. Then she shook her head, just the once, her hair floating and settling. Her jaw tightening.

"I brought coffee." She held one out to him, at arm's length. "Do you still take yours milky? Sweet?"

He slowly shook his head.

"Oh." She pulled the coffee back into her side, her expression flagging. Her bottom lip disappearing beneath her top teeth.

She'd never been any good at hiding her feelings. It used

to terrify him how readily she entrusted all that vulnerability in his big, rough, dirty hands.

But that was then. This was now. And his hands weren't going near her vulnerability.

Since it was clear she wasn't going anywhere till she did what she had to do, he figured the best thing was to let her get there as fast as she could.

He held out a hand. "Just give me the coffee, all right?"

She looked up. Her bottom lip came free, glistening. Plump.

His solar plexus tightened. If he wasn't running hot before, he was now.

With a grunt, he stepped forward, tugged the coffee out of her hand, then turned and walked back to the Airstream.

Sable fell into step beside him. Easy enough when he was barefoot and she in knee-high boots that hugged her calves as if she'd been sewn into them.

"I'm not going to shake you, am I, Sutton?" Rafe said.

"Nope."

"Because you have something to say."

"Yep."

"Then say it."

She opened her mouth. Closed it. Opened it. Closed it.

He might have enjoyed watching her squirm, if not for the tension gripping him as if his skin were three sizes too small. For while she was a pace to his right, he could feel her. The warmth of her. The peculiar, golden light of her.

"Fine," he said, his spare hand gripping the back of his neck. "I'll say it. I accept your apology. For leaving the way you did. In fact, I'll go so far as to thank you. Thank you for leaving."

She blinked at his bluntness. But he was on a roll now.

"You had an opportunity and you took it. You did what I'd never have had the foresight to do: you saw beyond the hand we'd been dealt, and demanded more. I demanded more too, once you were gone. I demanded more of the town. Of myself. And it paid off. I have a good life now, Sutton. Janie too. So…thank you."

He stopped to take a breath. It was a heck of a lot more words than he was used to saying in one go. And as he breathed, something dark and dicey skittered behind Sable's eyes. Ghosts in her gaze.

Reminding him that this wasn't the naïve seventeen-year-old he'd once known.

He owed her nothing. And to be honest, she didn't owe him anything either. Things had ended, not in the most ideal way. But were endings ever ideal?

She was no more to him than a memory, now. No longer his responsibility. No longer his to protect.

"So, are we done?" he asked, no longer concerned if his words made dents. "Have you got what you came for? Because I really need to get on with my day."

She gripped her coffee hard. Her fingers long and lean, the nails almost blue.

Unprotected, a memory swarmed over him. Taking those cold hands in his, blowing warm air onto her palms, rubbing heat back into her fingertips, kissing the tips…

"This must be so strange for you," she said, snapping him back to the present. The feathers on her coat fluttering and settling, as if the ripples of her return now affected the very air around them. "My, just showing up, after all this time. And the last thing I want to do is seem obtuse. Or as if I don't appreciate how nice you're being."

Nice? If this was her version of nice, he wished he could come face to face with the jerk who'd skewed her opinion on that score.

But no. Again, she was no longer his to protect. Perhaps he ought to set an alarm on his phone. Repeat hourly. Till she was gone.

"Rafe," she said, taking a step closer, those vivid eyes

flickering with more thoughts than he could possibly translate. "You want to know what I came for? Fair enough. What I want…"

She stopped. Glanced over his shoulder as the sound of the quad bike rolled up behind the caravan and shut down.

Knowing Janie, knowing how ripples messed with her composure, Rafe moved closer to the Airstream.

"I'm hungry," said Sable, matching his steps. "Are you hungry? Of course you are. You were always hungry. Can we go get breakfast somewhere? My shout. Or at least let me get you a coffee you'll actually drink."

"I don't remember you being this pushy."

"That's the LA in me, baby. It's the quick and the dead."

A smile hooked unexpectedly at the corner of her mouth. He'd forgotten how it did that. First a dimple appearing in her right cheek, a lift at the right corner, then the rest followed. Like a sunrise.

Her beauty had been more subtle back then. *She'd* been more subtle. A little shy, a silent witness to life rather than the kind to dive right in. Deeply sensitive, which was what had made her such a great photographer. The ability to see richness where others saw nothing at all.

The kind of person you'd notice out of the corner of your eye. Till one day you realised they were no longer beside you, and the loss was like a crater in your gut.

Add a dash of confidence, a splash of experience, and honed edges and the effect was like a sledgehammer. A sledgehammer who wasn't going anywhere till she'd said her piece.

He took another step towards the Airstream. As did she.

"Wait here," said Rafe. "The alternative is you following me inside while I get dressed."

Her chest lifted and fell. Her throat worked so hard he was surprised she didn't pull a muscle. "I'll wait. Not moving from this spot."

Rafe jogged up the stairs. Nudged his way through the small galley kitchen to the smaller washroom. Listing, in his mind, all the things he'd already missed by sticking around even one extra day.

Three impending sales of completed vintage car refurbishments that he had to physically sign off on. Requests to eyeball several possible restoration commissions. Council paperwork for the local car show Janie helped him organise. He was known not only for his workmanship, but his professionalism. He did not let things get out of control.

So, coffee. A little food. He'd hear her out. Shake her hand. Make her think all was forgiven. And get on with his life.

For it was a fine life. Perfectly satisfying.

He imagined Janie rolling her eyes at such a comment. Her voice dripping in sarcasm: *Sounds like a dream come true.*

As a kid contentment hadn't even been in his vocabulary, much less his plans. As for authority? Respect? Success? Big words for better people.

But now he had them, and nothing was taking them away.

Rafe turned off the water, skin prickling with goosebumps. He grabbed one of the small floral towels Janie kept on the "guest" rail and ran it hard over his hair. Stopping when he thought he heard voices. Female voices.

Janie had found Sable. And let her inside.

"Dammit."

The Airstream was hardly guest friendly. It was compact, open plan. Meaning he either had to hide in the tiny washroom, till they gave up and went outside. Or he had to head out there, squeeze past them, to get to the clothes he'd forgotten to take into the bathroom.

Sydney, he reminded himself. *Ticking clock.*

So, he wrapped the towel around his hips—a Janie-sized

towel, barely enough to cover his rear end—and went unto the breach.

At the sound of the door opening, both women looked up.

Janie, eyes the size of saucers, said, "Rafe. Wow. Um… you knew Sable was here, right?"

"I did. Thanks," he said, saying a hell of a lot more with *his* eyes. "Though she assured me she would stay outside."

"But it's freezing out there! Much more comfortable in here."

"Nice to know you're so concerned about everyone's comfort," said Rafe, lifting an eyebrow. Skin damp, hair dripping, he could feel his nipples puckering. The hairs on his legs standing on end.

Janie bit back a grin.

While Sable blinked at him. Once. Twice. And he felt the connection he'd been trying to pretend did not still exist twang, as if they were tied together with some invisible lasso that had just tightened around them.

"Janie," Rafe growled when the knot of the towel began to slip.

"Right." Janie moved to block Sable's view, to usher her back towards the door. "Come to think of it, that coat does look very warm. What's it made of? Crow?"

"Ah, nothing real," Sable stammered. "It's fake. Fluff. Stuff. But yep, definitely doing its job. Feeling pretty warm right now. And happy to wait outside."

Janie opened the door, and said, nice and loud, "Sorry about that. He's not usually such an exhibitionist."

Sable's fading voice wafted to him as the door slowly swung closed. "Could have fooled me."

Sable didn't want to blink in case it rid her of the vision currently burned into the backs of her retinas. Acres of hard male chest. Naked. Rippling. That magical vee of muscle she'd only ever seen in underwear ads. And a happy trail leading beneath the edge of the minuscule towel held precariously at lean hips.

"Earth to Sable."

"Hmm?"

Janie watched her, head cocked to one side. "I was saying… Have you decided how long you're staying?"

"Staying?"

She wasn't *staying*. She was on a mission. For Rafe.

Not all the bits she'd just seen. Ogled more like. Other bits. A single healthy, hearty sperm would do her just fine. He'd never had any plans for them so he'd never miss it. Not that she'd put it quite that way.

"Sable?"

"Right. Staying. How long? Depends."

"On? Mercury's alignment with Mars?"

"Sure. Let's go with that."

Sable stamped her feet, the dew having seeped through the bottoms of boots that had not been made for the great outdoors. "What's he doing in there, do you think? Curling his hair? Sewing his clothes?"

Janie laughed. Then, in the same tone one might use to ask where they might go for breakfast, she said, "Just don't hurt him, okay?"

"I'm sorry?" said Sable, though she'd heard just fine.

"My big brother might never say so out loud, but he's really made something of himself since you left. He's respected. Settled. And a raging success. I'm sure you can imagine the amount of work he had to put in for all of that to come to pass."

Sable blinked. "I'm really glad to hear that."

"Mmm. The thing is, as a kind of cosmic payment for all the good that has come to pass, he has this thing about responsibility. About not turning his back on anyone. His staff, the townspeople, me. He takes that obligation *very* seriously. To a fault. Our very own St Jude, Patron Saint of—"

"Lost Causes," Sable finished.

Janie clicked her tongue and pointed at Sable. "That's the one."

Sable tried hard not to swallow. Not to let Janie know that every word felt like a barb, snagging on her vulnerable underbelly.

For a few months back she had felt like a lost cause. Humiliated, broken-hearted, and appalled at how she'd let herself become a passenger in her own life, she'd felt about as strong as a single strand of dandelion fluff.

But while she might look a little thrown together, and was deliberately vague in voicing her intentions, Sable was *not* lost. She was *exactly* where she was sure she was meant to be.

"Janie," she said, "I can assure you, the last thing I want to do is hurt anyone."

Janie cooed, "Gosh, look at those doe eyes of yours. So beseeching. So earnest. Just make sure you don't do it anyway." With that Janie jogged up the stairs and pulled the door open. "Come on, pretty boy! Your date is waiting!"

Rafe growled something from inside the van that sounded like *Not a date*. Then appeared in the doorway in dark jeans, slick dark boots, dark Henley, dark hair curling damply around his ears. Just big, and dark and so beautiful it hurt to look at him.

Sable might actually have sighed. Out loud.

"Yeah," Janie muttered. "This isn't going to end badly at all."

Rafe picked his sister up by the upper arms and deposited her inside the caravan. "Be good," he growled. Then he gave her a kiss on the cheek and closed the door in her face.

Janie's words skittering about inside her head, her feet

cold and wet, her belly empty, Sable found herself caught in Rafe's tractor-beam gaze as he ambled down the steps.

"Hungry?" he asked, hands rubbing together.

"Mmm-hmm," she managed.

"As I remember it, you're buying. So, lead the way."

CHAPTER FOUR

BOTH BRANDISHING FRESH COFFEE—Sable's hot and dark, Rafe's cool and bitter—made by an exceedingly curious Bear, they found themselves strolling into Radiance Reserve, a series of parks bordered by dense forest at the far end of town.

Rafe took the outside of the path, his strides shortened so she could keep up, and Janie's "he has a thing about responsibility" speech niggled at the edge of Sable's brain.

She only hoped this expanded sense of responsibility of *his* didn't get in the way of her very good plan.

"So, this town, huh," she said. "A few interesting new faces about."

Rafe spared her a glance over the top of his coffee. Her throat came over all tight, her heart threatened to twinge. She told it to get a hold of itself.

"Bear, for instance," she went on. "Met him yesterday, love him already."

"You do know he's gay," Rafe said, sliding her a telling glance.

"Sure. Apparently, we have the same taste in coffee. And men."

She earned a double-eyebrow lift for that one. Then a chuckle, deep and rough and delicious. She'd forgotten quite how much she loved it when that serious face lit up.

"What's his story?" she asked, before clearing her throat.

"Rode into town a year or two back," said Rafe, "hoping my team could wield some magic on his favourite Harley: a 1974 Shovelhead."

"Your team?"

Another sideways glance, then, "Didn't Mercy tell you?

I took over Stan's old garage a few years back. Renamed it. Expanded a little. Made a bit of a name for myself, bringing broken-down vintage cars and bikes back to life."

"Well, that's just fabulous! And no, Mercy did not tell me. Turns out she's very good at not telling me much at all. Such as the fact that your father passed away. I'm sorry, by the way. It must have been a rough time."

Eyes front, Rafe offered up a single chin lift by way of acknowledgement. And nothing more. Stoic as ever.

Mulling that over, she didn't realise where they were till they got there.

"Oh!" she said, her boots scraping to a halt as a pile of crunchy autumn leaves caught in a whirl of wind and swept across the cracked grey path. "I didn't remember this place being so close!"

Open during spring and summer, and during the autumnal Pumpkin Festival, Radiance boasted an old-style fairground named Wonderland Park. Complete with Ferris wheel, a carousel with the most amazingly detailed horses, and a hand-painted wooden Chair-O-Plane.

Not one for group events, or capitalism, or fun in general, Sable's mother had flat out refused to ever give her a cent to attend, so she'd watched from the sidelines, listening to the clatter of machinery and the squeals of joy, on many a balmy summer evening from a spot in the playground nearby.

In fact, the playground had to be close… Searching the gaps in the frail-branched bushes, she found it. There—the ancient rusty slippery slide, and wonky wooden swings—

"Our first kiss," said Rafe.

Sable jumped at his nearness, at the words he'd said, the rough edge to his voice. "What's that, now?"

He angled his chin towards the playground. "Over there. That's where we had our first kiss."

"No, it wasn't."

She remembered, vividly. It had been the night of her seventeenth birthday when she'd seduced him. If dragging him up to the loft in his father's barn, where she'd set out a dozen battery-operated candles around a picnic blanket, and pressing him against a tattered old hay bale and kissing him for all she was worth could be considered seduction.

She remembered being so impatient for her life to begin back then. So impatient for a future with Rafe. A future and a family. It had taken her a long while to truly believe Rafe when he said he would never have a family of his own. A while longer still before she'd left.

Rafe's gaze swung to hers. "Do you really not remember? It was a week before the park was due to reopen that spring. A bunch of us came down here. Jimmy Dale had snuck a six-pack from his dad's stash."

Sable blinked and just like that it all came back to her.

She'd been fifteen, perhaps. Rafe a couple of years older. Jimmy had taken a shine to her, invited her along with a bunch of senior kids to "hang out". She'd never have gone if Rafe hadn't mentioned he'd swing by.

There'd been beer. Someone had brought a guitar. They'd built a fire. Stupid, what with all the winter kindling littering the scrub.

She remembered wishing she could go home. Feeling angry with herself for not having a richer vein of rebellion. Why did she flutter and float on the whims of others? Couldn't she stand up and say what she wanted? What was she so afraid of?

Then Jimmy had dragged her from the swing and started to dance. Spinning and spinning her until she thought she might faint.

Till he'd spun her out to the end of his arm and let her go.

There'd been a moment of pure panic, when she'd been

sure she'd trip, or fall, when her sense of balance would truly fail her, until a strong hand had taken her by the fingertips, curled her back in, gathered her close.

Rafe's hand. Calloused, and enveloping and so very warm.

They had been friends for a couple of years by that point. Best friends, really. He being her silent protector as she scoured the forest for junk to photograph, she his adoring acolyte, watching over him as he fixed radios, washing machines, cars.

And while he'd held her hand a million times, to help her navigate a path across a stream, carried her piggyback all the way home from the base of Mount Splendour the time when she'd twisted an ankle, they'd never been face to face, body to body, nose to nose.

Her hand on his chest, she'd felt the racket of his heart. His hand at her back had tightened, gathering her dress in his grip.

"Rafe?" she'd whispered. Bewildered, hopeful, on fire.

And then he'd kissed her. A light, sweet sweep of his lips over hers.

The catcalls had begun. Whistles and howls and laughter.

Not that Sable had cared. For Rafe had been kissing her. Kissing *her*. Till her muscles had melted and her insides had sung. Fulfilling the deepest, most secret wish she'd ever wished in a lifetime of wishes.

When Rafe had pulled back, he'd looked as glazed as she'd felt. Until a shutter had dropped over his face, as impenetrable as steel. "Was Jimmy watching?" he'd asked.

"Who?"

A small smile, then, "Jimmy Dale. The bloke who's been trying to paw at you all night."

She'd glanced sideways to see Jimmy watching her glumly. "He saw."

"Good. He'll leave you alone if he thinks you're with me."

"If he *thinks*— Are you *kidding* me?" Mortified, all the way to her very toes, she'd made to shove him away.

But Rafe had only held her tighter still. Warm and protective. Even then. "Stop fighting me," he'd ordered. "He's trouble, Sable."

"You're trouble."

Another crooked smile. Another arrow to her heart.

"The difference is, I'm only trouble for anyone who tries to mess with you. Don't you ever forget that. Okay?"

Feeling tingly from the kiss, achy from the knowledge Rafe had only kissed her to protect her, Sable had rolled her eyes. "Fine. Whatever."

From there the memory blurred at the edges, bleeding into a hundred other summer nights. A hundred other delicious kisses.

"I can't believe I'd forgotten," Sable murmured, her thumb tugging at her bottom lip.

Or more likely she'd blocked it out. A talent she'd inherited from her mother.

"Flattering," Rafe rumbled.

She shot him a look to find him leaning against the side of the slippery slide, watching her. Expression still guarded, but there was a little crack there now, a glint. Subtle as it was, she felt it. Like stepping out of the shade into a patch of sun.

"I got a black eye for my efforts," Rafe said.

Sable pulled a face. "You did not."

The hairs on the back of Sable's neck sprang to attention as Rafe pushed away from the slide, his moves slow. Measured. Focussed.

"After I saw you home," Rafe said, "waiting for you to shimmy through your bedroom window being one of my favourite pastimes, Jimmy and his mates came around. My father was home. So was Janie. He had her hold the money as he took bets. Took three of them to hold me down for Jimmy to get one good hit."

Sable's chest rose and fell. If Ron Thorne was still alive today, she'd give *him* a black eye. "Rafe…" she breathed.

But the telling tightness in his jaw took her back. When it came to his father Rafe had never wanted sympathy. Or help. She wondered how good it had felt to tear down the bastard's house.

"Hang on," she said. "I remember. I couldn't track you down for a few days. I thought you were avoiding me, because of the kiss. Then I refused to go to school, in case you showed up at home. When my mother found out I was skipping, she shrugged and went off to some herb festival in Yackandandah for three days."

Rafe's father had not been a nice man. But her mother's lack of warm and fuzzies had left their own marks too, like an old break that made itself known when the weather turned. She found it hard to trust when people seemed to like her. Constantly held her breath, waiting for them to snap.

Her ex-partner's therapist—the same one who'd told his client to come clean about his indiscretions, his lies, so that *he* might feel cleansed—had told The Chef that he believed Sable had "mother issues" that meant she deliberately put herself in situations that were doomed to fail. As if that excused The Chef's behaviour. As if she'd asked for his dishonesty.

As if she found it a secret thrill when those who professed to care for her spun her out to the ends of their fingertips…and simply let go.

Shivering, she tucked her cold hands into the warmth of her fluffy feathery coat.

Was that what she was doing here? Hoping Rafe might still be the one person she could count on to catch her before she spun completely out of reach?

No. It wasn't. This, coming here, was her way of catching herself.

"You okay?" Rafe asked.

She nodded.

Rafe tossed his empty coffee cup in a nearby recycling bin, and strolled away towards the fairgrounds, giving Sable a moment to collect herself. To rev her engine. To focus.

She took a deep breath and looked up. Looked around her. Letting the uniquely wondrous landscape of this place infuse her with the energy she needed. And it didn't disappoint.

Right now, the fairground looked like something out of a Stephen King novel with the dormant contraptions looming over them beneath the low-slung pale blue sky. The Chair-O-Plane chairs drooping sadly. The horses' faces on the carousel pulled back in heightened emotion as if they'd been turned to stone mid gallop.

Sable didn't realise she had the box Brownie camera in hand until her finger slid over the shutter button. The pad rough beneath her fingerprint. The box cumbersome as she shifted it to waist height.

Muscle memory coming to the fore, she set her feet a little wider, softened her shoulders, let the camera sink into her hand, then squinted to look down through the small viewfinder. She moved so that the spindles of the Ferris wheel peeked perfectly through a gap between a clump of orange leaves overhanging above and rows of evergreens in the distance.

She tilted the box a fraction, knowing it always shot high, took a breath, held it…

Then let the camera drop, till it caught on the cord around her neck.

She shook out trembling fingers. Blinked back into focus. And blew out a long slow breath through a small gap between her lips.

How long had it been since she'd taken a photograph because it called to her? Her reputation had led to commissions. Portraits. Fashion gigs. She'd been paid an obscene amount of money to shoot a famous rapper's dogs in an abandoned tyre yard. All of which was as far from those that had started her career as possible.

Her inspiration had waned correspondingly. Her ability to tap into her instincts disintegrating. Her confidence with it. She'd never been sure if it was age, waning talent, the different light, the lack of time, her lifestyle…

Or if she'd simply lacked her original muse.

Sable looked around to find Rafe over by the carousel. He'd hiked the sleeves of his black top to his elbows. Raked his dark hair off his face. He played with something he'd plucked along the way.

Sable's hands went to the camera once more. Gingerly at first, before the heft in her grip felt right. She nudged the focus until the vision was a blur of shadow and light. Then again until it was sharp, in her sights.

There was no zoom on the thing. The negatives huge. Perfect for taking poster-worthy shots. But she imagined Rafe's face in the distance. Such a good face. Strong. Serious. Achingly handsome.

Then he turned, looked dead into the lens.

Sable held her breath and…

Click.

She slowly let the camera drop. Her breath out a euphoric rush of air. When she looked up, the light, the edges of the vision, the reality beyond the iris, swarmed back into focus, like ink through water.

Rafe held his ground. Resting his elbows on the fence. Watching her across the distance as she watched him. Surely it defied the laws of physics, the way electricity seemed to crackle and arc through the air between them.

Then Rafe blinked, frowned and reached for his phone. Answered. And Sable's next breath out shook.

The longer she left this, the more likely the hum between them would blur the lines. And she needed them to be crystal clear.

It was time.

She reminded herself, chances were he'd say no, right up front. Which was understandable. It was a huge ask.

But she had counter arguments. She had research. Doctor's reports showing the bare facts of the uphill battle she was facing fertility-wise. But also her general excellent health otherwise. Financial records. Photos of neighbourhoods with great schools and hands-on programmes and parks...

She was ready for this. She *needed* this.

"Can't make it happen if he's twenty metres away, kid," Sable muttered under her breath before slinging the camera rope over the other shoulder, then making her way to the carousel.

"Right," said Rafe as she neared. "Leave it to me. I'll see you in a bit." He hung up, slipped the phone into his back pocket.

"You have to go?"

"I do."

"Work?"

He nodded. Yet he didn't walk away.

She moved in beside him, mirrored his position leaning on the railing. Tried to appear nonchalant while her heart thundered and her palms began to sweat. And said, "Have you ever wondered what your life might have been like if I'd stayed?"

Rafe's entire body stilled. Big effort for a guy that tall. "Sable, I don't think this is smart—"

"No," she said, holding out a hand. "It's okay. In fact,

it might be healthy to play out the disaster we would have become."

His face shifted, just enough to glance her way. All dark eyes, and suspicion. "Disaster?"

"Total disaster! Don't you think?"

His grunt didn't actually give away what he thought at all. But she went with it.

"I'll start. Okay, so you would have got a job with Stan. No doubt. You were always a magician with cars, and Stan was smart enough to see past the Thorne thing, even back then. While I would have probably ended up working at the Shop and Go."

Rafe winced, as she'd hoped he might.

"Taking photos on the side, of course. During summer, if it was still light when I got home. On weekends. Maybe branching out to photograph newborn babies. Family sessions. School photos. And that's if the townspeople let the witch's daughter anywhere near their kids."

Rafe was facing her fully now, slowly twisting and untwisting the long blade of grass over and around his fingers. "Sounds…dire."

"Right? So you're working, I'm working. We're earning a little money. Saving for a place. Or a holiday. A trip to Queensland maybe. But we're content. Because we have each other. So content we'd have been knocked up in a year. Probably had three in three years."

Oh, the ache in her chest as those words came out, so light, so blithe.

"So no holiday. No place of our own. I'd have had to stop work to look after the bubs. Which I'd have loved. Except we'd have had to move in with my mother." She let that thought sit for a good long moment. "How's that for a pretty picture?"

Sable glanced at Rafe to find his frown had deepened. The curling grass had unfurled from his finger, and lifted on the light breeze. His gaze was faraway as he said, "No kids."

"Hmm?"

"No kids. The rest, maybe. But no kids. Not for me. You knew that."

The ache in her gut grew serrated edges. Even while it was *good* news that his determination not to raise a child of his own was still prevailing, the fact that he still felt that way, a man with his kindness, and goodness, and genes. He'd have been a great dad.

"Right," she said, shaking her head before she turned it into a nod. "That's right. So this, now, the way things worked out, your life is better, right? Janie's life is infinitely better. Just as it is."

He looked into the middle distance and said, "All true."

Had his voice trailed off a little there? No matter. Things were falling into place. Exactly as she'd hoped.

Till he said, "How about you?"

"Hmm? What now?"

"Is your life better now?"

She opened her mouth and closed it, trying to figure how to twist his question to get back on track. Instead she found herself comparing her mess of a life to her life back then: home fires and forest walks, creativity rushing through her veins, lazy afternoons spent with Rafe in the loft of the old barn. No, her life wasn't better, not right now. But it would be and *that* was the point.

He moved then, slowly turning to face her, his gaze intent. And he said, "I know a little. Of what happened. In LA."

"Oh?"

"I know that it's been more than a year since you've released any new work."

More than a year? Was that possible?

"And you and that famous chef of yours…you're done."

Hearing Rafe mention her ex was so unexpected, she flinched.

"Janie liked to keep tabs, kindly sprinkling me with news every now and then. Bear brought me up to date, when he heard you were in town. And fine, I might have searched the Internet on occasion."

A quick flush rising in his swarthy cheeks, he looked down. He tossed the blade of grass to the ground and leaned back on the railing. When he looked back at her again, his gaze was intense. Enough it made the backs of her knees tingle.

"If that's what this is all about, Sutton, if you've come back here looking for a soft landing, looking for me to make you feel all better, I can't give you that. I won't."

Sable found herself caught in Rafe's dark eyes as he talked about "making it all better". A euphemism that set off a plethora of memories inside her head—warm, tender, knee-melting memories—as if they'd been waiting to be set free.

She had to physically shake herself back to reality. "That's not what I'm here for, Rafe. You can relax on that score, I promise. What I want…"

This was it. From here there was no turning back. She looked to Rafe, her past, present and future concertinaing till her throat tightened.

She fought past it, pressing her feet into the ground, firming up her foundations, as she said, "Rafe, I'm here because I want a baby."

Rafe's hand snapped back to his side as if burned. "You want—"

"A baby. *Your* baby."

Now the words were finally out she breathed deeper than she could remember breathing in years. Lungs filling and emptying. Spilling glorious oxygen through her body, her brain, until she felt strong, light and, oh, the blessed relief.

"I don't understand."

When Sable realised Rafe was physically backing away from her, she reached out and grabbed him by the hand. His warm, brown, strong and scarred hand. Held on tight. Using it to anchor her.

"Rafe. I was hoping—I *am* hoping—that you will agree to be my baby's father. Well, not *'father'*. Because I *do* know that kids are not in your life plan. It's what makes this plan so beautiful. I want you to be my donor. I'm not asking for you to sleep with me. There would be doctors—"

"To sleep with you?"

"No! To take care. Of your sperm."

He looked so pale, so stunned, it was almost funny. Though she knew that was the adrenaline making her feel giddy. She'd never been more serious in her life.

"It's all very safe. Clinical. And quick. Especially on your part. Once you…do your bit, that would be it. I wish for nothing more—no financial outlay, no physical help, no visitation. Nothing. No strings. Not a single one."

She was saying all the right things, all the things her research said might sway him, but she could tell she was making no headway.

Realising how tight she held on, she let him go. His hand whipped back, and he with it, putting even more space between them as he paced away from her.

Though he didn't bolt. That was something. Right?

"Rafe?"

His back remained facing her. He had one hand on his hip, the other in his hair. Tugging. As if he was trying to yank his thoughts to the surface.

Sable moved a little closer still. "I know you never wanted kids, Rafe. And I always understood why, even while I struggled to accept it. That's why we would never have made it. You and me."

She could have sworn she saw him flinch. But then he didn't move. He stood there. Breathing. Listening. His face turned just enough she could see his eyes were closed.

"Because it has been *my dream* since as far back as I can remember. No matter what else had changed in my life, that instinct, that *yearning*, has been a constant."

He moved a little then, his eyes opening. His face turning. His strong profile her focus as she said all the words she had to say.

"So why I'm asking this of you? And not some random donor? Or any other man I've met since?"

Something shifted deep behind the daze in his eyes. A flicker of discontent. An echo of possessiveness. It sent a shiver down her sides. She shook it off. Focussed.

"I considered," she went on. "Of course I did. I'm not here on a whim. My reasons for asking this huge thing of you are two-fold. Firstly, most importantly, you were so good to me, Rafe. I look back on that time with such fondness. Such gratitude. I would not be who I am if I had not had you in my life. But a baby, my baby—I've come to re-alise it's something I want to do on my own. No outside pressure from interested parties, no raising by committee. Just me and all the love that I plan to pour into my kid.

"It's all but fate for the women in my family to do this alone. My mother managed, in her own way. My grand-mother too. I know I can take what they did right, and what I believe they could have done better, and I can do this well. This is my time, Rafe. It's now, or never."

Rafe's eyes grew dark, his body a study in stillness. Then he turned. Slowly. Face first, then torso, then feet.

His jaw was tight, his eyes dark and a*pologetic*.

He was going to tell her *no*.

"Sable—"

"Stop," she said, moving in to quickly slam a hand over his mouth. "Just…think about it. For a day. Or two. I know you owe me nothing, not a single thing. If anything, I owe you. So much. Yet here I am. Asking. Even while knowing I've set myself up for ridicule, censure, rejection."

Doom.

She closed her eyes, told her ex and his dodgy therapist to stay out of this. "It's that important to me, Rafe. So please, think about it. And, as a bonus, once all is said and done I will walk away, and this time you'll never have to lay eyes on me again."

His breath blew hot against her palm, and ripples of heat rolled over her skin like creeping vines.

Slowly, a finger at a time, Sable removed her hand from Rafe's mouth.

His nostrils flared as he licked his lips. His eyes drilling into hers.

And despite the intense emotion, she felt a curl of attraction so strong it nearly knocked her sideways.

Not now. Not *that*. There was no place for it here.

Ironically. For jumping him would be far easier than the rigours of fertility drugs, and risky timing, and the ache of implantation. She'd read all about it. Talked to people who'd been through it. Even joined a support group in LA when her doctor had given her diagnoses. Plural...

But falling into bed with Rafe would only make a mess of things. And she was *not* about to sabotage whatever slim chance she had.

The Chef's enabling therapist would be so proud.

Sable didn't breathe as the leaves skittered at their feet. Rustled in the trees above. As if even the wind was mirroring the restlessness surging through the both of them.

Then Rafe's phone rang, buzzing in his pocket a moment before the sound split the heavy silence. It rang again and Sable flinched.

"Answer it," she said.

Rafe slowly slid his phone from his pocket and answered, eyes not once leaving hers, as if afraid of what she might do if he didn't keep an eye on her. "Rafe Thorne."

Then, before he had the chance to ask her to wait, or tell her no, she walked away. As fast as she possibly could.

Rafe barely remembered getting off the phone with his Sydney team, and making it out of the park, for his brain was shooting sparks in every direction like a faulty firecracker.

A baby, he thought as he turned onto Laurel Avenue.

Sable wanted a *baby.* Not just any baby. *His* baby.

And it wasn't some euphemism for *How about we take up where we left off?*

That he *might* have been able to get behind. For the attraction between them was thrumming so loud it was hard to hear over it. Chemistry had never been their problem. Only everything else that was against them: youth, family, the whole town, timing…

A *baby.* His baby.

No strings. Not a single one.

Was she out of her mind? Possibly. She'd lived in LA for years. Who knew what weird foods she'd eaten. Or substances she'd taken.

He might even have grabbed onto that notion and left it at that, had it not been for the fact that he knew her so damn well. The only thing they'd ever openly argued about was her dream to be a mother and his vow to never be a father.

He remembered one such time—or maybe it was several memories merged into one—wrapped up in an old blanket in the loft of his dad's old barn, dust motes floating through the air, on the verge of sleep as her fingers traced the hairs on his chest, her soft voice going through the alphabet, listing possible names for their future children.

Annalissa with the blonde curls and obsession with kittens. Benjamin with the grumpy frown and kind heart. Carys who thought she could fly…

He'd never felt as torn as he did in those moments, soul-deep, right to his marrow. He'd been so deeply smitten with her, desperate to give her everything she could possibly hope for, but the thought of having a child to take care of made his head spin, his lungs squeeze to the size of raisins.

He'd had to tell her, time and time again, in the loudest voice he'd allow himself to use, to stop. That it was *never* going to happen. That he'd do anything for her, but he would never give her that.

For he'd still been a child himself, thirteen, and Janie no more than three, when his own mother had left, leaving the pair of them in the care of their father—a turbulent man who wasn't to be trusted with his own welfare, much less that of two children.

So Rafe had raised his little sister as there had been literally no one else to do so.

That first couple of years had been the hardest. Keeping her fed with no money. Keeping her safe when she'd had a tendency to run.

As she hadn't even been in school attending himself had been nearly impossible. They'd called him a truant, a brooding, troubled kid, when really he'd been doing his best, while his head had been constantly in seven different places at once. None of them good. How had his mother left them? What mood was his father in? Could he keep Janie alive?

But they'd made it, the two of them. A little rough around the edges, but thick as thieves. And while their lives were now solid, secure, safe, he had not forgotten a second of the hard work needed to make that happen. How sometimes even that wasn't enough. That bad things happened—kids got sick, authorities intervened, life got in the way.

He had no intention of going through that again.

All of which Sable knew better than anyone.

His heart twisted, like a wrung-out rag, as he tried to

understand what on earth had made her think he'd even consider the idea of having a baby with her—

Not what she asked, his subconscious piped up.

Rafe rocked forward. Looked down at his feet to find they'd stopped. He scuffed a boot against the footpath, dirt and decaying autumn leaves shifting under his sole.

Seriously, though. To come back here, after cutting and running, not speaking to him in years, where the heck had she found the nerve to ask him to father her child—?

That's not what she asked.

What *had* she said, exactly?

That she'd found some kind of loophole? She didn't want him to *father* her child. Didn't want him to participate in the raising of the child at all. She wanted nothing from him bar his swimmers. Clinical. Safe. And quick. No support required, or wanted by the sound of it. And he'd never have to lay eyes on her—or presumably any offspring forged from the endeavour—again.

She'd left that bit till last. As if never having to see her again would be the clincher.

Rafe laughed out loud, the sound catching in his tight throat.

A day, he thought. *She's been home a day, and you can't stand still. Nor can you move forward. And now—because you didn't immediately say, hell, no, flat out, clear as day, unequivocal—she's out there, believing that you are actually thinking this ridiculous plan over.*

And *why* hadn't he said no?

Because she'd tucked her hair behind one ear over and over again. She'd looked up at him, unblinking, with those vivid eyes. She'd been so earnest, so hopeful, and so utterly *Sable* it had taken him back with a yank that had all but upended him.

Realising he'd stopped in the middle of the footpath again, Rafe rubbed a rough hand over his face, and told his feet to move. He grabbed a leather tie from around his wrist and pulled his hair back. Hard. Till the roots hurt. And made tracks to Radiance Restorations.

The scent of oil, the clang of steel on steel, the mutter of hushed voices, the tinny sound of Stan's filthy old radio playing country music from its place on the top shelf in the workshop ran over him like quieting hands. If any place could calm the tornado in his head, this was it.

For this was his home.

His father's old place had been a prison. The Airstream was Janie's happy cave. His Melbourne apartment, his London place, the hotels he stayed in when meeting clients around the world were simply places to sleep between jobs.

Work, endeavour, taking something broken and putting it back together better than it ever was—that was his happy place.

"Boss!" That was Fred McGlinty—tufts of sweaty red hair poking out of the edges of his grey on black Radiance Restorations cap as he ambled over.

Rafe nodded, not quite ready for words.

"Good, thanks," said Fred, oblivious. "Check this out."

Heading to a Charger up on blocks—only a polish and new tyres from completion—Fred popped the lid, slid behind the wheel, left the door open and gave the engine a rev.

It sounded great. Throaty and rough, but clean. A dream compared to all the other stuff in Rafe's head right now. "Again," he demanded.

Grinning, Fred revved and revved and revved.

And Rafe's twisted heart slowly but surely came down from the ledge.

Sable had meant something to him once. Strike that—she'd meant everything. Ensuring her happiness had been his number one goal in life. But the choices she'd made had changed all that. Irrevocably. She'd broken him when she'd left. In a way his mother's leaving and his father's volatility never had. But he'd put himself back together—with determination, and guts, and by sticking to the choices *he'd* made in his life.

And while it was patently clear the attraction still hummed beneath the surface of every word they'd uttered, it was not, and never would be, the same.

He was no longer accountable for her dreams.

Ed, Fred's twin, poked his head over the engine. "Gorgeous, right?"

Utterly, he thought, then realised Ed was talking about the car.

The engine cut off. The guttural growl echoing in their ears for a few moments before the soft strains of Stan's radio once more took over.

A cough came from the corner of the garage, where Stan himself sat. All weathered skin, and bristling silver moustache. Local newspaper open on the small table before him. "You still in town, boy?"

"So it seems," Rafe said.

Stan closed the newspaper and shot him a glance. "Wouldn't have anything to do with Mercy Sutton's girl being back in town."

Rafe's fingers clutched into fists at his sides, nails digging into his palms. Hell, he couldn't even hear about her without feeling that *whump* of heat rush through him.

"Who?" Ed asked.

"Rafe's old flame," said Stan. "First car he ever worked on with me he was building for her. A hunk of junk VW Beetle they dragged out of the creek and called Rosebud. Or Periwinkle or some such thing. Whatever happened to that thing?"

Ed blinked. And Fred cleared his throat.

The muscle below Rafe's right eye jerked.

"Boys," said Rafe, his voice like sandpaper, "take an early lunch. Grab some petty cash and head to Bear's."

Fred and Ed didn't have to be asked twice; they left so fast they practically laid rubber. Leaving Rafe with Stan and Neil Diamond crooning in the background.

"You okay, boy?" said Stan, eyes narrowed his way. "You don't look yourself."

Rafe held his gaze and considered his answer.

Stan had seen Rafe through plenty. Had stood beside him at his father's funeral. Had sourced the jackhammer that had destroyed the foundations of his father's house.

A single man, like himself. Never married. No kids of his own. And content with how he'd lived his life. Stan had been a role model in the way his own father had never been.

But this? Sable's request? It felt too big. Too private. Even if he was unquestionably going to say no.

"I'm fine."

"Fine, you say," Stan grumbled., shaking his head. "Most dangerous word in the English language. Let me know if you need a hand?" He cocked his chin toward the cars that still needed tending. But Rafe knew the old man really meant he had two ears and would listen to anything Rafe had to get off his chest.

"Will do," said Rafe, then he made a beeline for the rusty old Road Runner languishing in the end bay, hitched his jeans, lay himself down on the tray and slid underneath.

In the shade and the cool, surrounded by metal and rust and oil and purpose, Rafe made his decision.

He'd find Sable, and tell her no.

And then he'd head off to Sydney quick smart. Without her nearby, the mud in his head would clear, the unrelenting work ethic that had ground to a halt the moment he'd seen her sitting in the café would swing back into overdrive, and he'd get back to living the perfectly *fine* life he'd been living before she'd swept back into town.

CHAPTER FIVE

SABLE MANAGED TO work her way through two more espressos at Bear's before he questioned why she was sitting in the window seat, watching the street as if it would disappear if she blinked.

"It's the only patch of sunlight in your joint," she returned.

He leaned in beside her, making a play at watching the street with her. "Sure you're not waiting for a certain brooding, dark-haired hunk to wander by?"

She glanced right, trying to remember the layout of the town.

"Wrong way. His place is that way," said Bear, pointing left.

"Oh, shush."

When her phone buzzed, an incoming call from her agent in New York, she shooed Bear away and this time jumped on the chance to answer. Only to find herself looking at the original Norman Rockwell painting that lived behind her agent's desk.

"Nancy?" Sable said.

"Sable, darling!" Nancy slid into view. "Is that really you?"

Sable waved a hand around her face to prove that it was she.

"Oh, my dear girl, how I missed that beautiful face! How's Hicksville?"

Bear shot Sable a look. Sable just shook her head. "*Radiance* is...overcast."

"Lovely. But not as lovely as Greece, I'm sure. That job is still yours if you want it!"

"Not the right time."

"Darling, it's always the right time for a paid trip to Greece."

"I am fine, Nancy. Really."

"Fine," Nancy scoffed. "The most loaded word in the English language."

Sable smiled. For there was no heat in Nancy's words. They'd known and adored one another too long for all that. Nancy had been gifted to Sable as a part of the international art prize that had taken her to the States in the first place. She'd been the only one in Sable's circle who'd never warmed to The Chef, despite the heightened profile he'd provided. The only one who'd stood by Sable when his truth had been exposed.

Nancy was more than owed a little sweetener. "What if I told you I found my old box Brownie camera in my mum's house?"

Nancy's mouth sprang open.

"With film in it."

Nancy's eyes narrowed. "Don't mess with me, kid."

"What if I also told you I'd taken a few photos on it too. Small town. Fall foliage. Hyper-nostalgic."

Nancy grabbed the edges of her monitor, her face filling the screen. "What's the name of that Nowhere Town, again? I'm coming to you. On the very next flight. So I can hug you. And steal that film and develop it myself."

"No, you're not. And I'm not letting you anywhere near my film."

Nancy sat back, grinning from ear to ear, her cosmetic procedures making sure the smile only went as far as her eyes. "Fine. If Nowhere Town is your way back to finding your spark, then you stay right there, for ever and ever if necessary."

"Oh, no. No, no, no." Sable glanced out of the window at the pretty oak-lined avenue right as a flurry of autumn leaves drifted daintily to the ground. Then a pair of little girls in tartan dresses and wintry tights skipped past, holding hands. "Not staying. Just…passing through."

"Stay as long as it takes, then. Call me any time you need a hit of culture. Or an accent other people can understand. Deal?"

"Deal," Sable said on a laugh. They said their goodbyes then both rang off.

And Sable's gaze went to the window once more.

It was a truly pretty town. All park benches and picture windows and overflowing flower pots on the footpath that were still there the next day.

Picturesque and patently photographable as it was, she couldn't stay. Not for much longer. She'd spent no more than ten minutes with her mother so far, and had already ground a layer off her back teeth.

Then there was Rafe, and her promise he'd never have to see her again.

Just thinking his name had her feeling warm tumbles in her belly and nervous jitters skipping over her skin. Needing to walk it off, Sable stood and slid her arms back into her big coat.

"You off?" Bear asked. "Need me to point the way to the nearest brooding, dark-haired hunk?"

She shot him a look. "No, thanks. I'm all good."

Besides, the longer she could leave Rafe to think over her proposal, the better. Meaning she had to keep herself busy lest she spy him, drop to her knees and beg. "I think I'll go check out the sights of the town. See what else has changed around here."

The sights included a hill that called itself a mountain, a thick twisty forest in which tourists often famously got lost, a closed fairground, and the few local shops she could see from Bear's front window, which was probably why the big guy snorted his response.

And yet, Sable kept herself busy. Checking out the ancient thrift store, the wool store, the sweet new community library, the cool bike shop.

Most people she met were friendly. Asking if it was cold outside. If they could help her find what she was looking for—and meaning it. But she also felt a few dark looks hit between her shoulder blades, saw a few locals whispering behind cupped hands.

She'd lived in Hell's Kitchen when she'd first moved to New York. Then spent a year photographing nature, finding life between sidewalk cracks in South Central LA. Small towns really did do hostility like nowhere else.

After a long, long day, jet lag now tugging at her eyelids, emotions having run the full gamut from euphoria to panic, once the sun set behind her, the half-moon casting a smoky dark blue tinge over the hills beyond, she dragged her feet towards the top end of town.

The shops had all closed. Radiance was tucking itself in for the evening.

As if her footsteps had set off some switch, the street lamps along Laurel Avenue flickered to life. Then a zillion fairy lights—strings of orange, strings of purple, twirled prettily around the trunks of the big old trees lining the avenue—sparkled against the inky backdrop of the twilight sky. It was beautiful. Magical. Oozing small-town charm.

Then, right as she wondered if she'd been going the wrong way, as her sense of direction was shocking, there it was. Radiance Restorations. And any feelings of magic, and ease, and charm dried up in a snap.

From memory Stan's old garage had been a third the size, an old wooden building with a single petrol pump out front. Now it had swallowed the plots either side, boasted a huge flat-fronted building, painted matt black, with several big silver roller doors, one of which stood open, and an office door tacked on the side. Five gleaming, retro petrol pumps were lined up along the far end of the neat block. With a handful of fabulous-looking vintage muscle cars tucked along the fence line.

The name of the business was displayed across the entire top of the building, pressed tin in a chunky vintage font, then again down the side of each pump in fluorescent bulbs.

This was no small-town garage. It was the kind of place that made reality TV show producers salivate.

She moved in closer. Pale golden light spilled from the only open garage door. Her heart skittered at the sounds of metal on metal. The shuffle of wheels on concrete. The tinny sound of an old radio.

She suddenly felt nauseous. As if the rest of her life was hinged on the next few minutes. Which, in all honesty, it was. For if Rafe said no, she had no back-up plan.

She knew there *were* other options, of course. That a refusal wasn't the end of the road.

But from the moment she first had the idea—sitting in a booth in an old diner in Encino, dried tears making her cheeks feel tight, deciding her recent troubles weren't a loss so much as a gift, giving her a chance to create the life she truly wanted—it had felt right. As if everything she'd done, everything she'd gone through, had always been leading her back here.

Sable took a deep breath and strode into the garage where she found the husk of an old muscle car with a pair of legs poking out from underneath.

And it took her back so hard, so fast, to the times she'd walked in on Rafe in the exact same position—body hidden under a car, left foot flat to the floor, right foot resting on a heel—she was overcome with flutters in her chest, tingles over her skin, the echo of a soul-deep yearning she'd felt every time she'd seen him.

The scrape of the old rubber wheels broke the silence as Rafe rolled himself out from under the car and Sable held her breath as his long, strong body appeared, an inch at a time.

His belt strained at his hips, his now dirty black Henley clung lovingly to the rises and dips of his broad torso. Most of his dark hair was held back off his face with a tie. His jaw hard, rough-hewn, with just enough abrasive shadow to make her fingers curl into her palms so as not to reach out and touch.

Rafe hauled himself to sitting, his shirt lifting to reveal a hint of rigid stomach muscle, clenching as he moved. His eyes, when they met hers, were dark and full.

The air between them rippled with history and tension and things unsaid.

"Sable," he said, his voice deep. Ragged.

"Rafe," she managed. Then—because looking at him too long made her feel as if she might combust on the spot— she glanced around. "I can't believe how much this place has changed. Care to give me the grand tour?"

He wiped his hands on a dirty rag, pulled himself to standing and said, "There's cars. Tools. Spare parts. Front office. What you see is what you get."

She wished.

No. No, she didn't. She didn't want what she saw. She wanted…other bits, currently not in view. Nothing more.

She searched frantically for something else to draw her focus lest he see the heat flushing her cheeks. "So, what are you working on here?" she asked, motioning to the car.

With a huff of breath he lifted the bonnet to show a sleek, clean engine, light glinting off the gleaming metal.

She leaned in closer. Their shoulders were a few inches apart but the hair on her arms stood on end, as if even they remembered what it felt like to be close to this man. "Tubes, wires, battery. Everything looks to be in the right place."

His voice was deeper, grudgingly playful, as he said, "You have no idea what you're looking at."

"Sure, I do. That's what those in the know call an engine. How many afternoons did I spend watching you fix cars? Years and years of afternoons before we became… a thing. I could probably strip this thing down and put it back together. If I wanted to."

She looked up to find him close. Really close. Those dark eyes of his were too shadowed to read, but the shift of his mouth she saw, its edge kicking up, just a notch, hitting her like a thunderclap.

Sable knew she should look away before she did something stupid, like reach up and run a thumb along the new line at the corner of his mouth. Or grab him by the shirt front and haul him in for a kiss. To break the insane tension. Or simply to remember what it felt like to be held.

And then she did something stupid anyway.

"Fine," she said. "I wasn't watching you fix cars. I was just watching you."

Rafe might have laughed it off. Or told her off for playing with fire. Instead—as if he was also done fighting the urge—his gaze dropped to her mouth.

Giving it the okay to run away from her.

"Something I've always wondered," she said, her voice only a mite above a whisper, "did you know I had a crush on you, all those years before I finally did something about it?"

His gaze slid back to hers. "Yeah," he rumbled, "I knew."

The heat in his eyes, no longer banked, no longer coiled, had her heartbeat singing, *Danger! Danger!*

"Even when you kissed me that night? At the playground?"

He breathed in. Breathed out. Nodded.

"And it still took us another two years after that to *actually* get together. Wow. That was some admirable restraint I showed."

"*You* showed?" he muttered.

But before she had the chance to respond, to push, he

motioned for her to move back, and then he shut the bonnet with a metallic crack.

And he stalked over to the industrial sink and washed his hands.

Giving her a chance to breathe. And give herself a good talking-to.

What the heck is wrong with you, kid? You know that flirting with him is counter-productive! Is it the reflections in the oil spills you find overly stimulating? Or the winch chains waving in the breeze?

Next time she tracked him down, she'd do so in daylight. *With* an audience. And she'd certainly make sure she kept physical distance between them as well. Whatever it took to keep the heat blooming between them at bay.

She couldn't let herself fall for him again. Even a little bit. Because when she fell, she had a bad habit of becoming who she thought her partner wanted her to be. Surpressing her needs so that they might love her back. A survival skill learned living by the changeable whims of her dearest mother.

That was how things had gone down with The Chef. Even while he'd turned out to be a liar and a cheat, the break-up wasn't entirely on him. If she'd stood up for herself sooner, if she'd laid claim to her life from the very beginning, things wouldn't have ended as they had. In all likelihood they'd have ended before they'd even begun.

But the harder truth was, she'd probably been that way with Rafe the first time around too. *The only time around,* she reminded herself. They'd been so close, she'd not known quite where Rafe ended and she began.

Feet firmly back on the ground, she watched Rafe move about the space. Switching off machinery. Lights. Checking everything was safe. Secure. So self-assured, capable, resilient, sturdy. No wonder she'd been so smitten.

But now those qualities were no longer reasons to want him, but reasons to want her child to be half him.

When he looked over, and the darkness in his eyes made her blood go from normal to full sizzle in half a second, she took a step back.

"I should go," they both said, at the exact same time.

Sable laughed, the sound a little strained. While Rafe simply looked at her. Into her.

Then he slowly strode her way.

She held her breath, waiting for his next words. Bracing herself. Readying to battle, if she needed to.

When he surprised her by saying, "I'm meant to be in Sydney right now."

"Oh?"

He ran a hand up the back of his head, catching on the hair tie and yanking it loose, his curls falling around his face making him look a complete rogue. "There's a re-furbed Pontiac in my Surry Hills shop, owned by a Texan ex-pat who is road-trip-happy. Paid extra to make sure I signed off on the completion, in person. Yet here I am."

Sable had no idea what to say.

Rafe, on the other hand, wasn't done. "Later tonight, I'm meant to be on a flight to Dubai where I was to have first eyes on a Mustang GT Cobra Jet, which one of the royals found under a tarp in his father's other palace."

Lots to digest there, but Sable found herself stuck on the "Was? Meaning no longer. Because you're here. You're here because of me."

He nodded. But he didn't look disapproving. Or disappointed. Or stunned and confused as he had back at the fairground that morning.

He looked as if he could hear the whump-whump-whump of the blood pulsing through her. As if he too could taste the sensual tension in the air, above and beyond the tang of oil and steel. He looked as if it was taking every ounce of restraint to hold himself back too.

Then Rafe muttered, "To hell with it," before he took three long strides, reached a hand around her waist and hauled her close.

Sable's breath left her in a whoosh. Her thoughts following straight after. Until she was nothing but nerves and heat and a frantic pulse.

Then with a growl that sounded as if it came from the very deepest place inside him, Rafe leaned in and kissed her.

No hesitation. No softness. No finding his way.

He kissed her with a decade's worth of built-up heat. And anger. And frustration. She felt it all. Every feeling, every drop of heartache, every wave of disbelief.

Sable couldn't have prepared herself for such a kiss if she'd had a lifetime to try.

Sliding a hand around his neck, delving into his curls, she found herself swept away on an ocean of sensation as Rafe held her tighter. Kissed her harder. Heat rose within her, like a storm. A volcano. A rush of memory. And want.

This, her heart sang. *This is what you've been missing for so long. This is what you want! Him.*

All her sweetest memories were wrapped up in this man's smiles, and she wanted to have his baby, and it had been eons since she'd been kissed with such…thoroughness. Who said she couldn't have her cake and eat it too?

Her hand gripped the front of his shirt to drag him closer as the kiss deepened. Fuelled by regret and sorrow and punishment and mistakes they both clearly needed to fill with something more joyful.

Rafe's hand moved. She whimpered at the loss. Only to feel it slide back around her waist, beneath her coat, beneath her jumper, to find the edge of her waist. Bare skin.

The rough pads of his fingers—familiar yet changed—created waves of sensation, rocketing through her.

How long since she'd been touched like this? Since she'd felt wanted. For nothing but her skin, her warmth, her kiss.

It was heady. A rush. A wondrous thing. She hadn't even realised how much she missed that part of herself. Raw and honest and needy. Rich veins of need. Needing to be closer, to be a part of him, she lifted her leg to wrap itself around his.

Rafe growled, the sound echoing in her chest. Taking her under, till she could no longer hang onto a single thought—

Sable froze, hand at his chest now pressing flat as she tipped her head down, as she drew in a much-needed breath. It took every ounce of effort she had left to cleave herself away.

Rafe's hand slid out of her hair, his fingers so deeply entangled they caught. His hold disappeared from her waist. The loss of each touch felt a little death.

She waited for him to move back, away, to curse himself for giving in. But his hands lifted to hold her by her upper arms, gently, kindly, and she realised how wobbly she was on her feet.

"You okay?" he asked, a glint in his eye as if he knew exactly what he'd just done to her.

"No! Of course I'm not okay! I don't want this. Not from you."

She felt his fingers lift a smidge.

"Could have fooled me."

Sable squeezed her eyes shut. "I didn't mean it that way. I mean, I *did*. But we can't be kissing, Rafe. Kissing complicates things. And I need this—*us*—to be as clear-cut as can be."

A muscle twitched under his right eye. "Because all you want from me is my sperm," he said, his voice a rough burr.

"Yes," she countered. "Your sperm!"

Okay, Sable, perhaps a little less enthusiasm on the sperm front.

"I don't want to be a distraction, Rafe. I don't want Janie to feel as if she has to look out for you. Or for people to whisper behind their hands about you because I'm back—"

"What people?" he asked, his fingers tightening once more.

"A few people in town today. You know what they can be like—"

Her words dried up at the concern in his dark gaze. Rafe, standing so close, his strong hands holding her, his dark eyes on hers, his familiar scent curling through her making her knees melt, and making it hard to put her true wants into precise words.

Then she closed her eyes, shook her head. "That's not the point. Don't worry about *me*. I'm totally used to it. Water off a duck's back." *Yeah right.* "The point is, I know we can do this right. If it's direct, honest, simple, clear-cut."

Rafe breathed out long and hard, his eyes shifting between hers. Then he slowly let her go. Took a step back. And said, "Sable—"

Knowing, to the very innermost threads of her marrow, he was about to deny her, she cut him off. Searched frantically through the arsenal of arguments she'd prepared, for something that might stay him. "It's sudden. I get that. I wish I could give you all the time and space you need to sort through all of this. But as well as being an overwhelming ask, it's also time sensitive."

Hands lifting to rub the spots he'd late been holding, Sable took another breath. This next bit never got any easier to say out loud. The last person she'd told was The Chef. And the way he'd taken it… As if it was a blessing.

But this wasn't The Chef. This was Rafe. A good, kind, strong man—which was why she'd come to him.

"I saw a doctor a few months ago because my cycle has

been seriously out of whack. I assumed it was stress-related as things hadn't been good for quite some time. When she took my medical history my burst appendix came up."

"Your *appendix* burst?" Rafe moved in, hand out to steady her.

"When I was little," she quickly added, quietly telling her heart to chillax when it began to thumpity-thump at the concern in his dark eyes. "Before we moved here. Anyway, it turns out there's damage. Incidental scarring to one of my fallopian tubes means it no longer does the job. That, plus another underlying condition, it's all a bit of a mess in there. If I don't do this, and soon, my chances only go downhill, rapidly."

She finished with a shrug. Refusing to give in to the hopelessness that came with the litany of reasons why a child might never be in her future. No matter how well she planned it out.

Right now, hope was all she had.

Rafe remained quiet. Too quiet. It took every ounce of restraint she had not to ask what he was thinking. Especially when she wasn't sure she'd like the answer.

"What kind of condition?" he finally asked, his expression grave.

"It's called primary ovarian insufficiency, which basically means my egg-release mechanisms don't work properly or stopped working earlier than they ought."

A shadow passed over his face. Then he ran a hand over his chin and looked away, before leaning back against the closed bonnet of the muscle car and crossing his arms over his broad chest.

"I thought I was handling this rather brilliantly," he said. "You. Being back. I told myself I was fine."

"Are you *not* fine?"

He watched her and said nothing. Stoic. Controlled. Emotions hidden behind a tough facade. It was a side of

Rafe she'd conveniently repressed when putting together her plan. His determination to keep such a tight check on his feelings, when hers spilled out of her pores whether she wanted them to or not.

"Rafe," she said. "Talk to me."

Whether it was the crack in her voice, or the fact she held eye contact and refused to let go, something yielded in his gaze.

"You walk in here as if we're in the middle of a conversation from ten years ago. As if all that has happened in the last decade is moot." He glanced down at his shoes then back at her, as if he needed a break between all the words. "I can *feel* myself wanting to accept it too. Just forget all the bad and welcome you home. It's unnerving. You unnerve me, Sutton. I nearly ran over Fred's foot this afternoon, backing a car out of the garage, because my mind was elsewhere. I lost it at him. Poor kid had no idea what he'd done wrong."

"Ouch." Then, "What were you thinking about?"

The look he shot her was direct. A warning. The sudden memory of his mouth on hers, his tongue sliding over the seam of her lips, strong enough her knees buckled.

"Don't sweat it," she said, flapping a hand to distract him from the thoughts no doubt written all over her face. "Someone today told me they believed *fine* was the most loaded word in the English language. I think it's overrated."

"Really?"

"Mmm-hmm. Who needs *fine* when we could do something truly unique? We can do this and come out the other end better than fine."

His gaze dropped to her mouth again, right as she stopped talking to lick her lips. He pressed away from the side of the car. "Let's take this outside."

"Sounds ominous."

"I think a little air is necessary for this kind of talk. Space."

Right. Good call.

She turned and headed out. Night had fallen fast. She blinked into the darkness when the golden light of the workshop switched off, then the groan of the roller door closing echoed over the night.

Rafe followed her through the doorway till they stood, two lone figures in the great gaping concrete entrance. Pale moonlight poured over his broad shoulders, the waves in his hair. There was so much unspent energy coiled within him he practically glowed.

She didn't think it would serve her cause to tell him that they could be in the middle of a field, a desert, a shopping centre car park and it wouldn't make a difference. Any time she was near him space was irrelevant.

Then, his hands delving into the pockets of his jeans, his shoulders lifted to his ears before he let them drop. "I've listened. I've heard you. Now I need you to hear me. You've come looking for something that just isn't there."

"What do you mean?"

"The kid you once knew, the one you came here to find, I left him behind a long time ago. The scourge that came with being my father's son, the pressure to never set a foot wrong, the burden of keeping Janie alive. That's so far in my past I barely think about it any more. But then the moment I saw you, it all came rushing back."

Rafe's words hit—*snick-snick-snick*—like arrows to the chest.

Sable looked down, knowing she wouldn't be able to school her features. Unlike him, it was a skill she'd never figured out.

It wasn't a no, it was a plea. But could she heed his words and walk away? Should she? In her past, it was what she

would have done. Bent to his will to ensure he was happy.
But now? She was on a mission here, to no longer bend.

Rafe swore beneath his breath, muttering something
about patience and strength. She felt him near right before
he nudged a finger under her chin and forced her to look
him in the eye.

"Know what else?" he said, his voice rough. "You're
not the same girl either. That girl was so tangled up inside—about her mother, about her future, about what people thought about her. But now..."

"Now?"

"Steel," he said. "Along the way you've found yourself
some inner steel. It suits you. A great deal." A quick smile,
then it was gone. "But the vision you've built up inside your
head, of how this idea of yours could ever work, it's based
on a phantom. It's not real."

Sable swallowed when tears suddenly burned at the
backs of her eyes. Panic rising in her throat, she dug deep,
connecting with those threads of steel that now wound their
way through her body, and said, "Let me prove you wrong.
Ask me anything and I'll show you I have it covered. I've
got this, Rafe. I promise."

"Anything?" he said.

Sable tried to ignore the skitters along her skin at the
warning in his voice. "Bring it."

"All righty, then. Where would you live? With your
mum? No. That would be a disaster. And not here, you
made that clear. So LA? From what I gather, LA might not
be a good fit right now. So if not LA, how will you find
work? Will you work? Do you still work? If you work, will
you get help? A nanny? If not, what if you get sick? What
if the baby gets sick? And when you say 'no strings' what
does that even mean?"

Once he'd stopped long enough to take more than a single breath, she said, "You done?"

"For now."

"All right, then. I plan to live in New York. Brooklyn, to be precise."

Rafe's frown deepened.

"There's community, neighbourhoods, without the claustrophobia of a small town. Urban suburbia: the perfect place to disappear and simply live. Which sounds pretty much perfect to me. I have a real estate agent on the lookout for an old brownstone in need of some love, near my agent, Nancy, who is also a great friend. There's a brilliant day care on her block and a great independent school. I will work."

As she said it, she knew it to be true. And after months of struggling to feel inspired, struggling to find her voice, it was a blessed relief to have the urge again. No more magazine shoots in Greece, though. She was doing something real.

"But I don't need to work. I've done well for myself over the years but haven't had need to touch much of it."

Her eyes having adjusted to the moonlight, she saw the shadow pass over his eyes just before he said, "Because you lived with him. Your ex."

"Do you have questions about that too?" she asked.

His gaze darkened. "Only one."

Her voice was gentle as she said, "I didn't hear a question."

"Am I your fall-back plan?"

"No!" she said, taking another step his way. Reaching out a hand to him, before curling her fingers back into her palm. "God, no. It's not like that."

One eyebrow slid north. Disbelieving.

But how could she possibly tell Rafe what she'd only come to realise since it all fell apart: that she'd stayed with her ex for so long out of habit? That after the excitement of her first year abroad—the prize, the show, the feting— had died down, she'd been so very lonely. Riccardo had contacted her a month after attending her show—asked her out to lunch. How could she explain that she'd taken that first crumb of attention and held onto it with all her might? Mistaking a roof over her head for a home. Mistaking scraps of attention for love.

When she should have known better.

For here, before her—all dark coiled energy, all strength and drive and goodness—was the man who'd shown her what it meant to truly feel at home. What it meant to be loved. And she'd thrown it away.

But Rafe was onto something. She *was* different now. She had moved on. This was all about her future.

"You were right," she said, choosing her words carefully. "I have changed. More in the past few months than the rest of my life combined. That's what your twenties are for, right? Taking leaps? Making mistakes? Figuring out who you are?"

She must have hit a nerve, as he grunted. It sounded as if it was in agreement.

But then he asked the hardest question of all. "Would you have stayed, would you have had his child, had he not…?"

"Cheated on me with a plethora of women?"

Rafe made no response.

"I'd thought, at one time, that would be the case. A time when I was lonelier than I'd ever imagined I could be. I wondered then if a child might be the answer. Might fix us. But I held back. I thought I wasn't ready, when the truth was I knew it wasn't right."

She lifted her shoulder in a shrug. "Turns out he'd had a vasectomy. Years ago. No intention of letting an accidental pregnancy get in the way of his career. He told me the day I found out about my fertility issues. As if it was a good thing."

"Sable," he said, his voice subterranean.

"Dodged a bullet there, right? Literally!"

Her joke fell flat. For beyond the inviolable, unblinking facade, Rafe's whole countenance was stormy. As if he was imagining all the places around Radiance one could easily hide a dead body.

"You are not my fall-back, Rafe," Sable repeated. Then took a calculated risk, saying, "You're the best man I've ever known. And I've loved this baby of mine, this baby that does not yet exist, in my head for so long, how can I not want the best for her?"

"Her?" he repeated, his voice rough.

Was that a flicker? A softening?

"Could be a him. We'd have to wait and see."

His eyes were so dark now, she couldn't make out the centre. But she had his complete attention.

A husky note threaded through her voice as she said, "Say yes, Rafe. Do this for me."

He laughed, though there was no humour in it. Then he growled, loudly, as he ran two hands over his face. "You're not getting a yes. But—and I can't believe I'm even saying this—it's not a no. What it is, is enough for tonight. I'm going to Sydney tomorrow to finish the Pontiac deal. To get some distance so I can think straight. But for now, let me take you home."

For a moment she thought it was an invitation—and all her girl parts jumped to attention. Till she realised he meant *her* home. Her mother's place.

"Thanks. But I think I'll go it alone." Things had ended well, but precariously. She did not want the chance to ruin it. She turned on her heel, wrapped her coat about her, and walked. Throwing, "Come find me when you get back," over her shoulder.

Rafe caught up to her. "Never know who might be out on a night like this. Werewolves. Abductors. The McGlinty brothers."

"Don't the McGlinty brothers work for you?"

"Right. So they do. And they're actually great boys. If they saw you out and about they'd likely offer to drop you home too."

"Radiance. It's gone all mellow in its old age."

"No place like home," said Rafe, and Sable felt a clutch in her chest.

"You're really going to walk with me unless I let you drive, aren't you?"

"Mmm-hmm."

"Fine. Drop me home. Where's your car?"

Rafe motioned to the astounding line-up of muscle cars under the awning on the other side of the petrol pumps. "Take your pick."

It was Sable's turn to laugh, but hers was real. Like air bubbles popping in her chest. "Seriously? Are they all yours?"

"Till we've done them up and someone buys them."

"Are they safe out here?" She couldn't imagine them lasting a day in LA. Even in the Hills cars like these would be kept under lock and key.

He cocked his head. Said, "It's Radiance."

Which, she figured, was answer enough.

"Lead the way."

She did. In the end choosing a midnight-blue Charger with enough grunt when Rafe gunned the engine she felt it in her throat.

Glancing across the console, Rafe's profile in stark re-lief, shoulders relaxed, in his happy place, made her ache, just a little, for how things had been.

"Ready?" he asked, giving her a look. A look that made her mouth go dry.

She nodded, and sat back. No longer able to ignore the spark burning brightly between them. Now she simply chose not to act on it.

CHAPTER SIX

By the time they rounded the bend, and the peak of her mother's gabled witchy roof slunk into sight, Sable was ready to leap from the car.

All that moonlight pouring through the car windows. The warmth of the man beside her. The radio playing softly. It was like stepping back in time. Except she used to sit with one foot tucked up on the seat, the other on the dash, her head tilted to watch him. All cool and capable and hers.

She'd yabber on about some new spot she'd found on one of her forest walks, and he'd listen, an elbow on the window frame, a slight smile on his face. Or he'd glance her way, his gaze filled with enough promise to make her toes curl.

Back in the now, Sable kept both feet firmly on the floor, and her eyes front. But the snippets of their recent conversation swirling in her head did her no favours.

"You've found yourself some inner steel. It suits you. A great deal."

"You're the best man I've ever known."

"The moment I saw you, it all came rushing back."

Then there was the look in his eye when she'd spoken about her ex. The look in his eye when he'd said, "Her?"

The car slowed. Sable unbuckled. The car stopped, and she was out of there.

She leaned into the open door and said, "Thanks! I guess I'll see you when you get back?" But Rafe was already hopping out of the driver's side.

She stood so fast she got a head rush. Or maybe it was the sight of him over the top of the car as he ambled around the bonnet. Swinging his keys around a finger. His chin lifted, breathing in the chill night air.

When his eyes met hers, the edge of his mouth kicked north and she found herself stuck.

He looked loose, as if something she'd said had eased his mind. While she felt all tight and clammy with *You're the best man I've ever known* swimming about between her ears.

Remembering she was still standing with the car door open, she slammed it shut. And made to move towards the house.

"Sable," Rafe said.

She gave him a quick glance but kept on walking. "You can head off. No werewolves here. They'd be too scared of my mother to come close." Then she lost her footing and slipped on some damp leaves. He spun her towards him, an arm sliding behind her back, so that she wouldn't fall.

And suddenly there she was. In his arms again. Her heart beat so loudly in her throat, surely he had to hear it.

"We have to stop meeting like this," she said, trying to break the tension.

Only his hot gaze trailed slowly to her mouth. And he held her, in his big strong arms. It would take nothing at all to fist her hand in the front of his shirt, lift up onto her toes and kiss him.

It could be a goodbye kiss. A have-a-good-trip kiss.

Except he'd slide a hand into the hair at the back of her neck, the strands clinging to his fingers. His other arm slipping around her waist. And he'd kiss her right on back. Soft and sweet and slow, this time. A kiss full of longing and promise.

While she'd melt against him, her lips clinging to his, her body trembling.

Blooming slippery heat and swelling need. Till she could no longer feel the cold. Could no longer sense the night. Till she was drowning in him.

Some last thread of sanity had Sable curling her fingers

into fists and looking down, her forehead making contact with his chest. There she breathed for a beat or two. For she would not put herself in a position fated to doom.

Once she could feel her feet again, she disentangled herself from his grip, and ducked through her mother's broken front gate.

Waving over her shoulder, as if fearing even looking at Rafe again she'd jump into his arms, she said, "Thanks for the lift. And hearing me out. And the—" *Don't you dare thank him for the kiss.* "Have a good time in Sydney!"

Then she all but jogged down the driveway and went to heave open the front door. Only to find it wouldn't budge. For where there had been no lock, no handle, now there was both.

"Are you kidding me?" Sable muttered between gritted teeth.

Sable stomped down the steps, and—ignoring the dark shape standing not two metres away—she moved around the side of the house.

The ground beneath her boots squished, and slurped, sucking at her soles, while throwing up the occasional rock to attempt to twist her ankle. So long as she didn't meet a spider web, a toad, a snake, she'd be okay.

One window, two, three, there. Sable slid her fingers under the thin frame of her bedroom window, the wood twisted and gnarled like arthritic fingers, groaning under her efforts, before lifting a good foot in one heave, then jamming. It had to be enough.

She tore off her huge coat and shoved it through the crack. Then she stuck her head inside, followed by her shoulders, then with a leap she pushed herself through the gap, only to find herself stuck.

For her backside had wedged. She was nearly ten years older than the last time she'd done this after all. And now she teetered like a human seesaw.

Feeling all the feels—frustrated, embarrassed, fragile—she closed her eyes and yelled into the darkness. Then she huffed out a breath and let herself hang, her hair falling over her face like a wavy curtain, her legs dangling out of the window.

"Here," a deep voice murmured from behind her, close enough for her to squeak. "Let me help."

And then Rafe's hands were on Sable's backside, square and firm, one on each butt cheek as he gave her a shove. She gripped the window frame under her hips and wriggled as she began to shift, incrementally at first, then—like water through a hole in a dam—in a big rush.

Sable slid over the small white desk under the window and landed in a heap on the rough rug on the floor.

"You okay?" the deep voice said, humour lighting the dark.

Sable lifted her head, peeled her hair out of her mouth and found Rafe heaving the window open as if it was nothing.

Then he leaned into the gap, his strong forearms resting on the sill. Long fingers gripping one wrist, the other hand dangling over the edge.

Her breath caught as she took a mental snapshot. Moonlight casting a glow around his shoulders, shadows bleeding into the shallows of the brawny tendons in his forearms, the divots outlining his work-roughened knuckles, the gap between his lips.

Looking part caveman, part Viking, part poet, he was still the most beautiful thing she'd ever photographed.

"Sable?" Mercy called from somewhere inside the house, snapping Sable out of her reverie. "That you screaming blue murder?"

"Ah, yep! In...my room!" she called, feeling as if she were in some kind of vortex between the present and the past as she flapped a hand at Rafe, urging him to disappear.

But he only grinned at her. Adding crinkles to the edges of his dark eyes, a flash of strong white teeth in the shadows of his gorgeous face.

"I thought I heard voices," her mother said as she sauntered into the room, snapped on the naked bulb overhead, all but blinding Sable in the process. "Rafe?"

Rafe nodded. "Mercy."

Sable rubbed her eyes and squinted up at Rafe, then her mother, then Rafe again. Stunned to find both of them calm and smiling.

"You still here," Mercy said.

"Looks that way," he said.

"Unusual for you to stick around this long. Usually see the back of you before I even get the chance to say hello."

At that Rafe smiled. "Off to Sydney tomorrow."

"Right. Good. How's your sister?" her mother asked.

"She's doing all right," said Rafe with a quick smile. Then, "Thank you. And your tomatoes?"

"Thriving. The marigolds really did keep the grasshoppers away." Then a strained, "Thank you."

Sable leant back against the saggy couch. "I feel like I'm in *The Twilight Zone*."

With an exasperated sigh her mother said, "And why is that?"

"You. And him. Having a conversation. Like normal people."

"As opposed to abnormal people?"

As opposed to you telling me to stay away from the boy next door if I had any hope of making something of my life. That he would be the end of all my hopes and dreams and I'd end up just like you.

"What are you doing on the floor?" her mother asked.

"The front door was locked."

Another ever-patient sigh from her mother before, "Well, you were the one who was so insistent I get a lock. There's never been any pleasing you. Give my regards to your sister, Rafe," she said over her shoulder as she wafted from the room.

"Will do," Rafe called back.

Sable scrubbed both hands over her face, before hauling herself to her feet. She winced at a pain in her hip. Another in the heel of her palm.

"You okay?"

Not even close. "Sure," she said, wincing again as she shifted. "Peachy."

After a moment he nodded. And offered up a smile. With crinkly eyes.

Funny that the brooding dissatisfaction had done it for her as a teen. But as a grown-up, this new-found assuredness of his had her feeling all wired and warm.

Rafe's mouth moved, a slight twitch, and she realised she was staring.

She cleared her throat, glanced away. "How long till you're back?"

"Not long," he assured her.

"Okay. We can talk then, then. About…things."

"Yeah," he said, blinking a moment before drawing away, figuratively and literally, rubbing a hand over the back of his neck as he backed away from the window. "Goodnight, Sutton."

"Goodnight, Rafe."

And then he was gone. The window empty bar darkness and moonlight and a light breeze.

Still feeling a little wobbly after the whole kisses in the garage, drive through the moonlight, Rafe's hands on her backside thing, Sable wasn't sure she could cope with her mother. But she went in search anyway, finding Mercy in the kitchen, cleaning what looked like home-grown kale.

"Hungry?" Mercy said.

Sable grimaced as she pulled up a wonky kitchen stool, the bruise on her hip smarting. "Nope. I'm all good."

"Mmm," said Mercy. Then, "So, you and Rafe."

"There is no me and Rafe. Not in the way you mean." Okay, they were in discussions about him fathering her child but, apart from that, nothing to see here.

Mercy snorted. "You keep telling yourself that."

Sable bristled. "I've struggled to catch you these last days, but now we're both here, why don't we catch up? Fill me in—what's the haps in Radiance these days?"

Mercy just kept washing her kale. It would be the cleanest kale ever at this rate. But that was how she went about things. Loud then silent. Keeping Sable in a state of constant vigilance.

It reminded her so much of The Chef she wished she could go back in time, grab her young self by the scruff of the neck and say, *Wake up to yourself!*

At least now she could not be bothered to play her mother's games any more. "You know what, I'm bushed. I might go to my room for a bit. Unless you want help with dinner?"

She made to push back the chair when Mercy said, "Sit down, kid. You know full well I'm happy to see you. But I also wish you'd stayed away."

Sable laughed. It was either that or cry. Then she sank her head into her hands and rubbed her face hard. When she looked at her mother from between her fingers, Mercy was giving her a look.

"I just never wanted you to end up like me, falling for some small-town boy before you even had the chance to know who you were without him."

"I know that. I do." For Mercy had told her so every single day of her life. Her mother's heart was in the right place, even if her parenting methods were less warm and fuzzy and more steamroller. "So, I went away. And I made mistakes anyway. Some really big ones, in fact. But that's okay, because that's how it goes. That's life."

"Mmm."

"I need you to know, though. To really hear me on this. Rafe was never a mistake. He was kind to me. He looked out for me. He respected me, and wished the best for me. He liked me, just as I was. He was my very best friend."

"And now?"

"Now he's a good man I once knew."

The kale lay limp on the cutting board, as Mercy looked off into the distance.

Sable's heart kicked as it did those rare moments her mother didn't school her features. When she was spent. Or late at night when she had nothing to keep her hands busy. Or when she opened the mail box to find it empty.

Then Mercy collected herself and shot Sable a look. "Don't fool yourself. I'll admit, Rafe isn't one of the worst, but they are good at appearing good, till they get what they want."

When she went back to the kale it tore between her fine fingers.

Sable imagined it would have taken a strong man to dare even approach Mercy Sutton, much less gain her trust. Meaning her mother must have fallen hard for her father. Not that she knew for sure. Mercy had rarely ever mentioned him directly. But it was clear—from her obstinacy, her reclusiveness, the way they'd moved around constantly when Sable was a kid—Mercy had held onto the hurt of losing him ever since.

Till it defined her.

And if that wasn't a life lesson to be gentle with yourself, to forgive and nurture and let yourself grow beyond your follies, Sable didn't know what was.

Feeling a rare moment of connectedness with her mother, Sable pushed back her chair, moved around the kitchen bench and leaned in to kiss Mercy on her cool cheek. Her mother leaned in to accept it. A bare quarter inch, but it was something.

"Dinner's in ten minutes," Mercy grumbled. "Come sit with me even if you're not eating."

"Okay, *Mum*."

Mercy sent Sable a tight smile.

Back in her room Sable saw that the rug had buckled when she'd fallen in through the window. She gave it a yank, only to expose a slat of old wood a different colour from the rest. A slat with a missing nail.

She crouched, and jimmied the thing loose. And below the floorboards she found a small tin box. Inside it a treasure trove of memories, sentimental things her mother would have thrown away in a heartbeat.

A pure white feather. A smooth pink stone. A postcard Sable had once found among the junk mail her mother had dumped on the bench.

It was from Greece, the return address a scrawl she could barely make out. When Sable had brought it to her mother, Mercy had taken one look, her face brightening, then crumpling, before she'd thrown the card in the bin. Sable had fished it out later that night, stuck it back together, spinning tales in her head that it might have been from her father. Kidnapped by pirates and sending secret messages so her mother knew she was not forgotten.

But the card wasn't what she was hoping to find inside the little tin box.

There, having slid down beneath everything else, a thin, gold-plated chain, the clasp of which was held together with a slim arrow half the width of her wrist. The bracelet Rafe had given her for her seventeenth birthday. The same night she'd pushed him up against a hay bale in the loft of his father's barn and told him he loved her and it was time to stop pretending otherwise.

As her thumb ran over the dainty curves of the arrow, she remembered opening the gift. And Rafe's voice came to her as clear as if he were whispering the words in her ear.

"You cast your spell on me the moment you looked at me, lying on the banks of the river, your witch eyes drinking me in. You shot an arrow through my heart. Also, I hope and pray the arrow magically infuses you with some small sense of direction, as yours is a shocker."

He'd been nineteen and magnificent as a cloudless midnight sky. She'd loved him for years, so fiercely she'd feared it might cleave her in half. The thought of spending a day apart, much less years, would have been unimaginable.

But if she'd stayed... What was the likelihood they'd still be together?

If she'd stayed, would Rafe have had the gumption, the time, the drive to buy Stan out? Would he have been as driven to make something of himself, to create the big life he now led? The life that had mellowed him, given him purpose. Or would he have poured every ounce of that energy into loving her?

Her mother had wanted her to leave. To protect her. And to forge her.

But Sable now knew leaving was the best thing she could have done for *him*.

Early the next morning Rafe hooked a left from his driveway, about to head to the airport, when he found himself pulling up outside the house next door.

He noted the broken shingles over the front door. The gutters in need of a clean out. He'd get on to that for Mercy. But that wasn't why he'd stopped.

"Just go," he said.

The car said nothing back.

Swearing beneath his breath, Rafe switched off the engine, and got out. Clueless as to what excuse he'd make for knocking on the door. Asking after her bumps and bruises following her fall through the window? Suggesting she check in on Janie if she was bored?

Or to tell Sable, now, so it was done, that while he'd heard her last night, while her words had made him see how serious she was, his answer had to be no.

And not for the reason he would ever have imagined.

Yes, growing up, "family" had been a dirty word. Just because someone was blood, did not mean there would be love, or any instinct to care, no matter what. It was a choice. One that you had to decide to make every day.

But the reason that had kept swimming through his head as he'd tried to fall asleep the night before? If he said yes, and if by some miracle Sable actually had his child, he could not imagine a world in which that child did not know who he was.

It was the "her".

When Sable had innocently let that slip, it had knocked him sideways. Leaving a crack through which a vision had slipped. The vision of a little girl.

Not dark like Janie, but fair like Sable. With her hazel eyes and his curls. He pictured himself, clear as if it were a real memory, holding her tiny hand as he helped her navigate the stones across the river. The same stones he'd used dozens of times, with her mother.

Picturing that little girl, out there in the world, knowing he'd agreed not to be a part of her life? He'd never agree to that. For he knew what it felt to be that child. To have a parent know him, and still turn their back on him. That wasn't the kind of man he was.

Rafe glanced down the side of the house. Once upon a time he'd have slunk through those shadows, and levered open Sable's window.

This time, he walked up to the front door and knocked.

A few beats later, Mercy answered. Gave him a quick

once-over. He gave one right on back, which made her laugh out loud.

She leant in the doorway and said, "She's not here."

Rafe would have bet the farm on the fact she'd chosen those words deliberately. For they were the exact same words Mercy had used on him to let him know Sable had fled to the other side of the world.

"That so?" he said.

"Don't panic, boy," she said, even while he thought he'd hidden the brief flash of it rather well. "She went off into the bush with her old camera an hour ago. Like stepping back in time seeing her with that thing around her neck again."

While Rafe breathed again. "What makes you think I'm not here to see you?"

A smile kicked at the corner of Mercy's mouth. For they'd formed a grudging friendship over the years. The only two people in the world who understood what it meant to have a Sable-sized hole in their lives.

Mercy pushed the door wider and padded inside. And while he wasn't sure he'd had enough uninterrupted sleep to take a Mercy conversation, he followed her inside.

"Water?" she called over her shoulder. "Tea? Tequila?"

It was eight in the morning. "Not for me. But you go right ahead."

Mercy stopped in the kitchen, pulled up a stool, and said, "If you're here to ask for my blessing to start something up with my daughter again you're not getting it."

He could have assured her that was far from the case, but found himself saying, "Don't need your blessing, Mercy. Never did."

"You sure about that? Didn't take much encouragement for her to leave you the first time."

Rafe's fingers went to the bridge of his nose. "I'd be really careful, Mercy. She left to make you happy. Make sure she also knows you're happy she's back."

Mercy's expression twisted before she looked away. "Sooner she gets back out there, the better. She was living the dream, you know."

"Not her dream." For Rafe knew all about Sable's dream. She'd spent the last few days drawing it out for him in painstaking detail.

Then Mercy surprised the heck out of him, her nostrils flaring before her face crumpled, her bottom lip quivering before she looked down at her hands. "I thought she was doing fine."

There's that word again.

Rafe leaned forward, resting his elbows on his knees. "I'm sure she was. For a time. But from what I can gather, she's been lost out there for some time. Did you not pick up on it? When you talked?"

"I wondered," she said, then rallied in true Mercy fashion. "But life is a struggle." Then she crumbled again. It was like an emotional roller coaster. "I never got the feeling that he—that man of hers—was bad to her. I figured he was merely ambivalent."

"And that was okay with you?"

She looked up, her eyes intensely green, with none of her daughter's softness, pinning him with a glare. "*You* were never ambivalent."

Rafe stilled. Not sure if that was an accusation, or a compliment. "Thank you?"

"You want to know why she left you?"

If he'd seen it coming, he might have been able to steel himself. Janie called it his balaclava look. Instead, his entire body jolted.

"I saw you," said Mercy. "In the jewellery store. You were looking at a diamond ring."

Rafe held his breath as his memories whipped back through time. In the silence, wind set the tree branches outside scratching against the sunroom windows.

He could tell Mercy was waiting for him to play dumb. But doing what was expected had never been his way. "I'd saved for it for months. Years, really. I was going to give it to her on her eighteenth birthday."

Mercy's face worked. "My problem with you, Rafe Thorne, was never personal. My daughter was always too naïve. She needed grit. Resilience. She could never find that inside of her when she had you making things too easy for her."

Sounded pretty personal to him.

"So I told her to go. Told her she'd never forgive herself if she didn't. That I was prime example of what it felt like to live too small a life."

Mercy's background had always been a mystery. But he wasn't going to bite now. This was about Sable. And about him. "Here's the thing neither of you seemed to grasp— I'd never have held her back if I'd known about the prize. Even if it meant letting her go."

Mercy's mouth flickered.

"Not that it matters now," said Rafe.

"Rubbish. Watching you together, last night, the look in her eyes, the look in yours—" She exhaled hard. "If you care for her at all, and I know that you do, let her go. Let her go for good."

Rafe let Sable's mother sling every charge she needed to sling. For he knew that Mercy's hardness grew from a deep, instinctual love for her daughter. The kind he'd never had with his own parents. But even while he could have put her mind a little at ease with assurances, or a blood oath, the promise simply refused to come.

For she wasn't entirely wrong. There was a significant connection between them. Whether it was chemical, or electrical, or some force he'd never understand, it was a connection that distance, time and heartache had not severed.

Deciding to act on it, or not, that was where free will came in. She'd chosen to leave. She'd chosen to return. While he was choosing to…bide his time till he'd cleared his head.

He rapped a knuckle on the edge of her bench and said, "I'm late. Have to go." Then he turned and walked back down the hall.

"I won't tell her you came by!" Mercy called.

Rafe waved in response. Fine with him. He wouldn't know how to explain that conversation to Sable if he'd wanted to.

He'd go to Sydney, pick up the Pontiac, drive it to Melbourne. A good long car ride was the best way he knew how to clear his head.

He might even get onto the mob in Dubai, negotiate an extension. He could check in with his London branch for a few days, leaving Janie to keep on with the prep on the upcoming Pumpkin Festival car show that was happening a few weeks after that.

Give himself some solid time to put his decision into words he could live with.

Sable would just have to wait.

CHAPTER SEVEN

TWO DAYS LATER Rafe rumbled through Radiance in the restored Pontiac Parisienne he'd driven down from Sydney.

The window was down, his arm resting on the windowsill, as he breathed in the crisp autumn air. No other place in the world smelled quite like it. Fresh, clear, with a tangy edge.

Home.

But it wasn't the promise of clean air that had him driving a smidge over the speed limit the entire way back from Sydney. Or the promise of light traffic making him take a left at Albury rather than taking the straight run to Melbourne. It also wasn't the reason he wasn't on his way to Dubai, or London for that matter.

It was the same reason he'd been on edge for the past two days, spending more time under cars than buying or selling, only blowing his calendar out all the more.

He needed to get the Sable issue sorted.

His phone burred. He answered, hands free. "Janie, what's up?"

"Wanda rang, she said she saw you trundling down the avenue, and could I send you her way as soon as possible as her oven light isn't working. Aren't you meant to be in Abi Dhabi?"

"Dubai." He slowed as a sprinkling of swallows swerved from the treetops and into his lane before flittering off into the sky. "I'm sending Jake from the London office in my stead."

Janie's silence was telling.

"You still there?"

"Sorry, just had to pick myself up off the floor. Did you just say that you're…*delegating*?"

Rafe rolled out a shoulder and ducked to look through the low-slung branches of an elm to see if he could find a familiar blonde head in any of the Laurel Avenue shops. "It seems so."

"Am I allowed to hypothesise why?"

"Nope."

"Okay. Look, I wasn't going to say anything, but since your entire world is going topsy-turvy already, you should probably know it's been a little rough here for her the last couple of days."

Rafe didn't need to ask to know who the "her" was. "How so?"

"Some American tourist recognised Sable, walked up and snapped a photo right in her face while she was eating a pie at Bear's. Big Bear lived up to his name, shooed them out, gave them the fright of their lives, but it was all over the tabloids within the hour. Headlines such as *Shamed Star's Girlfriend Celeb Shutterbug Sable Sutton Seen Stuffing Her Face in Small-Town Hideaway as She Laments Loss of Famous Foodie Lover.*"

Rafe flinched. It was rough stuff. On many levels. Not least of which the jumbled alliteration. "Please tell me you're reading that and didn't memorise it."

"Want to hear the others?"

"That would be a no."

"Okay. There's more. Trudy refused service at the wool store, telling Sable she didn't belong around here."

Rafe tapped the brake hard enough the car nearly stalled.

"I took care of it," said Janie. "Swung by when I was picking up wood from the hardware store to start making the signs for the car show, asked Trudy what the hell she thought she was doing. She blanched like an almond. Said she'd heard Wanda tell Carleen that Sable had done you wrong, and this town looks after its own. I told her Sable *was* our own and to send her some free wool in apology. The good stuff."

"*You* did that?"

"Yup."

This from Janie, who would never leave her cosy little cave if she had the choice. If he wasn't around to nudge her. Make her feel safe. "I'm impressed."

"We Thornes stick together. And now that I'm soon to be an auntie it was my duty."

Rafe tapped the brakes hard that time, the tyres protesting. He glanced in the rear-view mirror to find not a soul behind him the entire way up the avenue. "What's that, now?"

"Ah, right. The auntie thing. Ed let slip when I had him over for dinner."

"Ed?" he parroted. She'd had Ed over for *dinner*? And, "What the hell does Ed know about anything?"

"Turns out he'd forgotten something at work the other night and when he turned up you and Sable were there. Talking. *About what?* said I, being sisterly and nosey. You should have seen his face when he realised he should have kept mum! So to speak. But it was too late. I grilled him. Poor guy folded like a pack of cards. So, you guys are thinking about making a baby, eh? That was fast."

Small towns, Rafe thought, his inner voice a fractious growl.

Sable's words from the other night came swimming back to him. Her dream to be somewhere with the comfort of community but also the private space to figure things out on her own. Somewhere to *"disappear and simply live".*

And in that moment he got it. All of it. Like a snapshot framed on the mantelpiece. He saw her dream as she imagined it, with a clarity that hit like a punch in the gut.

Rafe thanked everything good and holy when he hit the red light in town so that he could slow to a stop. Running a finger over his bottom lip, he tried to find the right words. Then decided the words weren't for Janie. Not yet. "You home this arvo? I'll swing by then. For a chat. About a brother's right to privacy. And staying away from Ed McGlinty."

In that moment, he felt a flash of affinity with Mercy.

Janie huffed out a breath. "Fine. I'll make a cake. Now go throw stones at her window. Or climb her tower. Or whatever it is you old folk do to woo one another."

"I'm not wooing her. And I'm not old."

"Whatever." With that his sister hung up.

The light turned green, the engine caught, rumbled winningly as it picked up pace. Rafe kept the speed down, checking every shopfront till he saw her.

In Wanda's Cakes and Stuff, of all places. Her hands making pictures in the air as she chatted with someone behind the counter.

Something inside him clutched, tightened, and released. Something that had been coiled in a hard knot since he'd driven out of town. Mercy's words, "She's not here," playing in his head like a broken record. As if deep down inside, he hadn't been entirely sure she'd be there when he got back.

He needed to drop the car at Radiance Restorations, fill it up before getting it to Melbourne, but instead he parked outside Bear's, eased himself up and leapt over the door.

"Look at her go."

Rafe turned, found Bear leaning in the doorway of The Coffee Shop. "Hey," he said, moving in to shake hands.

"Don't let that fool you," said Bear. "They've been giving her an awful hard time since you've been gone."

"It's been two days."

"A lot can happen in two days."

Rafe turned, saw it was Wanda herself who Sable was trying to charm. Though Wanda, arms folded, was having none of it. "What is she even doing over there?"

Bear slanted him a look. "You mean trying to charm the hostile locals when she'd much rather be enjoying a quiet coffee in my much nicer establishment? Come on, mate. Think."

Rafe didn't need to think. He knew.

From Janie's report Sable had every excuse for keeping out of the public eye right now, but knowing how hard he'd found being the subject of town talk as a kid, she was out there, smoothing the way. For him.

As if she was a ripple in the fabric of his existence. Rather than a seismic event.

Rafe took off across the street, pausing to let a single car cruise down the avenue, then jogging the rest of the way.

A half-dozen faces looked up from their conversations as he whipped open the door. Sable turned at the last. Her hands mid move. Her mouth half open.

Then she smiled. Her eyes lighting up, as if inside someone had flipped a switch.

As if *he'd* flipped a switch.

Rafe's lungs emptied in a rush. He felt more than a little light-headed. And the urge to go to her, to drag her into his arms and kiss her till that sunshine filled him too was strong enough he had to press his shoes into the floor.

Because that wasn't why she was back. It *would* only complicate things. Just as she said.

Only, now, none of that held quite the same sway as it did a week ago. None of it was enough to negate the power, the charge he felt just being near her. Making his *fine* life look two-dimensional in comparison.

"Rafe Thorne!" That was Wanda, coming at him with open arms. She enveloped him in a hug that smelled like lanolin and icing sugar. "You here to fix my oven light?"

"Not today, Wanda. I've got a sweet Pontiac outside and I promised Sable a ride."

The customers all craned their heads, oohing and aahing at the slick car gleaming across the road. One of them muttered, "I bet he did."

And Sable's smile slipped, her gaze lowering. As if all the work she'd put in the past two days to try to smooth things over, for him, had been for nought.

Done with overthinking things, Rafe did the one thing that had always served him, had never let him down. He followed his gut.

Holding out a hand, he said, "You ready, Sutton?"

Sable looked at it, then at the customers who were all watching the interplay with bated breath, then back at him.

He gave her a nod. A subtle wink. All but daring her to take it.

Finally, her hand reached out, cool fingers sliding into his as the sleeve of her jacket slipped back, revealing her wrist. And the fine, gold bracelet wrapped around it.

When she saw the angle of his gaze, she went to pull her sleeve back down, but he took his chance to tug her in close, tuck her hand into his elbow.

He ran a thumb over the fine gold chain. Turned her wrist to find the arrow he'd known would be there.

And something inside him locked into place.

Like a lost puzzle piece that had been missing for years.

He opened the door for her, made room for her to walk through before him. Together they crossed the street. Hips bumping. His hand still resting over hers, his thumb tracing the curve of her wrist.

Bear gave them a smile before he slipped back inside his shop.

A few locals walking down the street slowed, gave them a long look before heading on their way.

"Everyone's staring at us," she murmured as they reached the car, taking care to slip her hand out from the crook of his arm.

"Nah," he said, no longer sure what to do with his arm, now she wasn't holding on. "They're staring at you."

Her gaze locked onto his. Beautifully baffled. Rich, mellow hazel. Flecks of grey and gold. The colours of the trees behind her. Of home.

Rafe, buddy, he thought. *If you don't rein this in, you're gonna find yourself in a world of trouble.*

But it was too late. It had always been too late where she was concerned. The connection between them was inescapable.

If they were on opposite sides of the planet, or not. If they had a child together... Or not.

"Rafe?" she whispered, disoriented. "What happened to Sydney? Dubai? Janie mentioned London. I expected... I don't know... That you'd be gone. A while."

"Mmm," he said, taking the time to drink her in in a way he hadn't let himself do, not properly, since her return. "Thought the same myself."

"So what are you doing here?"

"This." He moved in, slid a hand behind her neck.

When she didn't demur, he pressed her gently against the side of the car.

When she didn't push him away, or call him out for complicating things, he leaned in, slowly, deliberately, his entire body aching in protest until—with the people of Radiance his witnesses—his lips met hers.

She stilled at the contact for half a second, before he felt her give. Moving to meet him. Melting in his arms.

Then her hands delved slowly into his hair, sending shards of heat down his spine. And he knew he wasn't alone in this. In the connection, or the missing. In the disarray, or the realisation it was what it was. Change or not, they were who they were.

Yet the kiss remained slow. Tender. Tinged with yearning. Their lips brushing. Lingering. Tasting. Sipping. Offering. Relearning the shape of one another. Lost in a kind of hazy bliss, yet teetering on a knife's edge. As if it could tip over into an inferno any second.

A few seconds later the kiss gentled, and they pulled apart.

Sable's eyes took several moments to flutter open. The surprise, the wonder, the heat in her gaze, the way she remained plastered against him, struck something deeply primal inside.

Inevitable.

"What was that for?" she asked, but there was no castigation in her tone. Merely wonder.

"I heard they've been mean to you."

"They?" she asked, her eyes still not quite focussed.

Rafe cocked his head towards the old men on the park bench outside the barber, then the women with their noses against the window of Wanda's Cakes and Stuff.

"The wool-store lady, thing?" She waved it off. "I've been on the receiving end of far worse."

"Janie told me about the photograph."

Her brow furrowed before smoothing out as she began playing with a loose thread in his shirt. "Oh. That. That kind of thing used to happen all the time. I hated it, but had become…accustomed."

He tried to imagine having to inure himself to having strangers come at him, in vulnerable moments, and sell the spoils for entertainment. "How *do* you get used to something like that?"

"It's fine. Well, not *fine*. I used to smile and try to move on. This time I felt like taking her phone and dropping it in my drink." She shot him a smile that he felt, right in the solar plexus. "But it was clarifying. Made me realise I didn't belong in that space, and neither did I want to. Which made me *really* think about what I did want. And…here I am."

"That doesn't make it right, what Trudy and Wanda

pulled. This was your home, once upon a time. You are one of us, no matter where in the world you might be."

She blinked up at him, her eyes coming over a little glossy. Before she swallowed and shook her head. "Don't worry about it. They're just looking out for you. Which makes me appreciate how far they've come. In fact, I wouldn't be surprised if a couple of those women have shrines to you in their basements—"

And from one blink to the next her gaze cleared.

"Hang on a second. Is *that* why you kissed me like that, in front of the whole town? Because you were trying to *protect* me? Just like our first kiss all over again?"

Was it? Partly. And partly because he couldn't *not* kiss her. Which was becoming a problem. One he was apparently willing to take on.

"I can look after myself, Rafe," she said, her face mutinous. "I'm not your responsibility."

But he refused to be pushed away. Not without the chance to have his say. He tucked her in closer. She glared up at him. But made no move to disengage. Her finger was still playing with the loose thread near his heart.

This push and pull, this constant humming tension, it had been their hallmark. For their relationship hadn't happened overnight—it had been built over years. Layers and layers of discovery and demand, differences and insecurities, trust and surrender. Some of which had been swept away by her departure, but not all. The foundations had been too well laid.

That foundation had been the one thing that had kept him upright when she left. For all that her leaving had shattered him, the fact that she'd been in his life at all was the reason he'd come as far as he had. She'd seen such good in him, with her ability to see beauty in places others saw only despair.

Would he ever have been able to realise his dream without her?

Without him would she be able to realise hers?

Her finger slid out from the grip of the cotton and laid over his chest. Her fingers curling gently against his shirt. He felt his heart thump, once, twice, a solid, sure, steady decided beat. A response he'd learned to trust when he'd had nothing else to rely on.

And he heard himself say, "Yes."

"*Yes?* Yes, I can look after myself?" Her eyes widened. "Or yes, as in…?"

Rafe glanced over Sable's shoulder to find the over-sixties walking group standing in a clump, gawping at them. The men in the barber shop had now spilled onto the footpath as well. Bear was out there, trying to hustle them all into The Coffee Shop, but they were all far too immersed in the show playing out before them.

"Can we go for that drive?" Rafe asked.

"Don't you have to get the car to Melbourne?"

"I'll get someone else to finish the trip. In a bit."

"Oh."

"Shall we?"

She nodded, her eyes still wild and wide, her head bobbing like a marionette. When he moved her aside just enough to open the passenger door, she spilled bonelessly inside.

While Rafe felt as if the next hour might well determine the course of his life from that moment on. Not only regarding the possibility of a child out there in the world, but the woman who'd stormed back into his life.

With the roof down, the wind was bracing. But Sable barely noticed for her mind was all a spin as Rafe drove out of town, up into the hills, round and around, till she lost her sense of direction.

Rafe, elbow resting on the windowsill, a finger sliding back and forth over the seam of his lips, his other hand relaxed on the wheel, had a faraway look. Serious.

Her heart clutched as a wave of tenderness, of heat, swept over her. Followed by a swift chill as the word *Yes* swam through her head like a fever dream.

For a second there she'd thought he'd meant… But no. Maybe? She'd thought her arguments were very convincing, so why not?

Sable risked another glance. What was he thinking about? His grocery list? Maybe he was still mulling over how he could make sure the people of Radiance treated her right.

For he was a protector at heart. Always had been. Protecting Janie from the mess she'd been born into. Protecting the memory of his mother, a woman she'd never heard him speak ill of, even while the pain of her departure was written over every line in his face. Even protecting his father, mostly from himself.

He'd kissed her, it seemed, to protect her too.

But it hadn't felt that way. It had felt as if a storm that had been brewing for days had finally broken. It had felt like coming home.

And this time, no single part of her leapt up and said, *Stop! We can't! Too complicated!*

Because for a few beautiful moments it had been such pure relief to slip back to a much simpler time. When she was an anonymous girl who loved nothing more than taking photos of things that other people neglected, and falling for the brooding boy next door.

Sable coughed on her thoughts. Then coughed some more.

Rafe shot her a look. "You okay?"

She gave him a thumbs up, even though she wasn't sure that was entirely true.

She'd only been caught up in a memory of feeling, not actually feeling those feelings, right? For surely the worst time to realise you were falling in…*something* with some-one, was not the time to have a baby with them. How twisty was that?

Were her crumbling defences inevitable, or was she self-sabotaging? Was this whole thing a prime example of her putting herself in a "situation doomed to fail", as her ex's enabling therapist had so kindly put it?

"I'm just going to put the car away," Rafe said, slowing as the edge of his property appeared. They'd come around the back way, not past her mother's house.

"Sure," Sable squeaked, then cleared her throat, not sure where "away" might be.

They trundled down his driveway, though he didn't stop at the Airstream, instead hooking a left, past a large copse of elms, and liquid ambers in all their autumn glory, which was when she realised where they were heading.

In the direction of the old barn.

A thrill of anticipation—and trepidation—shot down her spine. If she was worried about how her memories were mixing dangerously with the present, the barn would show her exactly where she stood. For, while she might have blocked out their first not-real kiss, she'd not forgot-ten a single moment they'd spent in the loft atop the crum-bling old ruin.

Memories flooded in so thick and fast she could barely keep up. Holding Rafe's hand as they ran inside to get out of a rainstorm. The scent of old hay. The ladder to the loft. Fake candles making the place look so cosy and romantic. The days and nights spent snuggled up together in their se-cret place, debating over what their future might look like.

Only when they rounded the trees it was to find the barn was no more.

While it took her head a few moments to take in its replacement—a massive two-storey utilitarian building the size of a small aeroplane hangar—Sable's heart got there all too quick. Squeezing so hard she let out a small noise. Like an ache she couldn't contain.

It should have been less of a shock, for the thing had been held together by branches of the trees growing through it, littered with cracks in the walls, panels torn away by weather, the frame rotted over time. She wondered when it had finally collapsed. Or had Rafe torn *it* down too? Had he exorcised her from his life, the way he had his father?

Heart now beating in her ears, she watched in silence as a massive roller door in the side of the building opened with a loud rumble.

Rafe eased the car inside. And whatever trepidation and concern had been flickering about inside her disappeared as shock overtook it all.

Sensor lights flickered on revealing what amounted to a car collector's paradise.

Rafe pulled into a space beside an old Bentley. Beside that sat a deep red vintage Ferrari. A gleaming Mustang crouched beyond that. And another. Early models, seriously rare. Car after spectacular car. Some covered in tarps. Others gleaming under the bright lights.

Gaze absorbing all there was to see, she noted a workshop. Down the far end a small office and kitchenette and bathroom. The ceiling was a mile above, held there by a criss cross of metal beams, except at the far end where a second floor had been built in. At the top of a set of thin stairs leading to a closed door.

She swallowed. If memory served, that was also where the loft had been. Their loft.

The car door opened with a snick beside her and she looked up to find Rafe, hand out. She took it, tingles and warmth coursing up her arm. She gently disentangled herself before he figured out, by some kind of osmosis, that she was going all gooey on him.

Then she glanced across to the far wall and saw it. In the same pressed tin as the Radiance Restoration sign, a series of big letters across the workshop wall saying, The Barn. And her knees nearly went out from under her.

Recovering, as well as she could, she asked, "What is this place?"

Rafe laughed, all deep and rumbly, a boot scuffing the polished concrete floor. "The shop is where the bulk of the work is done. This is my display case. I bring clients here from time to time. Temperature and humidity controlled. Special air-conditioning units for dust prevention."

"Wow. The contents must be worth more than the land they're sitting on. Please tell me you have excellent insurance."

"An eye-watering amount."

"Are they all yours?"

"Some," he said with a quiet smile. "A few are here early for the Pumpkin Festival car show. I started it a few years back, with Stan's help, now Janie runs it every year. It's become one of the biggest in the country. Others are ready to be shipped off to their owners. That one," he said, pointing to the tomato-red Ferrari that looked just like the one out of *Ferris Bueller's Day Off*, "is heading to a tech billionaire type from Silicon Valley. The two Mustangs are a his-and-hers pair we brought up to scratch after finding the husks in a shed in Dubbo. Prince Alessandro Giordano of Vallemont choppered in to see them when he was here visiting with his new bride, an Aussie girl from just down the way."

"Who *are* you?" she asked.

He laughed, cheeks pinking, just a smidge, as he ran a hand up the back of his neck. "Now I feel like I'm showing off."

"As well you should! It's very impressive, Rafe. You

should be proud of what you've achieved here. Even if you did have to pull down our barn to do it."

She shot him a sideways glance right as his face flickered. His jaw worked. But he said nothing. Shutting down right before her eyes.

"So the Pumpkin Festival, hey?"

"Mmm." A beat, then, "So you'll be here then? Still?"

"I guess that depends." Blood suddenly beating in her ears, she looked up, held his gaze, and said, "That depends on you."

She waited for him to give her an inkling, some clue of what he was thinking, fully expecting him to shut down completely. To go all stoic and statue-like, when instead he held out a hand.

"Come on," he said. "I want to show you something."

Blood still surging, she took his hand. Fingers gripped protectively around hers, he drew her around the bulk of the cars till they stopped before a smaller lump under an old tarp.

"What's this?" she asked.

He tilted his chin. "Have a look."

She bent, found the edge of the tarp and lifted one corner. The hint of small white-walled tyres, with daisy badges on the wheel rims, was all she needed to know what was beneath.

She whipped the tarp away with a flourish to find a 1972 VW Beetle. Matt black paint dulled by time. Peace-sign-shaped gearstick in need of a polish. With its amateur finish, lack of polish, the dents not quite beaten out, it stood out among the cars behind her like a field daisy in a bouquet of red roses.

She'd been sixteen, maybe, when they'd hauled the VW frame, muddy and filthy and busted, out of the creek that traversed the gully behind their houses, after Rafe had seen the striking photograph she'd taken of the thing. The juxtaposition of progress and nature, of death and regrowth, gloomy greys and fresh greens, going on to become her schtick.

And, oh, the days, months, *years* she'd spent happily watching over him as he'd rebuilt the thing from scratch. Rebuilding—as she'd only later found out—for her.

Sable laid a hand on the cool metal, and every emotion she'd spent the past several days trying to keep at bay overflowed. A longing for the simplicity, the surety of those days, so strong it made her sway.

She moved to the driver's side. Hooked her fingers under the handle. It opened with a clunk. Breathing in the scent—new and old mixing into a heady cocktail—she slid inside. The leather seat squeaked as she sank into it. Her hands wrapped around the hard steering wheel.

When, a few moments later, Rafe hopped into the passenger side, their gazes caught.

"You *kept* it."

He closed his eyes and leant back against the head rest. His large body barely fitting in the small space. "Seems so."

"Why?"

"Thought about letting her go over the years, but couldn't seem to do it."

"Why?" she asked again, the word rough, full of questions she should not be asking. As it opened her up to more than complications. It opened her up entirely.

Rafe tilted his head to look at her. And said, "You know why."

Sable's heart leapt. Her belly dropped. And the rest of her no longer knew which way was up. "Rafe," she said, when she had no idea what else there was to say.

Turned out, he did. "Okay, then."

"Okay?"

"Yes," he said. "The answer is yes. To your request. I'll help you. I'll help you have your child."

"Oh, my God! Oh, Rafe!" She all but crawled across

the seat to throw herself into his arms, hanging on for all her might.

Slowly, inevitably, his arms went around her too. His big hands sliding around her back, his face buried in her hair. The shape of him was so achingly intimate. The heat, the overwhelming surety that with him everything would be all right. It felt like…well, it felt like pure happiness. And even while she knew better than to trust it could last, she let it infuse her, let herself enjoy it, another warm memory to tuck away and bring out on cold lonely nights.

When she pulled back, tears now streaming down her face, she found herself laughing. "Thank you. More than I can possibly say. Now I had a great doctor in LA, but still have to find some here. Or Sydney or Melbourne. Whatever suits you. A good one. The best. Whatever it costs. And I'm paying every cent. We'll need lawyers too, for the contract—"

Rafe stopped her there, with a staying hand. "I have provisos."

"Oh." She swallowed. The edges of her bubble of pure happiness starting to wobble. "Such as?"

"I never wanted kids. You know that. I was also nineteen when I made that declaration. Janie was a nine-year-old wildling, still under my care, my father was in as dark a place as he'd ever been and I had no clue if my mother was even alive. Back then, family was a four-letter word." He stopped, picked a stray fleck of peeling vinyl from the dash. "Now, things are different. I'm different. I'm settled. I have structure in my life. Success. Businesses, I've discovered over the past few days, that can actually run without my micromanagement."

When he paused, Sable took a moment before speaking. For she felt, right to the very marrow, that she was a breath away from feeling the first true spark of her dream coming true and she didn't want to ruin it.

"What are you saying exactly?"

"If we do this, we do it together."

A sudden vision filled her head of them "doing it to-gether", making her mouth go dry, and her palms turn damp. "Mmm?"

The edge of his mouth flickered. "Not like that," he said, his voice rough and raw.

Then something flashed over his face that made her wonder if he was imagining the same thing she just had after all.

"I won't walk away, Sutton. I would have to be involved."

"Oh," she said, when she meant, *No, no, no, no, no.*

This wasn't part of the plan! The whole point was, she was doing this on her own. She was finally claiming agency over her life.

She should have known he wasn't the kind of man who would simply walk away.

You did know, a little voice piped up in the far reaches of her subconscious. A little voice that sounded far too smug. She could all but hear it clapping happily at this turn of events.

She shook it off. She *couldn't* possibly have been sure of anything after all this time.

Except him. You were always sure of him.

She pushed the voice deep, deep down inside and said, "Involved?"

"I can't imagine having a child in the world knowing I chose to be uninvolved." A pause, then, "I know what it feels like to be that kid, Sutton. And so do you."

Sable blinked so hard she had to stop in order to disen-tangle her lashes. "Then again it was the parents who stuck with us who made our childhoods harder still."

She let that sit for a beat.

"Kids are clever. They know when a parent is there under protest. But I won't be that parent. I'll be the mum who loves their kid so deeply they never doubt it. Who shows them and tells them, every single day, how wanted they are. How important. How loved. You know I have that in me, Rafe. You know how it feels to be loved by me."

Oh, God... She heard the words before she could stop them. Saw the heat and the hurt ravage his gorgeous face.

"My point is, if a child is seen, heard, guided, understood, and wanted so patently, surely it doesn't matter if they have one parent, or ten?"

Rafe's gaze was hard on hers as he listened. Really listened. No dismissing her, or deciding instantly that his opinion mattered more. Considering the myriad people she'd had to deal with in her life who did the opposite, it was a hell of a thing. And while bigger things were at stake here, she found another piece of herself falling into his hands.

"What was it you said the other day?" she said. "That romantic vision you had of me heading out into the world and—how did you put it?—*demanding more.* Well, the truth is, until the past few months I'd demanded very little for myself. It was all so foreign, so fast, so lonely—I went along with anything offered. So, this is me demanding more. Demanding I do this on my own."

Her final words were super husky. But what could she do? There was no hiding this was fraught. No hiding this was emotional. That they were both on the verge of something life-changing.

"And this is me, demanding that if we do this, we do it together. You don't get to disappear this time. You don't cut me out."

The word *again* hovered in the tense air between them.

She'd come with a plan, with bullet points, and preparedness. And oodles of rediscovered hope. Her expectations higher than any sane person had the right to feel. Now she wavered between panic and possibility. Disappointment and utter joy.

Rafe was offering up her dream. With addenda.

The next step, the next *yes*—or no—was up to her.

"So what do you say?" said Rafe, his voice wry. "Initial thoughts are fine."

Sable breathed out a laugh as Rafe tossed her the line she'd already used once on him.

And she said, "Yes. It's a yes. Yes, please. And thank you. And, oh, my God, I can't believe this is actually happening!"

"You're telling me."

Sable laughed again. "I imagined this moment so many times, certain I'd be leaping for joy. But instead I feel like I might never stop shaking. This is a big thing, Rafe."

"About as big as things get. Shaking is smart. Parenthood should be humbling."

"Humbling." He was right. Right and good and strong and generous. She couldn't wait to see how all that translated into a brand-new little person in the world. "Can you imagine? A girl with your eyelashes?"

"A girl with your terrible sense of direction."

"Yikes. A boy with your sense of justice."

"A boy with your terrible sense of direction."

She grinned. He grinned back. And she felt it. Like that arrow on her wrist, right through the chest.

Rafe reached out, found her fingers and entwined them with his. Then used them to draw her in. And she went to him. For it felt right, as right as any part of this plan, that they should seal their bargain on a single sweet kiss.

When she pulled away, he had a look in his eye that had her all but ready to ask why the hell they needed doctors. They *knew* how to make babies the old-fashioned way.

But her reach for independence, for autonomy, her determination to hold true to herself, could not waver.

Yet here they were. Holding hands and gazing into one another's eyes.

She cleared her throat, took back her hand. And remembered she was sitting inside the car he'd spent years building. For her. It was all suddenly a little too much.

She hopped out of the car. Breathed deep. Happy to have a little distance from the man.

Though distance wasn't a luxury that would last long.

Though they had to work out the exact details, saying yes would likely mean visits and catch-ups and holidays and birthdays, having his input, his help. Being connected to Rafe for the rest of her natural life.

It would also probably mean sticking in Radiance for a little while longer, at least. Meaning more time with her mother. Having to face the Wandas and Trudys out there. To accept that the people around here *would* care about her business whether she wanted them to or not.

She should have felt twitchy. Trapped.

Instead she felt her feet grounding. Her skittish heart settling.

She could handle waking to the sound of birdsong for a little longer. The crisp feel of autumn leaves crunching underfoot. The taste of home-made cherry pie and fresh whipped cream made from the milk of a cow living just down the road.

More than that, the juxtaposition of light and colour, foliage and bark, trickling streams and the violent beauty of a forest reclaiming fallen trees had relit the fire of inspiration inside her. Her daily walks with her old camera slung around her neck had reminded her, up close in full colour, why she'd taken up photography in the first place. Before it had become a job.

Back here at the site of the original crossroads, she was now officially taking her road less travelled. The road to motherhood. Not only settled on who her child's father would be, but getting closer and closer to being sure of who her child's mother was too.

CHAPTER EIGHT

"THIS IS SUCH an LA thing to do," Mercy grumbled.

Sable turned towards her mother, who was chopping vegetables with such vehemence she'd made sure to keep her distance.

"It's so not," Sable chided.

"So why are we doing this?"

"Asking friends over to dinner is a regular grown-up thing to do. It's just that you were never a regular grown-up."

The fact that she needed one of those "friends" and her mother to get along as well as possible because they soon might be related was something she didn't plan to own up to just yet. The others she'd invited as mere window dressing.

It was a few days after the Big Yes, as Sable called it in her head, and Rafe was due back any minute. In the end he *had* driven the Pontiac to Melbourne, probably trying to keep things as normal on his end as possible. He'd also promised to see a specialist there that Sable had found. She hoped the invasive nature of what she was asking wouldn't send him running for the hills.

His words came floating back to her, as they had over the past few days.

"If we do this, we do it together. You don't get to disappear this time. You don't cut me out."

Clearly she'd taken on the "running for the hills" mantle in their relationship. Not that they had a *relationship* so much as an agreement. Terms still under construction.

She glanced at her mother. The queen of disappearing, walking away, cutting people out. "You okay over there?"

Mumble, mumble. "Can't cook and she throws a dinner party." *Mumble, mumble.*

"I lived with a world-famous chef for years. Chances are I picked up a thing or two."

Mercy stopped, shot her a sharp look, thoughts tumbling over behind her vivid eyes. "And how was that?"

"Which part, exactly? LA? Living with a chef?"

"Take your pick." Mercy waved a hand her way. The one holding a knife, naturally.

Sable found herself looking for her mother's motivation in asking. The ulterior motive. For she never—ever—asked such open questions. But this was her future child's grandmother. If there was ever a time to accept an olive branch, this was it.

"New York was great. But LA? The light was different somehow," said Sable, starting slow, "which made everything feel a little unreal. For quite a while, actually. As to living with a chef..." She shrugged, feeling a little squally. She pressed her shoulders back. That part of her past was done.

While Rafe's part in her past, present, future, would never be done.

There it was, that cheeky little voice again. It had been piping up more and more over the past few days.

She glanced at her mum to find Mercy still watching her. Carefully.

"Was he kind to you at all?" her mother asked, gripping the knife handle tighter.

Sable blinked. "Um, yes. Of course. I wouldn't have stuck around so long if he wasn't. He was...nice. He told me he loved me, but I think what he loved was my work. He raved about my photographs. But with me he was... detached. A complete turnabout from how intense everything had been back here. Which, at first, was a relief. But

after a while I craved the rawness, the honesty, the direct-
ness I was used to."

Sable nudged a hip against the bench.

"And while we may have different ideas on what my life
should look like, I've never for a second doubted your love.
So thank *you*. For that. I now know just how much better
that is than the alternative."

Mercy swallowed. Sable gave her mother a smile.

"Now get out of my kitchen," Mercy said, quickly swiping a finger beneath each eye. "Before you do something
truly LA and skip the salt and sugar."

Everyone arrived en masse, right on the dot of seven, as
if they'd all heard about dinner parties but this was their
first. Stan, moustache trimmed for the occasion. Bear, looking twice as big as usual without his apron. The McGlinty
brothers and their mother Carleen bearing bottles of wine.
And lastly, Janie.

And Rafe.

Dark jeans, dark jacket, white T-shirt. Dark hair curling about his cheeks. Dark eyes boring into hers. He could
have been the poster boy for bad boys who grew up good.
And the moment his eyes met hers, Sable felt the floor dip
under her.

"Hey, Sable!"

Sable flinched as Janie leapt in between them, giving
her a huge squeeze. And a wink.

She knows, Sable thought, her heart suddenly hammering. *How does she know? Did he tell her? Surely not.*

Then Janie was off, heading into the kitchen. To Mercy.
And soon the two of them were chatting and laughing like
old friends.

Leaving Sable and Rafe. Alone in the entrance. Starlight
poured through the gaps in the overhanging trees beyond,
darkness and muffled laughter at Sable's back.

"Hi," she said, her hammering heart now at full gallop. Then she said it again, and felt instantly foolish.

Until Rafe's hard-hewn face broke into a charged smile. Then she felt giddy, and fizzy, and seventeen years old, all over again.

Funny that she'd gone nearly ten years without seeing him, now a couple of days apart felt like an eternity. At least she hadn't said *I missed you*, the words that she now held tight behind her lips.

Rafe leaned in, placed a hand on Sable's lower back and murmured, "Can we find a minute tonight? Alone?"

"Everything okay?" she said, her voice more than a little husky, hoping his visit to the doctor had gone well. What if it hadn't? What if he had issues too?

"Mmm-hmm," he said. "Everything's fine."

She leaned back to catch his eye, and his hand turned with her till it rested on her waist. His thumb traced circles over the bone. His little finger slid up and down her hip.

"Fine," she said, her voice a little croaky as she found herself all caught up in his dark eyes, his beautiful face, the way he looked at her as if he could keep doing so till the end of time. "There's that word again."

He laughed, a deep, sexy chuckle.

And she thought back to her conversation with her mother in the kitchen and wondered how she'd ever managed to convince herself that what she'd had with The Chef was in any way enough. When, on the other side of the world, once upon a time, she'd had this.

"Rafe!" Janie called.

And Sable jumped. Reminded herself that they were not what they were. What they were, what they would be, was to be affirmed. And that was what Rafe no doubt wanted to hash out tonight. In private.

Sable turned to find Janie holding a jar of pickles that looked as if they were a hundred years old, the younger girl all smiles as she took in how close her brother stood by Sable.

"I need your muscles, bro."

"Later, okay?" Rafe said, his breath catching on her hair, and it was all she could do to stay upright. His hand slowly trailing over her stomach, leaving spot fires in its wake before he sauntered away.

Breathing out hard, Sable looked over to find her mother watching. A silhouette at the end of the hall. Her expression fierce. The knife gripped in her hand once more.

This was going to be a long night.

Sable sat diagonally across from Rafe at the dinner table, watching him over her glass of wine, while trying not to look as if she was watching him. Unable to keep her gaze from swinging his way.

Bear, seated beside her, said, "Hey."

Sable flinched, her knee hitting the underside of the table. "Mmm?"

"Did Janie and your mother do all the cooking?"

Sable managed a nod.

"Then none of us are getting out of here alive."

Sable lifted her glass in salute, and he clinked it with his, then turned to talk to Fred on the other side.

Leaving Sable to not look at Rafe. Her leg jiggling so hard under the table she worried it might jiggle right off.

For her mind had been spinning in circles ever since he'd walked in the door. Ever since she'd allowed herself to admit she'd missed him. Ever since she'd let herself acknowledge what she'd had with him, back then, was irreplaceable.

How had she possibly been strong enough to come back to him, put herself out there, open up, exposing her most vulnerable self, if not for the surety that a single moment of Rafe's unbroken attention had always been worth more to her than an entire city of lights?

For she'd never loved anyone—*anyone*—the way she'd loved this man.

Loved. Past tense.

This, this feeling swarming over her right now, it was gratitude. Anticipation. With a healthy dash of lust. Not the other thing.

"Best dinner I've had in as long as I can remember," Stan professed, his plate squeaky clean while the others were barely touched.

"You eat at mine three times a week," Bear protested.

Stan shrugged, then sent a moony glance towards Mercy. "You're a fine hostess."

Mercy waved a hand his way. "It's inedible. But thank you."

"So, what are they going to call you when the bairn arrives? Nanna? Grandma?"

Leading Sable to spit a mouthful of wine fair across the table.

Carleen gasped, her white top covered in splatters of pink. The boys leapt up, fussing over her. Bear turned to Sable, his eyes near bugging out of his head. While Stan sank down into his seat.

How the heck did Stan know? Sable glanced around the table; Janie looked at her lap, while Ed looked chagrined. Did they *all* know? And *how*?

No. Not all. For Mercy glared at her like a thing possessed.

"You're *pregnant*?" Mercy managed. "To him?" A long bony finger pointed towards Rafe, her tone acidic enough to burn through metal.

"No!" said Sable. And Mercy exhaled so hard she seemed to shrink. "I wouldn't be on my second glass of wine if I was." Or was it her third? "But—"

"*But?* There's a but?"

Sable glanced at Rafe, who, frustratingly, sat back, arms crossed, expression unreadable. Having gone full self-preservation mode.

Well, it was out now. And from her extensive experience with deeply uncomfortable conversations, Sable had learned it was always better to be honest, and just push through it.

"But that is our plan. We've found some excellent doctors who think there's a good chance they can help make it happen, so hopefully, soon, yes, I'll be pregnant with Rafe's baby."

"What the heck do they need doctors for?" That was Ed.

Janie shrugged. "Beats me."

The faces around the table ranged from shock to discomfort. How had they gone from *"Please pass the salt"* to this?

"We're not together," she went on, in it now. "We're not in a relationship. Rafe has kindly agreed to do this for me. It's a…" What was it they were doing exactly? "It's a transaction?"

If Rafe looked rock-like before, at Sable's *transaction* comment, he now looked positively petrified.

"They want to have a baby together without the fun part?" Ed muttered, though loudly enough for everyone to hear. "Makes no sense."

Janie's, "I know, right," just as clear.

Before Sable could dig herself deeper into a hole of too much information, Mercy pushed back her chair with such vehemence it wobbled, spun and crashed to the ground. Then she swept from the room, her skirt floating behind her.

"Excuse me," Sable said, motioning to Bear to take over. Which he did, his voice following her down the hall, "Right, people. Anyone know if Mercy stocks soda water?"

Sable found her mother in her bedroom, a hand on the

desk beneath the window, fingers splayed over a slew of early photos Sable had taken that she'd found in a box at the top of a cupboard. "Mum?"

Mercy looked up. Her face pinched. Pained. "What the hell are you thinking?"

Sable moved slowly into the room.

"You had it so good," her mother muttered. "Away from here. Away from him."

Sable shook her head. "Maybe I was too subtle before. Things were not good for most of the time I was over there. Most of the time I felt as if I couldn't move, couldn't smile, couldn't breathe."

"Then go somewhere else! Try something else!"

"I am trying something else. I'm trying listening to myself. Listening to my needs, to my voice. I'm trying what I want for once. I want a child, Mum. More than one, if the fates decide. I want a home, with a backyard, and a sprinkler my kids can play under. I want to put down roots. I want my local barista to know how I take my coffee because I go to his coffee shop every morning, not because he saw a picture on Instagram."

The fact that the house that flashed into mind looked very much like the kind you'd find in the small snow towns of Victoria, rather than a Brooklyn brownstone, sent a little shiver through her.

Her mother sniffed. "So this is how you choose to rebel."

Sadie threw her hands in the air. "Oh, damn it, Mum, this is not about you!"

"It's always about the mother."

"Did you get pregnant with me because of *your* mother?"

Her mother slanted her a look that said maybe she had.

"Then tell me so," Sable said. As she knew less about her grandparents than she did about her father, which was saying something. "Throw me a bone here."

Mercy turned, leaned against the desk, her long fingers gripping the top. "*Fine.* My mother was terribly conservative. All baking and aprons and gingham curtains. It was claustrophobic. I couldn't wait to leave home. I had that scholarship to study agriculture at Melbourne Uni. I'd imagined myself a vintner. Then your father came along, all wilful and wild. I saw my way out."

Sable's heart clutched at the tragic note in her mother's voice even while she tried so hard to appear unmoved by her own story. Her story, which did not end well, Mr Wilful and Wild leaving her when he found out she was pregnant.

Sable's voice was raw as she said, "Funny. That I was so desperate to *have* a home, to stay in one place for any length of time, I'd have happily sewn my feet to the floor."

Mercy's right eye flickered. "Sable. Don't do this. Don't place your happiness in the hands of a man."

"I'm not. I'm placing my happiness in my hands. I just need Rafe to help me. And he's agreed. Because he's that good a guy. Just because my father didn't keep his bargains, doesn't mean Rafe would do the same."

Mercy finally looked her way, dismay etched into her features. "You love him, don't you? You love him still."

Sable didn't answer that. She'd only just started wondering the same thing herself. It would mess things up terribly. And if it turned out to be true, that was a conversation to be had between Rafe and her. If she told him at all.

"A baby," Mercy said, her eyes glazed. "How did *they* all know? While I was left in the dark?"

Sable went to her mother and took her by the hand to find the fingers cold, lean, rough. "It wasn't deliberate, I promise. I actually have no idea who knows or how. For this is all very new for us too. And I didn't talk to you about it, because I knew you wouldn't approve."

"Since when have you ever cared about my approval?"

"Since always! You just never wanted me to."

Mercy gave her a look then, as if she'd only just realised how thoroughly she'd hobbled her own efforts.

"Do you know why I left? Why I chose to go to New York?"

"Well, the prize, which you totally deserved. And because I saw Rafe buying the ring and made it crystal clear you would not have my blessing."

Sable shook her head. Then she crouched to the floor, lifted the corner of the rug, and unhooked the floorboard. Pulling out the small metal box, she found the postcard from Greece.

The look on Mercy's face as she took the card in hand was one Sable had never seen before. Shock, heartache, and joy. "Where did you—"

"I took it out of the bin after you threw it away. You were so miserable that week. And I knew the signs. You were about to pack us up and leave again. But I knew how much you loved it here. That you'd put down roots in a way I'd never seen before. So I left instead."

Mercy stared at her daughter.

"I'd seen them over the years, the postcards. No signature. I usually found them torn in half, in the bottom of the bin. It's from him, isn't it? My dad."

"How could you possibly—" Mercy slapped a hand over her mouth. Then her face crumpled.

So shocked was she at seeing her mother in tears, Sable moved in beside her, wrapped an arm about her mother's bony shoulders.

Finally her mother said, "It's his way of letting me know he's still around. But he was worse at sticking than even me."

Oh, Mercy. "But you loved him anyway."

"A little."

"Still?"

That earned her a smile. "Touché."

When the air in the room settled, Sable drew back. "I'd better go out there, see to our guests."

Her mother waved her away. "Go."

At the door Sable turned. "There is one guest I know would be devastated to think he'd upset you."

Mercy sniffed.

"Stan's pretty hot, don't you think? In a silver fox kind of way."

Mercy shot her a look, and the vulnerability behind it gave Sable hope.

Sable left her mother with the postcard and went back out into the fray.

The McGlintys were gone. Bear too. As he'd been their designated driver.

Janie was saying goodbye to Stan who gripped his hat hard in his hand.

Sable gave him a wave. And a smile. Mouthed, Not your fault.

He nodded, then hobbled out of the front door and was gone.

"Rafe?" Sable asked.

Janie pointed towards the back door, then headed into the kitchen to wash up, singing under her breath. High drama her base normal.

Sable found Rafe in the yard, holding a rope swing that was now a frayed rope, squares of light from the sunroom windows making shapes on the patchy dirt. His fingers gripping tightly, his shoulders a hard line, his profile deadly serious.

Her scalp prickled. Her chest tightened. And everything that had felt so certain an hour before felt wobbly.

He was an intensely private man, who hated nothing more than people sticking their noses in his business.

They hadn't discussed if or how they'd let anyone know, even their families, and in an effort at assuaging her discomfort, she'd just blurted their most private news to some of the biggest gossips in town. She, who knew how it felt to be on the receiving end of whispers and stares.

Badly done, Sable.

And while she'd told her mother Rafe would never back out on a promise, she felt a frisson of very real fear that she'd ruined everything. That it *was* a thing she did! Had her plan to try to bring everyone a little closer, to consolidate the relationships between those who would be a part of her baby's life, instead blown it all apart?

Sable took a step his way and felt time shimmer.

In her mind's eye the blackberries disappeared, the swing was fixed, and Rafe stood barefoot on the lush green grass, shoulders relaxed. She moved in and all but felt herself wrap her arms around his waist, lay a kiss on his shoulder, tuck her head into the warmth of his back. Then came the happy squeal of a child, and a head full of floppy blonde curls came bouncing their way...

Another step and the vision fractured, the grey autumnal evening gloom of this timeline slamming sharply into focus. And she ached, all over, from the loss.

"Rafe?"

He turned, his face unreadable. "Hey."

"Before you say anything, please let me apologise."

"For?" Rafe asked, his voice soft and rough in the semi-darkness. But closer. It definitely felt as if he'd moved closer.

"My unintended announcement! Stan feels so awful, I ruined Carleen's dress, my mother is sitting in my bedroom being all sentimental—"

"Mercy," he deadpanned. "Sentimental."

She shook her head, her throat too full to speak. "Rafe, stop. Let me say this, please." As if a veil had been lifted she finally let herself see just how much she'd imposed on this man. Not only in the last weeks, but her entire life.

"I'm sorry…for everything. My intention was to quietly slip back into your life, and instead I landed like a bomb. Disrupting your business, your reputation in this town. I've forced you to relive a past you've taken great pains to put behind you. And I've asked something of you no sane person would ever ask another—"

"Sable."

"No. It's me. It's my MO. Best of intentions, worst choices. My ex's therapist claimed I deliberately put myself in situations that are doomed to fail. I thought he was a sham, but I'm starting to wonder if he was right."

"Sable."

"Yes?"

Sable looked up to find Rafe had indeed moved closer. Moonlight poured over his back, creating a halo of silvery light around his big shoulders. His strong arms. How her libido could still yearn for him, even as every other part of her ached for the loss she felt was surely coming, she had no clue.

"Don't much want to talk about your mother right now. Or your fool of an ex. Or his therapist, for that matter. I do want to talk about us."

Sable closed her eyes. To think they'd come so close… "I knew it. You've changed your mind."

"What? No."

"Oh." *Oh!* Her eyes sprang open. "Really?"

"Sable. Once I've made a decision, I stick to it. Simple as that."

"Oh, thank you. Thank you, thank you! I love you so much! I mean, I don't *love* you…" *Oh, heck, how had that slipped out?* "I'm just…" *Mortified!* "Grateful. So deeply grateful…"

Her voice trailed away pathetically at the end, while the tension between them only built as the word she'd dropped swirled around them.

His voice was deeper, lit with a thrum of tension that sang in her blood, when he said, "When I collared you in the hall, I asked if we could find a moment alone."

"Mmm-hmm?"

"I wanted to talk to you about my visit to the doctors in Melbourne—"

"Are you okay?"

"I'm fine. My swimmers are strong and plentiful."

Of course, they were.

"But as I went from listening to the psychologist, to being poked by the fertility specialist, prodded by the ultrasound guy I wondered more and more what I was even doing there."

Sable felt as if she were driving on a never-ending roundabout. Was he about to tell her something good or something bad?

Rafe stepped in, took her by the hand. "Can we agree any attraction between us is not completely in the past?"

Sable blinked at the change of tack. Her gut cried out, *Deny, deny, deny!* But she'd have looked like an idiot. "It's not in the past."

"Great. Now whether it's an echo of what we had, or a glimpse of something new, I'm not sure. But it's there. Constantly. A hum keeping me awake nights."

"Like tinnitus?"

Rafe's face broke into a rare grin and the backs of Sable's knees tingled.

"It's driving me crazy, Sutton. You, being so near, and me not able to touch you, to hold you, to kiss you. Tell me you feel it too."

Feel it? It was rocketing through her like a sugar rush.

She nodded, feeling as if she'd just taken some huge step into the great unknown space beyond the borders of her plan.

Rafe's chest rose. And fell. "Great. Then I have a proposition for you to consider. I can't believe I'm saying this, but Ed made a good point. Why are we looking at intervention, unless we find, down the track, it's absolutely necessary? When the regular way of making a baby is less invasive, less crazy expensive, less stressful and far more fun than being poked and prodded by strangers."

Why? Because I'm falling for you, Thorne. All over again. And falling into bed with you would have to complicate things beyond anything I can contain.

"Are you hitting on me, Rafe Thorne?" She'd never felt less like making a joke in her life but if she didn't cut through this tension, she'd self-combust.

He shook his head. "See, that's the thing. I'm not. This is a time for rational decisions, not romance. And with this thing simmering between us, untended, unreleased, we are only going to blow." He reached up, tucked a swathe of hair behind her ear. "So what do you say? How about we make a baby, the old-fashioned way?"

His argument sounded so seductive. But could she separate the action from the result? Would being with him let off steam or show her a glimpse of a false life from which she might not recover. "Rafe—"

"No strings, Sutton. Just as you ordered. Only no prescriptions either. No pressure. We let things happen naturally. And if that doesn't work, we seek intervention."

"No strings." She looked from one eye to the other, searching for a glimmer of the feelings that had begun to overwhelm her, pull her under. But all she saw was pragmatism. And lashings of banked heat.

He meant it. He was being grown up about all this. Use the attraction simmering between them to bring about the result she so desperately wanted.

Rafe... No, *Rafe's baby.* A child. Her child.

It was a very sophisticated ask from a country boy. But he'd been around. He'd lived too. Not that she wanted details. Was this how he felt when anyone talked about her life? Her ex? It wasn't fun.

But speaking of fun, she wanted him. So bad. Even standing this close to him she felt feverish with need. "Is this even possible?"

"Only one way to find out?"

Rafe brought her fingers to his mouth and kissed them, one by one, before turning her hand over and resting his lips on her palm. Then his other hand slid under her chin, tilting it just so, so that he might lean down and kiss her.

There was none of the hesitation of their other kisses. Or the penance. Or the relearning.

It was sweet and luscious, full of longing and promise.

It was real.

So real, tears welled in the backs of Sable's eyes, clogging her throat. Too many to spill.

Rafe wasn't pulling back, he was all in.

After being at the lowest point of her life only a couple of months before, here she was, kissing Rafe, her first love, in the moonlight. It felt so terrifyingly close to getting everything she'd ever wanted it shook her to her very core.

She pulled back from the kiss, sucking in a breath. Looked into his eyes. And found herself drowning in the heady mix of emotion she saw within—care, want, need, lust and determination.

"So what do you say?" he asked.

Rafe. Rafe was asking her to be with him. Something he'd *never* done the first time around. She'd been the one to make the first move, seducing him in the barn on her seventeenth birthday. She had no idea how much that had played on the more vulnerable corners of her mind until that minute.

Then some creature deep down inside her slithered giddily to the surface and said, "Why the hell not?"

Rafe laughed, then, with a growl, he picked her up and threw her over his shoulder.

She squealed, then laughed, then struggled to speak for she could barely catch her breath as he loped around the side of the house. "Where are we going?"

"This is not happening in your old bedroom. There's only so far I'll go for the sake of posterity."

"This?" she asked, holding onto his backside for purchase. And because it was just right there. Asking for it.

His hand reached up and smacked her on the backside in recompense.

She glanced at the house as Rafe carried her up the driveway. "Won't Janie be wondering where we are?"

"Don't care."

"I am the host—"

"Do you want to go back in there?"

"God, no."

Rafe slid her down his front till her toes landed on his boots. She luxuriated in the feel of him, hard and spare and big.

He took her gently by the chin. "I've wanted you from the moment I saw you sitting in Bear's café, with a ferocity that has eaten me from the inside out. I tried to ignore it, then to fight it. I'm done. I don't want to wait any more."

"Then don't."

Hand in hand they walked down the footpath, towards Rafe's place. Past the Airstream. Towards the shed. Was this going to be a back seat of a Chevy deal? Or maybe the Ferrari? Did she care?

No strings. Not a one. Just two people with a twisted past littered with battered hopes and two-way heartache agreeing to a no-strings fling in order to make a baby.

As the adrenaline of the past hour began to fade, she waited for sense to kick in. For the bites and stings that had left scars on her heart to pull her up. But this was Rafe's hand she was holding.

She curled her fingers more tightly around his.

They slowed as they reached the big new shed.

"Old barn fell down about a month after you left," Rafe said. "As if it was holding on just for you. Took me a good three years before I was ready to lug the rotting lumber away."

Sable leant her head against his meaty shoulder. So he hadn't torn it down. Hadn't exorcised any memories of her. He'd held on. Perhaps he was still holding on. Perhaps she was too.

Only now she knew she'd never let go. Not if he couldn't go through with it. Not if this experiment failed. He'd always be a part of her. Her Rafe.

Needing to show him how much she was feeling, she drew him in, and kissed him with everything she had.

He slid a hand under her knees. Picked her up and carried her over the threshold. In the back of her mind she saw sensor lights, zillion-dollar cars and stairs, but nothing mattered bar the heat and shivery skin and heavy breaths.

He pushed open the door and carried her into the new loft space.

"Our window," she whispered, spying the large round window filling much of the far wall.

Rafe glanced over his shoulder. "Our window smashed into a thousand pieces when the building went down."

"And yet that one looks very much the same."

Sable's gaze swept back to Rafe, who didn't deny it. He could have put anything on the space the old barn had been, but had chosen to rebuild. Modernising, yet keeping the parts that had been special to him. To them.

He'd loved her once. More than she'd ever thought it was possible to be loved. And she'd left him. Sacrificed what they'd had to give her mother the sense of place Mercy had always craved.

Now it was her turn.

As that last grip on her past self fell away, Sable felt free. Free to want and ask and be and feel.

And if she hadn't already known she was falling for Rafe Thorne, the bad boy next door, all over again—if she'd ever really fallen out—she knew then.

Rafe tossed her onto a big soft bed.

She reached for him as he climbed over her, teeth nipping at her hip, then tugging at the edge of her top, sending her senses scattering.

When she got the chance, she tore his jumper over his head. Went for the fly of his jeans. He stopped her with a smile, with a waggle of his eyebrows, then a kiss that made her boneless.

Only then did he undress her. Slowly. Deliberately. Reverently. Following every slide of fabric with a trail of kisses. His gaze hungry. His touch tender. Till she could no longer think.

Just enough to do the same to him. Fingers trailing over the strong muscles of his shoulders. A scar on his left pec, another, longer, on his side. Marks of a life lived hard. Tough. A survivor.

When she shivered, he drew the blankets over them both, and slid down her body, kissing her neck, her breasts, each rib as he made his way down.

Sable reached back, one hand gripping a heavy iron railing on the bedhead, the other clutching a hunk of blanket as his tongue dipped into her belly button. Licked the edge of her hipbone. Lower.

The scruff of his unshaven face. The give and take of his clever mouth. It was the Rafe she remembered. Times a billion.

She'd been seventeen when she'd left, their love life new, sweet, fumbling, only just figuring one another out.

This was grown up. Edged with knowledge, determined forgiveness, and a steady heady beat of hope.

Sable's eyes slammed shut, every sense sighing, screaming, holding on for dear life as Rafe took her to the edge and right on over.

Damp and hot and reeling—in primal shock—she forced her eyes open when she felt Rafe come out from under the blankets.

"Hi," he said, a smile lighting his face, lighting his eyes.

"Hello to you too," she managed.

Then she lifted her head and kissed him, wrapping her legs around him, holding him close. Near. Dear.

This was the time to reach for protection. But neither did.

"We're really doing this?" Sable managed.

"Doc gave me a clean bill of health. Call her, if you're concerned."

"Now?"

Rafe lifted his head a fraction to look deep into her eyes. "If that's what you need. Of course."

"I trust you," she said. And meant it. "You'd never hurt me, Rafe. But that's not what I meant. I mean you and me and a baby?"

Rafe moved his hand to sweep a lock of hair from her cheek. "In the past week I've spent more time than a man should picturing how to adapt this space with a kitchen upstairs, bathroom, a nursery."

"You have?" she asked, all the while thinking that didn't sound like "no strings". It sounded like all the strings. But with Rafe pressing occasional kisses along her neck she couldn't remember why that was a problem.

"Bringing up Janie, I know how unspeakably hard parenting can be. And how breathtaking. First words. First

steps. First time she said thank you without being asked."
He ran his thumb over her cheekbone. "We're doing this,
Sutton."

"You're gonna be a father," she said, her voice breaking
at the vision she'd had of him in her mother's backyard. The
vision she'd thought she'd never live to see.

"I'm going to be a dad."

Her heart swelled so fast she laughed, though it felt more
like a sob. The kind that started right deep down inside.

Then Rafe's expression darkened, his eyes smoking over
as he leaned down and kissed her.

It was the sweetest kiss of her entire life.

And was soon subsumed by the heat that engulfed her
as they came together.

As if they'd never been apart.

She only realised later, as she drifted off to sleep, that
while she'd told Rafe she trusted him, trusted he'd never
hurt her, he hadn't said the same to her.

CHAPTER NINE

RAFE STOOD IN the small utilitarian kitchen on the ground level of The Barn.

A few cars still remained downstairs, but the workshop had been moved out, readying to turn it into whatever he decided to turn it into.

He scratched his bare chest with one hand, as he waited for the coffee machine to heat up. And he looked up, towards the loft.

Until a few weeks ago, he'd never even slept there, as Janie liked having him nearby when he was home. Now he wondered if he'd put it in out of some kind of wish fulfilment. *If you build it, she will come.* So to speak.

For there Sable slept now, face down, her hair splayed out over her pillow, and half onto his.

The fact that she took up three quarters of the bed and a long while to fully wake in the morning was new to him. They'd been close for years, and officially together for months before she'd skipped out, but it had been all about stealing time. They'd never spent the night together. Never woken to find the other still there.

And now they had… He'd miss it when she was gone. He'd miss *her*.

For that part of the plan hadn't changed as far as he knew.

Once he'd kissed her, swung her into his arms and all but carried her over the threshold of the barn, they'd made few concrete agreements as to what happened after she fell pregnant. As if neither had wanted to jinx it. Or question the halcyon spell that had descended over them.

The coffee machine beeped. He slid two espresso glasses

under the spouts, pressed a few buttons and the scent of freshly brewed coffee filled the air.

How normal this had become. The porthole window cracked open of a night, waking to birdsong. Him making two coffees and taking first shower. Her padding downstairs, late, to pack him a lunch to take to work. For he'd not strayed far since things had shifted between them, working at the original workshop most days. Managing remotely. Watching, with immense gratification, Janie take up the slack.

Rafe winced.

Truth was, he didn't want her to leave. Not that he could tell her. She was her mother's daughter after all. Skittish, unsettled. But the way things were going it felt…possible. As if they finally had their timing right.

He'd work up to it when the time was right. Tell her that he wanted strings. And always had.

Because he was that fully committed to this project: Project Baby.

As for that small voice in the back of his head that perked up every time they were apart, wondering if when he looked back she'd once again be gone? He did his best to ignore it.

Rafe rolled his shoulders.

She wasn't going anywhere. She was in this, as much as he was. He could *feel* it. In her newfound calmness and in her easy smiles. As he listened in on the video chats she had with her agent, Nancy, who seemed like a cracker of a woman. Watched her talk through the test shots she'd taken on her phone, saving the film images taken on her old camera for when the new series she was working on was complete. In the way she looked at him when she thought he didn't notice. In the way she looked at him when she did.

Rafe heard a creak and cocked his ear.

They were heading to Melbourne today—a final day trip before the Pumpkin Festival was due to take up a whole lot of time. He'd check in with the Melbourne operation, while she visited a photography specialist she'd made friends with, and they'd stop at their favourite Italian Place in Lygon Street for lunch before heading back.

He'd built the Melbourne spot, three times the size of the Radiance shop, from absolutely nothing. In a city in which no one judged him beyond the value in his work.

Sable had been the first person who'd ever looked at him as if he was worthy of a chance. Without her he might never have given voice to his ambitions. Or believed they might actually be achievable.

Not that long ago she'd said, "You know how it feels to be loved by me."

It had been a throwaway line, but it had hit him like a Mack truck. Whipping away any last defences he'd held against her. For he'd known how it felt to be loved by her. It was a feeling he'd chased the rest of his life. The feeling of being seen, understood, heard, trusted.

Then she'd left.

"Come on, man. Enough already," he said, gripping the counter. Closing his eyes and willing his lizard brain to shut the hell up.

For all that he was over the moon that she was back, the second-guessing was wearing at his edges. The looking over his shoulder.

From what he remembered of the time before his mother had left, his father had been exactly the same. Skittish, jumpy, waiting for it all to go wrong.

And it had.

How much was chicken, how much egg, he had no idea. He only knew it wasn't healthy.

And he'd worked damned hard to make sure he didn't follow in his father's footsteps. Any of them.

Including falling for a woman with itchy feet.

Rafe scrubbed a hand over his face, as if that might shake this internal conversation loose.

What happened, happened in the past. And he'd forgiven her. Otherwise how could he have asked her to stay? How could he possibly have considered starting a family with her if he wasn't sure that she was stronger now? That she had changed?

He grabbed the coffees from the machine, dashed a little milk into his, and padded out of the kitchenette, making a beeline for the stairs to the loft.

The sooner he found her where he'd left her, in his bed, *their* bed, every worry would melt away.

Taking the last stairs two at a time, he hit the loft floor and stopped.

The bed was empty.

The sheets were in disarray. The scent of her was sweet, warm—ripe in the air.

She had to be near. He'd only been gone a few minutes. But the gnawing in his belly—and the knowledge that if she'd left once without warning, without reason, she could do it again—bit so hard he winced.

Then the plumbing hushed as the bathroom sink water ran downstairs.

The air left his lungs in a rush.

One thing he'd learned about making broken cars look brand-new: a lifetime of damage left marks that would always be a part of the car. Niggles. Bruises that would linger deep in the belly of the beast.

And while he would have willed it to be different if it were possible, people were very much the same. Meaning this feeling, this knot in his belly where Sable was concerned, might never ease.

He spun and padded back down the stairs.

Sable knew the feeling all too well. The ache in her back. The slight fuzziness of her brain.

Her trip to the bathroom confirmed.

Her period had started.

She wasn't pregnant.

She'd read up, a lot, on this part of the journey, and she knew how rare it was to fall pregnant on the first go. Or the second, or the third. But the ache—the loss of something that had only existed in her head—was acute. Like nothing she'd ever felt.

Groaning, Sable fell into a crouch and wrapped her arms around her belly.

The vision she'd had of that flaxen-haired child had felt so real. So raw. So right. She'd felt as if it were a fait accompli. As if it were meant to be.

And she and Rafe had certainly tried hard enough. Often enough. Their no strings baby-making fling having blossomed into what had fast felt like something a whole lot more.

Rafe.

She closed her eyes tight and sank to the bathroom floor.

How was she going to tell *him*? Now that he'd committed to Project Baby, as he called it, he'd been reading books on fatherhood. Talking to Mercy about their experiences raising girls. She'd seen him stop a mother with a pram on the street the other day to ask what kind of nappy bag she was using.

The man was an utter doll. No wonder these weeks with him had been some of the best of her life. A glimpse into what things might have been like if they were doing this for real. If they were actually together. Building a life. Starting their family.

It had been a kind of lovely she'd never dared hope might be possible. The way he fell asleep with a book on his chest. The way he bartered for control over the remote. The way he played with her hair as they fell asleep.

Sure he grumbled that she took up too much of the bed.

And he was a total morning person whereas she was a night owl. And she smiled at the way he wanted her to check in at least once a day when she went on her walks, just to make sure she hadn't been kidnapped by forest pirates, or tripped over a knotty tree root and bumped her head.

Or run away again.

She closed her eyes tight.

And there it was, that single dark thread running through everything they did. The fact that he didn't quite trust her. It showed in the way he breathed out when she came downstairs. The way his eyes lit up when they found one another after work. As if he could only relax when he knew she was still there.

She'd thought she was the one putting herself out there in asking this of him.

But he was too. In agreeing to her request, he'd risked derision from his friends and family, he'd risked the chance of being the focus of town gossip, and he'd risked letting her into his life again. While he might not know it yet, he'd risked the agony of starting to want this too. And watching it fail.

The thought of putting him through that made her feel physically ill.

Maybe this was a sign, the fact that she wasn't pregnant. A sign to slow things down. Maybe even put it on hold for a bit. Despite the difficulties she faced in falling pregnant at all, that felt secondary to everything else right now.

"Sable?" Rafe's voice, warm and deep and wonderful, came to her from the other side of the door.

She squeezed her eyes shut tight. *Keep it together.* "I'll just be another minute."

"All good. Though we have not a thing to eat. Bear's for breakfast before we head off?"

She had to tell him. The thought of having this conversation in public was mortifying. But the thought of telling him here, in this place that had begun to feel like home, felt worse.

"Can we grab something to go? Picnic breakfast in Wonderland Park?"

"Not exactly picnic weather."

He was right. The wind had picked up overnight, bringing with it a wintry blast all the way from Antarctica. Like an omen. "Let's live on the wild side."

He laughed, the sound smoothing its way down her spine, like a caress. She closed her eyes, but not quickly enough to stave off the tear that slipped through.

Then she heard a light bump and she could picture him leaning his forehead against the door. "Sure. Why not?"

She closed her eyes, letting the tears flow fast and furious down each cheek, before she swiped them hastily away. "I'll have a quick shower and be ready in ten."

She was ready in seven. Tears washed away. Game face on. Tougher than she looked. Tougher than she felt. Well used to making big mistakes by now. Used to having to face them.

She'd never been more scared to face up to one than she was right now.

As they crunched through the piles of dead leaves on their way to Wonderland Park, an icy wind whipped through Sable's jeans, and Rafe's leather jacket that he'd made her wear when she'd forgotten to grab one for herself.

Turned out they couldn't go into the park itself, as city engineers were running final tests on the rides, readying them to run during the Pumpkin Festival that weekend, so they headed to what they now called "their" playground.

Sable walked over to the swing and sat, the chains creaking ominously under her weight. And she shoved her hands deep into the wool-lined pockets of Rafe's jacket. It smelled like him. All warm and clean and delicious. She drank it in deep, knowing that, depending on how this conversation went, it could be the last time she would have the chance for a long while.

Digging her nails into her palms so that she didn't cry, when she looked up at Rafe he was standing over her, holding a tray of coffees from Bear's. And he looked…uneasy.

"It's freezing out here. And I'd love to get on the road soon so we can be back before dark. Maybe we should just take these home."

Home. The Barn. Too many memories, new and old, swept over her, making her feel nauseous. "Not hungry."

Rafe's eyes narrowed. Then he placed the coffees on the dip at the bottom of the slide. Rubbed a knuckle over his cheek. Eyes locked onto hers. Waiting. As patient as time itself. Always giving her every second she needed to get to where she needed to be.

Why did he have to be so wonderful?

This was going to hurt like hell.

But keeping on as they had? Falling deeper and deeper? Watching him learn to love her again, while knowing he didn't fully trust her, would only hurt the both of them more.

"I've been thinking," she said, her voice cracking.

"About?"

"You know the new series I've been working on?"

She earned a single nod.

"Well, Nancy's been bugging me about heading back over there, to New York. To talk about the concept with a couple of galleries who are showing interest. And while I'm there I thought I should really start looking at some places in Brooklyn."

"Brooklyn."

"In the street I told you about. Near the great schools."

Rafe crossed his arms over his chest and looked out into the distance. Then he laughed. At first it was a shot of breath through flared nostrils, then it was actual laughter, then he finished with his fingers pressed into his eye sockets.

Sable nibbled on the inside of her lip and waited for him to speak.

"I guess I ought to be grateful you're actually telling me this time."

"Excuse me?"

"Come on, Sutton. We're right back where we started. Is this some kind of test? Do you want me to tell you not to go? Do you want me to beg you to stay?"

His gaze flickered to her belly, where he thought she might be building a baby inside her right now. His baby. And the hope in his eyes was palpable.

She didn't move. Not a single muscle. She was hurting so badly at the thought of having to tell him there was no baby, she couldn't see straight.

If only she'd kept to her original plan. For it had been cool, calculated, devoid of attachment. It had put *her* needs front and centre. And now she was practically living with Rafe. Sharing her needs with his. Getting used to falling asleep in his arms. Falling for him all over again.

Falling? She'd fallen. Slowly at first, trying so very hard not to, and then all at once.

How could she not?

He was Rafe. Her Rafe. Once and always the absolute love of her life.

So if she cared for him that much, why was she putting him through this at all? How could she trap him into being connected to her in the most real way for the rest of their lives?

He'd not wanted this. He'd *never* wanted this! Yet he was doing it for her.

She was more upset about telling Rafe she wasn't pregnant than she was about not being pregnant at all. Because deep down she knew, he'd always known, that she was the absolute love of *his* life too.

But if they were meant to be together, it shouldn't be because of a baby. It should be because they wanted it. Despite any obstacles, or promises, or family influence.

This? Being together but not together. Pretending they were so sophisticated, mere friends with benefits. It was cruel and unusual treatment of someone she cared for more than anyone else in the world.

If he had changed, if he truly wanted this, he should have the chance to do it for real. To fall in love with someone he trusted implicitly, someone who had never broken his heart. To have kids when he was ready. The story of how his kids came into being one that would make them feel safe and wanted and loved.

If she truly loved him, she had to set him free. For good.

While Sable's mind spun, Rafe swore, then pushed away from the slide. He came to her, grabbing the chains of the swing. "What do you want me to say, Sable? Do you want me to tell you I was so devastated when you left the last time that I broke three fingers when I punched that big old tree in your mother's front yard? How I didn't get out of bed for a week. That it took for Janie to finally get me up by asking for food when she hadn't eaten for a day."

Sable tried to swallow but her throat had closed up.

Rafe looked deep into her eyes. And said, "Stay. These past weeks… I didn't expect, when I asked you to be with me, that it would be like this. I'd thought we'd be scratching an itch. That all that tension would dissipate over time and we could both move on. Instead it's shown me what my life can be like, if I let it. That I haven't been fully alive since the day you left."

Sable's soul sang, while her heart wept. If he'd said such words a decade ago, if he'd looked her in the eye and let his feelings pour out of him the way he was now, everything might have been different.

Only now it made her more determined to take care of him. To put his needs before hers. Not because it was easier. Or because she'd been brought up to make people like her. But because she loved him.

"I want you to stay," Rafe said, his voice a deep rumble.

And he meant it. She was sure of it. Making this all the harder still.

Sable sat taller, held eye contact and said, "What if I told you there was no baby?"

Rafe flinched. "What do you mean, no baby?"

"What if I wasn't pregnant?"

A shadow passed over his eyes. His gaze dropped to her belly. His brown furrowing as if he was trying to ascertain her truth.

Sable waited for his gaze to lift to hers. "Back at the beginning of all this, I said I trusted you but you didn't say it back. Do you trust me now?"

His pause was telling. "Trust you in what way?"

"Every way."

He ran a hand over his face. "Have I ever woken up, found the bed empty, and for a second wondered if you've gone? Sure."

Sable felt heat rise in her cheeks. "More than once?"

Rafe sank into a crouch. His hands went to her shoulders, sliding down her arms to hold her by the elbows. His gaze locked onto hers and refused to let go. "You're starting to really scare me now, Sutton. What's going on in that head of yours?" he said, his voice rough. "Talk to me."

She swallowed. "I'm not pregnant, Rafe. There is no baby. I got my period. Just this morning."

His eyes squeezed shut. Holding back emotion with such vehemence a vein bulged in his neck. "So why didn't you just say that?"

Rafe's eyes caught hers, searching, begging her to speak. To open up. But she was at the bottom of a well. His face at the top the only light she could see.

He swiped a hand over his face, stood, and turned away.

"What if—?" she started, then stopped.

He turned back to her, his face ravaged. "What if what?"

"What if a baby hadn't been on the cards? Would you have let me in? Would you have taken me back?"

A muscle flickered at the edge of his eye. "Maybe. No. I don't know. But haven't these past weeks made it clear? You and me…we never needed a baby to bring us together. To be happy."

Sable swallowed. Believing him. And hating it.

She blinked away the grit at the backs of her eyes. Her voice small as she said, "But a baby is what I want, Rafe. Not a relationship. And while I know we both came at this thing from the right place, I think, deep down, we both know what this really was."

"And what is that?"

"Closure."

Rafe reared back as if slapped. "So that's it? One miss and you're giving up on us?"

"Rafe, there is no us." How she kept her voice gentle, she had no idea. For she could barely believe the words even as she said them.

"Harsh, Sutton. That's too damned harsh." Rafe looked as if he wanted to drag the thunder from the clouds hanging low and ominous overhead and throw it down upon the earth. "You know what? In all the years I've known you, that's the first time I've ever looked in your eyes and seen your mother looking back at me."

Sable pushed the swing back and twisted out from under the chains. Away from Rafe. Away from his glinting eyes. She felt so fragile, so pained. It was nearly too much. So she went into "Rafe mode". Full statue. Giving nothing away.

Something *he'd* learned at the feet of his father. Not that she'd tell him so. She had hurt him enough.

"There's nothing I can say to change your mind," Rafe said.

There was. But she was not about to ask him to tell her he loved her, that he'd always love her, that they were meant to muddle their way through whatever life threw at them, together. She'd asked too much of him already.

She shook her head and took a few steps away before his voice stopped her in her tracks.

"Where are you going?" he asked.

"To pack. Book my flight. Nancy will meet me when I get to New York."

"Call me," he said, his voice like sandpaper. "When you get there. Let me know you arrived safe."

And this time Rafe was the one to walk away. In the opposite direction. Into the park.

His shoulders were hunched, his strides long. The mist in the air had turned to drizzle until it filled the air with grey, turning Rafe into a smudge in the distance.

Leaving Sable a clear path to head back towards town. Feeling empty. Lost.

But in cutting Rafe loose, in giving him a chance to find all that he truly wanted in time, she was certain she'd done the absolute right thing.

Maybe even for the first time in her life.

CHAPTER TEN

Rafe had no clue how long he'd sat on the stool at the end of The Coffee Shop counter.

But when he looked up, it was dark outside. The rain had eased. The lights inside were turned down low. The front door sign was turned to closed. And his face felt hot from having been smooshed into his palms for ever.

"Another?"

Rafe turned his head on a heavy neck to find Bear at the end of the counter, hand-drying latte glasses. "Hmm?"

"You want another?"

Rafe looked down at the empty mug in front of him. Remembering, a sluggish beat later, it had contained gin and tonic. Perhaps more than one. Not his drink of choice. But it had done the trick. "Are you even licensed?"

"Are you a cop? I'm closed. I'm not selling it to you. Want some or not?"

Rafe pushed the mug out, asking for more. Bear wandered over and filled it halfway. Then filled a mug of his own, and held it out for a clink.

Rafe blinked at him. "Don't much feel like celebrating."

"Really? I'd never have guessed. You've been such chipper company this evening."

"I'm never chipper."

"I'd have agreed a couple of months back, but ever since a certain someone came back to town, I'd go so far as to say you've been downright giddy!"

Rafe shot Bear a look. It took his brain a few seconds to catch up to his eyes.

He was sloshed. Well and truly. Not something he'd let happen in a very long time, considering his father's predisposition for drowning his sorrows. But right then, numb was better than the alterative.

Stunned. Sideswiped. Laid to waste. And so damned angry at himself for letting it happen all over again. By the same woman. And he'd been ready. He'd been *waiting* for it to happen. Not that telling himself *I told you so* made him feel any better.

"She's gone," he said, barely recognising his own voice.

"That so?"

A pause, then, "I've told you already?"

"Once or twice."

"What else did I tell you?"

"Not much." Though Bear's eyes flickered away, meaning there had been plenty more.

Rafe figured he was unlikely to remember the conversation the next day as it was, so said, "You know we were... trying to fall pregnant."

Bear smiled, a sad smile. "Whole town knows, mate. It's the way these things go."

"Well...it didn't take."

"Ah, man. That's rotten luck."

It was worse than rotten luck. It was soul-crushing.

When he'd told her he thought they could be happy if it was just the two of them, he'd been telling the truth. She was it for him. She was the one. Consuming and confounding and crazy-making as she was.

But once he'd crossed that bridge, he was in. All in. He'd *wanted* to have a baby with Sable. Not to donate sperm. He'd wanted to be with her as her belly grew. To fall out of bed exhausted at three in the morning to get her whatever weird food she craved.

To hold her hand, her gaze, her heart, as she gave birth.

To look into that baby's face—he'd pictured his dark hair and Sable's witch eyes—and feel the kind of love he could barely imagine. The love of a father and child. The love he knew he had within him, despite the lack of an example to look to.

He'd dreamed of them all together, snuggled up in a big soft bed. Sable more beautiful than ever, despite the dark smudges under her eyes from lack of sleep. He'd imagined baby gates and pet guinea pigs and presents piled under a real pine tree at Christmas time. While Sable took photo after photo after photo.

A life laid out before him like an old home movie. A life he'd craved so ravenously as a kid he'd have given a limb to even glimpse it.

"Sable saw it as more than bad luck. She saw it as an out. Wasn't as keen to go the distance as she'd first intimated. So that's the end of it."

"But you don't see it as bad luck."

Rafe's instinct was to go still, self-protect. But the gin had loosened up his usually rock-solid inhibitions. "I do not. I see it as…an experience shared. The kind that binds. That deepens."

"You love her," said Bear.

Rafe did not deny it.

Bear put his mug down, leaned on the counter, and looked out into the middle distance. "Life can be wholly unfair at times."

"Preach," said Rafe, reaching for his mug, only for the scent to make his stomach turn. He pushed the thing away.

Bear gently replaced it with a very strong, very black, very sweet coffee. "So what now?"

Rafe breathed. And hardened. Adding yet another mental layer to the hard shell around his person. "Learnt from a very young age that life goes on. I wake up tomorrow, slide under the chassis of a beautiful old car and I do what I do."

As he said the words he waited for the usual relief that came with work, and routine, and accomplishment to come with it. The counterbalance to the erratic instability of his childhood.

He waited to feel that sense of closure Sable had insisted they'd both been looking for.

But it didn't come.

Sable. Miss Erratic. He'd never been sure if she'd turn left or right. If she'd say yes or no. If she'd stay or go. She should have been the last person to make him feel at home. But with all that came a huge heart. Emotions so close to the surface there was never any mistaking how she felt. An abundance of vulnerability that slayed him.

It must have hurt her like crazy, finding out she wasn't pregnant.

Rafe had been too caught up in his own hurt to imagine how devastated she must have been. To wonder how much that had affected her decision to push him away.

Rafe ran a slow hand over his face, the callouses on his palm catching on the bristles on his chin as the heavy truth filtered through the fog filling his head.

The first time Sable had left had been on her. Her youth, her inexperience, her desperate desire to make her mother happy. She knew it. She owned up to it. Said this is me, this is how I roll, take it or leave it.

But this time? That was on him.

Do you trust me? she'd asked.

And he'd all but said, *No.*

He'd fallen into the trap of believing that the constant ache in his chest meant he didn't trust her. When the truth was he had been in panic mode. In free fall. Falling in love with the woman in his bed.

Not the love of a messed-up teenaged boy, but of a man who knew the import and the rarity of such a connection, with the innate stubbornness to mess it up.

Rafe had always looked to his father as the anti-example of how to live a life. Doing everything not to be like him.

But he'd neglected to realise the impact his mother's leaving had had on his make-up.

Stubbornly holding back on starting up with Sable for years before she'd finally demanded he give in. Then refusing to even entertain her desperate desire to have a family. Had he always looked at her expecting rejection? Expecting her to disappoint? Had he always held back a piece of himself? Punishing her for his mother's mistakes? So that he might never be cut that deeply again?

Sable was insanely sensitive to vulnerabilities. It was what made her art so touching. Meaning she had to have sensed the wall he'd kept between them.

No wonder she'd left. No wonder she'd left again.

It must have hurt like hell to put herself out there, to lean on him, to trust him, to open herself up to him, and to have known that he wasn't doing the same.

The bell above the door tinkled, then, "Is he ready to go?" Janie's voice.

Rafe's shoulders dropped. "You called my sister on me?"

"Thought she could roll you on home."

"Hey, brother," Janie said, scraping the stool noisily beside him. "You okay?"

About to say he was *fine*, instead he went with, "Nope. I'm not in any way fine."

"Well, it shows. You look like hell. What happened?"

"Sable happened." That was Bear.

Rafe raised his hands in question. "Really, man?"

Janie tugged on Rafe's sleeve till he turned to her. Her face was distraught. And...and disappointed. As if she knew it was his fault.

Rafe shook his head. "Don't hate her."

"Hate her? How could we hate someone who loves the someone we love so very, very much? We love her to bits."

"Good," said Rafe. "She's my one and only."

Janie made a little mewling sound beside him. Rafe,

big brother to the end, lifted a dead arm and hauled his sister in tight.

While Bear's voice turned gruff as he said, "Hell, yeah, she is."

"She has to know that, right?" Rafe asked the big guy. "I mean, if you guys know it, she does too?"

Bear shrugged. "Did you tell her so?"

Rafe opened his mouth to tell of a time he'd told Sable she was everything he'd ever wanted, but couldn't think of one.

He'd *shown* her, in every way he knew how. Feeding her, holding her, protecting her, standing up for her, spending every available second with her, opening his home to her, letting her have control over the remote…sometimes.

She'd known how it felt to be loved by him.

But had he said the words? *Ever?*

No. Because he'd grown up knowing the sway of words. Powerful words. How they could not be taken back.

"Could it be possible she doesn't know?"

Janie made another pathetic sound beside him. Rafe shot her a frown. *Not helping.*

While Bear said, "If not, only one way to make sure."

Rafe pushed the stool back, only to discover he was not so good on his feet. The world swayed. The ground with it.

"Can you…?" Janie asked.

And there was Bear, an arm around his waist helping him out to Janie's tiny little modern car with its aluminium frame and sorry excuse for an engine.

"When are you going to let me build you a real car?"

"Get in so I can drive you home, you stupid lump," Janie said with a growl. "And you'll see how real my perfectly lovely car is."

The rest was a blur bar Janie and Bear rolling him into the sofa bed in Janie's Airstream. Someone taking off his shoes. Opening one eye to find Janie, laughing and pushing Bear out of the door, telling him she could take it from there.

Then Bear's deep voice at the door. "Will he be okay?"

"He survived losing her once, he can do it again."

At which point his brain gave up and unconsciousness kindly took him under.

Sable hadn't gone back to Rafe's to pack. She'd snuck into Mercy's house instead, needing to be near her mother. Even if her mother was as mothering as an ice cube. After crying till it gave her hiccups, she'd fallen asleep for most of the day, and had woken to find a blanket draped over her and a cup of cold tea on the desk in her room.

The next day she couldn't have bought a ticket out of town if she'd tried, for it was the opening day of the Pumpkin Festival and every bus, car, bike and horse and cart within fifty kilometres was heading in, not out.

All slept out, Sable trudged into town when the sun had only just risen, her hands tucked deep into the pockets of her jacket—Rafe's leather jacket, to be precise, as all her clothes were still in his loft.

There was enough light to see the entire town had been decorated in orange and purple streamers, orange and purple flowers. Even the street lights in the centre of Laurel Avenue flashed a permanent, thematic amber.

Every shop window boasted signs talking up pumpkin soup, pumpkin pie, pumpkin spice coffee, market stalls, live music, and re-enactments harking back to early days of the town when the gold rush and bushrangers were the talk of the day.

If she weren't feeling so rotten, it might have seemed delightful. A marked improvement on the town parade and pumpkin-judging contest that were highlights of the festival a decade before. Right now, all that orange just gave her a headache.

Sable dragged her feet into Bear's, the bell ringing cheerfully overhead. She breathed out in relief to find the place empty and sat at the counter.

"I wondered when you might show your face," said Bear, eyes roving over her bed hair, her old jeans, her oversized Cure T-shirt—also Rafe's. She'd decided she wasn't giving that one back. A spoil of war.

Slowly, slowly, Sable's head sank until it hit the counter with a thud. Even the scent of a freshly brewed strong hot coffee placed next to her barely registered.

"Like that, is it?" Bear asked.

Sable sat up and ran both hands over her face, tugging the skin over the bones before letting it spring back into place. "Very much so. What did you mean by, 'I wondered when you might show your face'?"

"Mmm?"

"Bear," Sable growled. PMS and heartbreak having sapped her of her civility.

"Rafe was in here yesterday. And last night. In fact, Janie and I might have rolled him home only a few hours ago."

"Bear! Did you get him *drunk*?"

"No! Maybe. How was I to know he was such a lightweight?"

"His father only drank so he never drinks."

"Oh. Oops."

"How was he?" *Angry? Sad? Chatty? Inconsolable? Fine...* "What did he say?"

Bear shot her a wry glance, before picking up a perfectly dry glass and drying it some more.

Fair enough. But why couldn't he be the town gossip? Sure, she was glad he wasn't before, but now it would be so helpful.

Sable reached out and grabbed her coffee, wrapping her hands around the hot glass. She drank deep, letting the smooth dark roast fill the parts of her tears had sent dry.

Then someone broke into her peace and quiet, slipping into the seat to her left. Another someone sat in the seat to her right.

"Coffee," said Mercy.

"How 'bout adding a nip of that Pumpkin Spice liqueur I know you have stocked back there?" That was Carleen. The two had become firm friends after the dire dinner party, connecting over disappointment in their respective children.

Bear baulked. "Sun's barely up."

"Meaning it's practically still night time," said Mercy.

Carleen laughed. "As your Queen of the Pumpkin Parade, I decree it's time to get the party started."

"Yes, ma'am."

While Bear moved to the back room, Mercy threw an envelope on the counter in front of Sable. "This came for you."

Sable opened it up to find the name of a Melbourne-based specialist photo developer on a package. The photos from the original film in her box Brownie. She'd sent it to a specialty developer in Melbourne when she'd hit the end of the roll a couple of weeks back, and had been planning on taking her second and third rolls in person the day before. Before their plans had changed.

Sable tore open the envelope, saw the large negatives spilling out. The feel of them—crisp and cool—gave her a sweet little thrill.

The pictures had been loaded back to front. Starting with the ones she'd taken over her first few days in town. The contrast was heavier than she'd have liked, something she'd work on with the next film, but the composition was fair.

Her critique came to a full stop as she saw the photo before the first she had taken.

"Mum?"

"Hmmm." Mercy took one look before screwing up her face.

The photo was of her mother's sunroom—a ray of buttery summer light pouring through her drying lavender hanging from the ceiling.

The next—Wanda and Carleen and Old Man Phillips sitting around a poker table, laughing till you could see their back teeth.

"You took these," Sable said, knowing it to be true.

Mercy waved a hand her way. Called, "What's taking you so long, Bear?"

The next photo was a stray kitten, sitting on Mercy's front stoop, looking right into the lens. The next, Mercy's view looking down at her skirt with her shoes poking out, the wild colours of the clothing contrasting with the raw rough streaks in the wooden floor.

Smiling, Sable shifted to the next photo, then lifted a hand to her mouth.

For there was a photo of Rafe, putting up the tomato trellis on the side of Mercy's house. He'd built that? Neither had said. His hair was shorter, the dark curls cut closer to his head. The roping muscles of arms were brought into sharp relief by the black of his T-shirt, the hard midday light.

Mercy must have called his name, as he'd turned towards the camera, a small smile on his face.

It amazed her still that over the years they had found a way to put aside their differences. But over the past weeks she'd come to understand why—they'd missed her. And in one another had found a way to keep her close.

Carleen asked if she could have a look, so Sable went through them all again. Happy with the stunning contrast of brilliant autumn leaves against a harsh grey sky. The old red McGlinty truck, the back filled with pumpkins. Loving the photo of the shops of Laurel Avenue as evening hit, right after a rain shower, light spilling onto the street creating puddles of gold on the footpath. The view thorough The Barn's new porthole window.

Markers of her time in Radiance. Memories she'd take with her as she left.

While she felt as if she'd been hollowed out with a spoon, the pictures reminded her that her time there had been pretty wonderful.

As she scrolled through the last shots, and hit the last picture, she had begun to see a theme. Different from the one she'd described to Nancy. There was none of the discord that had given her career such a great start. No focus on things lost and broken and cast aside. Quite the opposite.

Every single one of her new photographs exuded warmth, nostalgia, harmony, comfort.

She ran a thumb over the corner of the picture of Rafe leaning against the railing of the carousel. The dappled light. The warm foliage. And could all but see the exhibition title written on the marquee outside her favourite little New York gallery: *Home*.

Sable reached out blindly for her coffee and took a sip. Only to find it no longer tasted quite like coffee. "What am I drinking?"

"Clove," said Mercy, sipping her own coffee as if it were manna from heaven, "spice, cinnamon, nutmeg, pepper, ginger and pumpkin."

Sable grabbed the bottle of home-brewed Pumpkin Spice liqueur and read the label. "And vodka."

"Which is made from potatoes. Wholesome as can be. Unless… You're not pregnant, are you?"

Sable coughed on her next sip. "No. Not pregnant."

Though she'd thought she'd kept her voice normal, her mother paused. Looked at her like a hawk. Even Bear seemed to stop breathing.

Sable looked his way. Saw the sorrow in his face.

Rafe… Rafe must have been *really* toasted if he'd told Bear that much. And for Rafe to even go near a drink, well, he must have felt truly wounded.

"Not pregnant," she repeated. Then, "Not living with a guy. Not in a relationship. Just not."

What a mess.

"Drink up," Carleen insisted.

And Sable did as she was told, figuring she had nothing else to lose.

An hour and two espresso cups later Sable was nursing a bruised heart *and* a sore head. The constant low roar of vintage engines, as entrants in the classic car show rumbled down the street, didn't help the latter. The almost empty bottle of liqueur had a lot to answer for.

Including the words *Not pregnant. Not living with a guy. Not in a relationship* flipping and twisting inside her head.

"You know what my problem is?" Sable asked, expecting no one to answer.

"Where do you want to start?" That from her mother.

Bear shot Mercy a look and she held her hands up in surrender. Then he looked back at Sable and said, "Tell me."

"I go about things all backwards."

"What things?"

"My career, for one. I started out on a high—gallery show, prize money, fame—and only then did I have to work like crazy to earn a reputation."

"Right."

"And then, there's…the other thing. If you love someone, you don't ask them to have your baby first. You ask them if they'll have you."

The one time she would have liked for her mother to perk up with a sharp comment, Mercy remained all too quiet.

Sable licked her dry lips. Leaned towards Bear and, voice low, said, "But I couldn't do that. Because I didn't come back here for him."

"Please." *Now* her mother perked up.

While Bear said, "But you just said you loved him."

"What? No, I didn't!"

"Yeah, you did," said Carleen, most helpfully.

Bear gave her a soft smile. "You said, and I quote, 'If you love someone, you don't ask them—'"

Sable flapped a hand at Bear till he stopped talking. Till the café was deadly quiet.

"She did," said Mercy, "didn't she?"

Sable's breaths were suddenly hard to come by.

"Sable," said Mercy, waiting for her daughter to look her way. "Answer me this: if you had to choose, right now, would you pick Rafe, or Rafe's child?"

Bear sucked in an audible breath and held it. Mercy looked so hard into Sable's eyes there was no hope of faffing her way out of the question. While Carleen began singing "Stand By Your Man" under her breath in what amounted to a gorgeous singing voice.

Sable's voice shook as she said, "You told me my whole life *never* to believe a man is more important than my dreams."

"No," said Mercy, pointing a finger Sable's way. "I told you to figure out what those dreams are, before you even think about finding yourself a man. Unfortunately we had to move in next to Rafe Ruddy Thorne. And that was it. One look and you were a goner."

A muscle car revved its engine as it ambled slowly down the street, the noise shaking the windows.

Rafe, Sable thought, her heart now thundering so loudly she could barely hear herself think. *Rafe* had been her dream. Wanting a child, a backyard, a home, that had all come later, when she'd begun believing that life might actually be possible, with him.

And yet she'd pushed him away.

So as not to hurt him. Because she thought he was better off without her. When she hadn't stopped to ask what *he* wanted. What he now thought was possible.

"Quick, I need Janie's number."

"Why? What are you going to do?"

"Really? You want me to say it out loud? Fine. I'm going to enlist her help in doing whatever it takes to show Rafe how much I love him. And want to be with him. For ever and ever. If he'll still have me."

"Hallelujah." That was Bear, his voice hitching with emotion.

A beat later, maybe two, Mercy sighed. Then she called out Janie's mobile number by heart.

Thank you, Sable mouthed as she held her phone to her ear.

Sable gave her mother a big kiss on the cheek, before she waved to Bear, who was swiping a tear from his cheek, and bolted out of the door.

It took Janie another hour to open The Barn, move some exorbitantly expensive vehicles, find the keys to the VW and drive into town, giving Sable time to drink copious amount of water.

She sat in the passenger seat, running a hand over the dimpled dash, the old junkyard seats, wondering how she hadn't realised—seeing it kept under a protective cloth next to Ferraris and Lamborghinis and Mustangs that were near priceless in value—how precious it was to him.

Because *she* was precious to him. Even after what she'd done. Even after how she'd left. He'd held a flame for her. And he'd forgiven her.

Only now she realised, she had never forgiven herself.

It explained why she'd let herself fall into such one-sided relationships. Why she'd convinced herself Rafe was better off without her. Why she'd been so ready to push him away at the first hurdle.

Because she loved him so much she only wanted the very best for him.

Never stopping to wonder if she might be the best for him!

She wasn't perfect. Mistakes would be made. Differences navigated. Disagreements hashed out. And bad things might happen, to them and theirs.

But she loved Rafe. Deeply, wholly, ferociously. So much it expanded to encompass the people around her. Bear and Stan and Janie and this town. This beautiful, charming, crazy little town.

They hit Laurel Avenue, right as one of the McGlinty boys was cordoning it off, sending any traffic on a detour. A detour away from Rafe.

Sable wound down the ancient window. *Squeak-squeak-squeak.* "Fred? Ed? Let us through!"

"Can't, Ms Sutton. Mumma said we need to start putting out the cones for her parade."

Squeak-squeak-squeak. Janie wound down her window too. "The parade is *tomorrow* afternoon, you goose!"

Fred—or was it Ed?—blanched. "But Mumma—"

"Let 'em through!" Carleen and Mercy stood outside Bear's, holding one another up.

"Thanks, Carleen!" called Sable.

Carleen lifted a fresh bottle of Pumpkin Spice liqueur in salute.

Janie shot Sable a grin. "What happens during the Pumpkin Spice Festival stays— Nah, who am I kidding? Whatever happens today will go down in town folklore for ever."

The McGlinty boy hopped to it, moving traffic cones so that the VW could sneak through. And they were off once more. Heading towards the Radiance Reserve.

It was stop start traffic as they hit the path leading into Reserve. Over the tops of the trees Sable could see the tip of the Ferris wheel turning over, and she thought she could even hear the fairground music. And where the day before there had been acres of fresh green grass, there was now row upon row of sleek European sports cars that would look more at home in Monte Carlo, along with dented old Datsuns with their owners shining them up with pride, and more FJ Holdens than she could count.

Spying a gap in the low wooden fence lining the path, Janie hooked left, bumped over the small gutter and hit the grass.

Gripping the window frame, Sable said, "Do you know where you're going?"

"Yep," Janie insisted, eyes scanning the crowd as she bumped over the grassy ground. "I helped create the mud map for every car coming today. Rafe has me on the payroll as Bossy Little Sister."

Someone official-looking suddenly jumped in their way, holding a glowing arrow. Waving madly that they head off to the left. Janie rolled her eyes, but did as she was told, and they soon found themselves in a sea of Beetles and Kombi vans, all splashed in bright, hippy colours and motifs.

Janie parked, and they both hopped out of the car.

Sable strained to see Rafe through the streams of cars and the burgeoning crowd. It would be like finding a needle in a haystack. Standing on tiptoes made no difference. But what if…?

She walked around the car, pressed her hands into the bonnet. "Think it'll hold me?"

Janie grinned. "Never know till you try."

Sable kneed her way up onto the bonnet, pausing for a second when it made a light crumpling sound. If the thing buckled, she did know someone who could fix it.

She redistributed her weight and slowly stood atop the curved roof of the old Beetle. And wondered what the hell she'd been thinking.

Rafe. She was thinking about Rafe.

Eagle eyes on high alert she scanned the crowd. Looking for dark curls. Broad shoulders. Sending out sensory feelers for a man of strength and goodness. A great big beautiful forgiving heart. And hotness that surpassed all hotness.

There! By the big rigs. Dark chambray shirt and jeans while everyone around him was rugged up in scarves and beanies. All that glorious inner heat keeping him toasty warm.

Sable shivered, wrapping the leather jacket around her T-shirt. Wishing she could wrap herself around him. Hoping, if she hadn't screwed everything up so badly in her effort to do right, she might yet get that chance.

He was distracted, phone to his ear. Other hand on his hip. Frowning off into the distance.

Sable's next breath in was a shaky one.

"Hey!" called Janie from way down below.

Sable didn't dare look. She couldn't take her eyes off Rafe lest she lose him. Again.

"I found her! She's here! With the Kombi vans."

"You talking to Rafe?" Sable asked.

Janie gave her a thumbs-up.

In the distance, Rafe spun on his heel, his gaze glancing off the cars in between them and the growing groups of people who were now turned her way, pointing at the crazy lady standing atop the car, as if expecting some kind of announcement. Or catastrophe.

Rafe's hand flew out to the side as he shrugged. Sable imagined she could see his frown deepening. Oh, how she loved that brooding frown. Proof how seriously he took himself, and his place in the world. How deeply the man felt.

"Tell him to look up," Sable said.

"Look up!" said Janie.

Rafe did just that. Stilling the moment his eyes found hers.

"Give me the phone," Sable said, carefully crouching down and holding out her hand.

Janie reached up and slapped the mobile into her palm.

The phone was warm when it reached her ear. Or maybe her ear was warm already. She felt hot all over. Feverish. But determined.

She had no plan of what she ought to say. In fact her entire future felt blank. Beautifully so. No plans, wants, wishes, dreams, hopes, regrets or fears bar what she might do in the next minute. Bar convincing Rafe to give her another chance.

"Rafe," she said into the phone, her voice little more than a breath.

His voice came to her, deep and dubious. "I thought you'd gone."

"Still here. Can we talk?"

"Kinda busy right now."

Sable blinked and the hundreds of cars still streaming into the park came back into focus.

"Right. Of course," she said. "Yeah. Me too."

His laughter came through the phone all tinny and far-away. But she could feel him thinking. Considering. Weighing up what was more important.

And the sense that she had pulled away, right to the very outer reaches of the invisible rubber band that had always held them together, softened, just a little.

"What the hell are you doing on top of the car, Sutton?"

"Not just any car. My car. The one you made me. With your own bare hands. Because you were smitten with me. Even back then. Even when you kept telling yourself you couldn't be. When you were so convinced you—that wild Thorne kid—didn't know how to be happy."

"Sable—"

"I had to see you and it felt like the quickest way."

She heard him breathe in deep. Saw him, even at a distance, do the same. Then his head dropped, his hand went back to his hip.

She waited. The whole world waited. Trapped between breaths. Between heartbeats. Then he lifted his head.

"Sable," he said, only this time his voice was a rough, sexy, surrender.

The urge to go to him, Hollywood style, leaping from car rooftop to car rooftop, was huge.

"Don't even think about it," he said, his voice a low growl.

She felt it in her spine. Her veins. The tips of every hair on her body.

She teetered but stayed upright. "You can't possibly know what I'm thinking."

"I can. And I do."

Yeah, she thought, doing a little of her own deep breathing. He really could. He really did.

Her heart trembled, her knees shook, as she said, "So what am I thinking?"

He ran a hand over his mouth. Then looked at her. Right at her. She felt it, like an arrow through the heart, even from so far away. "You're thinking that maybe you were a little hasty yesterday, pulling the rug out from under us."

"Really? What else?"

"You're thinking you didn't give my plan, my request, proper consideration."

Sable sighed. "Then tell me. Tell me what you think I should do."

"Stay," he said as he took off, his long legs eating up the ground between them. "Don't move."

"But you're busy."

"Story of my life. Though clearly that word takes on less meaning when you're in the picture."

"You're welcome?"

Another laugh. Another skitter of sensation down her

spine. This one scattered all the way to the ends of her fingers and toes. She shuffled her feet a little wider in case her knees gave way, only to feel the roof of the car strain.

She wobbled. Then the car wobbled back. Her foot slipping an inch.

"Rafe?"

He must have heard the panic in her voice as he began to run. Towards her. In slow motion.

Well, not in slow motion, but that was how it felt. As if he were now the one pulling out the Hollywood stops. Only she couldn't run towards him too, as she was stuck on top of a car, in slippery city-girl boots.

One wrong move and the car would go full Herbie and send her flying.

And then there he was in all his dark-curled, broad-shouldered, unshaven glory. His perma-frown in place, the phone still at his ear.

She made to crouch, to go to him, only to be met with a creak. And a groan. The ground seemed to swell and keel. And it suddenly felt a longer way down than it had been up.

She froze, knees bent, one hand out to balance, the other holding Janie's phone to her ear.

"Sable," Rafe's voice murmured in her ear a split second before she heard it in person.

"Hi," she said into the phone, to him.

"Everything okay up there?"

"Yep. I'm fine."

"Meaning you're in straight-out panic mode, right?"

"Mmm-hmm."

He put his phone in his back pocket and held out a hand.

She tossed him Janie's phone. He looked at it, passed it on to his sister and gave her a look that sent her off in the direction from whence he'd come. Chatting to the car owners, directing, taking over. Bossy Little Sister in action.

Rafe climbed onto the car as if it were nothing. A mountain goat. Or a man who knew his way around the load-bearing walls of a car chassis.

When he reached the roof he took her around the waist and drew her to her knees, then her backside. Weight distributed over the windscreen frame, she sat, legs sliding down the window. While he uncurled his long self beside her.

"I thought you'd gone," he said, looking down at his hands, playing with a blade of grass he must have nabbed along the way.

The constant movement of his hands was so familiar, she near choked on the feelings spilling through her. "I thought about it."

"Couldn't get a bus ticket?" he asked, glancing her way.

She nodded. Slowly. Mesmerised by the emotion in his eyes. The heat. The hope.

That hope was everything. Her touchstone. Her true north. The hope that she'd finally, truly found her way back to him.

It was enough for Sable to stop prevaricating and leap. Figuratively. For she was clutching every muscle in case the entire car deflated underneath them.

"Rafe." She swallowed. Watched his dark gaze follow the small movements in her face. "When you asked me to stay the night of the dinner party, I know you said you wanted it to be a 'no-strings' thing, but the thing is…"

She dragged her eyes from his before she found herself lost in his eyes. "The thing is, I've spent so much of my life on the run. First with Mercy, dragging me from town to town. Then from my own shadow as I struggled to figure out where I fit every time we stopped. Then you came along and for the first time in my life I knew what it meant to stand still. To simply be. It was a heady thing. Magical really. Overwhelming. So much so I ran from you too."

She glanced up at Rafe to find his eyes on her. Gaze full,

dark with emotion. Then his hand slid slowly around her back, hooked her around the middle and drew her in. His chin landing on top of her downcast head.

It was so sweet, so tender, her throat threatened to close up. But she had more to say.

"I came here with a plan," she said. "But a little voice kept telling me that it was an excuse. That I was still running away. From LA, sure, all those opinions of people I'd never met. But mostly from the anger I felt at myself for all those lost years. And when I found out, yesterday, that I wasn't pregnant, it felt like a slap from the universe."

Sable scratched at a loose thread in Rafe's jeans. Before her hand landed on his knee. He took her fingers in his, turned them over, entwined them together.

"I promise you weren't the only one."

She slid her head out from under his, shook her hair from her face and looked back at him.

"I was caught up in the romance of it all. Your return, the feelings still between us, the notion of a ready-made family. When you told me it didn't take… I'm so sorry, Sable."

He lifted his hand, ran his thumb along her cheek, gathering a tear she hadn't even felt drop.

"Do you know how rare it is to fall the first time you try?" she asked.

"I'm thinking, pretty rare."

"Even the healthiest people in the healthiest relationships can struggle. So much comes down to luck and timing."

"I can imagine."

"And…" She stopped. Swallowed. "And the thing is, I don't want to stop trying. With you. For as long as you'll let me. And if it never takes, if it's not meant to be, then…we can find another way. Or not. We can take it as it comes. I can handle that. I can handle anything, so long as we do it together. For the truth is, in coming back here I was running. But I was always running back to you."

Then there was nothing—no colour, no sound, no people, no light, not one thing in the entire universe bar Rafe. The glint in his dark eyes. The way his fingers gripped hers. The way his eyes drank her in, as if he couldn't quite believe she was real.

He lifted his hand, this time sliding it behind her neck, cupping her, owning her. His words were a blur amongst the sensations taking her over at his nearness, his touch, the rumble of his voice, the heat of him. "Then *stay*, Sutton. *Be with me.* No rules, no promises, no transactions. Because you want to. And because you know that I want you to, too. Stay. For ever."

Sable threw herself into Rafe's arms. He rocked back as he caught her, the car rocking beneath them too. Sable scrambled to find purchase, the heels of her boots scraping against the windscreen.

"I've got you," Rafe murmured into her hair. "I've got you."

And the words hit so deep, she could have sobbed till she was nothing but a husk.

"Well, I've got you too," she said when she could finally find her words. Holding onto his shoulders, she leaned back. Heart fierce, throat tight, filled with such certainty she barely recognised herself. And yet felt more fully herself than she had in years.

"I love you, Rafe," she said, the words she'd held back for fear she'd made it impossible to ever hear them back falling from her lips with ease. "I always have. Being away from you, I was only ever half of myself. And I thought that was enough. But now… I'm back. And I love you. And it's everything. No matter our luck. No matter our timing. No matter where we live. No matter if we are blessed with a baby. Or not."

When she stopped to take a breath, Rafe pressed her hair

away from her face, and held her cheeks and looked deep into her eyes. His voice gruff as he said, "Ditto."

Man of few words, her guy, but the words he said, he meant.

She pressed forward and kissed him. Lips to lips. Eyes slammed shut. A promise. And a thank you. Everything she felt releasing on a rush of breath. A rush of realisation. Of admitting something she'd always known.

He pulled back. Said, "I wasn't done."

"Oh. Right. What else is there to say?"

Rafe laughed, the move lighting up his whole face. "Just that I love you too. Loved you since the first moment I saw you. Loved you more every day you let me near. I loved you when I first kissed you. Loved you even when it pained me to give you time—to grow up, to be sure that you really wanted a lug like me. I loved you as you glared at people who dared hold their bags tighter when I walked by. When you stood up for me against my father. When you took to Janie like a sister. I loved you even as I lost you. Twice."

Sable felt the tear fall that time. And the next. For she'd been more than forgiven. She'd been seen. Understood. And given the space to figure out what Rafe had known from day one.

That she was his and he was hers and they were more together than they could ever be apart.

Sable was ready, aching, by the time his lips met hers.

It was a slow-burn kind of kiss. The kind that lit a fuse, trickling deep, burning heat through every part of her until she was alight. Melting. Desperate for the heat to be quenched.

She threw her leg over his, gripped his glorious hair, moaned into his mouth—

A cheer woke her from the dream, to find it wasn't a dream.

Sable's eyes snapped open to find herself sitting on

top of a dented black VW, in the small alpine town of Radiance, Victoria, surrounded by strangers—cheering strangers—and classic cars as far as the eye could see. The scent of wet leaves and damp dirt and petrol filled the air. The scent of home.

"We have an audience," she murmured.

Rafe glanced out over the crowd, looking far less discombobulated than she felt. Until he ran a hand through his hair, a shaky hand. Big, strong and in demand, he was a quiet small-town boy at heart. One who needed few and loved fiercely. It made her smile.

Till he said, "You stood on top of a car, waving me down like an idiot. What did you think would happen?"

She thumped him on the arm. Then flapped her hand towards the crowd. "I didn't think *that* would happen."

Only it didn't make her stomach churn the way it had when people stared at her in LA. Or when she walked through town. Because she *knew* she had nothing to be ashamed of.

Then, seeing his gaze was on her mouth, hungry and intense, she sank back into another kiss. A warm kiss. Lingering. Full of promise. And forgiveness. And lots of lovely, fresh, blooming new feelings.

People cheered a little more, clapping and catcalling, before they eventually moved on. The cars beckoning their attention.

"You taste like cinnamon," Rafe said eons later.

"And cloves," said Sable, in between kisses she now rained over his cheeks, his jaw, his neck. "And pepper. And pumpkin. And vodka."

He shook his head. "Ah, Pumpkin Festival. You do bring out the crazy."

Right on cue, a cheer split the air. Sable tipped her head to follow the sound. A tunnel of people in the Mustang aisle whooped and clapped. And between them came flashes of bare skin as Carleen McGlinty ran stark naked through the crowd.

"No two guesses as to who else has been into the vodka," said Rafe on a laugh, pulling her deeper into his arms.

Sable grinned. Lifted her other leg to drape it over Rafe's. And settled in. The groans and creaks of the metal no longer a concern.

If this car fell apart, they had others. One of the benefits of being with a brilliant car restorer.

Feeling as light as air, Sable breathed in the colour all around her. The lush green of the grass, the purple of the mountain peeking out over the bursts of oranges and reds and rich autumnal brown of the trees. Above it all the sky— light and bright, a soft velvety blue peppered with tufts of fluffy white clouds.

And then there was Rafe, the hot, dark, solid presence beside her.

Smiling, with every inch of her body, she breathed out fully, and closed her eyes.

Feeling safe, and happy, and home.

EPILOGUE

SABLE STEPPED OUT through the front door of The Barn, tucked her light summer wrap around her nightie, and curled her toes into the warm wood of the new deck beneath her feet.

The sky above was a clear blue dome. Mount Splendour covered in the green of fresh spring growth. The air was cool but by midday it would be scorching.

Sensing movement, Sable found Rafe standing over a pile of dried wood, T-shirt dripping in sweat as he chopped the logs for next winter. The new fireplaces they'd put in the lounge and the sitting room when they'd converted The Barn into a home were possibly her favourite additions.

Well, that and the nursery.

Feet bare, she padded over the lush green grass outside their back door. As often happened when she came within touching distance of Rafe, she felt the world shimmer around her.

She reached for him, wrapping her arms around his waist, laying a kiss on his shoulder, tucking her head into the warmth of his back. A vision flashed inside her head, a memory of another such moment, or a wish she'd once had. Then it was gone. Reality being so much better.

And the air kept on shimmering, with the warm buzz of coming summer.

"Good morning." Rafe's voice hummed through his back into her ear.

"Isn't it?"

"Eaten yet?"

"I just woke up. What time is it?"

"Does it matter?"

Sable smiled, and felt it blossom through her. "Not a jot."

Rafe was in town for a few days, with a big old Cadillac to keep him busy and a wife who had plans to keep him busier again. Mercy and Stan would be coming over for lunch, but not for a few hours yet.

"You looked too peaceful all tucked up in bed," said Rafe. "Snoring away."

"I don't snore."

"You didn't snore. Since munchkin came on the scene, it's another story."

Sable glared at him as she tried to see if he was kidding. Then—

"Oh!" she said, her hand moving to her growing belly.

"Sutton?" Rafe spun to face her. Throwing the axe aside. Dark eyes worried, before his gaze dropped to her hand. "What's wrong?"

"I keep telling you, don't call me Sutton. It's Thorne now."

"Hell, woman, you're as bad as your mother."

She went to glare at him when… "There!" she said, grabbing his hand and laying it under hers. "Wait for it."

She felt it again. Like bubbles popping.

Rafe's eyebrow kicked north. "You snore. And now you have gas. If I'd known this was how things were going to be—"

"Shush, you big doofus. It's a kick. Those bubbly feelings, that's the baby kicking."

Rafe's eyes grew comically wide, before his gaze dropped once more to her belly. Then he dropped to his knees, jeans sinking into the dewy ground. His hand moving a little to the left so he could rest his ear against her belly. His other hand wrapped around her wrist, the one sporting her arrow bracelet, his thumb running over the thin charm.

They stood there, the morning sun filtering over them,

their land beneath their feet, pollen floating on the warm air, birdsong wafting to them from the copse of trees giving them privacy from Janie's Airstream—

Bubbles! One after the other.

Their eyes met. And they laughed as one.

Before Rafe pressed to his feet, and kissed her long and hard. Basking in the surety that their baby, their little girl—or boy—was happily, healthily moving around inside Sable's womb.

For all their big plans it had taken them a full year to fall pregnant.

Which was, actually, pretty perfect. As it had given them a whole year to find their new normal.

Sable liked to sleep in—heading out into the wilderness in the afternoon light, to find angles and damage and regrowth to photograph.

Rafe was up before the birds, answering correspondence from all over the world as his reputation grew and opportunities bloomed. When he travelled in search of cars that needed tending, needed care, it was with alacrity, making time to check in several times a day. Sable liked him checking in.

And together they'd converted The Barn into a warm, spacious, two-storey space, filled with homey rugs and plush furniture.

There was an art studio bathed in natural light, and a five-car garage in which to keep Rafe's most precious cars, and one VW Beetle—newly panel-beaten, freshly painted in a deep rich glossy black. They'd kept the stairs leading to the loft.

"You know that envelope the doctor gave us?"

Rafe didn't have to ask which one. He drew himself back to his feet, a hand still on her belly. "What about it?"

"I reckon we should open it."

Rafe had wanted to know the gender, Sable had not.

Having witnessed such impasses many times over, the doctor had gently suggested writing down the answer and popping it in an envelope. Just in case.

But here, now, with Rafe holding her with such tenderness, such strength and solidity, Sable knew she would give him anything he ever wanted. No questions asked. No strings.

"Are you sure?" he asked, dark eyes gleaming with such hope it made her laugh. "Because I can wait."

"Come on." Sable took him by the hand and led him back towards the house.

The envelope was currently attached to their fridge with a magnet Mercy had made. Sable's mother was trying out all kinds of creative endeavours these days. Sketching. Ceramics. Silversmithing. It was odd. But lovely. Softening. But if the baby ever called her anything but Mercy, there'd be hell to pay.

Sable took the envelope from the fridge and handed it to Rafe. "You do the honours."

Breathing deep, his big chest rising and falling with emotion, Rafe gently tore the lip of the sealed paper.

"So," Sable said, "if it's a girl, Mercy, if it's a boy, Stan?"

"Not for all the oil in the Middle East."

"Carleen or Bear?"

Rafe shot her a look that made her knees go weak.

Sable grinned and said, *"Fine."*

"I don't trust that word a jot."

"Mmm. Smart man. You ready for this?"

"Hell, yeah. But are you?"

"More than ready."

She leaned over and placed a kiss on Rafe's beautiful mouth. The kiss deepened near as soon as it began. She hooked her fingers into the front of his sweaty T-shirt, the scent of him, the taste of him, filling her senses until she was drunk with it.

Rafe groaned as he pulled her into him.

In the back of her mind Sable heard the sound of paper hitting the floor. The envelope. The news inside it unread.

The baby's gender… They'd get to that.

They had time.

All the time in the world.

* * * * *

HIS PLAN
FOR THE
QUINTUPLETS

CATHY GILLEN THACKER

This book is dedicated to my longtime editor,
Kathleen Scheibling. Thank you, Kathleen, for
always believing in me, always encouraging me
to do my very best and making the often
arduous process such a delightful journey.
This is a tough business to be in,
but a great one with you by my side.

Chapter One

"I wish you had told me you were coming back to Laramie to take care of this today." Gabriel Lockhart strolled up the driveway of the home Susannah Alexander had inherited six months before. Exuding the cool masculine confidence of a born-and-raised Texan, he met her at the rear door of the half-filled U-Haul truck, next to the loading ramp. "I would have organized a group of people to help you move."

Wasn't that just like her old frenemy, Susannah thought resentfully. Ready and willing to volunteer *others* to get involved. While simultaneously emerging the hero without really giving *anything* of himself.

She propped her hands on her hips and tipped her head up at the ruggedly handsome doctor, wishing she hadn't had a secret crush on him since, oh, forever. It would make brushing him off that much easier. She stared into his eyes, trying not to get lost in the mesmerizing depths. "What makes you so sure I haven't already done that?" she asked sweetly.

He scoffed, as if he knew her better than she knew herself. Squinting down at her, he let his gaze rove over her face and challenged softly, "Have you?"

No. Of course she hadn't. That would have made this situation far too sentimental. And it was hard enough as it was.

All business now, Gabe reached for the cell phone in his pocket. "It's not too late for me to make some calls…"

Glad her new golden retriever puppy, Daisy, was still asleep inside the house, and therefore would not distract them, she lifted a staying hand. "You don't need to do that, Doc. I've got it." And she did.

He regarded her skeptically, looking big and tough enough to manage all her problems. "You're really going to clear out the place and load this entire truck by yourself?"

The air between them crackled with sexual tension. Her pulse racing, she inquired, "What are you talking about?"

He shrugged. "I assume you're going to put Brett and Belinda's home on the market, now that the will has cleared probate and the property is yours, free and clear."

He really had been keeping up on her business. Then again, Laramie, Texas, was the kind of community where everyone knew everyone else's heart-break. As well as their joy.

The legal finalization of her twin sister and his former best friend's estate would have been remarked upon. A lot. Although she had gotten the bulk of the married couple's financial holdings—the payout from the lethal accident, their life insurance, real estate and two cars—some of the belongings, like Brett's CD and vinyl collection and his sports memorabilia, had been left to Gabe.

While she considered just how much to tell her late brother-in-law's best friend, Susannah tried hard not to notice how great Gabe looked in a rumpled blue button-up that casually draped his broad chest and worn jeans that did equally nice things for his long legs and muscular thighs. His boots were scuffed and cowboy tough, and in deference to the hot June afternoon, his sleeves had been rolled up to his elbows, revealing strong, sinewy forearms. As usual, his thick, golden-brown hair was in need of a cut, his square jaw clean-shaven. With effort, she returned her gaze to his captivating whiskey-brown eyes. "I'm guessing you're here to take your things, then?"

Seemingly as mesmerized by her as she was by him, Gabe shook his head. "Actually, I was just driving by to see if you had shown up yet." His expression gentled, and his voice dropped another low, husky notch. "I wanted to see how you were doing."

Not as well as she would like. That was for sure. Knowing it would do her no good to fib to someone who knew her as well as he did, she admitted, "Probably as well as you would think."

"Still grieving," he presumed.

A wave of emotion had her swallowing around the sudden tightness in her throat. Determined not to cry, she fought back her feelings and said, "Aren't you?"

The look in his eyes said the answer to that was yes. Lifting a noncommittal hand, he pointed out in a low, rough tone, "It's only been a little over six months."

Susannah blew out an unsteady breath, recollecting what a tsunami that had been. "And the first year is the hardest. At least that's what people always say."

He looked past her, at the Craftsman-style home on Laurel Avenue that had held all the late couple's hopes and dreams.

"Nevertheless, life goes on," he countered.

The two of them knew that better than most, Susannah mused sorrowfully, having both tragically lost their parents during their early teens.

After a few rocky years, Gabe and the rest of his seven other orphaned siblings had eventually been fostered, then adopted by Carol and Robert Lockhart and brought here to Laramie County. Whereas Susannah and her twin had been moved from Beaumont to Wichita Falls, where they had been raised by their elderly aunt Elda, who had done her duty while privately considering them a burden. Susannah and Belinda had left her home when they turned eighteen, headed for college, and, because it was what their aunt had seemed to prefer, had never looked back.

Now she, too, was gone. Killed by a chronic lung ailment.

Which left Susannah with no family whatsoever. Except for the golden retriever puppy she'd just adopted. While Gabe was still part of a big, lively, loving crew. Not that he seemed as attached to them as she would be, in his position. Instead, he seemed eager to leave the country completely and make his own way in the world.

"Which is why," Gabe continued, oblivious to her thoughts, "I assumed you were selling Brett and Belinda's house, so you'd be able to make a fresh start."

His cool authority rankled. "Well, as usual, Doc, you're wrong about a lot of things." She took hold of the handle and pushed the two-wheeled hand truck back up the ramp, into the rear of the U-Haul. "I'm not selling this home." She paused to look at him long and hard. "I'm moving in."

Gabe stared at Susannah in shock. She was standing in a wedge of summer sunlight, her face pale except for the riot of color spreading across her cheeks. She had lost weight in the months since the funeral, looking almost too thin in a scoop-necked peach T-shirt, tan knee-length cargo shorts and sneakers. And yet her natural beauty shone through, in her silky, shoulder-length honey-blond hair and oval face with delicate features. Her sea-blue eyes. And kissably soft lips...

"What about your life in Houston?" he asked, walking up the ramp to join her in the bed of the U-Haul. Which seemed to be packed with boxes of what he assumed were her belongings and a mattress and box spring. Nothing else.

Turning her back to him, she reached over to add a carton marked *Books* to the base of the hand truck. "I sold my condo."

Not about to stand around idly when a lady needed help, he reached for a second carton and set it atop the first. "And what about your job?"

She added a third. "I quit." She tried to turn the wheels, and just as he had predicted, found it too heavy for her to maneuver. With a frown, she looked down in frustration and said, "I hated being a graphic designer, and life is short, so…"

He took charge of the dolly for her and wheeled it down the ramp, toward the house. He paused at the bottom of the steps leading up to the spacious front porch, with the cushioned wood furniture and chain-hung swing. "Do you really think this is the place to start over?" Where every square inch reminded her of the twin sister and brother-in-law she'd lost?

She put out a hand to stop him from taking the boxes up onto the porch and moved to block his way. The tension that had existed between them from the very first moment they'd met, years before, simmered between them now. "Do you really think *you* should be asking *me* that?" she challenged, a flash of annoyance crossing her face. "I mean, it's not really your business, is it?"

Actually, although she didn't know it, Gabe thought sagely, it was his business. Thanks to the promise he had made to Brett and Belinda right before they'd left on their ill-fated second honeymoon. At a time when the usually fiercely independent Susannah had been incredibly, unexpectedly vulnerable. A fact that had fired up his valiant side and made him want to protect and comfort her. "Someone has to look after you."

Without warning, temper flashed in her eyes. "Well, it shouldn't be you, Doc, of that I'm certain."

No question, he wouldn't have volunteered. But since Brett and Belinda had drafted him to do so, and he'd agreed, he had no choice. Not that Susannah'd made it easy on him the last six months or so, in steadfastly avoiding his attempts to get in touch with her since the funeral.

Her delicate blond brows lowering over her pretty eyes, she flashed him a smile that was filled with both fire and ice. "Especially given the fact that you're about to go off to another part of the world with Physicians Without Borders. *Again.*"

Funny. Most people saw his efforts to bring medical care where there was none noble. Scoffing, he folded his arms across his chest. "You really resent me for that?"

With equal parts determination and grit, Susannah tried to move the hand truck up the porch steps. And again it was way too heavy. "I *resent* the fact that you tried to get Brett to join you on your first mission when he was just about to marry Belinda."

Except it hadn't happened. His best friend and fellow physician had been as devoted to the community where they had grown up and completed their residencies as he was ready to venture away from it.

He elbowed her aside and easily accomplished what she could not, taking the loaded hand truck all the way up the steps and leaving it where she pointed. Finished, he continued to defend his actions. "It was only for two months, and our expertise was needed in Indonesia."

Looking skeptical, she stepped closer to peer into the living room windows. Gabe followed her glance to the gorgeous golden retriever puppy still snoozing inside a metal crate. Satisfied all was okay with her pet, she countered, "I don't doubt that your medical skills will always be needed elsewhere, Gabe, but there are infectious diseases in Texas and plenty of people who need care here, too." She paused to give him a pointed look beneath her fringe of thick golden lashes. "For those who want to be close to their friends and family and share in life's challenges, anyway."

He wasn't running away from their mutual loss or his complicated family, no matter what she thought. "And your point is, darlin'?"

"Brett found a way to serve his community and provide much-needed medical care at the hospital here in Laramie."

No doubt his late best friend had been a saint. The kind Susannah had been looking to lasso for herself— at least according to her twin. "Yeah, well, I'm not Brett," Gabe returned gruffly. Which was why he had just quit his regular hospital job in nearby San Angelo, and signed up for his first five-year stint with PWB. So he would be free to concentrate on international medicine full-time. Instead of just a few months every year.

"Oh, how well we all know that," Susannah retorted.

Gabe understood why Susannah was lashing out. She had so much pain locked inside her, she had to put it somewhere. He also knew he was tough enough to take it. He watched her navigate her way down the steps with the hand truck and back up into the bed of the U-Haul, long, sexy legs moving purposefully, her silky skin gleaming in the sunshine. Reminding him he'd always wanted to make a move on her, but had known better, then and now. "You want to clarify that?"

"Brett knew how to really be there for the people in his life. Especially Belinda."

He caught the wistfulness in her low tone. Knew her sister's intensely happy marriage had been a source of relief, amazement and heartache for her. Guessing how lonely and inadvertently left out she'd often felt in the wake of such contentment, he narrowed his glance at her and goaded her into revealing more of her feelings, "And you think I don't have Brett's gift for getting close to others?"

"Not really, and especially not in a romantic way. I mean—" she surveyed the moving boxes still left to be unloaded, waving an airy hand "—it's not that I think you're a monk, mind you." Her eyes sparkled with sudden mischief. "I'm sure you have had your share of the ladies."

Choosing not to delve too deeply into her remark,

he provoked, just as languidly, "And I'm sure you date, too."

Regret battled with the sorrow in her expression. "Not...successfully." She sighed. "Which is why I'm back here," she continued, her usual stubborn optimism returning. "Because I'm going to forget all about trying to find the one and pursue having a family on my own."

"With...?" he asked, fearing he already knew the answer to that, given the terms of her sister and brother-in-law's will and the controversial property contained therein.

Her lips quavered slightly, leaving her looking achingly vulnerable once again. "The embryos Belinda and Brett left behind."

He knew she was heartbroken and bereft, and he privately worried she'd never find the bliss her late family had left behind, but this was *crazy talk*, pure and simple. No way a woman still in the throes of mourning should undertake such a risky, life-upending proposition. Especially when a happy result was far from guaranteed. "Whoa, whoa!" He lifted his hands in emphasis. "Just because they left you their embryos does not mean you have to personally use them, Susannah."

"And what would you have me do, Doc?" she shot back angrily, leaning in close and going toe-to-toe with him. "*Destroy them?* Because Brett and Belinda were quite clear that they did not want that to happen, *even* in the event of their death."

Reminding himself she was still grieving and that

he needed to tread carefully here, he suggested quietly, "You could donate them to another infertile couple."

He watched her lips open in a round "oh" of distress.

"As was also offered as an option for you, if this situation ever came to pass," he continued. And sadly, it had.

She shook her head, stepped back, distraught. "The thought of strangers taking on their embryos…" Moisture sparkled in her eyes. "No."

"You don't have to be related by blood to be a good parent," he reminded her gruffly, knowing it to be true. Carol and Robert Lockhart had been wonderful to him and his seven siblings, loving them every bit as fiercely as his biological parents had. First through the foster-care system, then adoption.

Yes, there were still underlying issues for all of the siblings, he admitted to himself reluctantly. How could there *not* be, after experiencing a lightning strike on their Houston home during a terrible thunderstorm, the frantic escape that followed, followed by the eventual roof collapse that had killed both his folks in an instant?

Yet, at the end of the day, he and his sibs were still family. Emotional scars and all. Fiercely loved and protected by their adoptive parents.

Susannah pulled herself together and studied him, the tenuous politeness they had managed for the sake of their late loved ones showing signs of fracture yet again. "I wasn't trying to insult you or your folks, Gabe."

"And yet," he couldn't help but point out, feeling a little resentful himself now at her attitude, "you said it. And meant it." *Thereby implying that nonbiological ties are inferior to biological ones.*

Susannah raked her teeth across her lower lip and tried again, choosing her words carefully. "I'm sorry if I hurt your feelings. I know you and your siblings were lucky enough to find a really wonderful second set of parents. But after Belinda and I were orphaned, we landed in a situation with an actual blood relative where that wasn't the case. Which makes me a lot less trusting that everything will turn out all right, just because a situation looks good on paper."

"Meaning?" he asked, aware this situation was becoming far too personal, far too fast.

Briefly, a flash of emotion that seemed to go far deeper than the situation they were in flickered in her gaze. "I have no intention of signing Brett and Belinda's embryos over to someone else to raise. Not," she said emphatically, coming close enough to inundate him with the wildflower scent of her perfume, "when I am still here to do it for them."

Chapter Two

"You don't know what you're getting into," Gabe told Susannah gruffly.

As their eyes locked, the interior of the moving truck became unbearably quiet. Susannah wasn't surprised Gabe didn't understand the bond she'd had with her identical twin sister. Nonmultiples rarely did. Connected since they had been in the womb, they had been able to communicate without even speaking. Had been able to predict each other's actions and finish each other's sentences. And the pain—or joy—one felt, the other did, too. Which was how she knew, even if Gabe didn't, *exactly* how Belinda would want her to proceed.

"I beg to differ with you there, Doc." Having held her sister's hand every step of the way to this point, she said, "I'm *well* aware of the many difficulties of IVF."

Ignoring his negativity, she turned toward him, inhaling the brisk masculine fragrance of his cologne and the soapy-clean scent of his hair and skin.

"Then you also know," he told her quietly, "being a gestational carrier will be incredibly time-consuming."

Feeling self-conscious beneath his frank perusal of her, she removed the elastic band from around her wrist and used it to put her mussed hair into a ponytail. "Got plenty of that on my hands these days," she said, wishing she'd taken time to put on some makeup before setting out that day.

His attention dropping to her bare lips, his gaze narrowed warningly. "As well as very expensive."

Aware her heart was suddenly racing, Susannah turned back to the rows of remaining boxes. Deciding it might be a good idea to organize them before she took any more off the truck, she shoved the cartons marked *Bedroom Lamps* to one side, next to the box that held the linens.

"Their estate plus the sale of my Houston condominium has left me with a tidy little nest egg."

He came closer and, noting what she was trying to do, stacked all the boxes marked *Kitchen* on the other side, the muscles of his broad shoulders and arms flexing tautly as he worked. "Are you prepared to go through all the invasive medical tests and procedures alone?"

Of course she wished she had a husband or even a devoted lover by her side! She didn't have either and was not likely to find one any time soon. But that didn't mean she had to go through the rest of her life alone.

Aware she was suddenly so parched she could barely swallow, she walked over to the cooler filled with ice and electrolyte drinks. She knelt down to open it up, gesturing for him to help himself. "Of course I'm prepared to be a single mom to more than one child. Otherwise I wouldn't even be considering this."

"Okay, then." He leaned down to pull out a lime-flavored beverage. Keeping his eyes locked with hers, he used the hem of his shirt to remove the moisture dripping from the plastic bottle.

Susannah averted her eyes from the brief view of flat, suntanned abs. Tried to act unaffected by the tufts of hair arrowing down the center of his chest and disappearing into the waistband of his jeans. "What about the fact that the implantation of the frozen embryos might not take?" Gabe continued, upping his pessimistic view another notch.

That was a little harder to deal with, Susannah thought, biting her lip. Since she only had enough cash on hand and emotional fortitude for one all-in attempt. Having decided not to dwell on that, however, she plucked a grape-flavored beverage for herself from the ice and shut the cooler lid.

Like him, she used the hem of her shirt to blot the moisture dripping from the bottle. Unlike him, she made certain no skin showed. "I'm not going into this with an adverse attitude, Doc." Finding her knees suddenly wobbly, she sat down on a stack of book boxes. "And I would appreciate it if you didn't, either."

To her irritation, he continued playing devil's advocate rather than honor her request. "You know that if you implant more than one embryo at a time, you also run the risk of having more than one baby."

That would be fine, Susannah thought happily. Even as she knew that statistically the odds were against that happening. Which was why most couples elected to implant more than one embryo at a time—so they would end up with at least one baby in the end.

Aware he was still studying her over the rim of his bottle, she settled more comfortably on her perch and took a long, thirsty drink of her icy beverage. "These embryos were created with love. They are also the last family that I have, if you don't count that puppy I just adopted, so yes, I'd be happy if that happened, too."

He lounged against the side of the truck. "This isn't some romantic ideal, Susannah." Disapproval vibrated in his low tone. "You really need to think this through."

His skepticism wasn't the first she had encountered, but for some reason she couldn't quite fathom, his rankled the most. Maybe because the people at the fertility clinic were just doing their jobs, whereas he…he was injecting his own detached life view into the situation and interfering in her personal business.

"Actually, Doc, I've given it quite a bit of thought. And it's not as out of left field a notion as you seem to think. Belinda and Brett and I had already discussed the possibility of me being a surrogate if she was unable to carry a child herself." As her twin had feared she might be after the number of miscarriages she'd had.

He looked surprised. "And you were willing to do that," he mused, pulling a couple of boxes over and settling down opposite her.

"Of course I was," Susannah told him, flushing self-consciously despite herself. "Just as Belinda would have done it for me if I had been in a similar situation."

"It's not the same thing," Gabe countered gently. He was so close, their knees were practically touching. "If you'd simply been a surrogate, you would have been giving the child—or children, if they chose to go the twins route—over *to them* to raise."

Ignoring the heat emanating off of him, Susannah held on to her composure by a thread. Calmly, she returned, "And if they had died *after* the babies had been born, instead of before the embryos were implanted, I would have been left to raise their children *then*, too."

"You don't need to do this to continue to feel connected to your sister, Susannah."

Once again, he had intuited what she was feeling, deep down. "What if I want to do it?" she demanded, warmth flowing from her chest into her face. "What if carrying on this legacy for my sister and her husband, via those embryos, is the greatest gift I could ever give them?" she said, looking long and hard into his eyes. "What then?"

Their gazes clashed as surely as their wills, and a heartbreaking silence reverberated between them. Gabe could see that Susannah thought following through on Belinda and Brett's dreams of having a family would somehow alleviate the deep, unsettling nature of the loss. He knew better. And it was time, he decided firmly, she did, too.

He reached over and took her hands firmly in his. "Listen to me, Susannah," he rasped. "As tough as it would be for you to go this alone, in a physical sense, emotionally it would be even more difficult. Especially if there were..." He paused, taking in the hurt gleaming in her pretty eyes, still searching for the right way to phrase this. "...complications."

Her lower lip trembled even as her eyes gleamed damply. She shrugged off his grip and shot to her feet. Ponytail bouncing, she lifted her chin. "Do you think I don't know the risks here? Of course I do! Probably better than anyone." Agitated, she began to pace.

"Brett and Belinda spent years trying to get this far. Suffering so many disappointments over their initial inability to get pregnant, plus several miscarriages— the last an ectopic pregnancy that nearly took Belinda's life. It was the *joy* they felt over the success of their last IVF attempt that prompted them to take the second honeymoon to Hawaii before embarking on the implantation process." Her voice broke, and she looked so distraught he longed to take her in his arms and offer her the kind of comfort she clearly needed. Sensing she needed her physical space, however, he merely stood and continued listening and watching her from a distance.

Susannah shook her head miserably, recounting, "Had they not taken the helicopter tour that tragically ended in a crash that killed everyone onboard, they would both be here now, Gabe. Going through with the final phase together."

Gabe felt the enormity of the loss, too. It had caused him to reevaluate his life. Stop part-timing it with PWB, and devote himself to the cause full-time. He closed the distance between them to square off with her once again.

"You still don't have to do this for them," he reiterated as they stood facing each other in the shadowy interior of the truck.

He knew grief could make you do crazy things. And this was crazy whether she realized it or not. He put his hands on her shoulders until she lifted her chin and met his eyes. Satisfied he had her full attention, he continued, more gently now, "They would understand you're entitled to your own children. Your own life." Which was what, he realized suddenly, he wanted for her.

Eyes shimmering, she withdrew her hands from his. "And what if that doesn't happen?" she continued, glaring at him as if he were a complete idiot.

He looked back at her in exactly the same way.

Knowing he would get nowhere if they started to argue again, he held on to his composure by a thread. "What are you talking about?" She was the most beautiful, sensual and intelligent woman he had ever met! The fact she'd always sent out signals forbidding him from asking her out, which he had reluctantly accepted, rankled even more. Why was she so loath to give him a chance? Was it the fact he was older than she? Not good enough for her? Too bent on helping others in the most effective way he could? *What!*

Her full lower lip shot out. "I'm thirty-two, Gabe! I haven't met the man of my dreams yet."

So he'd been right, he thought, surprised to find just how disappointed he was to learn there was no way he would ever be in the running for her potential boyfriend.

Oblivious to his thoughts, she stepped closer and waved a finger in his face. "I haven't even come close!" She propped her delicate hands on her slender hips and fumed even more. "The hard truth is, the way things are going, I may never get married! Never have kids of my own!"

Her slender body gave off waves of indignant heat. Beneath that was the wildflower scent clinging to her skin and hair. Aware just how important it was they get this emotion out in the open, he ignored the feelings of desire generated by her closeness and guessed sagely, "Unless, of course, you do this."

Put your whole life on hold to assume someone else's dreams. Out of grief, duty and quite possibly, loneliness. It was as wrong and as potentially life wrecking as his own family-induced grief and guilt.

Even worse was the knowledge that he, just like she, had let his misguided emotions rule the day and had inadvertently compounded one tragedy with an even more gut-wrenching mistake. The kind that, once undertaken, could not be undone.

He didn't want her to live with that kind of regret and heartache, the way he and all his siblings had done. He didn't want her to spend a lifetime trying to make up for the one life-altering misstep.

Unaware of the depth of his remorse, her expression turned fiercely determined once again. "I don't want to spend the rest of my life alone, Gabe, not when I could have at least this much."

He let his gaze drift over her, taking in her alluring, feminine beauty, wishing he could forget reasoning with her and simply take her to bed, show her firsthand just how desirable she was. But instead, he forced himself to continue matter-of-factly, "You're selling yourself short."

"What would you know about any of this?" she retorted bitterly, cutting him off once again. "You don't want to get married or have children."

That was true, too, but only because he knew, like the rest of his family did, that he'd make a mess of it. "But you do. So it will happen," he said firmly.

Susannah released a long, belabored sigh and flushed self-consciously despite herself. If only she could be half as optimistic as he was in this regard. She couldn't. No matter how much she wished the man of her dreams was waiting in the wings, ready to sweep her off her feet, the stark facts said otherwise.

No one she was attracted to was attracted to her. And there was no better example of that than the man standing right in front of her.

Noting her skepticism, he shifted so he stood with his feet braced slightly apart, then jammed his hands on his hips and waited until he had her full attention. "It will," he persisted, "if you give it time."

"And how do you know that?" Her patience thinning as swiftly as her willingness to listen to his advice, she pushed the words through gritted teeth. "Have you been visiting fortune-tellers? Looked into a crystal ball?"

If her sister's death had taught her anything, it was that time was the one thing she might not have. And frankly, she was tired of waiting for fate to intervene in a positive way. She wanted to take her destiny in her own hands—the lack of romance in her life be damned! Maybe she wouldn't have a man. But she could have kids, a dog and a cozy little home to call her own.

"I haven't, and you know why, darlin'? Because it's not necessary." He favored her with a challenging half smile she found even more disturbing than his sudden interference before confidently reassuring her, "All you have to do is be patient."

Talk about hopeless do-gooder syndrome!

"Yeah, well…" Unsure why Gabe was suddenly trying to be the dominant male influence in her life, she stepped close enough to glare up at him coolly.

Mimicking his posture, she propped her hands on her hips, too. "Someone would have to want me like that first." And that was definitely not happening. Especially not here, and not now.

Gabe blinked and edged even closer. "Is that what this is about?" he demanded, the heat from his body transferring to hers. "You think you're not attractive?"

Not the way she wanted to be. Not the way her twin had been. Belinda had always gotten the guys. Whereas she—she had been promptly put in the friend zone.

"You may not want to see it, Doc." Susannah whirled away as her temper rose. "Hell, even I don't want to see it," she muttered, swinging back to face him once again. "But the simple truth is that no one has ever looked at me the way Brett looked at Belinda." An ache clogged her throat as she leaned against the side of the truck, taking refuge in the shady interior. "No one has ever wanted me that passionately. Or ever fallen in love with me or wanted to marry me or, heaven forbid, even kissed me—" Her voice cracked as she thought about all the lonely years, playing second fiddle to her gorgeous, glamorous twin sister. "—like that…"

"Then maybe…" Gabe said gruffly, striding toward her until there was nothing between them at all but heat. He took her all the way in his arms, lowering his face slowly and evocatively to hers. His lips touched hers, and his low, implacable tone set her heart to pounding. "…it's high time someone did."

* * *

Gabe hadn't come here to put the moves on Susannah. For God's sake, he was supposed to be honoring his promise to Brett and Belinda by watching over her! Had she not confessed the real reason why she was about to make the biggest mistake of her life... he would have remained honorable to the core and kept his distance.

But knowing it was the misconception that she wasn't desirable that was forcing her to act as she was left him little choice but to show her otherwise, in the most potent way he knew how.

He brushed his lips over hers. Lightly. Seductively. His body hardened as he felt her shudder, and welcome him, in response. Another jolt of awareness arced between them.

"You're wrong about that," he murmured, lifting his mouth from hers. Gazing deeply into her eyes, he waited for permission to proceed. She curved her hands around the swell of his biceps, holding him in place. Uttered a soft, breathy sigh. "Because you're sexy as hell." He threaded his hands through her hair, releasing the ponytail from its band, then stroked his hands through the silky blond locks falling down around her shoulders once again. "You have to know that."

She laughed in disbelief, her hands clutching him even closer, the softness of her breasts trembling against his chest. "Oh Doc." She shook her head in wry disagreement, looking as if she wanted to hold that moment in her heart forever. "I wish..."

The desire to protect her increased tenfold. Sentiment swept through him, followed swiftly by a physical longing that was just as intense, and he tilted his head over hers again. Let his lips hover suggestively. And lower still, where their bodies touched, his hardness grew. "I know…" he said, his mind made up.

And still, she didn't believe that this was anything out of the ordinary, for her or for him. Whereas he knew they were on to something. Something wild… and wonderful…or at least it could be, if she'd finally give them half a chance.

"Oh yeah?" She threw down the gauntlet softly, her tone both taunting and deadpan. "Then prove it, Doc."

Clearly, Gabe noted, she didn't think he could. And that, as it turned out, was all the challenge he needed. He grinned down at her devilishly. "If you insist…"

Susannah caught her breath as Gabe's lips found hers for the second time. And just that quickly, all reasonable ideas of resistance left her brain. So many emotions poured through her all at once. Shock, that he had dared put the moves on her when she had been so sure he would not follow through on his softly spoken gibe. Amazement that she was letting him. She had never been wanted like this, never gotten so caught up in a single kiss, never melted in anyone's arms this way. But as the liquid stroking of his tongue, the unhurried pressure of his lips, worked together with a mixture of temptation and pleasure unlike anything she had ever felt before, the depth of her response to him shook her to her very soul.

She'd heard about embraces like this. Read about them. Seen them on TV and in the movies. But she had never experienced anything like the tumultuous whirlwind of pleasure and pure sensation that the taste of his lips and mouth and tongue were evoking.

And even though she knew he was only doing this to prove his point, that she was capable of getting a whole lot more out of life, without fast-forwarding to parenthood via IVF, the fun- and pleasure-starved part of her never wanted his embrace to end.

Had it not been for the sudden, sharp sound of her puppy's bark, who knew what would have happened?

But the fact was, Daisy was awake. Alone in the house. Probably wondering when she was coming back. And it was time for this foolishness with Gabe to end.

Susannah removed her hands from his biceps, planted them both on his chest, and pushed. As she had expected, he let her go immediately. "I've got to go." Tingling all over, she rushed past him.

Caught up short, he fell into step, all protective male. "I'll help."

She whirled and put up both hands, blocking his path. Angry now as well as hurt that he'd put the moves on her so shamelessly. When he had to know, as did she, that this could go nowhere...good. "Don't you think you've done enough for one day?"

"Obviously, I've overstepped."

For reasons she couldn't understand, the fact he could regret what had just happened, too, hurt even more. She shook her head, embarrassed and ashamed by her own romantic foolishness. No way was she going to be another notch on this doc's belt. "No kidding."

Daisy barked louder. Short, excited yelps. The kind that signaled she really needed to go out.

He walked down the truck ramp beside her, his shoulder nudging hers in the process. "I still think we should talk."

Bitterness welled inside her, even as her chagrin grew. It wasn't like her to lose sight of her independence. She knew better than most not to depend on anyone. "Now that you've proven me beddable, you mean?" she retorted.

"That's not why I kissed you, Susannah."

She studied the firm set of his sculpted lips and tried, without success, not to want to taste them all over again. Her heart pounded like a wild thing in her chest. "Then what was the point?"

"To show you that you have more of a future than you're giving yourself credit for," he said huskily.

Clearly, he meant without IVF.

Temper rising, Susannah stepped forward and poked her index finger in the center of his warm, solidly muscled chest. "Well, here's what I think you should know, Doc."

The beginnings of a satisfied smile tugged at the corners of his lips. "I'm listening."

"I want you to stop trying to meddle in my affairs and give me advice or…most of all…have anything at all to do with those frozen embryos."

His amusement faded. "So you haven't changed

your mind?" He seemed disappointed his ploy to prove her desirable hadn't worked to dissuade her.

The *arrogance*, Susannah fumed. But then, what should she have expected from a guy who cherished his career above all else? "Not one bit," she reiterated.

He released an irritated breath, warning, "You'd be a fool to try and do this alone."

She imagined he wasn't the only one who would think that. Not that it mattered. "Yeah, well, we'll see." And on that note, she turned on her heel and went inside the house to rescue her new puppy.

Chapter Three

June 1, five years later

Cade Lockhart swung open the front door of his Laramie, Texas, retreat and glared at Gabe. "I don't care what the folks told you to get you to come back from Africa," he said in a gravelly voice. "You don't have to babysit me."

Gabe looked over at his pro baseball–playing brother. Still recovering from arthroscopic surgery, his pitching arm in a sling, Cade had seen better days. His parents had been right to call him home to help out his younger sibling.

"Save your griping." Gabe shouldered past and set his duffel bag and backpack down. "After three bus transfers, a twenty-two-hour flight and a two-and-a-half-hour drive from DFW, I need a shower. A nice cold beer and food would be nice, too."

Cade clapped him on the back with his left arm. "You're really planning to bunk with me?"

Gabe strode through the luxurious digs and headed straight for the fridge, where he found plenty of beer and a plate of cold cuts. Aware Cade wasn't the only one who didn't want parental interference, he helped himself to both. "I'm not spending the next three months in my old room at the ranch." He grimaced. "Mom will be on my case constantly to get a job stateside and get married and have a family of my own. And Dad will have me up at sunrise chasing cattle every morning unless I've got something medical to do. So…my excuse is going to be that you need me to help rehab your rotator cuff, make sure you're not overdoing it or pushing too hard, too fast."

Cade rolled his eyes and continued watching Gabe's face. "You're really taking a three-month break?"

Although he would have preferred to keep the truth private, Gabe confessed, "It was not so delicately suggested to me by my boss at Physicians Without Borders that five years without a single trip back home to Texas was not good for the psyche. So, I'm on leave until fall, when I will get my next assignment."

And now it was his turn to ask, "How is your shoulder?"

"Hard to tell, since the only thing they've let me do since I had surgery last month is gentle stretching exercises. But they've promised I can start working out more soon. Hopefully, I'll be back on the pitching mound by August."

Gabe took in the bottles of over-the-counter vitamins and herbal cures. Some of which, he knew, should not be combined with the prescription meds Cade was taking. "That quickly?" From what he knew, it could take a rotator-cuff injury up to a year to heal. Six months would be pushing it. Three months…could be career suicide.

"Well—" Cade flashed an unrepentant grin "—there's what they tell me I can do and what I'm gonna do."

Exactly what the family was worried about, Gabe thought.

"Meanwhile, as you can see, I'm not suffering too badly." Cade waved his good arm expansively, indicating the baskets of flowers, gourmet goodies and home-baked treats on every counter. Some of which bore his team's logo.

Gabe helped himself to a tray of cookies. "This from the Texas Wranglers?"

"Some. The rest are from the ladies back in Dallas—" Cade flashed a sly grin "—who are constantly visiting me and bringing me care packages."

The problem was, Gabe thought, Cade wasn't interested in any of them, outside of the arm candy they provided him. His one *true* love was baseball.

Knowing how hard his brother had worked to accrue his fame and fortune, Gabe nodded admiringly. "Not too shabby."

Cade bypassed the beer in his fridge and poured

himself a glass of milk. "I could set you up," he offered generously.

"Nah." There was only one woman he was interested in, and she wouldn't give him the time of day.

Cade's lips twitched. "Still carrying a torch for Susannah Alexander, hmm?"

Gabe forced the image of the hot-as-hell woman from his mind. "What are you talking about?" he asked, as if he didn't know.

Cade chuckled with the inveterate ease of a true ladies' man. "I'm not deaf, blind and dumb. She's still single, you know."

Gabe took another slow sip of beer and tried not to think of this as another golden opportunity. That probably wouldn't end in an ill-gotten kiss. "Actually, I wouldn't," he said dryly. Since she hadn't returned any of the texts, calls or emails he'd sent her after he'd left. After six months he'd gotten the message. Loud and clear. So much for watching out for her. *Sorry, Brett and Belinda.* He sent a glance heavenward. *I tried. But Susannah wasn't interested in having me in her life in any way. So...*

Aware Cade was still watching him curiously, Gabe slid the cold cuts back in the fridge and shrugged. "Although I'm not surprised she's not married."

Cade nodded, in complete agreement this time. "Well, duh. I mean, five kids..."

Five! Whole body tensing, Gabe turned back to him. "What are you talking about?"

Cade scoffed. "She had quintuplets via her late sister and brother-in-law's frozen embryos, three and a half years ago. Don't tell me you didn't know that!"

He definitely had not.

"Mommy, doorbell!"

Daisy, their five-year-old golden retriever, yawned and rose from her place in the foyer.

Susannah stepped out from behind the easel she'd set up in her formal dining room. "Okay, I'll get it. You all keep working on your pictures," she told the quints.

"And then when we're done with our art, we get to go outside and play?"

Susannah wiped her hands on her cloth. "When it cools off after dinner, yes." She made her way to the door and swung it open. Stared at the handsome interloper on the other side of her portal, hardly believing that Gabe Lockhart was here after all this time. Looking tan and buff and sexy as sin. The crinkles around his eyes and mouth were a little more pronounced, but in her opinion, that just added to his rugged masculinity.

He was dressed, much as he had been the last time she had seen him, in a clean tan cargo shirt, worn snug-fitting jeans and boots. He filled out his clothes a little more, with the kind of brawn generated by a physically demanding profession. As she imagined medicine would be, out in the wilds.

As if understanding that the handsome do-gooder *should* be a family friend, Daisy left Gabe's side. Her expression alert but relaxed, she ambled over to stand next to Susannah. Her ears slightly forward, her head cocked curiously to one side.

"I hear congratulations are in order," he drawled, the grooves on either side of his sensual mouth deepening.

His husky tone intensified the sparks arcing between them. Trying not to recall how thrilling it had been to kiss him, she held on to her nonchalant stance. "For you or me?" She copied his deadpan quip, as Daisy eased between them, tail wagging.

Traitor, Susannah thought.

Grinning down affectionately, Gabe petted her dog's silky head before returning his attention once again to her. "You, obviously." His gaze traveled toward all five of her children, who were still busy working on their pictures at the dining room table, then back over to her. His gaze softened unexpectedly, and he continued to study her intently. "Why didn't you tell me?"

She folded her arms in front of her and lifted her chin. "Why would I, given how you felt about my plans to have a family on my own?"

He shrugged, whiskey-colored eyes darkening inscrutably. "Had I known, I could have helped."

Out of some misguided sense of duty to Belinda and Brett? That was the last thing she'd want. Because help like that usually came with strings. Which she would never want. Nor would she want to be the beneficiary of Gabe's unrelenting need to play hero everywhere he went. "Last I heard, you were prac-

ticing medicine in poverty-stricken areas of Asia and
Africa."

"So?" he said, with another curious look behind
her, as the noise level of the quints began to escalate.

Trying not to worry about what her children *might*
be getting into, Susannah kept her attention firmly
on their uninvited guest. And just how handsome and
sexy he looked in the late-afternoon sunlight. If only
he had been interested in her, not as the sort of obligation that had been thrust upon him by the deaths
of Brett and Belinda that everyone else in the community also felt, but for all the *right* reasons. But he
wasn't, so... "That's a little far to travel to come and
change a diaper, isn't it?" Although those days were
long past, thank heaven!

His lips curved into a laconic smile. "I get time
off, when needed, for personal reasons."

Except the situation between them wasn't personal, Susannah thought. Even if the hopelessly romantic part of her still wished it might someday be.
She blew out an exasperated breath. "Still not getting
your point, Doc."

He leaned in and spoke so the children would not
hear. "Had I known you were expecting multiples, I
would have returned to Texas to see you through the
labor and delivery."

And seen her sans clothing? At least from the waist
down? Physician or no... She fought back a wave of
heat at just the thought. "I don't think so," Susannah
retorted coolly, firmly and quickly nixing his desire
to play the hero to what he obviously perceived as her

damsel in distress. "Besides, I have plenty of friends here who helped out." Social worker Mitzy Martin McCabe, who was herself the mother of quadruplets, also conceived from in vitro, among them.

Mitzy, who'd embarked on single motherhood, too, before finding the love of her life, had understood Susannah's desire to have a family on her own better than anyone. Although, unlike Susannah, Mitzy had defied the odds and ended up having a wild romance with her new husband, Chase McCabe.

Gabe's gaze narrowed, and he eyed the living room behind her. "Maybe you should invite me in."

"Again," Susannah said in an exasperated tone, "I really have to ask why?"

Gabe gestured behind her.

She turned, almost afraid to look.

When the doorbell rang, her children had been seated at the dining room table, working on that day's post-nap art project, so she could get a little extra work in herself before starting dinner. Now, all five were engulfed in a soundless misbehavior. Abigail was leaning across the table, in her usual take-charge manner, bossily trying to correct Rebecca's drawing, to her shyest child's dismay. Connor was squirting glue out of a bottle at his brother, Levi. Who reacted by letting out a loud rebel yell and lobbing crayons and paper at his brother. Gretchen had climbed onto the center of the table and was hoarding the glitter, to her sisters' dismay.

Nearby, her own easel and paints were clearly in

jeopardy, as an entire uncapped bottle of school glue took flight.

Aghast, Susannah moaned. "Oh no, no, no..."

She raced across the room, stepped in to catch the glue with her open palm, just before it hit the nearly completed canvas. Her closing fingers didn't stop the white fluid from spreading outward, however. On the back of the easel, the floor, the nearby table and chairs. "What has gotten into you all?" she demanded.

Not that she didn't know.

Every time she talked on the phone, or spoke with someone at the door, or put her attention elsewhere, the quints had a way of directing her attention right back. Usually through mischievous acts like these.

"Levi started it!" Connor claimed.

"Did not!" Levi said loudly.

Abigail frowned. "They were all taking too long! We should have been finished by now!"

Gretchen stuck out her tongue. "I do not need any help! I can do it all by myself!"

Rebecca surveyed Susannah's expression, sighed quietly, and put her thumb in her mouth.

"Is it like this all the time?" Gabe asked.

Yes, Susannah thought, acutely aware how close to the edge of her patience she often felt these days. But not about to admit it to Gabe, she merely smiled and fibbed, "Of course not." Clearly, he didn't believe her. Which prompted her to add, a little haughtily, "Your presence has obviously upset them."

* * *

Gabe might have bought that had he not been one of eight very independent, rambunctious kids. Who were also close together in age. Although not *this* close.

The downstairs of the Craftsman abode had been opened into one large space, so Gabe was able to watch Susannah stride over to the kitchen, her body moving gracefully beneath her trim cotton T-shirt and matching shorts as she moved. She had cut her hair to just beneath her chin and filled out a little since she'd had the quints, but the curves were nice and womanly, as was the new maternal fullness in her face. She looked like someone who'd had all her dreams come true, he thought, and that was a good thing. Though he imagined she would be even happier if she had a loving husband on the premises to help her rear this rambunctious brood.

Susannah returned, paper towel roll and bottle of spray cleaner in hand. As she knelt to quickly dispense of the sticky mess, Abigail sidled up to Gabe and asked, point-blank, "Are you here to marry our mom?"

Taken aback, his jaw dropped open in surprise.

Susannah glanced over at him. Judging by the pink in her cheeks, she, too, thought it was a ridiculous notion.

"'Cause it's not going to happen," Connor chimed in.

Gretchen shook her head. "She won't even go on a date."

"And Mr. Bing keeps asking," Levi announced, edging closer, too.

"So does the plumber." Abigail stood between her brothers.

"And the electrician," Rebecca took her thumb out of her mouth long enough to say.

Wow, she really did have a line of suitors, Gabe thought, lifting a brow. That was no surprise, given she was as beautiful and elusive as ever, with her delicate features, silky honey-blond hair and sea-blue eyes.

"Don't forget that guy that brings our pizza and is always smiling real big at her," Gretchen said.

Susannah finished wiping up the mess on the floor and stood, her cheeks turning an even deeper rose.

"Those men are all just being nice, because they are doing a service for us. And I am nice to them because they are here helping us out. I don't think it means anything out of the ordinary. They're just people being kind and neighborly the way everyone in Laramie County is," she soothed.

The quints weren't buying it, Gabe noticed with satisfaction and something else that felt peculiarly close to jealousy.

The kids knew male-female interest when they saw it.

Connor stood on his head. His brother, Levi, immediately followed suit. Looking over, he informed Gabe happily, "But Mr. Bing asks the most."

Another waft of concern sifted through him. "Mr. Bing?" Did the guy have a chance with her? Gabe had never really envisioned Susannah with someone else. Given how independent she was, he had figured she would either stay single, or a damn miracle would happen, and she would end up with him.

With a harried sigh, Susannah soaked up a particularly big glob of glue on the dining room table. "Bingham Taylor. From the bank."

Gabe hovered close enough to Susannah to take in a whiff of her wildflower perfume. Her skin looked as touchable and soft as he recalled, her lips just as kissable.

Throat parched, he asked, "The Bing Taylor we went to school with?"

"Yes."

Miracles or no, Gabe rejected the notion out of hand. "Last I remember, he was about three inches shorter than you."

A squeak sounded behind them. Turning, they saw Rebecca holding open the screen door to let in their latest visitor.

Speak of the devil, who apparently had caught just enough of what was being said to add in a low, cultured tone now completely devoid of his homegrown Texas accent, "I grew when I went to Princeton for my undergrad and Harvard for my MBA."

He certainly had, Gabe thought. These days, Bing was almost as tall as Gabe. He also had the aura of big-city slickster. Yet Bing'd maintained the inherent kindness and compassion he'd always had, too.

But that did not explain his pursuit of Susannah. Not to Gabe's satisfaction, anyway.

"And yet here you are, back in Laramie." Gabe surveyed Bing's custom suit and tie, wishing he had taken the time to iron his own shirt and get a haircut, instead of just shower and shave.

Bing smiled and extended his palm. His handshake was firm, friendly. "I'm just here for a year or so to settle my dad's estate and manage the sale of my family's ranch. I want to make sure my mom gets top dollar. Then I'll be going back to my life in Chicago. Meanwhile, I'm working remotely out of the branch here."

Susannah informed Gabe proudly, "Bing is a vice president of private investments for Unity Bank."

"And the two of you are…" Dating? Trying to date? Gabe wasn't sure how he felt about that. It wasn't that Bing wasn't a decent person. He just wasn't right for Susannah. Did she know that? Hard to tell from her genial expression.

"Bing is handling the general welfare trust I set up for the children, with the funds Brett and Belinda left," she explained.

His demeanor suddenly all business, Bing looked at Susannah. "And we need to talk. Which is why I've been calling you."

Flushing guiltily, she carried the used paper towels over to the trash. "I know. I've been busy."

Bing nodded. "You're always busy." He grinned down at the kids, who grinned back. "And it's understandable. Which is why I want to set up a business dinner." He lifted his hand before she could get a word in edgewise. "It can be late. After the little

ones are in bed. I've already talked to your neighbors
Mike and Millie Smith. I know they sit for you all the
time, and they've offered to watch the kids whenever
it's convenient for us to meet. As long as it's not on
Wednesdays and Thursdays, when they're off galli-
vanting around the state with their line-dancing club."

Now Susannah looked irked—which wasn't a
surprise, given her highly self-sufficient nature, Gabe
thought. "You really didn't have to do that." She
forced a smile.

The kids looked back at Bing.

"I really think I do," he said, "if we're going to
make this happen."

Susannah slipped her cell phone from her pocket.
"How about I make an appointment and come to the
office instead?"

Good. She didn't want a dinner date, Gabe thought.
Glad she had enough sense not to go on a date bound
to go nowhere.

"Fine. As long as we set something up now," Bing
returned firmly.

Susannah sighed, looking anything but willing to
do just that. Surprised by the protectiveness surging
within him, Gabe stepped in. "Maybe you could do
it later." Or *never*, he thought grumpily.

Bing frowned and gave Gabe a highly frustrated
look that encouraged him to mind his own business.

Noting the simmering tension, Susannah stepped
between the two men, her back to Gabe. "I'm sorry.
I'm not trying to be difficult, Bing. I'll make time,"
she said quietly. "I can't meet with you until Friday,

but I will be there first thing when the bank opens, if that is agreeable with you."

Bing nodded in obvious relief. "It is. I'll see you then." He said goodbye to everyone and left.

Susannah turned back to Gabe with an arched brow. She glanced at her watch, noting it was near five. "I think that's your cue, too."

Gabe realized that. Their ongoing artwork now abandoned, the two boys took several plastic toy crates, turned them over to empty them onto the carpet, willy-nilly, and then began stacking them, one on top of the other, directly behind Susannah. Probably, he thought, so she wouldn't be able to see what they were doing and correct them. Again.

Aware their messiness wasn't his problem, but finding out what was really going on with Susannah was, he stepped closer, keeping his voice low, persuasive. "I'd like to catch up…"

She stiffened, the way she had after the one and only time they had ever kissed. Still holding his eyes with the heat of remembered passion, she said tersely, "I don't think that's possible, Doc." Chin up, her icy glare warning him away, she stepped defiantly backward.

Seeing what she didn't, and the boys hoped she would not, Gabe reached for her in an attempt to catch her before she stumbled into the teetering crates and the small metal vehicles scattered all around them. To no avail. She moved away from his hand, misinterpreting and dodging his chivalrous attempt to save her—at the exact same time her foot landed awkwardly atop a small toy ambulance.

Again, he put his arms out to keep her from falling. And again, she stubbornly evaded him, throwing out both her arms and shoving him away. For a second, she teetered, and it looked as if she didn't need his help after all. Then still off balance, she tripped and twisted her right leg on the way down.

Searing pain ripped through Susannah's ankle, simultaneously pushing its way up toward her knee and down toward her toes. She cried out in agony as she hit the floor, her leg twisted awkwardly beneath her.

Around her, everyone froze. Then the kids sprang into action. "Mommy's got a boo-boo!" Abigail shouted.

Rebecca's lower lip quivered. "Don't cry, Mommy!" She rushed forward to help.

"We'll fix it!" Connor declared.

"I'll get the Band-Aids!" Gretchen moved to the bathroom.

"She needs peas!" Levi yelled.

Gabe knelt in front of her leg while two of her daughters flanked her comfortingly on either side of her head. This time, to her relief, he made no effort to touch her. Yet she was quivering with awareness just the same. "Are you okay?"

Obviously not. Determined not to let him know that, however, she fought back a grimace. Shifted her weight off her ankle. Another searing pain shot through her, and there was no way to circumvent the helpless tears flooding her eyes.

"We'll get you a cookie!" Abigail leaped up.

"And some juice!" Rebecca followed.

All doctor now, Gabe took charge. "Let's see if we can get you up and over to the sofa."

Susannah wanted to refuse, but there was no doubt she needed his help. Maybe it wouldn't hurt so badly if she were able to straighten her leg. Plus, the kids were all starting to look very worried. "Okay." She swallowed around another wave of pain.

He laced his arm about her waist. Aware how big and strong and solid he felt next to her, she put her arm around his brawny shoulder. Carefully, he guided her to a standing position and helped her limp over to the couch. She sat back so her legs were stretched out in front of her across the cushions, alarmed to find the pain was even worse.

"Mommy, we're coming!" The quints raced back into the room.

Gretchen held Band-Aids, Levi a frozen sack of peas. Abigail had a cookie. Rebecca, a juice box. Connor had the *Mother's First Aid Manual.*

Susannah attempted a smile. "Thank you," she said as everything was pressed into her hands, all at once.

Meanwhile, Gabe was peering at her ankle, which was looking uglier by the minute. "Mind if I quickly examine it?" he asked.

Might as well. It was, she knew, the only way she would get rid of him. "Go ahead." She sighed.

He palpated it gently, turned it this way and that. Every action caused excruciating pain. She managed not to make a sound, but because he was watching her face, he knew. And so did, she realized unhappily, her kids.

"This has got to be X-rayed," he said.

She had feared as much. Acutely aware of their audience, adapting an air of nonchalance, she took a small bite of the cookie and ignored the wave of nausea that rose in her throat as a result. "I'll go in the morning."

He stood, all take-charge doc. "No," he said autocratically, already taking out his phone. "You'll go now."

Chapter Four

Fifteen minutes later, Susannah heard the car doors slamming outside her home. "I can't impose upon your parents this way, Gabe."

"You heard my mom on the phone. It's no imposition. My parents were going to have dinner in town, anyway, and now they'll just have it with the kids while I take you to the hospital. And besides," he continued when he saw she was about to protest further, "isn't this why you moved to Laramie in the first place? Because of the way neighbors help neighbors all the time?"

It was.

"Is Mommy's ankle going to be okay?" Abigail asked.

Gabe knelt down to reassure her. "It sure is, sweetheart. But we still need to get it X-rayed."

The doorbell rang. He strode over to open the door. Carol and Robert Lockhart came in.

They were a handsome couple in their midfifties. Legendary for rounding up and then adopting Gabe and his seven siblings, their big hearts and calm, practical natures had brought the brood back to health after the sudden devastating loss of their birth parents.

"We're so sorry to hear about your mishap," Carol said. A slender woman with short, dark brown hair and vivid green eyes, she was dressed in a sleeveless denim dress and flats. A cardigan was tied around her shoulders.

"But not to worry. We'll cover everything here while you get that ankle looked at," Robert added. The dark-haired, brown-eyed rancher had the perennial tan and build of a man who spent his life outdoors. And the kind disposition of someone who had spent his life tending to animals and helping others.

"Are you going to be our babysitters?" Connor asked.

Robert knelt down to bump fists with him. "We sure are."

"Do you like pizza?" Carol whipped out her phone.

"Yes! Cheese, please!" the kids shouted in unison.

"All right, then." Gabe's mom grinned, looking happy to have that decided.

"Need some help getting Susannah to the car?" Robert asked.

Gabe handed a set of keys to his dad. "If you can get the doors, that would help."

"No problem." Robert went on ahead.

Doing her best not to moan, because the slightest movement caused searing pain to skip up and down her leg, Susannah removed the bag of peas that had been numbing her ankle and gingerly swung her legs off the sofa cushions.

She managed not to cry out, but she felt the blood leave her face all the same.

"Just what I thought," Gabe murmured just loud enough for her to hear. The next thing she knew, he was sliding one forearm beneath her knees, the other around her back, and she was lifted up into his strong arms and held against his chest.

"Wow," Gretchen said in obvious wonderment. "Just like a princess…"

"Or a bride," Abigail sighed.

"The doc rescued our mommy," Rebecca said, taking her thumb out of her mouth.

"Our mommy doesn't need rescuing," Connor declared.

"Yeah," Levi said defiantly. "Mommy rescues *us*. All the time."

"I bet she does," Gabe agreed, still holding Susannah as if she were light as a feather, and moving sideways through the door.

She tried not to think how good it felt to be carried this way. Never mind how safe and protected she felt with him in charge. "You all be good for Gabe's mom and dad," she told her kids.

"We will," they said in unison.

Robert headed down the sidewalk ahead of them, then hit the electronic lock on the late-model Silverado pickup sitting at her curb. "Pretty fancy," Susannah remarked. A lot fancier than she expected Gabe to be driving.

While his dad held the door, he eased her into the passenger seat. "Yep. Thanks, Dad."

"You'll call to let us know how things are going?" Robert asked.

Gabe nodded.

Abruptly, Susannah remembered. "Oh! I need my purse. With my ID and insurance card and phone…"

"Where is it?" Gabe's father asked, every bit as naturally gallant and genial as his eldest son.

"On the desk in the kitchen, next to my laptop," Susannah said.

"I'll get it." Robert strode purposefully back up the walk.

While they waited, Gabe eased behind the wheel. Suddenly, it all seemed a little too intimate. "You really didn't have to carry me," Susannah said, still tingling all over from where they had brushed up against each other.

Gabe's lips turned up at the edges. "You really wanted to try and hobble and risk more damage?" he drawled, glancing down at her swollen, visibly bruised ankle.

No. She hadn't.

Pride made her reiterate, anyway, in an even more clipped tone, "It was unnecessary."

He chuckled and shook his head in silent remonstration, as if knowing the real reason why she was protesting. His actions had made her way too aware of him again. It had made her want to lean on him, made her remember what it had been like to kiss him, and both were the last things she wanted to be thinking about at a time like this. When he was here, trying once again to unnecessarily insert himself into her life.

Deciding they needed to move the conversation into more neutral territory, she changed the subject. "Is this your pickup?"

Gabe squinted toward the house, as if willing his father to appear. "Belongs to my brother Cade."

Susannah had heard about the pro baseball player's injury in late April. And knew Cade had come back home to recuperate in the privacy Laramie County afforded. "How's he doing?" she asked sincerely.

"He's stubborn. Like you."

Trying to ignore the brisk masculine fragrance that emanated from him, Susannah asked, "Doesn't he need his truck?"

"I don't know why he would." Gabe shook his head. "He's got another one here. A sports car. And four more in his garage at his home in Dallas."

Susannah did a double take as the front door on her house opened and Gabe's father strode back out. "Cade's got six cars?"

"It's a thing with athletes. They collect them like women."

Robert reached the truck and handed the purse

through the window. "Do you want us to order some pizza for you, while we're at it?"

Gabe nodded appreciatively. "Thanks, Dad. I'm sure we'll be hungry when we get back." Robert took their preferences, which surprisingly enough happened to be the same: sausage and pepperoni and mushroom. They thanked him, and he headed back up the walk.

Strong hands commanding the wheel, Gabe pulled away from the curb and drove toward the hospital.

Aware this felt oddly like a date, instead of an emergency situation, she tried to focus on the graveness of the situation at hand instead of how very attracted she was to him. "Do you think it's broken?"

Gabe kept his attention on the cars in the intersection. "Only an X-ray will tell."

She sighed.

He reached over to pat her arm, and another sizzle of sensation coursed through her.

"It's going to be okay," he said with a reassuring smile.

At that moment, in pain and barely able to get around, even with help, Susannah didn't see how. "Says the person without five three-and-a-half-year-olds to care for."

He gave her a look that reminded her he had tried to warn her before she fell. A warning she had promptly—and idiotically—ignored.

A fact that made her even crankier. "And don't even think about saying *I told you so*," she grumbled.

He slanted her a look of choirboy innocence that

she was tempted to believe despite herself. Which only made him look even more infuriatingly gallant in her eyes. "I wasn't going to," he said. "But now that you've brought up your need for rescuing in this particular situation, it just so happens that I am going to be around for the rest of the summer. So…"

Painfully aware it would be all too easy to end up kissing him again, she said, "I've got Mike and Millie across the street."

His golden-brown brow lifted. "Except on Wednesdays and Thursdays."

So he recalled everything Bing had said. And hence knew her neighbors across the street would not be back in town or able to help her and the kids until late the following day.

Ignoring the faint flutter of her heart, Susannah continued, "And all the other moms in the Laramie County Multiples Club…"

Eyes twinkling, he flashed her an audacious grin. "And like it or not, at least for now, you've also got me."

Susannah had no comeback for that. Luckily, they were turning into the ER entrance. Gabe parked under the portico and went inside. Then he returned a few minutes later pushing a wheelchair.

It was clear Susannah was going to need help getting out of the cab, but there was a limit as to what kind of aid she would allow. As he leaned in, inundating her with his clean masculine scent, she unclasped her safety belt and said, "Don't you dare pick me up!"

He chuckled.

Keeping her guard up, she grabbed her bag and held it against her. "Just help me move into the chair."

"Sure thing, princess."

Wary of letting him into her life in any way, she lifted a chin and speared him with a testy glare. "I'm *not* a princess." And she did not want to flirt with him. No matter how attractive and chivalrous he was, or how lonely or bereft she had been when it came to man-woman relationships.

One palm beneath her forearm, his other arm wrapped snugly around her waist, he eased her out of the car and helped her onto the wheelchair. As she settled, he knelt before her, looking tenderly into her eyes, to make sure she was all right. "Your children think you are." His tone was both conciliatory and deadpan. He gave her a flirty grin. "And I can't say they aren't right."

Damn, he knew how to seduce a woman. Provided that was his goal. She still hadn't figured out why he felt her situation was any of his concern. Especially after all the time that had elapsed since they had last seen each other.

All she knew for sure was that it felt like she was missing something about the situation.

Something that could be a game changer.

The triage nurse was waiting inside to talk to Susannah. She took the basic information, copied the identification and insurance cards, and then wheeled her back into one of the private exam rooms. "The doctor will be in to see you in a minute," she said after helping Susannah into a hospital bed.

"You want me to stay with you or bide my time in the waiting room?" Gabe asked, lounging against the wall, his hands stuffed in the pockets of his jeans.

Suddenly, for reasons she did not want to examine too closely, she did not want to be completely on her own. At least not until she knew what the situation with her ankle was. "Ah." Susannah shrugged haphazardly, wishing he didn't tower over her quite so alluringly or radiate such masculine energy. "Might as well stay here," she said finally. "Someone else might need the chairs out there."

His soft laughter was infectious. It was all she could do not to feel pleased she'd been able to make him laugh or smile back in return.

Without warning, his expression grew thoughtful. "When was the last time you were here?"

Recalling, her heart panged in her chest. "Not since the quintuplets were one and they all got bronchitis at once."

He moved closer to the hospital bed. "Whoa." His voice dropped another notch as his gaze met and held hers. "Sounds harrowing."

"It was. But my neighbors, Millie and Mike Smith, came, and so did a couple other mothers from the Multiples Club, and we got through it. The quints were all able to go home that same night, and a week or so later, thanks to the antibiotics and nebulizer treatments, they were all back to being healthy as could be."

Gabe looked at her with new respect.

A knock sounded.

Gavin Monroe, a cardiothoracic expert and ER doc, breezed in. Like Gabe, Gavin was also charming, good-looking and in his early forties. "Hey. Heard you were in town." Gavin slapped Gabe on the back.

"Good to see you, too." Gabe hugged his old friend from med school warmly.

Gavin looked from one to the other. "So, what's up with this? You two finally dating?"

Finally? As if such a thing were preordained, Susannah thought, on a huff. To her relief, Gabe seemed equally stymied by the assumption. "Why would you think that?" she asked.

Gavin moved to the end of the bed. "Because he brought you in and he's hovering around like a boyfriend."

Susannah worked to hold back a flush, wincing, as Gavin examined her swollen ankle from the front, side and back. "It's probably guilt," she quipped. "He's the reason I tripped."

"Ah. Got it." Gavin stopped palpating her ankle long enough to wink. "The old knock-'em-down-and-then-rescue-them trick."

Gabe, who had been keeping a close eye on the proceedings, scoffed. "That only works in bad romcoms."

Gavin gently checked the range of motion, then pressed the puffy skin in and watched it slowly bounce back. He looked up at Gabe. "You've tried it, then?"

Everybody laughed. The exam was finished. Susannah realized she had been successfully distracted by their banter. Gavin stepped up to the computer and quickly typed in an order. "You're going to need an X-ray."

Susannah nodded. "Okay."

To Gabe, the doc said, "When the tech comes to get her, come find me. I'll show you around. Update you on all the improvements the hospital has made since we did our residency here."

To Susannah's relief, the X-ray was conducted quickly. So quickly, Gabe was nowhere to be found when her stretcher was wheeled back into the exam room. The nurse brought her a ginger ale and some graham crackers while she waited to hear the results. Not long after that, she heard male voices approaching her room. "Think about it," Gavin told Gabe. "With Dr. Caldwell retired, we really are short staffed."

Gavin stuck his head in and smiled at Susannah. "I'm going to see if your report is back yet."

The ER doc exited, and Gabe strolled into her room. He looked slightly peeved. "What's going on?" Susannah asked curiously.

He took up a place against the wall. Ankles crossed, arms folded in front of him. "They want me to take a job here as an infectious disease specialist."

Why should that thrill her? "And you said no," she guessed, trying not to feel disappointed he wouldn't be sticking around.

He cocked his head. "I have a job with Physicians Without Borders."

"When do you go back?"

His poker face became even more unreadable. "Not until September."

Susannah paused. "That's a surprisingly long time."

He shrugged, not looking particularly happy about it.

Gavin Monroe walked back in. "Hey! Good news! There was no break, no torn ligaments. It's just a sprain. You're going to need to keep it wrapped and iced and elevated for a few days, but with proper attention, you should be back to hobbling around in no time."

Susannah sat up. "Hobbling?"

"Well, I wouldn't suggest running for a while. Not if you want to keep from reinjuring it." He paused to type something in the computer again, then turned back to her. "Ever used crutches?"

Susannah shook her head. The nurse came in to give her a quick tutorial and go over her discharge instructions. Then an orderly brought a wheelchair while Gabe went to get the pickup truck.

It felt a little like a date, as he cruised up and came to a stop, then jumped out to circle around and personally make sure she got in okay. Even though the orderly could have done just that.

Which made Susannah wonder, what would it be like if they *did* date?

Taking in the damp summer air whipping around

them, she pushed the thought away and asked, "Is it supposed to rain tonight?"

Gabe shut the door, then came back around to climb behind the wheel again. "Ah, yeah! That's all they could talk about on the weather this morning." He slanted her a curious glance. "I'm surprised you didn't hear."

Susannah sighed and waited for the ibuprofen they'd given her in the ER to kick in. "I try not to borrow trouble." She shifted restlessly.

He slid a glance toward her leg. "And rainy days mean?"

"Way too much pent-up energy for the quints."

"Speaking of which...think they're asleep?"

Susannah's ankle throbbed. "I hope so."

Upon arriving home, Gabe parked as close behind her car as he could, to give her the shortest path from the driveway to the front porch. Daisy had been taught not to bark when guests arrived, but Susannah could see her golden retriever silhouetted against the blinds, watching out for their return. Outside, thanks to the heavy cloud cover, the sky was a velvety black, without even the moon visible.

Gabe opened the passenger door for her, then gave her a gentle hand down. Waited while she stood up straight, with her crutches placed slightly forward and out to the side. The corners of his lips curving up, he watched her struggle to establish balance, move both crutches awkwardly forward, step forward with her injured leg and push down forcefully and equally on the handgrips. Trembling slightly with the effort it was taking, she stepped through the crutches with her good leg, then established balance once again. To her frustration, the one step alone took a great deal of effort and a good twenty seconds.

Gabe looked at the distance still to go, and shook his head in silent admonition. "I should probably just carry you to the front door, then come back to get the crutches."

Knowing she needed his help, whether she wanted it or not, she frowned. "Don't be ridiculous. What would your parents think?" she groused.

When they'd left for the ER, she hadn't had any way to get around—except for Gabe's arms. Now, she had a professionally wrapped ankle and crutches.

"That I was being chivalrous?" he returned, his expression as matter-of-fact as his low tone.

She lifted a brow in return, her heart tightening a little in her chest as she took another careful step forward. *She could do this. She really could. It was just going to take practice.* Feigning more confidence than she felt, she shot back lazily, "Or that you probably *don't* need to come to the rescue of every damsel in distress."

He gave her a long, steady look laced with compassion and moved next to her, seemingly ready to step in the instant she needed him. "What makes you think it's *every* damsel?"

His lazy quip brought heat to her cheeks.

"It could just be you."

"Your reputation in Laramie County says otherwise, Doc."

"Checking up on me?"

Boy, he was maddening.

Worse, she didn't know why she was letting him get under her skin. She'd dealt with bossy, overbearing people all her life.

"Plus, it's not like you grew up in Laramie County alongside me, you know."

That was true. She and Belinda had grown up in north Texas, in Wichita Falls. "I saw you plenty when you were in med school at UTSA. Belinda and I were undergrads there. Remember?" Susannah said, as she worked her way slowly and cautiously up the sidewalk. Despite her desire to make her journey look a lot easier than it felt, she was beginning to perspire. Huffing slightly, she continued, "You had no shortage of young women following you around the campus."

This time, he grinned. "Exactly. *Following* me. Not the other way around, and that's because I was a doctor. Or going to be. Every woman wants to marry a doctor."

Susannah inhaled deeply. Breathed out slowly. She gave him a warning glance. "Not me."

"Mmm-hmm. You're young yet—you could wise up."

The crazy thing was, if he had plans to stick around, she just might dare to give him a chance. But he wasn't going to do that, so... "Dream on, Doc."

Gabe sobered. "Please let me help you up the steps."

She could see it was killing him not to be able to rush to her aid. What he didn't know was that it would devastate her to accept it. She had already depended upon him way too much as it was.

"I got it." Determined to succeed on her own, the way she had for years now, Susannah turned around, sat down and levered her way up via the seat of her shorts, one step at a time. Finally, she reached the top step.

Which presented a problem, since she wasn't sure if she could actually get back up to a standing position on her own. Without toppling over, that was.

Gabe asked, "How about a hand up?"

Probably wouldn't hurt. Grudgingly, she relented. "If you insist."

She slid her hand into his. He clasped it warmly, and with the addition of an arm about her waist, brought her to her feet, just as the front door opened. Carol and Robert stepped outside. "Thought I heard something," his dad said.

Carol noted the absence of a cast. "So...no break?"

Susannah smiled. "Just a sprain. I'll be good as new in a few days."

"How will you manage in the meantime?" Carol asked in maternal concern.

"I'll call my mothers' club in the morning. How were the kids? I assume they are asleep?"

Robert nodded. "They went down about fifteen minutes later than what you texted us was normal for them."

"They were a little excited." Carol grinned. "But after a half an hour of bedtime stories, they were all yawning. And willing to close their eyes and snuggle with their stuffed animals, and once that was done, well…we haven't heard a peep since."

Relieved to be home again, Susannah eased into the closest chair and propped her leg up on the coffee table. Carol brought the baby monitors, with video screens, so she could see into both the boys' and girls' rooms. All five were curled up, snoozing away. Beginning to see where Gabe got his chivalrous streak, Susannah looked over at Gabe's mother and father gratefully. "I can't thank you enough."

Carol gently touched her shoulder. "Oh, honey, this is what Laramie is about. Neighbor helping neighbor."

"You probably should go on home," Gabe advised his parents. "You both look…"

"Our age?" his mom quipped, evidencing the famous Lockhart sense of humor.

Gabe chuckled. "I was going to say a little tuckered out. But, yeah, it is late. Almost ten. And since I know both of you have to work tomorrow…"

Carol glanced at Susannah. "Are you going to be okay? Because I could stay the night."

"That's not necessary, Mom," Gabe said as wind whipped up outside, signaling rain on the way. "I'm going to do that."

Chapter Five

"Why did you tell your mom you were going to be here tonight?" Susannah asked after his parents had left. She shifted toward him on the kitchen stool, invading his space.

Gabe folded his brawny arms across his chest, and let out a sigh that reverberated through his six-foot-three-inch frame. Intuitive whiskey-colored eyes lassoed hers. "Probably because I am, unless you decide to kick me out. And I really wouldn't advise that."

She wished he didn't radiate such potent masculinity or look so ruggedly fit in whatever he chose to wear. Never mind have such a sexy smile and such firm, sensual lips...

She could barely look at him and not wonder what it might be like to kiss him again.

With a huff, she planted both hands on her hips and declared, "I don't need a babysitter."

"Probably not. But your kids might."

Not if I can help it. Susannah shut her eyes briefly and rubbed at the tension in her temples. "They're fast asleep."

Outside, there was a very distant rumble of thunder, a lightning flash against the blinds.

He strode over to where her dog was standing by the back door. Gabe reached down to pet Daisy's head and scratch her behind her ears. "And it looks like Daisy needs to go out," he said.

Was that what was bothering him? He looked more concerned than she would have expected him to be about her beloved pet. It was also a situation easily remedied and help she could use. "Would you mind snapping a leash on her and taking her out front? She'll get down to business quicker that way. Then she'll be all set for the night."

"Happy to help." Gabe eased out the door, making pains not to make any sounds that might rouse the sleeping children upstairs.

As soon as he was out of sight, Susannah grabbed her crutches again and hobbled across the kitchen. She was just trying to figure out how to pull the pizza box out of the fridge without dropping it when Gabe came back in. He let Daisy off her leash, then went to the kitchen sink to wash his hands. "You must be hungry," he said kindly.

She was. Worse, his inherent helpfulness caused her heart to pang in her chest. She knew it would be far too easy to begin to lean on him. And where would that leave her when he left, as he inevitably would? Clamping down tight on the floodgates of emotion that threatened to open up, she forced herself to concentrate on her growling tummy.

Leaving him to retrieve the pizza, she perched on the stool again. Guilt flowed through her as she recalled, "Darn it! I meant to give your parents money for the pizza."

Gabe shrugged. "I'm sure they're fine."

"I don't want to owe them."

Gallantly, he brought another stool over and situated it so Susannah could prop her swollen ankle across the seat and still enjoy her meal. "I'll find out what the cost was and let you know."

Susannah smiled her gratitude. "Thanks. I also need to pay them back for their kindness tonight. So, what can I do in return? So your folks will know I'm genuinely grateful."

Gabe arched a brow in consternation. "I think they know that already, princess."

Susannah thought about the years she had spent with her late aunt Elda, how bad she had always felt, upsetting the older woman's life. She didn't want to go back to feeling like a burden. Not if she could avoid it. "I still need to do something to show my appreciation. So, what do you think? Could I take them to dinner or...?"

Gabe cocked a brow, considering. "They both love homemade cookies, and my mom hasn't had much time to bake lately."

"I can do that in a few days when I'm feeling better. The kids can participate, too."

"They'd love that. They're both really into grandparent mode."

"How many grandchildren do they have?"

"My brother Noah has three daughters. They're all in California. And my sister Faith is fostering an infant here."

"And the other six...?"

"Are all single. And childless. For now. Much to my parents' dismay."

And her children didn't have any grandparents. Wondering what his future plans held, she asked, "Not planning to supply them with any yourself?"

He offered a wry shrug. "Kind of hard to do when I'm constantly on the move and living overseas."

Before she could stop herself, Susannah inquired casually, "You don't want to change that?"

Gabe hesitated. Something indecipherable came and went in his eyes. "No. Not really."

Which was, Susannah reminded herself sternly, yet another reason why she shouldn't give in to the attraction brewing between them.

Changing the subject, she pulled the pizza box on the counter toward her. "You want yours heated?"

A single shake of his handsome head. "Actually, I prefer it cold when it's leftover."

"Me, too."

Rising and leaning on her good foot, she brought out two bottled waters from the fridge. "Sorry, I don't have any beer to offer you."

His eyes twinkled. "What makes you think I want beer with my pizza?"

"Back in college, you always ordered a pitcher whenever you got a pie."

"I'm surprised you remember that."

She remembered everything about him. But figuring he didn't need to know that, she shrugged. Then hobbled over to get two plates from the cupboard. He was instantly at her side, his shoulder nudging hers. "You should let me do that."

"I'm not helpless."

"No one said you were."

Their eyes met. And just that suddenly, she wanted to kiss him again. *Not good.* Figuring the more distance between them, the better, she relented. "Okay, Doc, if you insist…"

She moved around the island and sat down. He brought the napkins from the table. She told him where the silverware was. A companionable silence stretched between them. As they began to eat, he tilted his head at the wall of paintings in the breakfast area. They were all of Daisy, starting at eight weeks, and tracking her progress until the quintuplets were born. "Did you do all those?"

Susannah savored the crisp crust, flavorful tomato sauce and spicy toppings. "Kept me busy when I was going through the preimplantation process and waiting to see if the IVF took, and then during the months I was pregnant. The latter three months of which I was on bed rest. But I still managed to paint."

Gabe helped himself to another slice and continued admiring the art. "They're incredible. They seem to really capture her."

Others had said so, too. Susannah dabbed the corners of her lips with her napkin. "I worked hard to capture the essence of her personality as she grew."

Gabe's eyes twinkled. "I think you succeeded."

"Thank you," Susannah said, not knowing why his approval mattered so much to her, just that it did. "I'm glad you like them," she admitted.

He looked past the adjacent mudroom, to what had once been a screened-in porch and was now a sunroom, fully decked out with a tall drawing table, two easels, canvas and paint supplies. "This your studio?"

"Yes." The depth of his curiosity paired with his quiet admiration had her offering, "You can look around if you like."

While she finished her second piece, too, he stepped inside, in front of a half-finished painting on an easel of an exuberant Jack Russell terrier, catching a tennis ball in midleap. He studied it for a long moment. "Is this for someone else?"

"Yes. I have a pet portrait business now. People bring me their favorite photographs of their pets, and I paint them."

He came toward her. "Nice."

Her heartbeat picked up for no reason she could figure. Finished with her dinner, Susannah cleared her throat. "It allows me to stay at home with the kids right now, which is what I need."

He stepped in to clear the dishes. "You don't miss graphic design?"

"Not. One. Bit."

He laughed. Lounging against the opposite counter, he indicated her current work in progress. "Well, you're certainly capturing that little guy's personality."

"I take it you like dogs?" Susannah noted Daisy had joined them and was now gazing up at Gabe adoringly.

He petted her golden retriever on the head, gently rubbing behind her ears. "Oh yeah. We grew up with a lot of them on the ranch. We got a new puppy every year, until all eight of us kids each had a dog, and then a few more, for good measure."

Susannah couldn't help but be impressed. "Sounds... lively."

"It was." Gabe's expression turned wistful. His hands cupped the counter edge on either side of him. "It's the one thing I miss having now," he admitted ruefully, "but in my line of work, with me traveling, the places I go, I can't have a pet, either."

Outside, the lightning flashed. The thunder was getting closer. With a look of concern, he got out his phone to check the weather.

"How big a storm is it?" she asked.

He showed her the large green area on the radar map. The fifty-mile radius was peppered with isolated red and yellow storm cells. He hit the time-lapse button that predicted the next eight hours of activity and showed her that, too.

Susannah sighed. "Looks like it will last all night."

He glanced up, his expression inscrutable. "Will the kids sleep through this?"

Funny he'd even think to ask.

"They usually do, unless the thunder gets really loud. Or there is a power outage and the air-conditioning switches off and it starts to get really warm or something."

He walked over to the bay window and stood there, staring out at the rain beginning to come down. Then turned back to her, his expression more concerned than ever. "Are you going to be okay here tonight without help?"

Another peculiar thing to ask! "Of course."

Gabe frowned. "I really think I should stay. Just in case," he added hastily. "I don't mind."

Taking his savior complex to new heights, wasn't he? Aware the last thing she needed was to impose on him further, Susannah said, "First of all, I'm fine. Second, I can still comfort them with a sprained ankle."

Another flash of lightning appeared, followed thirty seconds later by a clap of thunder.

He challenged quietly, "But could you get them out of the house in an emergency if you're not able to move quickly?"

What in the world was going on with him? "Actually," Susannah returned just as confidently, "I could. We've practiced both in-school and at-home emergency drills. Their preschool requires it, and I need them to obey me quickly and quietly in an emergency, too, since as you just pointed out, it's usually just me taking care of them these days."

He came back to sit next to her and finish his bottle of water. "Was it always like that?"

"The first year, I had lots of volunteers coming to help diaper and feed and rock them. Now it's mostly just Millie and Mike and the occasional teenage babysitters. Although I always have to hire at least two sitters, so it gets kind of expensive and hard to schedule."

"I can imagine." Finished, he tossed his bottle into the recycling container and came to stand before her, Daisy still at his side.

"So. Back to your plans for the rest of the night... Princess, you really need to get some sleep."

As if she didn't know that! She met his level look with one of her own. "So do you, Doc."

"Except I never sleep during a storm."

"Why not?"

His lips twisted thoughtfully. "Just don't. The point is, I could be here, make sure you've got enough ice to get through the night. Set up a bed for you on the sofa."

"I'm planning to sleep in my bed upstairs. That way the kids will know where to find me if they need me, and I'll be near them, as usual. But if you're in a mind to help, you're welcome to fill a cooler from the garage with ice and the gel packs I have in the big freezer out there and carry that upstairs."

By the time he'd done that, she was halfway up the stairs, scooting stair by stair on her bottom. Crutches at one side. Leg straight out in front of her. Daisy bringing up the rear. It worked fine until she reached the second floor. Momentarily nonplussed, she tried to figure out how to get back to a standing position from where she was.

"Allow me," he murmured. Tucking his hands around her ribs, he lifted her to her feet, and she stumbled into his chest.

Gabe looked down at her. And suddenly she could tell he was thinking about kissing her again. The only problem was, she wasn't sure that if they started, they would be able to stop. And with the kids sleeping nearby, Daisy sitting there, looking up at them quizzically as if wondering what was going on, she knew there was only one thing to do—put an end to this before they did something they would both likely regret. So she whispered instead, "I've got it from here, Doc. There's a spare key in the kitchen. You can see yourself out and leave it in the faux frog holder slash planter on the front porch."

He paused, then regretfully bid her good-night, and did as she asked.

"Still in another time zone?" Cade asked the next morning, while making a smoothie with protein powder, fresh fruit, juice and yogurt.

Gabe scraped a hand beneath his jaw. Feeling the stubble, he went to pull his electric razor from his bag. "Why?"

"Heard you roaming around most of the night."

Gabe looked out the window. The rain had stopped and the sun was coming out. Looked to be a pretty day dawning. Gabe felt the relief he always did when thunderstorms ended. He switched on his razor. "Sorry."

Cade added a couple of handfuls of spinach and kale. "No big deal. I assume that was why you couldn't sleep."

Gabe rummaged through his clothes, pulling out a clean shirt and another pair of jeans. Straightening, he turned the tables on his brother, asking, "The real question is, why weren't you asleep?" If Cade had been, he wouldn't have heard Gabe pacing while studying the storm on the weather radar most of the night.

Cade fit the lid on the pitcher. Punched Blend. "I was texting with all three of our sisters."

Gabe waited until the concoction was mixed. "What about?"

"Dad's Father's Day gift. We went all out for Mom for Mother's Day, so we have to do the same for Dad, only no one knows what to get him. We can't exactly get him diamond jewelry, too."

Finished, Gabe switched off his razor and dropped it back in his bag. "He's not exactly a bling kind of guy, is he?"

"No, but he is sentimental." Cade poured half the blender's contents into another tall glass and handed it over.

That he was. As was their mom. "Any ideas?"

"The girls were talking about maybe doing a family portrait of all the kids. But that just seems so…" Cade frowned.

"Hard to arrange?" Gabe guessed, wondering how early was too early to appear on Susannah's doorstep, to check on her and make sure she'd made it through the night okay.

"Well, yeah, since half of us don't even live in Laramie anymore." Cade took his glass and stepped outside into the lavishly landscaped backyard, with the Jacuzzi and waterfall pool, and took a seat beneath an umbrella table. "I was thinking it should have something to do with the ranch, but Mom's already given him fancy framed photos, including an aerial view of the Rocking L Ranch."

Deciding he needed to wait until at least 9:00 a.m. before visiting Susannah and the quints, Gabe settled opposite his brother.

Cade exhaled. "Travis suggested we get Dad a new horse, but we already have a stable full and you know how much he loves Chestnut, so…" He rubbed the place just to the left of his right shoulder, as if it were hurting him again. Then dropped his hand.

"Actually, I might have an idea, but I need to talk to someone first," Gabe said as Susannah's beautiful face came to mind. "Make sure it's even doable."

Cade grinned. "That sounds mysterious."

"Provident, actually," Gabe corrected with another sip of the remarkably unsweet concoction. Since he needed to live up to his obligation and keep an eye on Susannah and the kids—at least while he was in the country—this would give him plenty of excuse to see her.

Assuming she agreed to his request, anyway. Gabe exhaled and put his glass aside. "In the meantime, I'm going to go check on Susannah Alexander, see if she needs anything."

Cade shifted his upper torso to the right and gently flexed his injured shoulder, as if testing it for pain. With a lifted brow, he reminded Gabe, "She's got friends, you know. Plenty of them."

Gabe finished the last of his smoothie. "I feel responsible. If she hadn't been so distracted talking to me, she wouldn't have tripped and fallen."

"Ahhhh." A wealth of innuendo in the single word.

Gabe tensed with irritation. "Don't read too much into it. I'm just being a Good Samaritan."

Cade chuckled. "Keep telling yourself that."

Gabe did as he made a stop in downtown Laramie. And then again, on the way to Susannah's place. He didn't see any other cars parked in front of her house when he shifted his gift to one arm and rang the doorbell. Susannah's melodic voice rang out in the sweet silence of early morning. "Come in!"

He eased the door open. Saw Susannah sitting on a dining room chair, her ankle propped up on another, a cold pack draped over it. The easel had been lowered to her height. She had a palette of paints in one hand, a brush in another.

He scanned her, taking in the healthy color in her cheeks, the denim shorts riding up her thighs and the oversize pink button-up shirt that covered her curvaceous breasts. He eased closer, unable to help but admire her long, lissome legs and bare, silky skin. Drinking in her wildflower scent, he repressed a sigh of pure lust and nodded at the canvas in front of her. "Working?"

Oblivious to the ardent nature of his thoughts, she sent him a cheeky grin. "Looks like."

His gaze moved over her soft, plush lips before returning to the tumult in her pretty blue eyes. The downstairs was as neat and quiet as it had been when he'd left the night before. He exhaled, still watching her intently, still keeping a careful distance. "Where are the kids?" he asked casually.

"Some of my girlfriends took them for the day so I could keep my ankle elevated and get some work done. What do you have there?"

Gabe put his offering from the Cowgirl Café down on the table. "Breakfast goodies, in case they were hungry." He gestured at the wicker basket containing an assortment of fruit, pastries and two coffees for the adults. "A vanilla latte for you."

Briefly, an ecstatic look overtook her delicate features. She gestured for him to make himself comfortable and have a seat. Took the stopper out of the coffee cup and inhaled the rich, creamy aroma. Then sighed as luxuriantly as she had when they'd kissed. Smiling, she took a small sip. "How'd you know that's what I like?"

He pulled up a chair adjacent to hers. Opening up his black coffee, he admitted, "It's what you always used to order at the coffee shop on campus."

"Well, thank you." She took another grateful sip. "You know, it's weird how much you and I know about each other when it comes to the mundane."

And yet they still knew relatively nothing about the important stuff, although he planned to rectify that ASAP.

"True," he said, as she continued to survey him curiously, "but now that I know you're a pet portrait artist, I may have a proposition for you." Briefly, he explained that he and his siblings wanted to gift his father something really special for Father's Day. "Which is where you come in…"

Susannah listened intently while she sipped. "So you're looking for a portrait of Robert's favorite dog?"

Gabe hedged. He and Cade hadn't gotten that far in their discussion that morning. "I don't think Dad could choose one pet, any more than he could choose a favorite kid."

"The first pet, then?"

His next idea hit with pleasurable speed. "How about all of them?"

Susannah set down her latte, her mouth opening into a soft "oh" of surprise. "Who've lived at the ranch?"

Gabe could picture it as readily as he could envision her painting such a tribute to their past family life. "Yeah." He exchanged excited grins with her. "That would be great if you could depict all the family dogs running and playing across the field in front of the ranch house."

Susannah picked up her cell phone. "How many dogs would that be?"

"To date?" Gabe counted. "Sixteen, although he

might have had a couple others before they adopted us. I'll have to ask my mom to be sure."

Susannah started making notes on her phone. "Wow."

"I know. They love animals as much as kids."

Thinking, she raked the edge of her teeth across her plump lower lip. "Well, it will be interesting, making that all work," she concluded with a happy sigh. "How large a portrait were you thinking?"

Mesmerized by the softness of her lips, as well as the escalating urge to kiss her again, Gabe gestured off-handedly, not sure about that, either. "Dad has an oversize leather sofa in his study. He spends a lot of time in there, and the pets' portrait would look great hanging above that."

For a moment they talked approximate dimensions. Susannah warned, "Anything that large would be expensive."

Gabe knew he and his siblings could afford to be generous. "Rough estimate?"

"If we included authentic renderings of all of the dogs, it would likely be five to six thousand dollars, minimum. And it would take some time, too."

"But you could do it?"

"Yes." She began to look as excited at the prospect as Gabe felt.

"Do you think we could have it by Father's Day?"

Just that quickly, her face fell. "In a little over two weeks? No. I'm sorry. I've already got several commissions ahead of you."

Undeterred, he asked, "Are they Father's Day gifts?"

She straightened in her chair, and the gel pack she had across her ankle slid off. "They are not." She frowned as it hit the floor. "But I do things in the order that they are commissioned, so…"

Gabe picked up the gel pack and, being careful not to touch her, draped it back over her swollen ankle. "What if I could get your other clients to agree to let us jump ahead with our gift?"

Susannah's pretty eyes narrowed. "First of all—" she let out an exasperated breath "—that's a big if." Her chin lifted, and their gazes locked. "Secondly, I still couldn't do a work that complex in the time frame you are suggesting since I'm only able to work afternoons, while the kids are napping, and then sometimes in the evening if I can get them down early enough." She released a breath. "A project like that would take at least seven or eight hours a day for two or three weeks, minimum. So, at my current work availability, we'd be talking the end of the summer for delivery."

Luckily, thanks to his mandated time off, he was planning to be here all summer. For the first time, that seemed like a plus instead of a minus. "But you *are* interested?"

"Yes," she promised readily. "I think it would be a real challenge as well as a way to repay your parents' kindness to me and the kids. I just can't have it by Father's Day. So, if that's the condition, I'm going to have to say no."

Gabe frowned in disappointment. He'd been so sure he had a solution that would work not just for his father, but all his siblings, too.

Seeing his displeasure, she attempted to appease him, the way any good businessperson would. "There are always other holidays, Gabe. His birthday. Christmas. Or we could just go with a much smaller, less inclusive pet portrait for now—like something that would work in a frame on his desk—and do something more expansive later."

Gabe finished his coffee. "I doubt that would appease my siblings—" who were committed to delivering the most special Father's Day gift ever "—but I'll talk to them. See what they say. Maybe it would work as an additional gift, but not *the* gift."

Susannah put her coffee aside, too. "I'm sorry I couldn't help you in the time frame you specified. But I can do something for you right now that has needed to be done." She reached for her crutches and stood with a lot more ease than she had used the evening before. "I have five boxes of things in the garage that Brett left to you. I'd like to give them to you now."

"Sure." Not wanting her to overdo it, he lifted a staying palm. "But I can get them if you tell me where."

She shook her head, her chin-length, honey-blond hair glimmering in the morning sunshine filtering in through the windows. "There's a lot of stuff out there." She adopted a defiant stance. "It will be easier if I just show you."

Together, they walked past her studio, outside via

the side door, out of the laundry room, nearly touching as he held the door for her and she maneuvered by him using her crutches. She even managed, with relative ease, the three steps down to the driveway that led to the detached two-car garage set just back from the house and built in the same Craftsman style.

She gazed over at him, wrinkling her nose. "I apologize. It's going to be hot in there. It's not air-conditioned." She rested her weight on one crutch and entered the code in the keypad. The overhead garage door slid open. Her van was parked in the center. The whole back wall and both side walls were filled with shelves and well-marked plastic storage containers and cardboard boxes. His five were clearly marked and placed at the very top. She pointed. "You're going to need the ladder to get them."

"What's in here, anyway?"

Abruptly looking a little exhausted from the jaunt out there, she perched on a step stool next to the wall. "Vintage record albums, CDs, DVDs…and a lot of UTSA med school memorabilia. Brett said you weren't very sentimental and didn't collect much of it in comparison to everyone else."

"That's because I knew, with my future plans, that it would end up in a storage facility with the rest of my stuff I couldn't take with me."

Abruptly, Susannah grinned. "But I heard you kept a futon."

The mischief in her eyes had him admitting, "And for good reason, princess. I spent a lot of years sleeping on that thing." He winked. "There was a desk lamp I was quite fond of, too."

She laughed outright.

And it was one of the best sounds he'd ever heard in his life. Mood lifting even more, Gabe asked, "Mind if I back my brother's pickup into your driveway?"

She couldn't stop holding his eyes, as if she were enjoying the sudden pleasurable rapport between them, too. She gestured expansively. "Have at it, Doc."

While she watched Gabe spring into action, an unexpected melancholy washed over Susannah. She didn't know why she was suddenly so sad to see those boxes go. Maybe it was because she had been holding on to them for so long. Or perhaps it was because it was another link to Brett and Belinda she would no longer have. Or it *could* be because once she had handed Brett's belongings off to Gabe, she knew she would have no official reason to see him again. Unless it turned out they wanted some sort of smaller pet portrait for his dad, or one in another time frame, but even that would not take anywhere as near as long a time as she had held on to these boxes for him.

But maybe, she thought, as she watched him climb the ladder nearly half a dozen times, retrieving one bulky cardboard container after another, the muscles in his broad shoulders, back and arms flexing beneath the weight of the contents, having his belongings out of her garage would be a good thing.

Heaven knew she was far too aware of the sexy doctor. She had spent way too much time thinking about the impetuous kiss they had indulged in, in the midst of their shared grief. And privately wished they might someday kiss each other again. Why, she wasn't quite sure, when they were still clearly all wrong for each other. Was it loneliness that seemed to be driving her to his arms? Lust? The forbidden? An attempt to recapture what they'd once so briefly tasted?

It certainly wasn't like her to daydream about a man like this…

"Penny for your thoughts, princess."

"Oh!" Startled, Susannah looked up, embarrassed by the direction of her thoughts. "Finished already?"

Amusement turned his eyes a darker bourbon. "Mmm-hmm."

Time to get out of fantasy land and back to reality.

With a beleaguered sigh, she struggled to get off the footstool. And, in the process, forgot to reach for her crutches at the same time. Consequently, as she lurched less than gracefully to her feet, she started to lose her balance completely. Would have, she swiftly and gratefully realized, had Gabe not reached out to grab her around her waist and steady her against him.

Just that quickly, the desire she felt when she was near him like this surfaced yet again. She flattened her hands across the solid warmth of his chest, jerked in a breath and glanced up. He looked down at her, his eyes shuttering. A shiver of desire swept through her, weakening her knees, causing her to lean against him even more.

And just that suddenly, everything that had felt off felt oh so right...

The next thing she knew, his mouth was on hers, giving her a kiss filled with passion and need, and he was tugging her even closer. He paused to lift his head ever so slightly. Grazed her earlobe with his teeth, touched his lips to the underside of her chin, her throat, her cheek and the top of her nose, before once again moving to her mouth. And this time when he fit his mouth over hers, she was ready for him.

Her lips parted under the steady, persuasive pressure of his, and his tongue swept inside. And then her hands came up to cup his head. He tasted so good, like mint and man and the unique flavor that was him. Her usual inhibitions fled. With a little moan of pleasure, she rose up on tiptoe and sank even further into the deeply satisfying, wonderfully evocative kiss. And to her delight, he responded, just as hungrily.

Gabe didn't know why he had given in to impulse and kissed Susannah again after all these years. But now as he flattened his hand against her spine and brought her even tighter against him, he couldn't *not* follow his gut and his heart or move boldly to claim her as his.

It was something about the searching way she looked at him whenever she thought he didn't notice. The fact he was taking those boxes, which were his last excuse to come and see her—that she would likely accept, anyway. That, coupled with the as-yet unfulfilled promise he'd made years ago, and the sweet and vulnerable way she felt against him, had brought out the even deeper need to protect her. She struck a chord in him like no other. And judging by how she was snuggling close and pressing her breasts and thighs against him, the hot openmouthed way she was stroking his tongue with hers and returning his kiss with sizzling intensity, it made him think she was feeling the same.

Had it not been for the sound of a car door behind them, followed by footsteps and a clearing throat, who knew what would have happened.

But someone was there, and so Gabe had to pull away. Just as Susannah did. He couldn't let her go completely, though, since she was still standing on one foot. So, one hand still firmly around her waist, he reached down to retrieve her crutches from where they had fallen next to the step stool.

As he straightened, he saw Susannah's face. Flushed. Embarrassed. "Hi," she said to their new guests.

Chapter Six

Susannah extricated herself from Gabe's sensual embrace and hobbled over to sit on the step stool yet again. She gestured cordially. "Mike, Millie, you remember Gabe Lockhart."

"Of course we do. We both had him in our classes when he was growing up here." Her neighbors from across the street smiled. The silver-haired former teachers were wearing their line-dancing clothes—a pretty Western dress with a flared skirt and boots for Millie, and similarly cut dress shirt with string tie and jeans and boots for Mike.

"What are you doing here?" Susannah asked in surprise. "You're supposed to be in Corpus Christi, visiting that new line-dancing place with your club."

Millie frowned, upset. "We heard about your accident!"

"You should have called us last night! We would have come straight home," Mike said protectively.

Susannah protested, "I didn't want you to do that. This is your special time together."

"We're retired, Susannah," Millie reminded. "We can have a lot of special times."

Mike studied her ankle, which was wrapped in an elastic bandage. "Do you need to go to the hospital?"

Susannah shook her head. "Gabe took me to the ER last night. It's just a mild sprain. I should be able to put weight on it again in another four days. Until then I'm on crutches."

Millie looked unconvinced. "Where are the quintuplets?"

"With some of the other mothers from my Multiples Club," Susannah soothed. "They'll be home this evening after supper."

"Are you going to need help with bath and story time?" Millie asked.

Susannah grinned. "Let's put it this way," she said drolly. "I won't say no if you want to come over."

"We'll be here," Millie promised. "In the meantime, can we do anything for you?"

Mike's glance narrowed. "Or is Gabe handling that?"

Ah. The query beneath the query. As casually as possible, Susannah related, "Gabe came over to pick up some boxes Brett left for him years ago. And he was about to be on his way. We were just saying goodbye."

"Well, then, let me walk you out," Mike told Gabe firmly.

"And I'll help you get back in the house," Millie volunteered.

Gabe knew a man-to-man talk coming when he saw one. He'd had plenty from his dad. And Mike was acting like Susannah's honorary dad...

"You know, she's been through a lot the past five years," Mike said.

Gabe nodded, glad she'd had the Smiths looking out for her. "I do know."

"Millie and I are so fond of her. We think of her like our daughter, and the quintuplets have become the grandchildren we would never have otherwise been privileged to love."

"I can see that."

"So you can understand our concern to see you putting the moves on this obviously injured and more-vulnerable-than-usual young woman."

The accusation stung. "I wasn't taking advantage of her."

Mike lifted a brow. "Then you're dating...?"

"Ah, no," Gabe was forced to admit.

"Then just trying to seduce her."

"No."

Mike waited, arms crossed.

Gabe cleared his throat. "It just happened."

Mike gave him a look that said it had better not happen again. "Are you back in Laramie for good?"

Gabe shook his head, knowing this was not going to go over well. "Just here for the summer."

"So then you'll be gone again."

"Yes," he admitted reluctantly.

Mike scowled. "Then you can see how unfair it would be to let Susannah become enamored with you, only to leave."

Much as Gabe did not want to admit it, the older man had a point. "I do."

Mike slapped him on the back. "I trust, then, that you will consider that the next time you're tempted to give in to the attraction obviously simmering between you…"

Susannah looked out the window at the two men standing in front of her house. She groaned. "Tell me Mike is not having a man-to-man talk with Gabe."

Millie spread her hands wide. "I have no control over what that man does. You know that. I do have a question for you, though. Did you see the UPS man come this morning?"

Susannah nodded. "He was here around nine. I saw him put the package in the milk box beside the front door."

"Good." Millie sagged with relief. "I was almost out of our special blend of sassafras tea, and I need it more than ever if I'm going to lose those extra ten pounds to get in the dress."

Susannah gave up on watching Mike and Gabe

in the driveway. She turned back to Millie. "How is the plan going for the reenactment of your first date with Mike?"

Millie assisted Susannah into the living room. "Aside from the fact that the restaurant we ate at and the movie theater where we saw our first show fifty years ago both no longer exist?"

Susannah half maneuvered, half fell onto the comfortable L-shaped sofa in the living room. She propped her injured ankle on the coffee table. "How are you going to manage it, then?"

Millie disappeared into the kitchen and returned with a bag of frozen peas. She looped it over Susannah's now-aching ankle. "I asked the Laramie Country Inn to reserve a private dining room, and they're going to recreate the menu for us. And then I asked the theater in town to have a special Tuesday-night showing of the Western we saw that night. They think *McLintock!* will bring in a lot of viewers. And I'm borrowing a restored '69 Mustang from a friend for him to drive. So that part is all set. I just have to fit into the little black dress I wore that night. And, uh, I still have at least ten pounds to go."

"You'll make it."

"I hope so." Millie smoothed a hand over her hip. "The last five pounds can be very stubborn. Now, enough about me. Why were you kissing Gabe Lockhart just now?" she asked in concern. "And not just kissing! I mean, *really* kissing! Are you two having a long-distance romance that you haven't mentioned?

Because I know you don't normally indulge in that kind of thing."

"That's the problem. I haven't kissed anyone since before the quintuplets were born, and sad to say, I hadn't really even missed it. I've been so busy, and then he shows up so hot and sexy and I don't know quite what happened…"

Millie nodded in understanding.

"But—" Susannah lifted a hand "—I know he's bad news for me, because he's not sticking around for long. So I promise you, Millie, you don't have to worry. I'm not going to get hurt, because," she swore solemnly, "it will not happen again."

Figuring Susannah had been right to break off their clinch and send him on his way, boxes of inherited stuff in tow…Gabe parked in the alley of the Laramie County storage center. He typed in the code to the cipher lock, lifted the garage-style overhead door, then began carrying all five of the boxes inside the unit.

The futon that had been with him all through college and med school was still there, as were the rest of the physical contents of his life that he could not take with him when he was working around the world. Memorabilia. Old clothes. The ten-speed bike he had used to get across campus in a hurry. And now these five boxes that Brett had left for him, too.

He sat down to go through them, the sadness he'd felt since they lost Brett and Belinda returning. The CDs and albums brought back bittersweet memories of some of the parties they had thrown. But it was the med school yearbook, with the program from the funeral and a postcard from Hawaii stuck inside, that conjured up the most grief.

There was a big, beautiful picture of Maui on front, a handwritten note from Belinda on the back. "Thanks for watching out for Susannah while we're away," she had written. Brett had scrawled, "Couldn't have taken this trip without you, man. Thanks…"

They'd been worried that Susannah had been sinking into a depression, because her sister was married and, thanks to the creation of the five healthy frozen embryos, about to be implanted via IVF upon her return. While Susannah was still very much alone. Wishing for that perfect man.

Gabe had arranged to go to Houston and unexpectedly drop in on Susannah for the weekend in the middle of Brett and Belinda's ten-day second honeymoon. He had never had the chance, because they'd gotten the call about the tourist helicopter going down. So he'd gone to Houston, and then Laramie, Texas, to help with the final arrangements, instead. And the promise he'd made to check in on her had been realized there. And again, six months later, when he'd dropped by to see how she was faring in response to the will making it through probate court.

Funny, when he'd found Susannah moving in, he'd thought she was making a huge mistake, planning to step right into the remains of their life and bear her sister and brother-in-law's children. It turned out she had been right to take the comfort where she found it. She was now happy, with a lively brood of her own, a cozy home, lots of good friends and a life that seemed brimming with possibility, despite its many challenges.

Whereas he…he was on a forced leave from five years of constant, grueling travel and third-world living conditions, secure in the medical care he brought to those who might not otherwise have it. But lonely as hell and emotionally wrung out, just the same. And still feeling guilty because he'd never really looked after Susannah or her biological kids—not the way Brett and Belinda would have wished, anyway.

Not that Susannah would ever know about the request. Or his barely realized efforts to honor them.

Until now…

Whether she knew it or not, Gabe decided resolutely, she needed all the help she could get bringing up those children. In her case, as a single mom, it really was going to take a village. And right now, he really did not have anywhere near enough to do. So as long as he was here, and could help out, even in seemingly small or insignificant ways, he would continue to do what he could to make her life a little easier…

In the meantime, though, with Father's Day looming and no big group gift decided upon, he had a family meeting to attend.

Thursday evening, they had all eight of the siblings on conference call. Cade and Gabe were at Cade's house; their other six sibs had joined them via video chat.

No one was happy about Susannah's refusal.

"I'm telling you, there is no way she could get the painting done in time," Gabe reiterated.

"Doesn't matter," his brother Griff, a Fort Worth attorney, said. "It was the best idea, by far."

"Griff's right," their sister Jillian, a botanist who specialized in saving antique roses, said. "All our other ideas were nothing compared to that."

"Just take her some flowers and sweet-talk her into doing the multi-pet portrait," Cade suggested.

"Spoken like a man with way too many groupies hanging around," murmured their sister Faith, who'd recently lost her Navy SEAL husband after he'd resigned from the military, and was now a new foster mom to a precious baby boy.

"You have to make a business case," their sister Emma said from Italy, where she was studying shoe design.

"Offer a lot more money," Noah, their recently widowed CEO brother—and father to three daughters—said. "And compensate her well for whatever time she thinks it will take to do the job right."

"I agree," their single brother Travis, the only cowboy in the bunch, added. "If she doesn't think she can do the job right, there's no way she will accept the commission, and Dad will happily wait if he knows he is getting the perfect gift from us."

"It's the love that counts," Faith said gently as she cuddled her son close, "and Dad knows we love him dearly, same as Mom does."

No one could disagree with that.

Their foster parents had saved their lives and given them much brighter futures when they had adopted them.

"But if we're going to do this," Emma added, "we

have to do the portrait right, and that means adding to the general idea, and making it even better..."

"Trust me, when it comes to ladies, flowers are always welcome," Cade said the next afternoon. He slapped Gabe on the back. "I already called the florist in town and told them you were in the market for something really spectacular, so remember, since we're all splitting the cost eight ways, money is no object. Make sure it's a statement. The kind that will have Susannah Alexander changing her mind." Cade winked. "About a lot of things."

"Why do I ever tell you anything?"

His brother gently flexed his sore shoulder. "'Cause you know when it comes to women, I know it all."

Gabe rolled his eyes. "You *think* you know it all."

Cade gestured at the many gift baskets. "The number of well wishes around this place confirm that I do."

Gabe shook his head and left. The florist was indeed waiting for him, and she had an arrangement that was so big and elaborate it was almost ridiculous. But if his siblings were right, if that plus the new terms they were going to propose did the trick, his dad was going to be one happy man.

He parked in front of Susannah's home, grabbed the flowers and went to ring the bell.

Two of the quintuplets answered. "You can't come in," Abigail reported sagely.

Connor nodded. "Mommy's upset."

Had their mom asked them to say that, or were

they doing this on their own? Or was something else going on? Like…she'd reinjured her ankle? "Is everything okay?" he asked in concern.

"No," Connor said, frowning. "Mr. Bing made her *cry*."

Abigail nodded. "He was mad she didn't go to the bank this morning."

What the…! "She has a sprained ankle!" Gabe said hotly.

Abigail looked equally peeved. "She called and left a message for him."

Which, Gabe thought, should have been enough.

"But he said she couldn't dodge him anymore." Connor frowned. "What does *dodge* mean?"

Gabe held on to the ridiculously big arrangement of flowers. "I really think I should see your mom," he told the kids seriously.

"But you can't!" Connor said. "She's crying in the laundry room."

Gabe was beginning to panic a little. "Are you sure she didn't fall down and hurt her ankle again?"

Abigail shrugged. "I don't know."

"We got her the frozen peas," Connor said, "but she said it won't help this time."

That was it. Gabe knelt down to eye level. "Kids. Please let your mom know I'm coming in just to make sure everything is okay."

Abigail sighed. "She's not going to like it. She told us to make whoever it was go away."

"Well, she's going to have to tell me herself," Gabe vowed stubbornly.

The kids looked relieved to have another grown-up on the premises.

"Follow us," Connor said.

They went through the living and kitchen area, down a short hall, toward the back door that led to the art studio. Past that was the combination mud and laundry room. And Susannah was indeed sitting on the floor, in front of the washer and dryer, a bag of peas over her ankle. The other three quints were sitting beside her. Gretchen was patting her shoulder, Levi was cuddled up beneath her other arm and Rebecca sat in front of her, sucking her thumb, a box of tissues held in front of her.

Susannah looked up and sighed. She was indeed crying.

"What happened?" he asked, thrusting the flowers aside.

"Nothing. I just forgot for a moment and got up too quickly and sort of stomped my foot, and it was stupid." She sniffed.

Gabe knelt in front of her. He might not know a lot about young mothers in the midst of an emotional storm, but he could patch up a sprain. "Do you mind if I examine your ankle?"

She lifted a hand and bit her lip as more tears flowed.

"May I get in here?" he asked the kids.

They rose and moved back to allow him entry into the small space. Not easy given how big he was and how many of them there now were.

He palpated her ankle, checking to make sure she

still had normal range of motion and no additional swelling. "I don't think you did any damage," he said, replacing the bag of peas.

"Good." She glared at the bouquet. It appeared to be as unwelcome as he had initially feared it might be. "What is that?" she demanded unhappily.

So he'd been right. She wasn't an extravagant-flowers kind of woman. To impress her, you'd have to do something that touched her heart. Although what that would be he had no idea right now. He carried the flowers into the kitchen and set them on a counter, out of sight and out of harm's way. Then returned to her side.

"Well?" she said, still awaiting an explanation.

He gestured, closing the subject—for now, anyway. "Long story. I'd rather hear yours. Was Bing here?"

"Yes."

Jealousy arrowed through his gut. He didn't like the idea of Susannah with the guy. Period.

Gabe handed her a tissue from the box the quintuplets had brought into the room. "I take it you weren't expecting him?"

Her temper rose. "I wasn't expecting you, and you showed up."

"Yeah." He flashed her a charming grin. "But I haven't made you cry."

"The day is young, Doc." Susannah sighed wearily.

A muscle ticked in his jaw. "Did he upset you this much? Because if he did, I'm going to find him and have a little talk with him."

"Oh, for heaven's sake." A hand on the floor on

either side of her, Susannah unsuccessfully attempted to get to her feet.

When she started to sink back down, Gabe intervened, easing her to a standing position. She then leaned against the washer, her weight on her uninjured leg.

"Don't you dare speak to him about this," she continued grimly.

Aware she couldn't be comfortable like that, Gabe wrapped his arm about her waist, putting her weight up against him, and helped her hobble the twelve feet or so to a chair at the kitchen table. "Then I'll get Mike and let Mike talk to him."

"Aha!" Susannah's index finger stabbed the air. "So Mike *did* talk to you!"

Gabe pulled out a second chair and positioned it so Susannah could prop her sprained ankle up on that. "Yes."

Susannah fumed. "What did he say?"

"Nothing that made me cry." Gabe shrugged off the fatherly third degree and the warning to stay away if he wasn't going to stick around. Mike Smith might not realize it yet, but he was not going to hurt Susannah. Help her, yes. "Although—" Gabe accepted the frozen peas the kids had brought to him and replaced them on Susannah's ankle. "When it comes to Bing… if he were to see the state that man just left you in…"

Susannah lifted a halting hand. "Okay, okay, no need to bring the neighbors into this."

The quintuplets seemed to realize their mother was

on the mend. "Mommy," Abigail asked, "can we go in the backyard and play?"

"Yeah," Levi chimed in. "Can we have Popsicles, too?"

Susannah smiled in relief. "That sounds like a really good idea. But remember what to do with the sticks and the papers?"

"In the trash can on the back porch?" Gretchen said.

"And your hands?" Susannah prodded.

"Use the sanitizer so they won't be all sticky!" Rebecca exclaimed.

"Great."

Susannah turned to Gabe. "Can you please help them get the Popsicles out of the freezer?"

Gabe nodded. "You want one, too?" She looked like she needed it.

Susannah flashed a wan smile. "Sure. Why not? And while you're at it, you might as well join us."

The quintuplets showed him where they were. Once the frozen treats were dispensed, he let the kids out into the backyard, instructing them to let him know if they needed anything. Then he walked back inside. Susannah was just where he'd left her, enjoying a pineapple Popsicle and looking at the flowers. She aimed her stick at the bouquet. "Are these an apology?"

Gabe unwrapped his tangerine-flavored treat. "More like an inducement."

She peered at him in stunned amazement. "For sex?"

Nice to know that she had considered that as an

eventual possibility, too. He pulled up a chair opposite her and sat down in a way that eased the sudden
pressure at the front of his jeans. "Whoa! Really getting ahead of ourselves there, princess."

She didn't think so. "The way you kissed me…"

"The way you promptly kicked me out."

She grinned. "Touché…" Then slanted him a
glance. "So. Picking up where we left off…what did
Mike say to you yesterday?"

"He doesn't want to see you hurt. Neither do I."

Susannah rubbed the hem of her walking shorts.
"That makes three of us, then."

"So." Gabe echoed her curious tone. Instinct told
him she was holding a lot back. "What did Bing do?
Was he pressuring you?"

"No." A faraway look came into her eyes. "More
like telling the ugly truth that I did not want to hear,"
she said sadly.

Susannah could see Gabe was shocked. Protective. Looking as if he needed to rescue her. And while
she had thought that was not what she wanted, she
was surprised to find that the vulnerable part of her
wanted that very much. Because he would be a great
man to lean on. Solid, strong, principled. Incredibly
giving. And while he might not be able to be there
for her in the long haul, he could be there for her in
this moment.

Which she very much needed.

"Truth about what?" Gabe prodded gently as they
continued to eat their Popsicles.

Susannah sighed. "The trust he is managing for the kids."

"I thought that was abundant."

"It was. With the inheritance I received from Brett and Belinda, along with the money from the sale of my condo in Houston and my severance package from my job there, I had almost a million dollars when we saw each other five years ago. The frozen embryos were paid for, but there were storage fees and all the medical expenses that led up to the implantation."

"I bet that cost a pretty penny."

She nodded. "And then, on top of all that, the pregnancy, the multiple births, the extended stays in the hospital for all of the kids since they were underweight at birth, and the many pediatric visits after that. I had health insurance, but as you can imagine, co-pays and monthly premiums for six were steep. Going back to work was not possible, and I put them in preschool last year, so that was times five."

"I gather it's dwindling faster than expected."

"By the time they are ready to be in full-day kindergarten, in two years, I'll have just enough left to pay the very basic expenses until they are eighteen. There will be nothing left to pay for their college. And if there are any unexpected expenses that come up, like a sudden severe illness, or all five of them needing braces or glasses, then I could be in real trouble. Because I'm not really going to have any nest egg to rely upon."

"You still own the house outright?"

She saw where he was going with this. The same

place Bing had gone. "Yes. And I could do a reverse mortgage if I need to at some point, and start taking funds out on a monthly basis to continue to help pay expenses. But then I'll be on a really slippery slope. And could easily end up flat broke unless I can do a lot more to supplement my living expenses now. Which means bringing in a lot more business and finding a lot more time in which to paint."

"Speaking of pet portraits… I might have some good news on that front."

She sensed what he was about to ask. "I told you. I can't meet a mid-June deadline."

"Then what if we extend it by however much time you need?"

Chapter Seven

Gabe could see Susannah was tempted.

"We're still talking about an oversize above-the-sofa portrait," she assumed.

He nodded. "And a commission of ten thousand dollars, or more, depending on how much time it takes you to paint the gift."

She looked both angry and insulted. Turning her head, she looked out the window to check on the kids. They were playing happily on their swing set, with Daisy watching nearby. "Is this some kind of charity?"

Gabe shook his head. "Far from it. You'd earn every penny."

She lifted her brow. "Gabe, the largest portrait I've done, which was of three Yorkies, was thirty-six by forty-eight inches and only went for a little over a thousand dollars."

"I imagine that was pretty straightforward, too. You had one photo you worked with?"

She squared her shoulders, the action lifting the soft swell of her breasts. "Three, actually. They could never get the expressions they wanted on all three faces simultaneously, so we sort of photoshopped it all together to get the design, and I worked off that."

Noticing she'd finished her Popsicle, he got up to take the empty stick and wrapper and throw both in the trash, along with his. He brought the bottle of hand sanitizer over to her. "Well, you'd be doing something similar here, but you'd be working with all seven of my siblings, and me, and my mom, because now she knows about it, and she wants in on the excitement, too. Which is good because we need someone to comb through the old family photos and come up with pictures of us when we were all kids and correlate those with the ages of the dogs that we want to portray."

Susannah pumped the citrus-smelling liquid into her palm. "Meaning?"

Gabe watched her rub it into her fingers, then did the same. "Every one of us gets to choose how old we want our dogs to be in the portrait. My three sisters are all leaning toward the puppy stage of their pets, whereas Noah wants to portray his Labrador retriever as a two-year-old, and Travis is all for seeing his dog depicted in the last year of his life, when he was half-lame with arthritis and having trouble seeing but still had this sense of regal dignity that is heartrending."

Her expression turned thoughtful. "Sounds really challenging."

"It will be. Believe me." Gabe carried the bottle back to where he'd found it and stood, leaning against the counter. "Which is why you'll earn every penny, and you might even go over our projected cost, just to get the design all laid out and a rough image painted. But we're okay with that, because we're splitting the cost nine ways, and we know how much this is going to mean to my dad."

She buried her face in her hands and moaned. "Now I'm worried about living up to expectations."

"Don't be. I've seen your depictions of Daisy. They're phenomenal. You really know how to capture the spirit of a canine. And think of what taking on a project like this could mean for future business. I mean, who knows, by the time the quintuplets are in school full-time, you could easily be making enough to live on, without dipping into the general welfare trust."

Susannah pursed her lips together, thinking. "That would be nice. Because then I could use what is left of the money in there for their college."

He stuck his hands in the pockets of his jeans. "You could use pictures of the work in advertising. We would all be glad to act as references."

Susannah shook her head in wonderment. "Wow."

"I know. You're solving my problem. I'm solving yours."

* * *

Susannah wished it were that easy. She reached for her phone and began to type notes into it. As excited as she was, she was also scared to death. "It's going to take a lot of time for me to get this done," she warned. She propped her elbow on the table and rested her chin on her hand. "Especially since the kids are off from preschool for the summer."

He sauntered closer, filling up the space, making her all the more sensually aware of him. "I'm off, too."

She speared him with a testy glance. "So you're, what? Offering to find me a babysitter, or two or three, too?"

He shook his head, his eyes drifting slowly over her face, before returning to her eyes. "Actually, I'm offering to be the babysitter a few hours a day so you can work. You already paint in the afternoons when they nap. So if I'm here a few more hours after that, that would double your time. If you did that five days a week, you could be done with the project by summer's end. Or possibly early fall."

For a guy who regularly avoided his own family, it boggled her mind why he was offering to spend quite a lot of time with hers.

"You'd prefer it to be summer's end, though."

He nodded, admitting this was so. "For selfish reasons. So I could be here to see Dad receive it before I have to go back overseas. But if it doesn't work out, that's fine." He braced his hands on the counter on either side of him. "The important thing is he get a gift that is as special as he is, and this will definitely meet that requirement."

"Where are you going next?"

"Africa or Indonesia."

Not sure why it mattered to her, just knowing that it did, she asked, "For how long?"

He gestured noncommittally. "It could be as long as a year, or as short as three to six weeks. Depending on what kind of medical crisis situation they are dealing with."

Curious, she asked, "Do you ever get tired of moving around so much?"

He exhaled and kept a poker face. "It comes with the territory."

Feeling a little irritated she had revealed so much of the private details of her life to him and he had revealed so little of his to her, she chided softly, "That's not an answer."

His gaze narrowed. "Up till now, no."

She studied the newly sober expression on his face. "What's changed?"

For a moment, she thought he wasn't going to answer. Then he frowned and admitted, with surprising candor, "Something about Cade getting hurt...having his whole career as a major leaguer in jeopardy...and me not even finding out about it until weeks after he'd had his surgery, was sort of a wake-up call. I need to be more connected to the other Lockharts than I have been."

She drew a breath, thinking of all she wished she still had. "Family's important," she murmured.

"Sorry." He straightened and sent her a deeply apologetic look. "Didn't mean to bring up your loss."

Susannah tried not to think how masculine and sexy Gabe looked in the sunlight pouring in through the abundant windows of her kitchen. "I think it all worked out the way it was supposed to in the grand scheme of things." She conjured up a mental picture of heaven above that comforted her and contrasted to what she witnessed now on earth. "Brett and Belinda are together and are watching over their kids, even now. In the meantime, I have them, and as a consequence have the family I always wanted and never thought I'd have. So…"

"So fate works in mysterious ways," Gabe said softly, understanding.

Susannah met his eyes. "Yes."

Deciding she'd sat and rested her ankle long enough, she moved to get to her feet. Gabe was at her side immediately to help her. She stumbled a little as she rose to her full height. He continued to focus all his energy on helping her, and that focus was wreaking all sorts of havoc inside her. "Where do you want to go now?" he asked, tightening his grasp on her waist.

Nowhere but your arms, Susannah thought wistfully.

As if he could read her mind, he looked down at her and smiled. Not just any smile, but one of pure gallantry and masculine need. Tingling all over, she said, "Doc…"

His sexy smile widened as he pulled her flush against him. "Yes, princess?"

She caught her breath as his lips captured hers, inundating her with the heat and strength and taste of him. Filling her heart and soul with everything she had ever yearned for. Everything she had been denied. She kissed him back and melted against him, her insides fluttering even as she struggled to keep her feelings in check. And still, over and over his tongue plunged into her mouth, stroking and arousing, kissing her hotly, ardently, until she wreathed her arms about his neck, pressed her body up against his and kissed him back with absolutely nothing held in reserve. Until there was nothing but need and yearning and unbridled desire. And that was when a door opened, and the kids burst in.

"Mommy and Mr. Gabe are kissing!" Abigail shouted.

"Yeah!" Gretchen enthused. "Maybe now they'll get married!"

"Are they always like that?" Gabe asked, minutes later, when she was packing up the cowboy cookies she and the kids had baked the evening before for him to take to his parents.

Her cheeks still flushed with embarrassment, Susannah said, "You mean aggressively matchmaking?"

Somehow Gabe didn't mind it when he was the target. If it were anyone else, though. The plumber, the electrician, Bing...

He was definitely *not* on board with that.

"Yes," he said.

She sighed. "It started last spring. Mother's Day was coming up. They were talking about that at school. And their friend Chloe, from preschool, was part of the wedding of her dad, Jack McCabe, and Bess Monroe. So, brides and grooms and happily-ever-afters are on their minds these days."

"You think they'd like to have a dad?"

"In a perfect world?" she returned skeptically. "Of course they would. But we don't always get what we want—they know that, too. In the meantime, all things considered, I'm doing pretty good on my own."

"You're a great mom," he said, glancing into the living room where they were now all working together to build a play village in the middle of the floor. "They're great kids."

She nodded, still seeming a little irked about the kiss.

Though she hadn't been irked when it had been in progress, he thought to himself. Only when they had been found out...

Aware he was going to have to be a lot more careful about when and where he put the moves on her, he cleared his throat. "Listen, about my offer to baby-sit while you worked on the portrait. I was serious."

"I know you were, but I can't possibly accept that, and especially not on a regular basis. Not to worry, though." She handed him the plastic-wrapped platter of cookies to take to his folks with a brisk, professional smile. "I'll figure it out."

* * *

"Was that Gabe I saw dropping by again this af-ternoon?" Millie asked the following Friday evening, after Susannah had put the quintuplets to bed.

Their home across the street had the perfect view of the comings and goings in her house.

Glad to be off the crutches, and finally have her ankle back to normal, Susannah bustled about, tidy-ing up with her usual speed. "He brought me more photos for the project I'm doing for his family."

The older woman unzipped the dress she'd worn on her and Mike's very first date from its garment bag, where it had been hanging for the last couple of months.

She got out the simple black jersey, with the scoop neck, cap sleeves and flounced skirt, and held it up to her with a sigh.

It had become her mission to get into it for the big night, and once every week she came over to Susan-nah's to try it on again in secret. See just how far away from fitting into it she actually was.

Millie slipped into the powder room. Spoke softly, through the crack in the door. "Couldn't he have just scanned them into a computer and emailed them, or brought them all at once?"

That's what you would think, Susannah thought as she continued folding that day's laundry. Espe-cially since she had been kind of putting him in the deep freeze since that last kiss. "He says he likes to do things the old-fashioned way."

Millie came back out, barefoot, her dress gaping

open in the back. She turned so Susannah could zip. "I gather you don't believe him."

Susannah recited what she had been telling herself. "I think he's just bored. And maybe a little lonely."

Millie frowned. "How is that possible with his family in Laramie?"

Susannah got the zipper up only an inch before it came to a dead stop. "Well, everyone is busy with their own work, and Cade is working hard with his personal trainer and physical therapist or going out with the number of hot women who keep driving in from Dallas to see him."

Millie reached around behind her and felt the progress. She frowned. "Couldn't Cade fix him up, then, if it was just female company he craved?"

"Probably not, since most of them are apparently vying for the role of famous major league ballplayer's wife."

Still frowning, Millie slipped back into the bathroom, where Susannah could hear her turning this way and that, to get a glimpse in the mirror. "Gabe said that?"

"Not in so many words, but it's clear what he thinks—that the women who are chasing after Cade now will not be chasing after him if he doesn't make a full recovery from his pitching injury."

Millie's voice was muffled as the dress came back over her head. "That doesn't sound nice."

"It's not. Which is why Gabe isn't interested in spending any time with any of them."

"Why is Cade, then?"

"Probably because *he's* bored, and he likes having a beautiful woman on his arm. Apparently, the social part of his life is pretty superficial. To the point it really annoys Gabe."

"Who, as a Physicians Without Borders doc, is used to a more serious existence." Millie came back out, the dress back on the hanger.

"One where he is constantly helping people. I think being here for the summer and not working is harder on him than he anticipated."

Millie put the dress back in the garment bag. "Hence his chasing you."

Susannah blushed, aware it felt like more than that. Even though the logical side of her insisted it probably wasn't. "He's not really chasing me."

Although there had been those kisses…kisses she still couldn't seem to forget…

Millie lifted a brow. "Looks like it to me."

"Only because he's not currently romantically involved with anyone, and neither am I. He's also enamored of the idea of the quintuplets. And they are certainly enamored of him."

Millie hung the black garment bag back in Susannah's front hall closet. "You could kick him out or not invite him in whenever he shows up unannounced."

Susannah sorted socks, matching them pair by pair, then turning the cuffs down so they would stay together. "I could, except that I accepted an advance and signed a contract for the portrait I'm doing for his family. So I feel obligated to let him drop by and check on any sketches I've done thus far, get his feed-back."

Millie picked up her iced zero-calorie sassafras tea. "Which he happily gives."

"Usually right before he gets involved with help-ing the quintuplets build a fort or put together a Lego creation."

Millie's eyes lit up. "So you like having him around, too."

Too much, actually. Susannah shrugged. "I mean, it's all fine now, but if he keeps this up and the kids get used to having him around a lot, and then for whatever reason he stopped dropping by on a daily basis, they would probably be a little upset by his sud-den absence." *As would I.* "So I worry about that."

Millie pitched in to help with the pajamas. "Is that all you're concerned about?"

Susannah paused. "It's complicated."

Millie's glance turned maternal, reminding Su-sannah that she was the closest thing to a mother she had these days. "How so?"

"I think he feels a little guilty or something, be-cause he advised me not to do the IVF way back when I was still reeling from Brett and Belinda's passing."

Millie's brows knit together. "Why would he do that?"

"Medically, he knew the odds were stacked against it ever working out. And he didn't want to see me risk that kind of devastating grief on the heels of the enormous loss I had already suffered."

"Yet you did it, anyway," Millie observed softly.

"I can't really explain it, but I had faith it would all work out. And it did. But I think he somehow feels bad because had I listened to his advice, as a physician and Brett's friend, then I wouldn't have the quintuplets. So he is trying to make it up to me now by being extra supportive. At least that's my theory." And the only one she could come up with, unless it was just pure lust driving him to spend more time with her. And given the responsibilities she had, she couldn't really have that.

Millie waggled a teasing brow. "You certainly have been doing a lot of thinking about this man."

"Only because I haven't thought about a man…in forever. But the thing is, even if I wanted to get involved with someone right now, it couldn't be him, because he's only here for a short time and I need someone who is going to stick around."

"I agree with you there. An absentee daddy would not work out in your situation."

No, it wouldn't.

"Have you spoken to him about your feelings on this subject?" Millie pressed.

"No." *Heavens, no!*

"Why not?"

"Because there is no way to do that without putting him on the spot. And that, in turn, could make working together on the gift for his dad really awkward."

"I remember Gabe when he was in high school, and Mike and I both had him in our classes. He was not just a stand-up guy, but always someone who knew his own mind, too. So if he is demonstrating an interest in you and the kids…it might be that he is more ready to settle down than you're giving him credit for."

"And it also might be that he thinks he is a family man, deep down, like all the rest of the Lockhart men are at heart. But the reality of the quintuplets is quite different than the romantic notion of them."

Millie grinned. "You want him to understand that before his demonstrated interest goes any further."

Susannah nodded. "I think that would be best." *For both of us.*

"Then give him what he wants and allow him to help Mike babysit for them tomorrow morning while we do our errands."

Gabe wasn't sure he heard right when Susannah called him a short while later. "You want me to babysit tomorrow morning?" He hadn't ever thought she would take him up on that offer.

Just back from a run with Cade, who seemed to be pushing too hard, he went to the fridge to get a bottle of water.

"Yes," Susannah replied. "Millie and I are going shoe shopping." He could hear the smile in her voice. "Naturally, I wouldn't expect you to do it alone. Five kids is five times too many on your own. But if you can, it would be helpful to Mike, who has already offered. Otherwise…" She sounded abruptly hesitant, "I can call around and see if I can round up another babysitter."

"No need for that. I'd be happy to help. What time do you need me?"

"How about 10:00 a.m., and then hopefully Millie and I will be back by the time the kids wake up from their afternoon naps."

Five hours? "It takes that long to buy shoes?"

"It does if you're a woman and you're looking for an exact replica of something you had nearly fifty years ago."

"Oh."

Susannah's voice dropped to a throaty whisper. "Please don't say anything to him, but she's trying to recreate her and Mike's very first date, and it's a little more challenging than she thought it might be. But she's determined, and I'm going to help her."

"Good for you."

"So, you can help Mike tomorrow?"

"Yes. See you then." Gabe hung up.

"That's a pretty big smile," Cade observed with a grin of his own.

"Susannah asked me to babysit tomorrow."

His brother wrapped his shoulder in ice and settled on the sofa, electrolyte drink in hand. "Now I really don't get it."

"Up until now, I don't think she has trusted me as far as she could throw me. So the fact she's willing to put me to the test with her kids is a good sign."

Cade squinted. "I thought you weren't trying to date her."

"I'm not."

"Then…?"

He still had a last request to follow through on. "She and the kids don't have a lot of people in their life who look after them, except Millie and Mike, and, of course, the other mothers in town, who are her friends."

Cade squinted. "So, where do you come in?"

"Brett was one of my best friends."

"Still not getting it," his brother said.

"If the situation were reversed, if they were my biological kids and former sister-in-law, he would look in on them whenever he could."

Cade nodded. "It still doesn't make them your responsibility."

While he was in Laramie, it did, Gabe thought. Although Cade was right about one thing—it was going to bother him when he went back to work overseas and was unable to check in on them the way he was now. He'd worry about them. And miss them a heck of a lot, too.

The next morning when he arrived, Mike was already there, and Millie and Susannah were champing at the bit.

Looking absolutely gorgeous in a knee-length summer skirt that showed off her legs and a lacy white sleeveless top that did equally spectacular things for her breasts, Susannah bustled about in a drift of wildflower perfume. "I fixed lunch for everyone. The sandwiches are in the fridge, along with the fruit cups. Chips and cookies are on the counter."

"But no cookies unless we eat all our lunch," Abigail said.

Susannah smiled. "You all be good for Mr. Gabe and Mr. Mike, you hear?"

"We will," the kids chorused. Millie and Mike kissed. And then the ladies headed for the door.

Chaos began soon after.

The boys climbed on the furniture and refused to get down, even when Mike directed them to do so. So Gabe plucked them off and carried them out to the swing set out back, where they began playing a game called Obstacle Course. He made up the drills, and the kids followed suit. Down the slide, in the swing, around the monkey bars. On the seesaw, back up and down the slide, then onto the swing and so on.

The three girls, who had been playing inside, came out and joined in the excitement. Half an hour later, all five were spent, and it was time for lunch. Gabe herded them back inside, where Mike had their noon meal set up on the kitchen table.

Gabe noted that the older gentleman looked tired and a little sweaty, which was odd, given how cool it was indoors due to the air-conditioning. And Gabe had been the one outside supervising the little ones in the June heat.

But then, maybe that was because Mike had also picked up all the toys that had been scattered about. It was easy to see how he could have gotten a little out of breath doing that. Especially at his age. Still, Gabe had to be sure.

"You doing okay?" he asked as he lined up the kids at the powder room sink for hand washing.

"Right as rain." Mike forced a smile. "Want some coffee? I'm going to brew a pot."

"No, thanks. Already hit my quota this morning."

Mike frowned. "I haven't had any yet. Millie's got us both on this sassafras tea regimen. She's been trying to lose a little weight, and she read somewhere that this might help. Plus it doesn't have any caffeine, so it's healthier. But it's just not working for me," he complained and went on to brew some of his favorite beverage.

And as the meal went on, and he consumed two cups of coffee, Gabe couldn't help but note that Mike did look a little better. While the kids watched a thirty-minute video, the two men cleaned up together.

"You're pretty good with them," Mike observed. "You want kids one day?"

Until now, Gabe hadn't. "Not sure," he said finally. "Maybe."

"If you do, don't make the mistake Millie and I did and wait too long, because if you do that, it just might not happen."

Gabe was still thinking about the older man's advice when the kids went down for their naps. As soon as they were out, Mike said, "Maybe Millie's right. We should cut out the caffeine."

"Problem?"

"I've got a little reflux. Plus, I just now realized that in all the excitement, I forgot to take my cholesterol and blood pressure medication this morning. So I'm going to run across the street and take my meds now."

Gabe noted that Mike looked pale again, and a little ragged around the edges. Like he hadn't been sleeping well. And was that his imagination or were Mike's legs and ankles a little swollen?

Gabe saw no reason for the older man to extend himself in the heat when he was already not feeling well. He rose. "You want me to get it for you?"

"Nah." Mike waved him back into his seat. "I know right where it is. It'll only take me a minute. Unless..." Mike flashed a teasing grin, more typical of his usual jovial nature. "You're afraid to be here alone with the kids?"

Yet another test? "Of course not," Gabe said.

"Okay." Mike clapped him on the shoulder. "I'll be right back."

Except Mike didn't come right back. And he had left his phone on the kitchen counter, so Gabe had no way to text him to see what the delay was. Not sure whether or not the couple had a landline or not—a lot of older people still did—Gabe looked that up on his phone. Found it and dialed. It rang and rang. And was still ringing when Susannah and Millie walked in, their arms laden with shopping bags. He'd never been so glad to see two women in his life.

Susannah took one look at Gabe's face. "What's up?"

"Mike went over to the house to take his meds about fifteen minutes ago, and he hasn't returned. I was calling him to see what was taking so long."

Millie scoffed. "That man! He can never find anything in the medicine chest, even when it's right in front of him. I'll be right back." She headed across the street.

"Is everything okay?" Susannah turned back to Gabe, tipping her face up to his.

He told himself he was overreacting. Probably because he hadn't had anyone to diagnose in a couple of weeks now.

Before he had a chance to answer, Susannah's cell went off. As she listened to the caller, her face turned white.

"Oh my God, Gabe! Millie thinks Mike might be having a heart attack!"

Chapter Eight

"Good news," Dr. Gavin Monroe told everyone gathered around Mike's hospital bed. Millie was on one side, Gabe and Susannah the other.

"Mike did not have a heart attack. His arrhythmia was caused by a combination of low potassium and high blood pressure."

"So does that mean he gets to go home?" Millie asked.

"Actually, we're going to keep him overnight. We want to run a few more tests on his heart, to make sure that there's no underlying cardiac problem. So we're going to be putting him in the cardiac care unit, but from what we see right now, we fully expect him to be able to go home by noon tomorrow." The ER doc gave them a reassuring smile. "We just want to make sure we cover all the bases before we release him, and we will also be sending in a dietitian to make sure that you all know how to keep his potassium levels up in the future."

Millie's smile quavered. Briefly, she looked as upset as she had when the EMTs had come to transfer Mike to the hospital by ambulance. "Will I be able to stay with him?"

Kindly, Gavin reassured, "As long as you want."

Millie breathed a sigh of relief. "Thank you, Dr. Monroe."

Gavin smiled. "The team will be in to transfer you upstairs in a few minutes." He slipped out.

Millie turned to Gabe and Susannah. "Thank you for being here. But you all need to go home and take care of the quintuplets."

Mike nodded. Since receiving the IV fluids and potassium, his color and demeanor had returned to normal. "We've got this," he said appreciatively.

Sensing the couple wanted a few minutes alone, Susannah moved to hug and kiss them both. "Let us know if you need anything." She held up her cell phone. "I'm only a text away."

Together, she and Gabe walked out of the ER. The two had followed behind the ambulance in his truck. "You doing okay?" He surveyed her tenderly.

He looked so strong and solid, so at ease in the medical setting, it was all she could do not to throw herself in his arms. "Why?"

"You look a little shaky."

Susannah's knees wobbled. Her need for comforting grew. She forced a watery smile. "I think I am."

He moved closer, his expression becoming all the more protective. "Low blood sugar?"

Susannah swallowed around the sudden parched feeling in her throat. "Maybe." She hadn't had anything to eat or drink since lunchtime.

Taking charge, he steered her into the hospital coffee shop off the lobby. "Let's get a drink and sit down a minute. Make a plan."

After the traumatic morning they'd all had, Susannah was happy to lean on him. She drew an enervated breath. "Sounds good."

They got two mango smoothies, a snack bag of pretzels for him and a crispy cereal and mixed nut snack for her. Because the courtyard was shady that time of day, and no one else was out there, they took their goodies out there and sat down on a bench before the fountain in the center.

They sat side by side, their bodies touching. "It was quite an afternoon."

When she had trouble opening her bag, he reached over to help her, then handed it back. "Amazing that the kids didn't wake up when the ambulance was across the street."

She nodded, already beginning to feel better. "They're all sound sleepers—have been since they were born."

He offered her one of his pretzels and took a bite of her snack mixture, too. "It's also amazing you were able to get someone to watch them while they slept, and then Mitzy and Chase McCabe to take them after that."

"The Laramie Multiples Club is fantastic." As was Gabe. She didn't know how she would have made it through the calamity without his help. Certainly, it would have been harder. "Speaking of which—" Susannah sighed, her own responsibilities coming to the fore once again "—I really should call and check on the kids. Let Mitzy and Chase know I can come and get them at any time. In fact," she said, already regretting her time alone with Gabe would soon come to an end, "I'll FaceTime her in case the kids need to see me to be reassured."

Gabe smiled. "Good idea."

Susannah took another long, thirsty sip of her smoothie, then set it down and made the call. Mitzy picked up on the third ring. "How are things?" the social worker and mother of quadruplet boys asked immediately.

Briefly, Susannah explained and found the recounting of Mike's attack almost as debilitating as the event itself. "So," she said, her voice trembling slightly with the pent-up emotion of the day, "we can come over now…"

"No, you don't." Mitzy's face was etched with concern. "The quintuplets are fine right where they are, and they will be the rest of the evening." Firmly, she continued, "You, on the other hand, are not."

"I am."

Mitzy looked past Susannah at Gabe. "You're not. And I'm sure Gabe will second me on this." Sternly, she reiterated, "You can't see them like this, Susannah. You need to get hold of yourself, have a glass of wine and chill out. Because if the kids see you like this, they are going to know something is up. And they don't need that."

Beside her, Gabe nodded his agreement.

Susannah capitulated with a sigh. "Okay. You're right…" She did need to get herself together.

"But in the meantime," Mitzy said, "to reassure you that everything is okay, I'm going to give you a glimpse of what is going on right now."

The social worker stepped outside her home and turned toward the backyard. Her husband, Chase McCabe, was standing on the patio, grilling hot dogs. The picnic table was set for the evening meal. All nine of the kids—their quadruplet boys and Susannah's quintuplets—were playing a spirited game of Father May I with Chase. They looked incredibly happy and excited to be just where they were.

"See?" Mitzy reiterated. "They're fine. And after dinner, we're going to have story time and then catch fireflies when it gets dark. So, you get here by nine, and then I promise they will all be so exhausted they will go right to sleep."

Susannah sagged in relief. "Thank you, Mitzy. You're a lifesaver."

The other woman waved off the gratitude. "Oh, come on, you've done the same for me and all the other moms lots of times. It's what we're here for, right?"

"Right."

After a few parting words, Susannah ended the call. And then, to her horror, promptly burst into tears.

Gabe did the only thing he could do. He gathered Susannah in his arms and hugged her close. "Hey, darlin'," he said in her ear. "What's this all about?" It couldn't be over Mike, since he was fine.

Tears continuing to spill from her eyes, she pushed away from him and let out a shuddering breath. Her chest rose and fell with each agitated exhalation. "Just…everything." She gestured helplessly.

"Are you worried about the kids?" Given what Mitzy had showed her, she shouldn't be.

"No." Susannah took another halting breath, still struggling to get her emotions under control. "You saw them," she said, making no effort to hide her aggravation with herself. "They were thrilled. They always are when they get to spend time with the other dads."

"Which is something they don't have."

She pressed on the bridge of her nose. "Right." Swallowed, and finally looked up at him again, remorse glimmering in her sea-blue eyes. "It just makes me feel guilty sometimes, because I know they're never going to have that."

He brought her back into the curve of his arm. "You don't know that," he said gruffly.

Taking the folded tissue he pressed into her hand, Susannah wiped her eyes and blew her nose. "I'm not saying guys wouldn't date me, if benefits were involved."

"Now you're really selling yourself short," he told her in a low, gravelly voice.

"But no one wants a ready-made family with five kids."

I would, Gabe thought, much to his surprise. "I'd take you all in a heartbeat," he said before he could stop himself.

Not taking him literally, Susannah wrinkled her nose. She rose gracefully and gathered up her trash. "Except you don't want to get married."

Not sure that was true any longer, Gabe paused.

Her back to him, she walked over to the trash can and dispensed with her empty cup and foil packet. "It's okay." She squared her slender shoulders and swung back to him, looking better now—stronger, more like herself. "I shouldn't have said that," she admitted with a self-admonishing shake of her pretty head. "It's just been an emotional day. I probably just need to go home and pull myself together, like Mitzy advised."

Gabe stood, too, and walked over to join her. He tossed his own trash into the bin. Then reached over and brushed a strand of hair from her face and tucked it behind her ear. "Or," he suggested smoothly, "you could have dinner and a glass of wine with me and my brother. I'm supposed to go to Cade's house and cook dinner with him tonight. He always buys enough to feed an army, so it'd be no problem to throw something on for you, too."

Finally, Susannah began to relax. "He wouldn't mind?" she asked.

Talk about an understatement. Gabe rolled his

eyes. "Please. He's at his best when he is entertaining a beautiful woman."

Susannah made a face at him. "Okay, Doc," she chastised drolly, "you don't have to lay it on so thick. I'll stop crying without the false compliments."

It was his turn to do a double take. "You *are* beautiful," he told her sincerely. "Even more so than when I saw you five years ago."

Her delicate brow arched. "I've gained weight," she said flatly.

She sure had! Gabe shrugged. "In all the right places." And to prove it, he let his glance drift over the lovely swell of her breasts, the nip of her waist and the curve of her hips, before returning to her eyes. "Sorry," he said, seeing the flare of feminine temper, "but you brought it up."

Her gaze narrowed even more. He had the feeling she didn't know whether to deck him, read him the riot act or both.

"It's the truth," he said, just as flatly, looking her right in the eye. "Before you bordered on being too thin. Now you're perfect." So perfect it was all he could do to keep his hands off her.

"Well, thank you. I think. Unless," she added hastily, "this is some new way of hitting on me."

Which would be forbidden, she seemed to be saying. "Of course not," Gabe returned automatically. *Only in my mind. And my heart. And my loins...* Once again, he pushed away the need to get her beneath him. "So, are you up for going to see Cade?"

Susannah hesitated. "Shouldn't you call him first and ask him if it's okay?"

Unsure whether it was celebrity wariness or shyness driving her concern, Gabe said, "He hasn't answered my texts all afternoon. So, no. I'm just going to drive over there and see what the situation is."

New concern lit Susannah's pretty face. "You think there might be a problem?" she asked, walking with him to the parking lot.

Gabe inclined his head. "He's been overdoing the post-op rehab and postsurgical workouts, so he might just be sleeping. At least that's what I'm hoping he's doing."

She tucked her hand around his elbow as they threaded their way through the vehicles. "Well, there's only one way to find out," she said with a determined smile. "Let's go see."

Although she knew him in passing, Susannah had never been in Cade Lockhart's home before. It was as luxurious a bachelor pad as one might imagine a famous major league pitcher would have, with large, open rooms, lots of dark wood and expensive leather furniture.

Seemingly oblivious to the richness of their surroundings, Gabe strolled in ahead of her. There were grocery bags on the kitchen counter, waiting to be unloaded.

"Cade?" Gabe yelled in warning. "We've got company."

Susannah smirked. "Afraid he'll walk out naked?"

Gabe groaned, not joking. "With that man, you never know." With a frown, he gazed around, then advised grimly, "Make yourself at home. I'll go see if I can find him."

Gabe headed up the stairs, then returned, swearing, what appeared to be a handwritten note in hand.

"Problem?" Susannah guessed.

"He drove to Dallas."

That was several hours away. Minimum. "With a bum right shoulder?"

Gabe snorted. Wadding up the note, he tossed it in the trash, then began unloading the groceries, which appeared to be some fresh fruits and vegetables and other staples and dry goods. "Apparently, my younger brother had some female 'help' with the driving."

"Well, that's good at least."

Gabe scowled. "He also said he's going stir-crazy here in Laramie County, so he's going home to Dallas to meet with the team doctors and see if he can't get off injured reserve any earlier. And he also wants to check on his home there, enjoy a little nightlife. Oh, and I'm welcome to join him, he said, but not before the first of the week. In the meantime, his place here is all mine."

Finished, Gabe took some wine out of the fridge and opened up the bottle of Bordeaux. "Now I need some, too." He poured two glasses.

Susannah accepted hers. Wordlessly, they touched glasses. "Are you worried about him?" She settled down at the island.

He lounged on the other side, still looking restless.

"I won't be as long as he makes a full recovery and can get back to where he was in his career."

Susannah knew enough about sports to realize that was never guaranteed. "And if the worst happens and he doesn't?"

His expression turned brooding. "You can't suddenly give up everything you have known and loved that has been your life's blood for years and not feel a tremendous emotional toll..."

Suddenly, Gabe didn't just seem to be talking about his brother. She sipped the delicious full-bodied wine. "Is that the way you feel about your work?"

He seemed surprised by her question. Brow furrowing, he looked over at her. "You mean what would I do if I weren't able to be a physician any longer?"

"A Physicians Without Borders doctor," Susannah clarified.

Gabe's broad shoulders tensed. "Well, that hasn't happened," he said.

Not exactly an answer.

He continued affably, "But I imagine I would figure out something."

That would not likely make him nearly as happy, Susannah imagined. Still, sensing Gabe needed comforting now as much as she had earlier, she turned the conversation back from him to his younger brother. "Just like Cade eventually would figure something else out if he couldn't resume his career the way he would like, and instead gets traded to another team or relegated to backup instead of star pitcher."

Gabe turned to Susannah with a half smile. "You're right about one thing. Cade is the kind of guy who always lands on his feet. So I probably don't have to worry about him."

Except he still was, Susannah noted.

Gabe surveyed her kindly. "But back to you. Do you want to have dinner here, or shall we go out?"

"In public?"

"Well, we could hide out in a cave somewhere and sneak a few sandwiches, but…"

She made a face at him. "I think if we were to be seen in a restaurant together, alone, that might raise a few eyebrows."

"Why?"

"Because," she said, irritated, "people would assume it was a date."

Grinning mischievously, Gabe spread his hands wide. "And that would be bad because…?" he taunted playfully.

Susannah flushed. "We're not dating, Gabe." *And won't ever be.* "And I don't want to deal with the speculation. Nor would I imagine that you would, either. It was bad enough when you brought me into the ER with the sprained ankle. And at least that could be explained away by the fact you were there when it happened and were just being neighborly."

Gabe regarded her with a poker face. "Mind helping me cook, then?" he questioned, deadpan. "Since no one will be here to see our teamwork or make something of that?"

* * *

This was going to be okay, Susannah told herself firmly, even if her heart kept racing and her entire body was on edge, with signs of an overabundance of emotion and too much residual adrenaline. She smiled. "Sure."

Gabe took another sip of wine. "I'll handle the steaks if you manage the sides."

She studied the veggies. "Sautéed carrots, yellow squash, zucchini and broccoli okay with you?"

"Perfect."

"There's also ready-made salad, which could be topped with fresh strawberries and almonds. Several different kinds of vinaigrette. Or poppy-seed dressing if you prefer that."

"I should bring you home more often," Gabe teased.

It was just a joke, but the image the words evoked—of the two of them making love—was all too real and enticing. Susannah took another sip of wine, then stepped to the sink to wash her hands.

Gabe did the same. "How about you take that side of the stove and I'll use the indoor grill over here?" he asked.

Everything had already been prepped, presumably by Cade, so all she had to do was add a little olive oil and butter to the skillet, let it heat up and then add the veggies. While they sautéed, she worked on the salad.

Gabe grilled steaks with the expertise of a man who knew his way around a kitchen.

Aware it had been years since she'd been with a

guy in such an intimate situation, Susannah tried not to make too much of it. "You were great today with Mike, by the way."

Glance narrowing, Gabe placed the seasoned filets on the sizzling hot grill. "Don't let my calm in a crisis fool you," he said soberly. "I was shaken up, too."

"But you're a doctor."

He exhaled and shrugged his broad shoulders offhandedly. "It's still hard to see someone you've known since you were a kid in the midst of a crisis."

And yet... "You seemed calm when you went over to assist Mike and Millie and await the EMTs."

Another sigh, deeper this time. "That's where my medical training kicked in."

Susannah took a moment to absorb that. She hadn't expected him to reveal this much about himself to her. Yet she was glad he had. It made him seem more human and accessible.

Nodding in empathy, she continued, "Thank God the kids didn't see him being loaded into the ambulance on a stretcher with an IV in his arm and an oxygen mask on his face. They would have freaked."

"We're lucky they slept through it," he agreed.

"Mind if I text Millie, see if she has everything she needs?"

"Go ahead." He turned the steaks and gestured at the stove. "I'll watch over all this."

For the next ten minutes, Susannah texted back and forth with Millie. By the time she finally put her phone away, she had another half glass of wine and a loaded plate of steaming food waiting for her.

"Everything okay?" Gabe asked.

Susannah sat down opposite him at the table. "Millie decided to stay the night with Mike over at the hospital."

As they settled in, their knees briefly bumped, sending an electric current racing through Susannah. Chivalrous as ever, Gabe asked, "Does she need us to bring her things?"

Susannah shook her head and took a bite of salad. "The nurses gave her the soft jersey pj's, nonskid slipper socks and toiletry kit for people who unexpectedly stay in the hospital with loved ones overnight. So she says she is good."

Gabe cut into his steak. "I didn't know the hospital did that."

She nodded, doing her best to concentrate on their delicious dinner rather than the ruggedly handsome man opposite her. "The overnight visitor kits are provided by the McCabe Foundation."

He sobered. "That's been around since John and Lilah McCabe passed, when I was doing my residency here. Their ranch was put in a trust and was being turned into the McCabe House when I left, which was going to be run like a Ronald McDonald House."

Susannah tore her eyes from the sinewy contours of his chest. "But they now do a lot of other little things, too, which are important to patients. All new babies go home with sleep suits and caps, as well as the traditional hospital newborn nursery blankets. Others who can't afford transportation to and from the hospital for treatment receive that free of charge."

Gabe smiled. "People in Laramie County really take care of their own."

"They sure do," Susannah agreed. "It's one reason I like living here. It would be a lot harder to raise the quintuplets in the city."

"Speaking of taking care of our own..." He gave her an admiring look and raised his wineglass in a toast to her. "You really care about Millie and Mike... and vice versa."

With good reason, Susannah thought. "They're family to me. Millie is sort of the best friend I had always hoped my mom would one day be, if she had lived, as well as a surrogate mom, and Mike is definitely the father figure in my life. They're both de facto grandparents to the kids. So much so that I would feel guilty for taking so much of their time and energy if I didn't know their situation."

Gabe locked eyes with her. "Mike mentioned to me he and Millie always wanted kids but it didn't work out."

"They met in college while they were studying to be teachers. They wanted to travel a lot while they were young and unencumbered, so every summer for the first fifteen years or so that they were married, they went off to see the world. When they finally decided they wanted kids, it didn't happen. They tried in vitro several times, but it failed."

"Damn. That must have been really tough to deal with."

"It was." Susannah sighed. "They thought about adopting a baby, but by then they were in their late forties, and they didn't think it would be fair to have a kid graduating high school when they were getting on Social Security. So they gave up on that dream and went back to traveling—until I moved in. And then," she admitted wryly, "they dedicated themselves to helping me…and eventually the kids…and now we're the family that we all always wanted."

Abruptly, she teared up. "I don't know what Millie would do if something happened to Mike," she said thickly.

Gabe squeezed her hand. "I know," he said softly. "She would be devastated, and vice versa."

Finished with her meal, Susannah sat back, studying him. His expression didn't change in the slightest, yet there was something in his eyes, some small hint of worry he had yet to express. "Is there something going on medically that you and Gavin haven't told us about yet?"

He shook his head. "No. It really was just low potassium and high blood pressure. The tests he is having tomorrow are just precautions."

"So if you don't expect anything else to show up, what's bugging you?"

His manner guarded, he stood and began to clear the table. "I should have seen it. Would have if I didn't like Mike so much and he hadn't been my teacher and track coach all through high school."

Susannah cleared the table, too, carrying the plates over to the sink, where Gabe stood. "You mean there were signs?"

Briefly, the sexy doc looked like he had taken a

punch to the gut. Recovering, he pressed his lips together tersely and admitted, "He looked a little off as the morning wore on today, but he'd been picking up toys and rushing around getting the meal set up while I had all the kids outside, so I chalked it up to too much activity. He also said he hadn't had coffee this morning, and he perked up when he had a couple of cups."

"But then…?"

"He needed his medicines, because he had forgotten to take them this morning."

"So he went across the street to get them," Susannah recalled.

Gabe nodded, even more unhappily. "He didn't come back right away and wasn't answering my calls when you came in. And, of course, that's when he had the incident that put him in the hospital."

Susannah curved her hand around Gabe's bicep, forcing him to face her. "You can't blame yourself for that," she said gently.

"I'm not taking responsibility for his missed medications or memory."

"Then…?" She studied his brooding expression.

Grimacing, Gabe went back to doing the dishes and sliding them into the dishwasher. "It's a problem I have when I'm close to someone. It's also why doctors don't treat their own families. They don't want to think anything is amiss with someone they love, so they convince themselves they are overreacting out of concern and believe everything is fine when it's not."

Susannah's heart broke for the pain she could see

he was in. "Has this happened to you with someone you love?"

Gabe exhaled. "My parents," he said wearily. "The night they died."

Chapter Nine

"I don't understand," Susannah said in bewilderment. "I thought your parents died when a water heater exploded and the house collapsed in on them. That you and your siblings weren't home at the time."

He never talked about this. But maybe she did need to understand the depth of his remorse. "Not at that moment, no, but we were all in the house that night when the thunderstorm hit and our roof got struck by lightning and caught on fire."

The color drained from Susannah's face. "Oh my God. Gabe," she whispered, aghast, "that must have been so terrifying."

It had been. The fear he had felt then came pouring back in a rush of adrenaline. "My parents got all eight of us kids out safely and across the street to the neighbors."

Her brow furrowed. "Then I don't understand what happened."

He took her hand and led her over to the sofa. Sat down next to her. "While we were waiting for the fire department to arrive, the pouring rain put out the flames. Or so we thought."

Susannah's hand mimicked the ice in his gut.

"My mother was worried about the stuff in the safe in the den, and she wanted to go back to retrieve it," Gabe recited numbly. "My dad wouldn't let her go alone, so he went with her. They thought it was okay, and maybe it would have been if the sparks from the fire hadn't ignited the gas water heater, which was located in the attic. But it did, and there was an explosion, and the house went up in a giant fireball," he said, ignoring Susannah's gasp of horror, "while we all watched, and then the house collapsed in on itself.

"If there is any blessing in it, it's that my parents were killed instantly. The fire marshal told us they never knew what hit them."

Susannah wrapped her arms around him and hugged him, hard. Then drew back, her eyes shimmering with tears. "Oh Gabe…" she whispered, "I am so sorry."

"Yeah, well that's not the worst part." He began to tear up. Having gone this far, he figured she might as well know the worst. "The worst part is that my brothers Cade and Travis saw what I didn't."

Susannah sat back, listening.

Gabe forced himself to go on. "They instinctively knew it was a bad idea and tried to stop my folks from going back across the street. But I had such complete faith in my parents," he recollected bitterly, "that they knew what they were doing and were invincible, that I intervened. Played the oldest sibling card and told them to let Mom and Dad do what they had to do. And I held them both back when they would have physically stopped them."

She jerked in a ragged breath. "How old were you?" she asked empathetically.

Gabe rubbed the knee of his jeans. "Twelve. Cade was ten, Travis eleven."

Susannah shook her head and covered his hand with her own, stilling its restless motion. "Everyone must have been so devastated."

An understatement. "They were. And angry at me," he related miserably, owning up to the aftermath of the mistake. "As they had a right to be. It was because of me that my parents perished."

Susannah tightened her grip, shaking her head in gentle disagreement. "You were just a kid, Gabe. A kid who was just trying to do what was best in the moment. You had no way of knowing…"

"I let my emotions get in the way of good judgment."

Never again, he promised himself.

Susannah gave him the space he needed and let go of his hand, then sat back. "What happened after that?" she asked quietly.

Gabe let out a rough breath. "My parents were

both orphans, and we had no family who could take us. Social services didn't have any place to put us all, so they had to split us up, starting that very night."

Susannah made a soft, empathetic sound.

Gabe plunged on. "We were scattered across six foster homes in southwest Texas. It was two years before Carol and Robert Lockhart could foster all of us together, and a while after that before they were able to formally adopt us all."

Susannah's voice quavered. "That must have been so hard on you."

"It still is." For once, Gabe made no effort to camouflage his sorrow. His voice caught at the unbearable pain of that memory. "I don't think I'll ever get over the grief and the guilt my actions caused my whole family."

"You can't let one mistake ruin your life," she told him fiercely.

"It hasn't." He echoed her firm tone.

"Really?" Susannah countered. "Because I think that's what is behind your constant need to be on the move and the long years you've spent away from your family and everyone in your hometown who really cares about you."

The unexpected accuracy of her intuition stung. "I go where I'm needed," Gabe said brusquely.

She looked him in the eye, long and hard. Seeing far more than he preferred. "What if you're needed here more?" she challenged, even more softly.

If she was talking about her and her children, he could see that was true. His heart took on a slow, heavy beat. But there were difficulties with that she still knew nothing about.

Her eyes softened, everything about her inviting him in. "Isn't it time you let yourself be close to someone again?"

Funny that she would be the one to sense that. "Oh, princess." Gabe exhaled. She was so smart on so many levels, and so naive on this one. He shook his head at her, stood and moved away, then told her what he knew she would not want to hear. "There's only one way I want to be close to someone," he confessed. And she was not cut out for a brief, meaningless affair. Which was the only kind he had. Where it was all about the sex and nothing else. And hence destined to end as soon as it began.

"Then be close to me," she urged sincerely, returning to his side.

If only it were that simple. But he didn't want to hurt her. "You don't know what you're asking, Susannah."

She arched a dissenting brow.

His heart twisted in his chest as his conscience intervened. "I'm never going to be the lover you want and need," he told her sorrowfully. "Never going to let you in…" And if the forbidden happened, and he were really close to her, he'd never be able to keep his promise and protect her…

She stood her ground, looking incredibly determined. "Actually, Gabe," she declared, shocking the hell out of him by stepping close enough to align her body with his, wrapping her arms about his neck and pressing her lips to his. She sighed softly, wantonly. "I think you're *exactly* what I need right now."

Susannah couldn't explain what propelled her into Gabe's embrace, never mind so impulsively. Except... the adrenaline of the day...the sense that life was fragile...the fact that their previous kisses had demonstrated to her that she had never been wanted like this, or wanted anyone in return...all combined to conjure up a reckless passion within her unlike anything she had ever felt before.

But damn if it didn't feel good, she thought as she felt his pulse skitter and jump and his body hardened all the more, and she wasn't about to let it go without exploring it further. Because if today had taught her anything, it was that moments like this could not be wished into reality...they happened or they didn't. And right now, as he began to kiss her back, deeply and evocatively, this was damn well happening, and she wanted to enjoy every single delicious second of it.

Gabe knew this wasn't what Brett or Belinda'd had in mind when they had asked him to watch over Susannah in their absence. He also knew, given the many barriers she had erected around her heart, that getting more intimately involved with her was the only way he would ever be able to fulfill that promise.

The fact she wasn't looking for forever from him complicated things, to be sure. But he also could tell by the way she was melting into his embrace and kissing him in return that she needed this kind of intimate physical contact and emotional connection, however fleeting, every bit as much as he did right now.

And that knowledge gave him the will to continue. When she unbuttoned his shirt, he slid his hands beneath her top. And the caress of her hands on his bare skin heralded the touch of his hands on hers.

He'd thought the first couple of times he had kissed her had been amazing. Sweet, hot, tempting beyond all reason. But those times were nothing compared to this. Her lips were soft and warm and sweet, and she kissed him with absolutely nothing held back. The blood thundered through him, and he reveled in the soft surrender of her body against his. "My bed okay?"

She grinned against his mouth. "Bed's good."

He danced her backward down the hall to the guest room, kissing her all the while. He loved the sexy, feminine scent of her, the way she opened her mouth to the plundering pressure of his.

She splayed her hands across the hardness of his chest, stroking and molding. Both of them were trembling as they made quick work of undressing each other and their clothes fell all the way to the floor.

He was hard and throbbing with need. She was flushed and gorgeous, her skin silky and delicate, and her curves every bit as womanly as he had imagined.

"My scar," she murmured shyly, her hand going to the line that started just beneath her navel and disappeared into the nest of honey-blond curls.

He moved her fingers, tracing the place where, with the help of the doctors, her babies had emerged to meet the world. He bent to kiss it, too. "You're beautiful. Inside and out. Don't ever let yourself think any different…"

Her hands sifted through his hair. She held him close as he claimed her as his. Exploring, loving until she was drunk with pleasure, whimpering and quivering.

Rising, he wrapped his arms around her and brought her close. The softness of her breasts nestled against the hard wall of his chest as his hands explored the silky-smooth softness of her inner thighs, the rounded curves of her buttocks.

And still they kissed. Their lips and tongues mating. Until she rocked against him, leaving him with no doubt about what she wanted. Needed.

He found a condom. Together, they rolled it on, then tumbled onto the bed. He hardened all the more. "Let me," she whispered, her lips and hands moving over him with utmost care. Tantalizing. Tempting. Drawing it out. Until they were almost there.

Then his hands were on her shoulders, and she was on her back. His gaze locked with hers as he pulled her legs to his waist and slid between her thighs. Her muscles tensed as he used his fingertips to pave the way before he slid home, claiming her as his, letting her claim him in return. And then their bodies melded in boneless pleasure. Yet still they kissed and touched. Rocking together. Rising to greet each other. Their union incredibly sensual, hot and wild. He took his time, possessing her with excruciating slowness, going deeper, harder, until she gasped his name and they both finally went spiraling over the edge.

Long moments passed as they clung together, both in awe at the abandon they had shown.

As they caught their breath, Gabe rolled so he was on his back and Susannah lay with her arms and legs still wrapped around him, her head against his shoulder. Raw emotion rocked through her. And thoughts. So many thoughts…

"What are you thinking?" Gabe asked quietly. He kissed the inside of her wrist, her elbow, her shoulder.

She turned to him, mischief in her eyes. "That even though this was incredibly reckless of me, I'm not sorry it happened." His sensual lips curved, encouraging her to continue.

She shrugged. "I can't say whether it will happen again or not." She kissed his shoulder, too, loving the solid male warmth of him. "All I know right now is that I needed to be with someone tonight, and so did you and we were here for each other."

He surveyed her, again seeming to like what he saw. "It's really that simple for you?"

She tingled in response, much the same way she had when they'd made love. "It hasn't been in the past." She frowned. "And I realized today when I was at the hospital that this has become a problem."

He sat up against the headboard. "How so?"

Aware their time together was dwindling, Susannah rose and began to dress. "I've had no difficulty taking risks when it comes to other areas of my life," she admitted as she shimmied into her panties. Pulling her bra over her breasts, she turned around so he could help her with the clasp. "When Brett and Belinda died and I inherited the embryos and I wanted a family of my own, I leaped into the IVF process."

His fingers brushed her skin as he fastened the bra.

"And when I was unhappy in my career as a graphic designer in Houston, I quit, moved to Laramie County and started a small business as a pet portrait artist." Susannah snatched her clothes up off the floor and stepped into them. "But when it came to my love life, I refused to settle for anything less than anyone who was perfect for me in every way. That hasn't worked out so well." She turned her back to Gabe again. "It's left me lonely and alone."

He obliged her with the zipper on her skirt, too. "So now you're ready to settle?"

I'm ready to take a chance. On you. Even if it means an intermittent affair. But knowing Gabe wasn't ready to hear that, Susannah tidied her hair with her fingers and admitted practically, "I decided I need to start taking some chances in this area, too." Drawing a deep breath, she continued, "I want to be with someone who can help me be more present in my life."

Gabe rose and began to dress, too. "Like me."

She sat down on the edge of the bed and slipped on her flats. "I'm so used to being responsible, to being focused on the chaos of the moment in the wake of the kids. I've got no time for pleasure. No time for an evening like the one we're having now." Rising, she straightened the folds of her skirt. "Maybe it's selfish, but I want to enjoy this part of my life, too."

His gaze locked with hers, Gabe buttoned his shirt and tucked it into the waistband of his jeans. "Even though I'm leaving in a few months."

Susannah shrugged, aware this was the point where she would have cut him out of her life completely in the past. Now, she didn't want to do that. She held her hands wide. "All the more reason for us to take the here and now and enjoy it to the max…"

He studied her, his own feelings inscrutable. Worried he might be about to end it, already, for both their sakes, she went up on tiptoe to deliver another kiss. Sweet and persuasive this time. "It doesn't have to be forever. It just has to be right, in the moment, and tonight it was…" she kissed him again, even more persuasively "so…right…"

Gabe gazed down at her for a long, thoughtful moment. "Promise me," he told her gruffly. "Whatever happens, there'll be no regrets."

Susannah gazed up at him resolutely. "Not. A. One."

"As much as I'd like to stay awhile longer," Susannah remarked shortly thereafter, "it's time for me to collect my van and go and pick up my kids."

Regret shimmered through Gabe, along with a flash of guilt. How could he have forgotten about the quintuplets? Another sign what a bad bet as a lover and potential family man he was? Or just a sign at how right he and Susannah were for each other, that they had temporarily managed to shut out the entire rest of the world…even if it had only been for an incredibly enticing and satisfying half an hour? "I can go with you." He put on his shoes, rose.

She paused. "I don't know if that's wise."

He couldn't let her go thinking a onetime hookup was all this was or would ever be. Not when they had just glimpsed the potential of their future. "It's late. They've got to be tired." He watched her hesitate. "Just wrangling them into your van could be a challenge."

"Good point. But just so you know, what happened here tonight doesn't change anything. I'm not expecting anything from you because of this. You don't have to date me or even call me again about anything but the portrait. I know this was a crazy day, and both our emotions are running high."

He fell into step beside her as they headed out to the truck. "You think that's why this happened?"

"Don't you?"

She was right. He was leaving. She was staying. There were five kids between them that could be hurt by this. Bottom line, the two of them couldn't be more wrong for each other in the long run. And yet, in the short run, over the course of the summer, he wanted it to work out. He wanted them to be able to bring happiness and passion to each other, for as long as they could. Even if it meant parting would be difficult in the end. And just how insensible was that?

* * *

"You're half an hour earlier than we were expecting," Mitzy greeted them at the backyard gate. "And you look a lot more chill than I expected you would."

Probably because she'd just made love. Trying to hide that, Susannah said, "A nice leisurely dinner with an adult will do that for you."

Mitzy studied her with a smile. "I'm just glad to see you and Gabe are finally getting along."

"Mommy! Look!" Levi shouted. "We're blowing bubbles while we wait for the fireflies to come out!"

Susannah looked at Mitzy. "Thanks for jumping in today." She reached out and caught Gretchen, who stumbled with fatigue. "I've really got to get them home."

The other woman watched her four boys try to play an overly boisterous game of leapfrog while waving their bubble wands. "Ours are fading fast, too."

Susannah motioned for her crew to gather round. "We're going to have to catch fireflies another evening," Susannah told the kids.

A chorus of groans followed.

"But Mommy!" Connor protested.

"I want to stay!" Abigail stomped her foot.

"So do I!" Levi yelled, while Rebecca put her thumb in her mouth, disappointed.

"Gosh, that's too bad, because I have to leave right now, and I was going to give you all piggyback rides to your mommy's van on the way out," Gabe said.

The kids all spoke in unison. "Piggyback rides! Whoo-hoo! Let's go! Me first! No, me!"

"First, say thank you to our friends for having you," Susannah instructed, while using gentle touches to their shoulders to line them up, tiredest first.

"Thank you," they all chorused together.

Gabe bent down to take Rebecca. She hopped onto his back, a giant grin on her face. Then did what she rarely did—verbally added her two cents. "You must be strong. Mommy says we're too heavy for her now."

"I'm really strong," Gabe declared with a grin, while Susannah went ahead to open up the back of her van.

And so it went. One after another. The rest of the goodbyes and the short ride home were equally easy. Until they pulled in to the driveway, that was. "I don't want to go to bed," Levi complained loudly.

"Me, either!" Abigail concurred.

Gabe looked at Susannah from the passenger seat, where his big body filled up the entire compartment. "More piggyback rides?" he mouthed.

Susannah would have liked to politely decline, but knowing how difficult the chore ahead was likely to be without his help, nodded and said, "Sounds good."

The kids were thrilled to get another ride up the stairs to their second-floor bedrooms. Susannah helped them get ready for bed, while Gabe entertained them with stories of monkeys and elephants he had seen out in the wild. By the time all five were tucked in, it was quiet once again.

"Night, kiddos," Gabe said from the hall.

"Night, Doc Gabe," the kids echoed drowsily. And seconds later, as eyes closed, all five were fast asleep.

Susannah led the way past her bedroom, back down the stairs to the front door. "Thanks for helping out," she said.

"My pleasure," Gabe murmured in return.

The next thing she knew she was in his arms. His head was lowering. And Gabe stole a kiss that felt very much like he was staking a claim.

"What was that for?" Susannah asked a little breathlessly when he finally released her.

"No reason." He rubbed his thumb across her lower lip, the single action making her ache for another kiss. "It just felt right."

That it had, Susannah thought, as she watched him go.

"So, how is the summer vacation going?" Lou Ellen Rafferty, Gabe's boss at PWB, asked over the phone the next morning.

"Great."

"Not going stir-crazy?"

Crazy for one woman, but that wasn't the question. "Nope. Feels good to be home for a change," Gabe said honestly.

"You're still coming back in September, though?" Lou Ellen prodded.

"Of course. Any idea where I'm going yet?"

"I think this once we'll let you have your pick of assignments. You can go somewhere for up to two years if you want or go back to the six-week gigs."

Susannah and the quintuplets came to mind.

"I might want to do something even shorter for a change."

"Well, then, I'll work on that. And Gabe? I'm glad you're taking this R & R seriously. You sound better than you have in a long time."

He felt better, too. "Well, what can I say? I love Texas."

"Well, don't get too attached, because we still really need you here, too."

"Good to know," Gabe said, ending the call and then heading to the community hospital.

"Hey, good news about Mike," Gavin Monroe said when he caught sight of Gabe in the hospital's main lobby.

Millie had told Gabe that all the additional tests had been negative.

"Yeah, I'm waiting for the paperwork to be finalized, then I'm driving Mike and Millie both home."

"You were really good with them yesterday."

Gabe had an idea where this was headed. "Next thing I know, you'll be telling me you all need someone with my congenial bedside manner around," he joked.

His old pal remained affable but serious. "And an acting head for the diagnostic team while we conduct our search. Not only do you have an infectious disease background, you've been all over the world. Seen things that most of our staff has only read about in medical journals." Gavin shrugged. "Who knows? You might like it and decide to stay. And if not, the hospital would have some coverage over the summer until we do find a permanent fit. Come on, Gabe, think about how glad the residents of Laramie County would be to have you back again as a practicing physician."

They wouldn't be so happy if they knew how he'd blown it yesterday with Mike's diagnosis, at least until it became clear Gabe's former teacher and coach was having a cardiac event, anyway.

Like it or not, having gone to school and done his medical school residency here, he was equally close to many other people in the area. He couldn't take a chance on missing it with anyone else. The situation the day before had proved once again he was better off treating patients who were strangers.

Gabe dipped his head in a grateful nod. "Thanks for thinking of me."

"But?"

"If I were to take the position, even temporarily, it would give my folks false hope that I intend to stay in Texas. I don't."

"I understand." Gavin extended his palm. "If you change your mind…"

If it were just Susannah and the kids under consideration, Gabe might do just that. But it wasn't. So… He exhaled.

Seeing Mike coming down the hall in a wheelchair, an orderly and Millie right behind him, he waved to let them know he was there, then said, "I've got to go."

As soon as they got Mike home and settled in

his favorite lounge chair for a nap, Millie sent Gabe across the street.

"Everything okay?" Susannah asked when she opened the front door.

"Millie wants to make sure you've got it covered. Apparently she and Mike come over to help out most mornings when the kids aren't in preschool. She was wondering how you were faring."

Not good, from the looks of it. The kids were out of control, and Susannah was so overwrought her hair was practically standing on end.

Calmly, she directed, "Do me a favor and text Millie that things are great. The kids are ready to go down for their nap."

Gabe watched them run circles around the entire downstairs, whoo-hooing at the tops of their lungs. "Really?" he challenged mildly. "'Cause it doesn't look like they're anywhere near ready for sleep."

"I want her to relax and concentrate on taking care of Mike and herself."

"Gotcha." He did as asked while she shut the front door behind Gabe before two of the quints could escape.

"So, what else is going on?" Even when the kids were misbehaving, it wasn't like her to look so frazzled.

"I promised your mom I would get her a rough sketch of the group puppy portrait today so she could give me some feedback, but the quintuplets aren't cooperating. At all."

He saw. "Want some help?"

She brightened. "You really wouldn't mind?"

Mind? He'd jump at the chance to spend time with all six of them. Thinking she'd accept it better if she thought it was no big deal to him—when in reality being included in her life was a *very* big deal—he shrugged. "I'm at loose ends, anyway," he said.

"Okay. Then I accept. First order of business is to get them all to calm down…"

"Will do," he promised.

An hour and a dozen stories later, all five were asleep in a puppy pile across the living room sectional, their lovies and blankets cuddled against them.

Susannah still hadn't managed any work on the portrait, but she had her weekly grocery order typed into the computer and ready for pickup later that day.

"What now?" he asked.

She chuckled. "You really are a glutton for punishment."

One hand on her waist, he brought her nearer, happier to be there than she knew. "A glutton for you, maybe."

Chapter Ten

Susannah didn't know how badly she had been waiting for him to do this again until the moment his lips brushed hers. But that touch told her everything she wanted to know. He cherished his time with her as much as she cherished her time with him. It didn't matter if this was destined to be short-lived or something that continued intermittently, whenever he was back in Texas. She only knew how right it felt in the moment. How right it felt, *period*.

Wrapping her arms about his neck, she pressed her breasts to his chest. Dancing him backward, still kissing him, she moved them even farther out of view of the still-sound-asleep kids. "I can't believe I'm telling you this. But I really want to be completely alone with you again," she murmured, resting her forehead against his jaw.

He caught her wrist and rubbed the inside of it with his thumb. "As in a date?"

She flushed at his light touch. Another spark lit between them. "Doc. Are you asking me out?"

He leaned down to whisper in her ear. "Hell, yeah, princess. Will you go?"

Susannah sucked in a breath. A date would formalize whatever this was that was happening between them even more, she knew. "If it can be something that fits with our lives," she said finally.

He drew back just far enough to peer into her eyes. "The fact is you have kids to consider. And I don't. And the fact is that if there is a health crisis anywhere in the world, I could be called to serve on a moment's notice."

"I know. I understand. And I don't expect or even want any of that to change because…despite what I said last night about you being away from Laramie…"

Once again, his hand was on her, this time pressed to the middle of her spine. "And it not necessarily being a good thing?"

She sighed. Continuing even more firmly, "You are who you are, Gabe, and I am who I am, and we've made our choices." She wet her lips. "But, at the same time…"

"Whatever this is that is happening between us…"

"It's awfully good." Trying not to notice how good it felt to be hanging out with him again, she rested her palms on his chest and said, "I know I said I would just roll with the outcome, whether we decided to see each other again in that way or not. But I thought about it last night after I came home and I realized, given the choice, I'd rather not just let this go by unrealized."

"Me, either." They smiled at each other. "So, when do you want to go out?" he asked.

"If I can get a sitter? How about as soon as the quintuplets are asleep tonight?"

He gazed down at her indulgently. "Where do you want to go? A late movie? Dinner? Dancing...?"

As long as it was going to be up to her... "How about Cade's place, if he's still in Dallas?"

She was ready when he picked her up at nine, and he caught the two teenage babysitters peeking out the window as he opened the passenger door for her. "I think we're being observed."

Susannah inclined her head to the house across the street. "By Millie and Mike, too."

He sent her an ornery grin. "Does that mean we're news?"

Noticing how handsome he looked fresh out of the shower, his jaw clean-shaven, Susannah met his humorous glance. "I guess we are. Does that bother you?"

"Not at all."

She caught a whiff of his brisk masculine cologne. "Me, either."

He squinted at her thoughtfully. "Although you've

got me wondering, bringing an artist carryall with you, as well as a handbag. Are you planning to work?"

The passenger seat gave her a nice view of his mouthwateringly good physique. Shoulders wide enough to lean on. Arms strong enough to hold her. Ripped abs and trim waist. Lower still, it was easy to see how well he filled out a pair of jeans. Heart skittering in her chest, she admitted, "I was hoping you wouldn't mind previewing the sketches I've done of the pets before I show them to your mom and siblings. I'm a little nervous about getting their reaction."

"No problem. Although, from what little I've seen so far, I'm sure they are going to love it."

He'd already made the salad and gotten the potatoes ready to go in to bake. While he started the outdoor charcoal grill—they were going old-school tonight—and waited for it to heat, they sat down outside with a glass of wine on one of the cushioned outdoor sofas.

The high wood fence that rimmed the backyard provided privacy, and the night was pleasantly warm. A full moon shone down on them, and stars abounded in the velvety sky. Lights from the patio gave them plenty of illumination.

He draped his arm along the back of the sofa as they settled in. Enjoying the comforting warmth of his body so close to hers, she asked, "So, when is your brother coming home?"

With a shrug, he let his gaze drift over her body before returning to her face. "Actually, I don't think Cade's coming back to Laramie any time soon."

Susannah tilted her head. "Why not?"

He caught her hand and locked eyes with her. "He's working out with the team trainers, as well as his own private physical therapist there. Apparently, his social life is a lot better in Dallas, too."

"Cade's really a city boy, isn't he?"

A mixture of pique and disappointment lingered on his face. "Certainly, since becoming a major leaguer. I kind of think it feeds his ego, being around all the fans instead of the people who knew him as a kid."

Susannah could see that.

Noticing the hem of her skirt had ridden up on her thighs, she tugged it lower. "What about you? Weren't you here to sort of be his support person over the summer? I mean, does this mean you should be in Dallas, too?"

His gaze shifted to her lips. "Well, first, he didn't ask me to come and stay with him. Here, or any-where else. I sort of invited myself here, at my par-ents' behest."

She felt herself flushing. "Then you could go back to work?"

He gave her a long look she couldn't interpret. "It's already been arranged for me to take the entire summer off."

There was definitely something he wasn't saying. "But the plan is still for you to go back to work in September?" Susannah persisted.

Gabe moved away from her. "Yeah, my boss called me today, and we talked about it." He paused to check the coals.

Ready to give aid if it was needed, Susannah stood, too. "Any idea where or how long?"

Gabe placed marinated chicken breasts onto the grill, then closed the cover. A smoky southwestern scent filled the air. "Depends on what the current need is, and we won't know until we see what area of the world is in medical crisis." He checked his watch and returned to sit down.

Aware it was likely going to be a lot harder to say goodbye to him this time than she'd thought, she nodded her understanding. Pushing her feelings aside, she reached for her portfolio with a smile. "On to the sketches I brought with me…"

They reviewed them.

"I love the drawing of my golden retriever, Traveller."

Interesting that when it came to pets, they had chosen the same breed. "Nothing you'd change?"

Gabe rubbed the flat of his hand beneath his jaw. "He was a little more gangly than what you've portrayed. I mean you've got the cheerful joie de vivre right. But…and I hate to say it…he was more goofy than smart. Daisy seems a lot more attuned to what is going on around her."

"I doubt she would ever have been as adventurous as the way you described Traveller in your initial notes to me."

"True. There was nowhere on the ranch or in Laramie he was loath to go."

Susannah typed a couple of notes into her phone.

"Okay, I'll give that another shot and show you what I've got tomorrow."

Gabe got up to turn the chicken. "Want me to take a look at the rest?" he asked over his shoulder.

"Actually, I think I should email what I've got on each pet and just let your siblings and your mom tell me what might be missing. Each person is going to know their own dog best. I was just worried over nothing, I guess."

He caught her hand and squeezed it reassuringly. "You don't need to impress us with your art. You already have."

"You've impressed me, too," she admitted before she could stop herself. "You're a real natural with kids. Have you ever thought about having any of your own?"

That, Gabe thought, was the kind of question he usually received from a gal who had marriage in mind. Not an independent-to-a-fault woman like Susannah.

He supposed an honest question deserved an honest answer. Forcing himself to meet her eyes, he turned toward her. "I've never wanted to have kids and not be there."

Her delicate brow knit together intently. "And you can't give up your work with Physicians Without Borders?"

Another complicated question. "I haven't wanted to yet. I guess my ideal woman would understand that working where I'm needed is as much a part of me as the color of my hair or eyes. I need to be needed. To feel I'm making a difference by being where I am."

For a moment, she went silent. Then she smiled and said softly, "I can understand that. And you're right. That is exactly who you are and always have been."

So why, then, did he think that had not been the answer she was looking for?

Luckily for both of them, dinner was delicious, and they finished it off with the triple chocolate torte he'd picked up at the Sugar Buzz bakery in town.

He looked at the clock and saw it was already ten thirty. Time went fast when a date started at nine instead of the more commonplace seven. He carried the plates to the sink. Turned to find her right beside him, doing the same. He relieved her of her burden. "How long are your sitters staying?"

She wrinkled her nose, looking beautiful in the soft light of his kitchen. "Midnight." She turned to face him more directly, and the look in her eyes was the same one he imagined was in his. "You know, when I turn back into Cinderella."

He wrapped his arms around her as she snuggled up against him. "Then no way are we wasting time with dishes, princess," he murmured back, just as playfully.

As their lips fused, Gabe's body ignited. He realized he wanted her to surrender to him, to this, heart and soul. And he could feel her melting against him, even as her spirit remained as feisty and independent as ever.

Resolving to make the night the most memorable one she had ever had, even if time was way too short, he tucked one arm beneath her knees, placed the other behind her back and swung her up into his arms, against his chest.

"I thought you were done carrying me around," she chuckled.

He set her down in his bedroom and backed her up against the wall so his hips pressed into hers.

"Never," he murmured back, engulfing her with the heat and strength of his body while absorbing the soft femininity of hers. He kissed her again, and she moaned as he rained soft kisses down her throat, across her collarbone into the open V-neck of her lacy cotton top. He traced the uppermost curves of her breasts with his tongue, felt her shiver, then zeroed in on her mouth once again. Her lips parted beneath the pressure of his, and he delighted in the sweet, hot taste of her. Kissed her long and wet and deep until she fisted both hands in his hair and murmured, "Gabe..."

She whimpered for more as he slid his hands beneath her top, finding the soft globes of her breasts and taut nipples, before sliding lower still, beneath the hem of her skirt, to her panties. Chuckling softly at her highly erotic reaction, he went on a little tour, unzipping, unbuttoning, easing everything off. Until she was as naked as the day she was born, and God help him if she wasn't the most intoxicating woman he had ever seen in his life.

He bent his head to kiss the tight, puckered tips

of her nipples, the valley in between her breasts, the dip of her navel, the flat of her tummy, her thighs. Her head was back, her eyes closed, as he found the sweet blossoming essence of her. She moaned again, and he kissed and explored and stroked some more, until she quivered in ecstasy.

And then she was saying, "More."

More of him.

She unbuttoned and unzipped with the same skill he had possessed, taking a leisurely tour that easily could have had them both climaxing had he not called a halt to find a condom. They moved to the bed and she arched against him pliantly. He moved her hand to the proof of his desire, wanting her to feel, *really* feel, what she did to him, too.

He palmed her breasts. She clutched his biceps. Already cradled by her open thighs, he slid into her.

Susannah cried out, shuddering in pleasure. And still they kissed and kissed. His strokes were long and slow, making them both want and need, and need some more. Until, finally, that was all it took. Her body sizzled with sensation; his followed suit. And as she came, she took him along with her, their locked gazes as steadfast as this moment in time.

"Any chance your babysitters could stay later?"

Susannah sighed and shook her head. "Nope. Like me, their evenings end at midnight."

"What about tomorrow?" Gabe dressed, too. "How can I help you then?"

She turned to face him, looking deliciously sated. Her pretty eyes widened. "Seriously…?"

He brought her closer for another kiss, then followed her out to his truck, where she slipped into the passenger seat. As he drove, she plucked a brush from her purse and began restoring order to her honey-blond hair.

"Yes, seriously," he said.

"Well…" She opened up a compact, plucked a lipstick from her purse and began applying a soft coat of rose just slightly darker than the natural hue of her lips. "Mike and Millie are watching the kids for me in the morning, so I can continue working on the sketches. And then the kids will be asleep in the afternoon, so hopefully I can work more then. But during the witching hour…"

"Witching hour?" Cade asked, parking in front of her house. He walked around to open her door for her.

Grinning, Susannah stepped out and linked arms with him. "The time before dinner when all their mischievousness seems to come out at once," she explained as they strolled up the walk. "I can always use help then." She winked as they reached the front porch. "If you're up to it, that is."

Loving the challenge in her eyes, he grinned down at her. "I'd love to drop by." He tucked an errant strand of hair behind her ear. "Three o'clock okay?"

"Three o'clock is perfect," she said softly.

Gabe bent his head, intending to steal a quick good-night kiss. She stepped in. Their lips met. And the two teenage babysitters opened the front door.

"Whoops," the shorter one said. "Didn't mean to spoil the moment."

Didn't they know? Gabe wondered. Nothing could spoil their evening. It had been perfect in every way.

Chapter Eleven

"Hot date last night?" Millie said as she breezed in the next morning shortly after breakfast.

The kids were lined up on the sofa, watching their allotted hour of their favorite show, *Paw Patrol*, which was the only way Susannah was able to get a shower and the breakfast dishes done in a timely manner every day.

Daisy was curled up next to them, her head on her paws, half dozing, half watching over them.

"Oh…" Susannah paused, not sure how to describe it without giving up her privacy. She walked into the adjacent laundry room and took a load from the dryer. She put the clean linens on the long counter that topped both units and began to fold. "You know…" She waved the air vaguely.

Millie took in the blush creeping across her cheeks. "I do. And I'm happy for you, darling, if it makes you look like that."

"Well, don't read too much into it," she advised, heating at the memory of her and Gabe's red-hot interlude. If only they'd been in love! Instead of just in lust!

Millie reached over to fold washcloths and stack them, one on top of the other, while Susannah concentrated on the towels. "What do you mean?"

"He has an ulterior motive. He's anxious to get the portrait done before he leaves for another PWB assignment in September, so he can be here to see his dad receive it. To ensure that happens, he's going to come by whenever he can in the afternoons to help me out with the kids, so I can get some extra time in on it."

Millie smiled. Finished, she began helping with the bath towels, too. "Sounds nice. And practical."

Susannah knelt down and began transferring damp clothes from the washer to the dryer. "It is."

"But?" Millie prodded, assisting with that, too.

I worry he'll get tired of spending so much time with me and the kids. Worry that will ruin what we have. Susannah added a softening sheet to the load. Shut the door and switched it on. "I worry about taking advantage of his generosity."

Millie moved out of the way while Susannah began putting in yet another load. "So repay him, the way you repay everyone else. With food."

They said the way to a man's heart was through his stomach. "You mean, bake him cookies?"

"Invite him to dinner. Whenever he's around."

Susannah added detergent and switched on the machine. "We have mostly kid fare."

"So add a few sophisticated side dishes for the adults, if you think that is what he wants. But honestly, if he works in the remote locations Physicians Without Borders is often known for, I imagine he is used to making do with everything from meals ready to eat to whatever the locals are having."

Susannah envisioned Gabe somewhere out in the jungle, all sweaty and gorgeous, looking all noble, doing his humanitarian work. She felt her heartbeat kick up another notch.

Aware Millie was watching her closely, she did her best to hide her desire and said, "That's true."

As they walked toward the living room, Millie reached in the front hall closet for her date-night dress. "Mind if I try this on again to see how much progress I'm making?"

Susannah shook her head, then, since Millie did not appear to be worried about spoiling her surprise for her husband, asked, "Is Mike not coming over this morning, too?"

Millie slipped into the downstairs powder room, which was tucked beneath the stairs, and left the door open just enough to be able to talk. "He'll be here later. He's still a little tired. So he's staying over there for a while to have an extra cup of coffee, and if I know him, to also sneak a couple extra of those Australian and/or Dutch candies he likes."

Susannah recalled how sick he'd been just days before. "Is the high-potassium diet helping him feel better?"

"I think so. Still, we decided to skip our line-dancing club trip this week."

"Really?"

Millie emerged from the powder room, looking pretty as could be in the little black dress. "I'll make it up to him on Father's Day. You know how we like to get out of town for that, do something distracting."

Susannah did, since she often felt the same, since losing her own dad and having quints without one. She cast a glance over at the kids, who were still engrossed in *Paw Patrol*, then turned back to Millie and said quietly, "About that… I had an idea that maybe the kids and I could do something for him, since he has been like a dad to me and a grandfather to them."

Millie's eyes widened in surprise, then began to glimmer moistly.

Guilt mingled with the emotion in Susannah's heart. "I know we didn't celebrate Mother's Day with you, even though the two of you came to my rescue this past Mother's Day to make sure that I had a good day. But we should have done something official for you that day, too, because you've been more than just my best friend—you've been a mom to me the last four years."

Abruptly, Susannah was so choked up she couldn't go on. Millie teared up, too.

Susannah forced herself to go on, revealing what was in her heart. "I really think that the kids should honor Mike on Father's Day this year, as their grandpa. In fact, they should start calling you Grandma Millie and Grandpa Mike, if it's okay with you all."

Joy exuding from her smile, Millie hugged her warmly. "Oh, sweetheart, we would love that."

As they moved apart, Susannah smiled over at her in relief. "Us, too."

That settled, they got back on task, and Millie turned to show Susannah the back of the dress. "So, what do you think? Am I getting any closer to being able to zip this thing?"

Susannah hated to disappoint, but she had to be honest. "I think it's still an inch and a half, minimum, from where it needs to be to close."

Millie's face fell in disappointment.

"Maybe if you took it to a tailor and had them let out the seams as much as possible. Or add a little strip of fabric along each side in the same black knit…"

"No. I want to wear it the same way I wore it then," Millie said stubbornly. "I know, I know, it's irrational, but I can't help it. I just really want to get into this dress. But not to worry. I have my special blend of calming antioxidant sassafras tea that is supposed to be good for weight loss, too. I'll just drink more of that. It really does curb my appetite. Who knows—" she smiled "—maybe it will help me stay away from Mike's stash of Dutch and Australian candy. In the meantime, you need to get to work while I'm here to watch the kids…and stop worrying—" she winked playfully "—about how irrational love can be."

Millie was right about that, Susannah thought as she took her sketch pads, photos and laptop computer upstairs to the desk in her bedroom.

Love *was* irrational.

Her feelings about Gabe were irrational, too. Not that it was love, per se, or ever would be, that the two of them were experiencing. But it was certainly attraction, and desire, and he was so great to be around. Of course it wasn't wise to be falling for him so hard, but she couldn't seem to help it.

Any more than Millie could stop wanting to re-create the perfect first date she and Mike'd had as an anniversary surprise for him.

So maybe that was a sign she should stop wishing for the impossibly perfect romance and accept what fate was giving her in the here and now instead.

Mike joined them a short time later, and although his color was a lot better than it had been, Susannah couldn't help but note that he still seemed fatigued, just as Millie had said. She mentioned it to Gabe when he came over later that afternoon to help her out with the kids.

"Is it something to worry about?" she asked when she finished explaining her concern.

Gabe helped her set out the afternoon snack for the kids. Breaking their graham crackers into quarters, just the way they liked them. "Not unless the low potassium and high blood pressure combination continues, and it shouldn't, as long as he takes his medication as prescribed and follows the diet the doctor set out for him."

Susannah portioned spoonfuls of vanilla yogurt into little dipping cups. "I know he's doing both those things."

"Then he should get better. Quickly," Gabe said, putting ice into the sippy cups. "If he doesn't, I'm sure his family doctor will run more tests."

"You're right." Susannah poured in the water.

Together, they snapped on the lids and set the cups at the places at the table. Now all they had to do was wait for the kids to wake up from their naps, which should be at any time.

Gabe lounged close by, his hands braced on either side of him. "Is Millie worried, too?"

Susannah settled next to him, inhaling the brisk masculine scent of his soap and skin. "Only about getting into her dress."

"Ah. I'm sure she'll find a way."

Wondering if she would ever be less physically aware of him, Susannah took in his easy smile and tall, powerful physique. "You don't think it's silly?"

His gaze tracked the careless way she had pinned her hair away from her face, and she could tell he was thinking about taking it right back down again. "I think it's sweet," he said. "How much she and Mike adore each other."

Trying not to think about the hot, hungry look in his eyes, Susannah swung away and busied herself making tall glasses of iced tea for them both. "Me, too."

"So did you need me to do anything else to help out…besides watching the kids while you work on the portrait?"

Susannah swallowed around the sudden dryness of her throat. "Stay for dinner?"

Gabe had been hoping she'd ask.

"I want to repay you for helping out by watching the kids this afternoon."

Not like that, as one commodity exchanged for another, however.

Still he knew that was how Susannah worked. She didn't accept one kindness without doling out another in return. He sipped his tea and wondered what it would take to get her to let him all the way in. And why it was so important to him to entice her to do just that. "How is the portrait going?" he asked casually.

Susannah picked up her iced tea and led the way down the back hall to her sunny studio. There, on a large bulletin board attached to the only wall without a lot of windows, were sketches of all the family dogs that she had done thus far. "See for yourself," she said, checking out his reaction.

"I mean, it's still in the planning stages," she added, pointing to the work in progress.

As well as eye-catching. "I really like what you've done so far," he said, meaning it. She was really talented.

She beamed with pride. "Thanks."

As she moved restlessly about the studio, her full cotton skirt swirled around her bare legs, drawing his attention to her slender ankles, curvaceous calves and taut hips.

Sobering, she began to talk about the work. "I heard back from all of your siblings, and they all had helpful suggestions regarding the personalities of their pets. Cade said his Labrador retriever was athletic as could be and loved playing Frisbee with him."

Because there was no place to sit down except at the drafting table where she was currently perched, Gabe took up a place against the windows. Watched the midafternoon sun catch the gold in her honey-blond hair. "Hercules did have some truly impressive moves."

She paused to study the sketches and the written notes and photos she'd tacked up beside each one. Blue eyes sparkling with delight, she recited, "Griff's malamute slept all the time and had to be coaxed into any activity."

"Also true."

"Jillian said her childhood beagle was very shy and was always hiding behind her legs."

Gabe laughed, recalling.

"Faith's Australian shepherd was very cuddly. Emma's boxer was adventurous. Noah's hound dog was steadfast. Travis's mutt was scrappy."

As was the woman in front of him, Gabe thought. To the point he wondered that he had ever imagined she couldn't handle life on her own.

Oblivious to his thoughts, Susannah came nearer

in a drift of her familiar wildflower fragrance. She paused to look at him in a way that made him want to haul her close and kiss her and make love to her all over again.

Her mind only on business, however, she raked her teeth across her lower lip and said, "What I don't have enough information on is your mom and dad's first two dogs, the ones they had before you all were adopted."

Gabe could see where that would be a problem.

"So—" she drew in a soft breath "—I was wondering if you could ask your mother if she knows anything in particular that might help me. Or, better yet," she pushed on, a little more reluctantly, as if she were fearful of crossing some invisible line, "if you could get your dad to reminisce and talk about what those pets were like. Maybe this Sunday—on Father's Day—because I imagine you're going to see him then?"

"Yes, I am," Gabe returned, letting her know with a look that whatever she wanted and needed was okay with him. He pushed away from the window and edged closer to her, enjoying her aura of femininity.

Wishing he didn't have to worry about the kids waking up and walking in on them and he could just make love with her again, he reined his desire in for later and said, "And in fact, I was going to ask if you and the kids wanted to go out to the ranch with me and attend the barbecue they're having. There are going to be a lot of people there. It would be fun."

Plus, his family wasn't just going to love the pet

portrait she was doing for his dad—they were already starting to love her. As a person, as an artist. Maybe, if he were lucky, even as a potential romantic interest for him.

Susannah's face fell. "Oh."

He had an answering arrow of disappointment. "Too much too soon?" he asked lightly.

"N-no." She flushed prettily and wrung her hands in front of her. "It's just we already have plans with Mike and Millie. We've decided to formalize our relationship a little more. They're going to be the kids' grandparents as well as our good family friends."

Aware all over again just how much he enjoyed spending time with her, he let his gaze rove over her face. "That's great."

"I mean, it doesn't make up for the quintuplets not having a daddy." She ducked her head shyly. "I know that. But it will make things more normal for them, so maybe they will stop trying to get me married off."

He tugged on an errant lock of her silky hair. "I can see where that would cut back on your embarrassment."

She wrinkled her nose. "You think?"

They exchanged grins, and he dropped his hand, stepped back. Wishing he didn't know she thought their lovemaking might be all about lust and loneliness and little more.

"Anyway, everyone is happy about that," she continued.

"Especially you," Gabe guessed, his protective

instincts coming to the fore once again. Because he knew they could have more, if she would allow it.

Raking her teeth over her lush lower lip, her gaze turned thoughtful as she agreed. "Especially me."

"I'm glad," Gabe told her tenderly.

He just wished he knew what that meant for him. *Was* Susannah inching toward having more family in her life, despite her outward denials to the contrary? And was he crazy to be thinking she might be wanting more from their fast-growing relationship, too?

"Any particular reason you didn't bring Susannah and the quintuplets to the barbecue this afternoon?" Carol Lockhart asked as the sun went down and the last of their guests left.

Gabe pocketed the additional pictures of his dad's late dog, Rocky, that she had just clandestinely handed him.

Briefly, he explained the plans they'd had with Mike and Millie. "That's wonderful," Carol enthused, hearing about their newly anointed grandparent status to the quintuplets. "You have to take family where you can find it."

Gabe nodded and gave his mom a hug. "Millie and Mike Smith are that to her, for sure."

The question was, would he ever receive enhanced status, too?

Gabe was still thinking about that as he drove back into town. Thinking it might not be too late to drop the latest pictures and information off, he headed over to Susannah's home. The lights were on. He parked at the curb and reached for his phone and texted her, I've got a couple of stories to tell you about Rocky that might shed light on his personality. More photos from his last years and puppyhood, too.

Terrific! she wrote back. When can I have them?

Now...?

There was a pause. More blinking dots on his cell phone screen that signified typing on her end. Where are you? she texted.

Fifty feet from your door, he wrote back.

The blinds shifted. The front door opened, and just like that, a widely smiling Susannah waved him in.

Susannah had been hoping Gabe would stop by this evening. It was why she hadn't changed out of the pretty sundress and sandals she'd worn earlier, and instead of taking off her makeup, had freshened her lipstick a little while ago instead. He looked nice himself, in a short-sleeved navy polo shirt that molded to the muscular contours of his broad shoulders and chest, dark jeans and boots.

"Kids asleep?" he whispered, looking more handsome than ever with a hint of evening beard lining his strong jaw.

Fighting the tingle of sensual awareness sifting through her, Susannah nodded. She moved away from his tall, sturdy frame, flashing a matter-of-fact smile that was so much less than what she was feeling. Casually, she reported, "They were snoozing before the sun went down." She met his gaze. "I was just about to have a cup of that special blend sassafras tea Millie has been raving about. Want to join me?"

"Sure."

While she poured two mugs from the kettle and set out the sugar and lemon, he looked at the sketches spread over her breakfast table. There were more laid out on the kitchen island. As well as a container of drawing pencils and a big sketch pad with the half-finished sketch of Rocky on it. Another, even larger drawing, with all the dogs romping across the meadow. "Wow, you have been busy."

Susannah sipped her tea, admitting happily, "The work is starting to take on a life of its own."

"I can see that." He walked around, admiring the progress she'd made since he last looked at her sketches, while sipping the tea that seemed to be a mixture of herbs and spices and some sort of candy-like sweetness. "It's nice."

"Thanks."

She glanced at the child monitors she had set up on the kitchen, saw her children sleeping soundly in their beds, the two boys in their room, the three girls in theirs. Satisfied all was well, she opened up the back door, switched on the outdoor lights and eased out onto the porch. The scent of the flowers she'd planted rose up to greet them. Although this wasn't a date... it was beginning to feel like one. Determined to get the conversation back to business instead of her increasing feelings for him, she asked crisply, "So, what were these stories you had for me?"

Gabe sat beside her on the chain-hung swing, leaving a little distance between their bodies. His voice low and sexy, he told a story of Rocky leaping onto the kitchen counter to devour a just-frosted coconut layer cake, his black muzzle covered in white. Then relayed another, of the year-old black Lab getting stuck while trying to hide beneath the bed, after taking off with a porterhouse steak that had been ready to go on the grill. "He was trying to hide it for later, but the trail of marinade gave him away."

Still sipping her tea, Susannah grinned over the photos of both incidents. She turned to Gabe, her knee accidentally nudging his thigh. "So all of Rocky's antics were related to food?"

Gabe chuckled. "No surprise there. Labrador retrievers are always hungry."

Susannah gazed up at the moon shining down on them, reflecting, "Well, then, it might be cute, depicting him taking off across the meadow with a steak in his jaws." She sucked in a breath as pain radiated across the center of her chest. "I'll run it past your mom, see what she thinks." Susannah paused as another stab of pain hit her and put her hand right above her sternum.

Gabe picked up on her discomfort. His brow furrowed. "Everything okay?"

Susannah moaned softly as she endured another wave of pain between her breasts. Unfortunately, this was all too familiar. "Reflux," she said.

"Bad?"

Was it ever. "Ah, yeah. It is." Embarrassed, Susannah rose and moved off the swing, the taste of acid rising in her throat.

Gabe followed, slipping into physician mode. "Do you get it often?" he asked gently.

Susannah shook her head and looked into the top of the kitchen cabinet for the box of prescription medications she kept on hand. She found what she needed and took a pill with a small sip of water. "The first time I had it was after Brett and Belinda died. The doctor felt it was triggered by grief. The next time was during the last two trimesters of my pregnancy with the quints. That was understandable, too."

"Because of the pressure the babies put on the stomach."

"And the stress of it." Going back into the kitchen, she got a container of yogurt out of the fridge. She put a couple of spoonfuls in a small dish, offered Gabe some. He shook his head.

Leaning against the counter, she took a small bite. Let it stay in her mouth a moment, to get rid of the acid taste.

Gabe regarded her tenderly. More friend and lover now than physician. "Was pregnancy very hard on you?"

Susannah took a deep breath, willing the reflux away. "Multiple pregnancies are hard in general—you were right about that."

His arm slid protectively around her shoulders as he took up a place beside her. "But Mike and Millie were there for you all."

Despite her trepidation about getting too close to

him, emotionally, lest it hurt too much when he eventually left again, Susannah relaxed into his comforting embrace. "As was all the rest of the medical staff at Laramie Community Hospital," she murmured, remembering fondly. "It was a very exciting time."

Gabe leaned over and pressed a kiss on her brow, picking up on all she hadn't said. "And yet...?"

Susannah turned to him wistfully. "There were plenty of times that I wished I'd had a boyfriend or a husband to see me through it and share in the joy."

Briefly, Gabe looked as if he wished that had been the case for her, too. "Did the reflux pass after you delivered the babies?" he asked eventually.

"For the most part." Susannah smiled. "I mean, occasionally I'll have a flare-up, but most of the time I am fine."

"What do you think is causing it tonight?" Gabe was in physician mode again.

Good question. Susannah took another bite of yogurt. She thought about the excitement the quintuplets had evidenced over now having a grandpa and grandma, and her worry that one day they would again focus on the fact they still did not have a father and would not likely get one, either. Although for now Gabe was a good stand-in for one. But he would be gone again at summer's end, too. "Probably stress," she said eventually.

"Over the work you're doing, or what happened to Mike this week?"

And us. What I might be letting myself in for, when

you eventually depart, as we both know you will. Will I be able to handle it? Will the quints?

"Probably a little of both, plus financial stress, maybe," Susannah said cagily.

Gabe frowned and moved to stand opposite her, his hands braced on the countertop on either side of him. He studied her face. "Have you had more conversations with Bing?"

Susannah sighed. "We talked on the phone. He still thinks I need a better long-range plan than just increasing my income through more commissions if we want to be really secure." But what that would be, Susannah did not know. Her options were pretty limited, unless she decided to sell the house and take all the equity out and invest it. And she did not want to uproot the kids and live elsewhere.

Gabe came closer yet again, all protective male, prodding, "And you think you should…?"

Be very careful of my heart.

Susannah shrugged, looked him in the eye and said, "For right now, I'm happy to take things day by day."

And she did not want to think beyond that.

Chapter Twelve

"Good to see you again." Several days later, Bing shook Gabe's hand in the bank lobby, then ushered him into his private office for their prescheduled appointment. "What can I do for you?"

Gabe sat down and got out his checkbook. "I'd like to set up education saving accounts for Susannah Alexander's quintuplets."

Bing slipped behind his desk, his expression genial but wary. "First of all, they already have a general welfare trust that she set up for them. And second, shouldn't she be here for this?"

Ah. The hard part. "She doesn't know about it," Gabe said.

Bing cocked a brow. "Shouldn't she? Given the fact these are her children?"

Gabe shared the other man's protectiveness when it came to Susannah and her kids. "Believe me, if I thought she would readily agree, I would tell her right now of my intentions."

"But she won't," Bing guessed with a frown.

"I don't think so, no."

For a moment, neither of them said anything. "I didn't know the two of you were that serious, romantically," Bing said finally.

Neither did I, Gabe thought, until he'd listened to her worries and nursed her through her bout of reflux. Then, all he had wanted to do was take care of her and the kids. Not just on a casual, daily basis while he was in town. But long term, in every way. Gabe exhaled. "Can I speak to you in confidence?"

Bing reached into his drawer and brought out a pamphlet. He handed it to Gabe. "Yes. The bank has strict rules regarding client privacy. Even if they didn't, I can be trusted to keep a confidence."

Aware it was past time he unburdened himself to someone, Gabe leaned back in his chair. "Susannah's twin, Belinda, and her husband, Brett, asked me to keep an eye on Susannah before they left on that last fateful trip. They also tasked me with caring for the embryos if something happened to them, and if Susannah did not feel up to dealing with the situation."

"But she did…"

"So I considered my commitments honored and backed off until I came back to Texas and found out what had happened in my absence, and the financial difficulties she's now facing. The bottom line is

I've got a lot of money saved up and nothing really to spend it on, and she and the kids could really use it. So I thought if I set up individual college savings accounts for each of them and added to them each year, they'd be in a much better situation when they do reach college age."

Bing nodded agreeably. "They definitely would be. And you would realize a tax advantage, too, in the meantime. But I have to ask. What happens if you and Susannah have a falling-out? Once you gift them the money," he warned, "you can't get it back."

"I wouldn't want it back," Gabe said firmly.

Bing lifted a skeptical brow.

Gabe went on, "I want to know that all the quintuplets will be okay. That they will have choices later on, the kind that Susannah is worried she won't be able to give them."

Bing tapped his pen. "This makes sense if you two were going to get married, but even then I would advise waiting until everything is official and the vows were said."

Without warning, Gabe had a fleeting image of Susannah walking down the aisle toward him, her beloved golden retriever and all of her children surrounding her. "We're not getting married," he said firmly. Although now that Bing had brought it up… Gabe had to admit he wasn't averse to the idea of joining forces with Susannah permanently in some way or other…

"Okay." Bing got out a pad of paper and began to make some notes. He paused to look up, asking,

"Well, what if you go on to marry and/or have children with someone else? How is a prospective spouse going to feel about you providing for someone else's children?"

Unable to see himself with anyone else, now or at any time in the future, Gabe shrugged. "Good, I would hope. Otherwise I can't see myself being involved with them."

Bing jotted a note. "What happens if she marries someone else?"

Honestly? Gabe couldn't see that happening, either. He gestured offhandedly. "She's pretty independent."

Bing chuckled ruefully. "Don't I know it. Still—" the banker sobered "—this is a big decision."

One that had already lifted a weight off Gabe's shoulders. And would make it possible—he hoped, anyway—for him to go back to PWB in September without worrying about the future of her and the kids.

"So if you wanted to wait, really think it over some more," Bing continued.

Gabe shook his head. "My mind is made up. I'm doing it. And I'm doing it today whether you help me or not."

When and how and where he would inform Susannah about what he had done was a question for another day.

"How come you don't have to work?" the kids asked Gabe later the same afternoon, when he went over to take care of them for a few hours in the late afternoon.

"My mommy has to work," Gretchen pointed out, sitting at the breakfast table and coloring in plain view of her mother, who was currently painting a portrait in the adjacent sunroom.

"Yeah," Connor added, coloring, too. "She says all adults have to work."

Abigail squinted. "Are you retired, like Millie and Mike?"

"No," Gabe explained. At the children's request, he was coloring, too. "I'm on leave."

Rebecca took her thumb out of her mouth and scoffed. "Leaves are on trees, silly."

"No. Leave..." Gabe found himself spelling it out—to whose benefit he did not know "...is like a vacation. Only it's a little longer, and it's because I didn't take any time off for a very long while. But, just so you all know, I am going back to work part-time starting tomorrow morning."

Susannah walked out of her studio. Pulling a drink out of the fridge, she asked, "Where?"

Gabe sat back in his chair. In painting attire consisting of a loose-fitting button-up and shorts, with her chin-length hair held back in barrettes, her face and lips bare, she was still as gorgeous as could be.

Aware she was still waiting for his reply, but not about to tell her what had really changed his mind about accepting the position...aka the college savings accounts...and the wish to put even more money in them, he said, "The hospital. They need an infectious disease person on their diagnostic team and offered me a temporary contract position until they find someone with the kind of international health experience that's required. Hopefully, they'll have a permanent person by the time I head back overseas at summer's end."

Susannah paused, her uncapped bottle of water halfway to her lips. "So does this mean no more helping me out?" she asked, a little panicked.

Not about to let her down, Gabe shook his head. "I'm only working mornings, from six until noon. Mostly, I'll be reviewing cases that have the rest of the staff stumped. I'll still be here every afternoon you want me," he said.

"Yay!" the kids chorused in unison.

"We like you, Dr. Gabe!" the boys yelled.

"And we love you, too!" the girls enthused.

Susannah blushed in a way that reminded Gabe it had been far too long since they'd had a date. And they needed one if they were ever going to make love again. Although he enjoyed spending time with her and the kids an awful lot, too.

Composed again, she looked at Gabe. "Can I get you anything?"

How about your lips on mine? "Not right now," he said, saving his private request for later, when they were alone.

She smiled shyly. "I'm really in the middle of something, so if it's okay with you, we'll delay dinner a bit this evening?"

"Sure."

"In the meantime…" Susannah set out an afternoon snack for everyone, including Gabe. "Back to the studio…"

As she headed into her multi-windowed art space, he couldn't help but note how happy she looked when she painted.

The kids went back to alternately coloring their pictures and eating their afternoon snack. And with it came a whole new slew of questions. "Dr. Gabe, how come you don't have kids?"

Because I've been a fool. Because had he been as adventurous as Susannah in this regard, Gabe knew he could have had what she had now—a lively, loving family of his own. Wondering if Susannah was still half listening to everything they were talking about, he directed his attention to the kids and said, "I don't know the answer to that."

Levi paused. "Couldn't you find any?"

Gabe blinked. "Ah…what?"

Abigail gestured importantly. "Mommy says babies are born at the hospital. And you work at the hospital now. You just said so. So, why don't you have babies? Couldn't you find some there and bring them home?"

The door to the studio opened yet again. The chagrined look on Susannah's face indicated she had indeed heard everything the quints had said. "Hey, kiddos! I forgot to mention it's not too hot to be outside today. So…when you finish your snacks and your drawings, you can go outside and play for a little while."

"Okay, Mommy," her children chorused happily.

"Sorry," Susannah mouthed to Gabe and slipped back into her studio.

"How come you're not married, Dr. Gabe?" Gretchen asked.

"Mommy isn't married because things are too complicated," Connor reported.

"Are things too complicated for you, too?" Gretchen asked.

Out of the corner of his eye, Gabe saw Susannah press the heel of her hand against her forehead.

Meanwhile, the kids were waiting. Gabe tried to come up with a reply that would satisfy them while not giving their mom any wrong ideas about him. "That's sort of why," he said eventually. Although in many ways his life was getting simpler. In ways he really liked.

"I'm done!" Levi shouted happily, waving his colorful picture of a truck.

"Me, too!" His siblings followed his lead. Chairs pushed back. Pictures were left out for their mommy to see. Crayons put back in the caddy. Trash thrown away. Abigail took the lead as group spokesperson. "We cleaned up, so can we go swing now?"

"Yes," Gabe said, holding the back door open for them. "I'll watch you out the window and be out in a second." They filed out and, her fluffy golden tail wagging happily, Daisy headed out with them.

Gabe moved to the window. Before he could decide his next move, Susannah was at his side again. Her soft hand curved over his bicep. "Had enough questions for one day?" she teased. "Or should I ask you a few more?"

Gabe turned toward her, realizing all over again how glad he was that she was now in his life. He looked down at her, caressing the curve of her cheek with the pad of his thumb. "I've got one for you. When are you going to make time to go out with me again?"

Susannah smiled. "If I can get a couple of sitters last minute, we could go out tonight after the kids are asleep."

"We can do this another evening," Susannah said five hours later, as what was supposed to have been a simple night out had turned into the Murphy's law of whatever can go wrong will go wrong type of evening.

Sensing something was up, they'd been uncooperative during dinner and bath time. And now, a little before nine o'clock, the quintuplets were still not asleep. And she knew if she and Gabe left the house before her children drifted off, they'd give their two babysitters nonstop problems and still be up when she got home at midnight.

The problem was, she'd forgotten to tell Gabe not to arrive until after she had given him the all-clear signal. So he had arrived, right on time, at eight o'clock, which had, in turn, made the kids go wild with excitement to be seeing him *twice* in one day.

"Are we going to play games, Dr. Gabe?" Connor had asked.

"Yay! How about Father May I?" Levi had shouted.

"Or Farmer in the Dell!" Gretchen had suggested.

"How about we all say good-night and go back upstairs to bed?" Susannah had asked, while Cindy and Susan, her sitters, stood by, looking a little overwhelmed.

"I don't want to stay with the babysitters, Mommy! I want to go out with you and Gabe!" Gretchen stomped her foot.

"Me, either!" her sisters said in unison, beginning to cry.

The next thing they knew, all three girls were weeping, while the two boys were hooting and hollering, "Watch this!" and running up the stairs and attempting to slide down the banister.

It was Vintage Kiddie Chaos 101. And then some.

"Whoa, there, fellas." Gabe plucked them off, settling one little boy on each hip.

"How come Dr. Gabe gets to carry them!" Abigail wailed, jealous and upset.

"Giddy-up!" Connor and Levi yelled.

Exasperated, Susannah looked at Gabe. "I'm serious. You don't have to stay and wait around for things to calm down." Which she knew very well they might not, at least not for a good while. Especially while he was still there. "We can try this again another evening."

He shook his head at her as if to say, *No way am I giving up on us.* Then looked down at the boys in his arms. "Tell you what, little wranglers. I will go upstairs with you if you promise to play the quiet game with me."

Levi snorted in derision. "Nah. You just want us to go to sleep!"

"Noooo," Gabe disagreed immediately, his expression serious. "The whole *point* of nighttime quiet game is *not* to fall asleep. You just close your eyes and *pretend* you are getting *really sleepy*, but then you don't fall asleep after all. When I was growing up, my brothers and sisters and I used to play it all the time. And guess who won?"

"You!" they shouted in unison.

"So," Gabe drawled, grinning encouragingly, "do you want to play it or not?"

"We'll play!" an overstimulated Levi shouted at the top of his lungs, while still hanging on to Gabe's wide shoulder with all his might.

"But I am *not* falling asleep!" Connor declared with an impish grin.

"Me neither!" Gretchen said.

And they didn't. Not for a good half an hour, anyway. Finally, though, the giggles stopped. Gabe's breathing was so deep and even, Susannah thought he might have fallen asleep. She looked over at him where he was sitting in the bedroom opposite the one she and the girls were in, his back to the wall.

All five of the children slumbered on.

Soundlessly, she slipped off her shoes and rose.

Just that suddenly, he opened his eyes. Smiled.

And they were free.

* * *

They practically danced out to his truck, they were so excited to finally be starting their date. Trying not to notice how wonderfully cozy it felt to be in such close proximity with him again, she settled into the passenger seat. As their gazes met, Susannah felt a shiver run through her.

He caught her hand, then flashed her a sexy grin. "So, what next?"

Good question, Susannah thought, watching her fingers mingle with his. Aware he was going to be very hard to resist, Susannah tried to slow her pounding heart and said, "Well, it's nine-thirty. Which means, since it's a weeknight, all the sit-down restaurants in town are getting ready to close."

He frowned. "Including the Wagon Wheel, where we had dinner reservations."

"So, what now?"

He shrugged and let her go to start the engine so they could be on their way. "The Dairy Barn is open until eleven…"

She grinned at the G-rated nature of their date. It wasn't exactly what she had been expecting. "Then the Dairy Barn it is."

Luckily, there was no line this late at night, so they got their burgers, fries and shakes and carried them to one of the outdoor picnic tables. "So, when do you start at the hospital?" Susannah asked conversationally as they began to eat.

He opened a ketchup packet and poured the sauce into a corner of the paper tray. "Tomorrow, 6:00 a.m."

She paused, aware she might have been inadvertently inconsiderate to him. "You want to make an early night of it, then?"

He laughed, the sound warm and throaty. "Actually, I'd like to make it an exciting night," he teased. "What time do you have to be back for your sitters?"

It was Susannah's turn to frown. "Midnight."

Gabe waggled his brows as he spread his napkin onto his lap. "I guess we're going to find out, then," he told her mysteriously.

Susannah paused, her cheeseburger halfway to her mouth. "Find out what?"

His whiskey-colored eyes twinkled. "Just how much fun we can pack in two and a half hours."

Quite a lot, as it happened. They talked as they ate, simultaneously watching the teenagers having a blast at the Putt-Putt course next door. When they finished, Gabe asked, "Want to play a game?"

Another time, the answer would have been a resounding yes. That evening? "I'd rather…" Feeling a little wicked and a lot adventurous, Susannah leaned over to whisper in his ear.

And this time, when Gabe laughed in response, it was with lusty anticipation.

The passion in his voice stole her breath. "We don't have much time," he told her when they got to his brother's home.

They kicked off their shoes and kissed their way through the living room, down the hall, toward the bedrooms. "You'd be surprised what can happen in an hour and a half, Doc—if you're determined, that is," she promised, guiding his face down to hers.

"And are you?" he asked, melding his lips with hers, evoking a wealth of lust and complex emotions she didn't want to admit existed.

She moaned, even as she kissed him back passionately. She hadn't allowed herself to want anything for herself for such a long time. But she found herself wanting this. Wanting *him*…

"Resolved?" she breathed, resting her head on the solid curve of his shoulder. Drinking in the scent and feel and warmth of him. "Oh, yes…"

"Good to hear." He shut the bedroom door and guided her up against the wall, his strong, hard body ensconced in the open vee of her legs. His eyes held hers with the promise of the passionate lovemaking to come. He reached beneath her dress, hooking his fingers in the elastic of her panties, easing them down her legs. She arched, her breasts brushing against his chest, as his lips found the sensitive place behind her ear.

Still driving her mad with sensation, he kissed her again, deeply and rapturously, even as his hands roved even higher. She trembled as he kneaded her breasts, caressing the tender crests through the silky-smooth cotton of her sundress and bra. And then slowly, ardently, his hands moved from her breasts to her thighs to the sweet spot between, and then back again. Overwhelmed by the pleasurable sensations, she returned his embrace with everything she had, easing her hands beneath the waistband of his jeans, finding him hot, hard, ready.

As ready as she.

With a low moan of impatience, she wrapped a leg around his waist, opening herself up to him. And still they kissed, soft and sweet, slow and deep, and all the ways in between.

Until she could stand it no more. With a low, shuddering moan, she felt her body go up in flames. Let him take her to his bed to undress her and wait while she undressed him.

He found a condom. Then tumbled back down onto the bed.

He lifted her overtop of him. She straddled his middle, then stretched her body out languidly over his, her heat cradling his pulsing hardness. Sank lower, tantalizing him, until he rolled her so she was beneath him. Hearts flooding with feeling, triumph rising in their throats, he finally slid home, and she trembled and clenched around him.

Claiming him. Loving him. New sensations spiraling and ricocheting inside her. Until it was all so hot and wild and free, and both of them were soaring in passion and pleasure, tenderness and surrender.

Afterward, they clung together, still trembling with pleasure. Then made love again, more slowly and languidly this time. When their tryst ended, Susannah knew the clock was ticking. That this would have to hold them, and that she was never so content as she was when she was with him.

Reluctantly, she got up, found her clothes and

began to dress. He glanced at the clock and did the same. Finished, she sat on the edge of the bed next to him. He pulled her to him for a long, thorough kiss that quickly had her tingling from head to toe. She splayed a hand over his chest, wishing they had more time, that they didn't have to go. And instead could remain together, sleeping, locked in each other's arms, only to wake and make love all over again.

But it wasn't to be.

Not tonight, anyway.

She let out a grateful breath. "You were so sweet with the kids tonight."

"It's not like it's a chore, you know." He grinned and shifted her onto his lap. "I've had more fun this summer with all of you than I've had in years."

"It's been great for all of us, too," she admitted contentedly. Then added, even more candidly, before she could stop herself, "The kids really love you, you know."

Their glances meshed, held for a long, heart-stopping moment. "I love them, too," he returned huskily.

Now, Susannah thought wistfully, if only he would love her, too. Her life really would be complete.

Chapter Thirteen

To Susannah's delight, the next few weeks took on even more of a satisfying routine. Mornings she worked, with the help of either Millie and Mike or teenage babysitters, and Gabe went to the hospital. Midday she was on her own while the kids napped. Which usually allowed her to get in a little more time to work on the pet portrait for Robert Lockhart.

Then, late afternoon, Gabe stopped by to help with the kids while she finished up in the studio. Sometimes they cooked dinner together; other times, one cooked and the other supervised the little ones. A few times they even went out to eat, either at the pizza place in town or the Dairy Barn.

One night a week, they managed to go on a date. No matter where it started, it always ended up in the same place—his bed. And that, too, was an event that became more and more satisfying with time.

The only drawback was the short-term nature of their liaison. A fact that did not escape Millie's notice one morning in mid-July, when she came over to slip into her dress and see if it fit.

"When is Gabe going back overseas again?" Millie asked while the kids watched their daily allotment of *Paw Patrol* from the living room sofa.

"The beginning of September."

Millie took a sip of her favorite sassafras tea blend. "The kids are really going to miss him."

I am, too. So much. "Your point is?"

Millie sighed in concern. "The two of you are getting awfully involved."

They were. And they weren't. Susannah did her best to hide her emotions, replying casually, "We know it's just a summer fling."

Millie slipped into the bathroom, hanger in hand.

"Are you sure it can't be more than that?" she asked through the slit in the door.

Actually, no, I'm not sure of that at all, Susannah thought in frustration.

She pushed aside the ache in her throat. "How about we worry about tomorrow, tomorrow?" she said to Millie, who walked out with a very big grin on her face. Then twirled.

Susannah gaped. "It zipped!"

Millie beamed proudly. "It sure did. All this sassafras tea I've been drinking is really paying off."

"I'll say."

The older woman slipped back into the bathroom. "Have you tried it?" she called out.

Susannah picked up some toys the kids had left on the floor and deposited them in the storage box. "Gabe and I both did one evening. Until I got reflux."

"You think it was the tea?"

Not wanting to hurt Millie's feelings, Susannah shrugged. "Any tea or coffee can trigger it." So she had gone back to drinking mostly water.

Millie came back out of the powder room, looking perplexed. "But it's caffeine-free!"

"Doesn't seem to matter." Susannah sighed.

Millie hung the dress back up in the closet.

"So, how are the top-secret anniversary plans going?" Susannah asked, wondering if there was anything she could do.

"Well, I..." Millie turned, suddenly looking alarmingly pale.

"Millie?" Susannah asked in alarm as the older woman lost even more color and swayed uncertainly. "Millie!"

An hour later, Gavin Monroe stopped in the doorway of the office where Gabe was reviewing files of as-yet-to-be-identified chronic illnesses.

"Hey, got a challenging case that just came into the ER." He handed over the paperwork identified thus far.

Gabe got only as far as the name. Millie Smith. "You want me to handle this?"

Gavin reminded him, "No reason you shouldn't, given the fact you've got temporary staff privileges."

Except... Gabe tensed. "I know her."

His friend shrugged. "So does everyone else who went to high school in Laramie County. That shouldn't make a difference."

It shouldn't. Gabe knew that. A little worried about letting his personal feelings get in the way of sound judgment yet again, he rocked back in his chair and warned, "We've become kind of close lately."

"Which makes you the perfect person to try and get the information out of her and Mike that will lead to the proper diagnosis and the end of their sudden heart arrhythmias."

Both Mike and Millie were suffering from heart arrhythmias? That was unusual. Intrigued despite himself, Gabe rose. "You said she's in the ER now?"

"Brought in by ambulance half an hour ago. We're working to bring them down, but her heart rate and blood pressure are both still really high."

"Who is with her?"

"Just her husband, Mike, although they mentioned Susannah Alexander will be here as soon as she gets her childcare situation straightened out."

Determined not to let any of them down, Gabe forced himself to put aside his fear of making another mistake and headed out the door, file in hand. "I'm on it."

"Thanks."

Gabe found the Smiths in Exam Room 10. Millie's face was tear streaked, and Mike looked equally shaken up. He said hello to both, explaining he'd been asked to consult on the case. "You want to tell me what happened?"

"I was over at Susannah's and just talking with her, and suddenly I felt very, very weak, and my heart rate went out of control. I thought my heart was going to pound right out of my chest. I tried to go sit down but I didn't make it to the chair, and I collapsed. She called 911 and here I am." New tears appeared in Millie's eyes.

Gabe squeezed her hand. "We'll figure it out. Just like we did with Mike. In the meantime, I need to ask you a few questions. Did you do anything out of the ordinary this morning?"

She shook her head.

"Have any more coffee or tea than usual?"

Again, no.

He had to ask. "I know you've been trying to lose weight. Have you been taking any diuretics? Or over-the-counter diet aids?"

Millie met his glance equably. "No."

"What about blood pressure medicine?" Gabe pressed.

Millie shook her head. "I don't take anything like that," she said straightforwardly. "My blood pressure is normally one hundred over sixty. So I don't need it."

"Any vomiting or diarrhea?"

"Also no."

Gabe looked at the blood work that had just been done on the computer screen. "Your plasma renin, aldosterone and potassium are all really low, though. And—" He lifted the sheet near her feet and looked down, pressing a finger into her ankle. It left a physical dent in her skin. "I see some swelling here."

Millie worried. "What does that mean?"

"You have pitting edema," Gabe explained. "Which is caused by an accumulation of fluid in body tissues."

"But you can fix all that, can't you?" Millie asked nervously. "By giving me some bags of potassium, like you did Mike, and some meds to bring down my BP and lower my heart rate."

"We can, but we're going to have to admit you to the cardiac care unit to do that. And we also need to figure out why you and Mike are both suddenly having this problem," Gabe told his former teacher kindly. "Because it's likely the cause is linked."

Susannah was walking into the ER just as Gabe was walking out, a set of keys in his hand.

"Up for a little sleuthing?" he said, explaining that he was about to head for Mike and Millie's home to have a look around, to see if he could locate the cause of the couple's strikingly similar cardiac events.

"Absolutely." Susannah changed direction. "If you think it will help."

Gabe fell into step beside her. "That's what the Smiths thought you would say."

Noting Susannah looked a little shaky—her face was as tear streaked as Millie's had been—Gabe worked to keep his mind on the task at hand. "How about I drive?"

Her lower lip quivered, and she turned her glance away. "Please."

While they traveled the short distance to the couple's home, Gabe explained what they had uncovered thus far. "We ran a quick blood test on Mike before we left. Turns out his potassium, plasma renin and aldosterone are all very low right now, again, too. And his heart rate and blood pressure were elevated, too, although not as high as before. But we're admitting him along with Millie—as a precaution."

The color left Susannah's face. "Oh my Lord. This is so scary!"

"They're in good hands, Susannah. But you and I need to figure this out as quickly as we can. And I am going to need your help to find the source of what they are ingesting that is causing this."

She bit her lower lip, and her expression turned thoughtful. "So you think it might be something they are eating or drinking?"

"Most likely. But there are other factors that could be playing into this, too. You're with them a lot. Do you know of any changes they've made in their lifestyle since the summer began and Mike had his incident?"

Susannah dragged in a calming breath. "Well, they haven't been walking as much as they usually do."

"How much did they used to walk?"

"Six miles total every day. Three in the morning and three at night, but it's been hot, so most days they're lucky to get in a mile if they both feel up to it." She shook her head in remorse. "And that is probably my fault."

Gabe gave her hand a reassuring squeeze. "Why?"

"They've been helping me with the kids a lot more. And you know how tiring the quintuplets can be."

"The quintuplets aren't going to cause hypokalemia."

She shot him a quizzical look.

"Low potassium level," he explained.

He looked around the kitchen, at the big bowl of bananas and oranges on the counter, the peels in the trash. The bundles of fresh spinach and broccoli and red meat in the fridge. "Their diet looks healthy and potassium rich, so something else has to be bringing it down." His expression thoughtful, he asked, "Where do they keep their medicine?"

"In this cabinet." She brought out two plastic storage boxes, one marked *Millie* and one marked *Mike*.

Gabe went through them. "Nothing here."

Susannah sighed in frustration.

His gaze narrowed. "That sassafras tea that gave you reflux. Is Millie still drinking that?"

Susannah nodded. "By the gallon."

"Can you find a box with the list of ingredients?"

She paused. "Maybe in the pantry."

Gabe kept checking out the contents of the kitchen, methodically going through everything. "Mike doesn't drink that, though, right?"

"Only if forced, and since he had his episode, she isn't pushing it on him. She's been making him decaf coffee instead. Which he drinks by the gallon."

"Got any of that? So I can check the label?"

"I'll look." Susannah knelt to check the cabinet beneath the coffee maker.

"What about energy drinks?" Gabe continued. "Some of those can have Red Bull–like ingredients in them."

In frustration, she checked out the fridge, then the pantry. Sighed. "I don't see any."

"Well, Mike must be indulging in something," Gabe said.

Susannah brightened. "Hang on." She moved the step stool to the far end of the counter and climbed on it to look into the top cabinet above the fridge. She pulled out a bag of candy, announcing, "Here it is! Dutch salt licorice candy coins and Australian black licorice."

Gabe looked up from the tea label he'd been reading. "Bingo!" he said.

"So it's been the consumption of black licorice in my tea and his candy that have been causing this?" Millie said in wonderment, half an hour later.

Gabe and Susannah stood at the end of their two hospital beds, which had been moved into the same room in the cardiac unit.

Had it been a purely social call, Gabe might have put his arm around Susannah's waist. But because he was there as a medical professional, he remained apart from her.

"Yes. It contains glycyrrhizin, which is the sweetening compound derived from licorice root. Overconsumption causes abnormal heart rhythms, potassium levels to fall dangerously, high blood pressure, lethargy, muscle weakness, kidney damage and even congestive heart failure. Although I am happy to report neither of you have the two most serious complications."

Millie and Mike exchanged worried glances. "What is the cure?" Mike asked.

Gabe advised sternly, "Stop eating or drinking anything with black licorice in it immediately. And you should both recover with no permanent health problems. You are going to have to stay in the hospital overnight again, but I think you should be able to go home tomorrow."

Millie nodded in relief. "Thank you, Gabe. Thank you so much."

He nodded, surprised and pleased at his own confidence, how he had handled the situation. "You're welcome." He flashed a brisk, professional smile. "In the meantime, promise me you two will get some rest."

Millie chuckled. "I don't think either of us is going to have any problem taking a nap this afternoon."

Gabe and Susannah walked out. Although the medical mystery had been solved, a recovery plan put in place, she still looked as if even the faintest breeze would knock her over.

"Where are the kids?"

Her hand trembled slightly as she removed her phone from her purse and checked for messages. There were none. "One of the other moms from the multiples club has them for the day." She stared at the cell phone screen. "I guess I should call her and go pick them up."

"You could," Gabe agreed, aware she still appeared as if her entire world were crashing down on her. "Or," he added gently, aware the older couple weren't the only ones who needed some tender loving care right now, "you could have some lunch with me and let yourself recover from what has been a very, very stressful morning."

To his disappointment, she looked as reluctant as she was tempted. "I don't think I could sit in a restaurant."

He persisted. "So we'll get takeout and bring it back to my place."

Meeting his eyes, she released a breath. "You can leave the hospital?"

This time he did touch her, taking her hand. "I'm on flex time." He squeezed her fingers reassuringly. "As long as I review all the cases they ask me to look at in a timely fashion, I'm good."

Her slender shoulders relaxed. "Then I accept your offer."

Susannah sat in the car and tried to collect herself while Gabe went into the restaurant to pick up their order. When they drove back to his temporary home, they unpacked the bags, got out the plates and silverware, and sat down at the dark ebony kitchen island with their meals.

"You're awfully quiet." He took a bite of his brisket sandwich.

She toyed with her smoked turkey on Texas toast. "I know. I'm sorry. I keep seeing Millie turn white, clasp her chest and then slowly crumple onto the floor."

"Were the kids upset?"

Guilt flooded her. "Initially, yes, because Mike and I were. But when the EMTs got there with the fire truck, two of the firemen took them out to see the big engine and the inside of an ambulance. They let them try on their hats and talked about how much fun Millie was going to have riding in the ambulance with Mike, so by the time they had her loaded up on the stretcher and ready to go, the kids were completely excited for her and able to wave goodbye."

Gabe smiled, as if envisioning the kids and all she had described. "Yeah, Laramie County has a great emergency services department."

"They do."

Looking into her eyes, Gabe persisted, "So... what's worrying you?"

Without warning, the tears she'd been holding back for several hours got the better of her. And suddenly, she needed him as never before. The way she had been fearing she would need him one day. "Oh, Gabe," she choked out.

He pushed off his stool, stood and pulled her into his arms. "Hey," he said fiercely, pressing his face into her hair and wrapping his arms around her. "Let it out, sweetheart. Let it all out."

And she did.

In the comfort of his arms, pressed against his big,

strong body, she let the tears fall and the sobs come, hard and fast and embarrassingly loud. Until finally, there was no more grief and fear left, and the tears were reduced to a slow, steady stream.

"I'm sorry you were scared," he whispered, still stroking her hair. "I wish I'd been there."

"You are here." She wept some more. "That's what is killing me. I'm starting to depend on you the way I already depend on Millie and Mike. And the kids are, too. I mean, I know you're leaving." She wiped her face and tried to get herself together. "I get it. I accept it. I know it's the right thing for you. And I want that for you, I do. I just... I'm scared for me, and the kids, and what will happen when something really does happen to Mike and Millie. Because we depend on them, too. So much."

"So maybe," Gabe said gruffly, pulling back so she had no choice but to look into his eyes, "it's time you started depending on me for more than just this summer."

Chapter Fourteen

Blinking hard, Susannah stared up at him. Was this some kind of proposal? Because if it was… Ignoring the butterflies jumping around in her stomach, she asked, "What are you talking about?"

"They need a father, Susannah," Gabe told her softly, all the affection and protectiveness she had ever wanted to see in his eyes.

Their gazes locked. "So they won't be forever dependent on just you," he went on to say. "And so that you won't have to worry that they'll end up orphaned one day, the way you and I suddenly were."

The pain of remembered grief glimmered in his eyes. "I mean, it could still happen. But the chances are much less if the kids have two parents, ready and willing to take on the challenge of loving them into adulthood."

He made a solid argument, one she had wished to see enacted many times, never more so than by him. "You would do that for them?"

He took in her hopeful expression. "And for you. Of *course* I would." Then, stepping close enough that she could feel his body heat, his voice dropped a husky notch. "Don't you know by now how much I care about all of you?"

If she hadn't, she certainly would have known the moment he took her back in his arms and kissed her. The feel of his lips on hers sent a jolt of electricity through her that brought her to life and tantalized her insides. Moaning, she wrapped her arms about his shoulders and kissed him back, letting him know everything she felt, everything she wanted, everything she could give him in return.

He flattened his hand down her spine, bringing her up against his hard-muscled thighs and the proof of his desire for her. The fiery intimacy of the contact robbed her of breath as the demanding feel of him scorched through her clothes. If this was what it was like now, she thought as he danced her toward his bedroom, heaven knew what it would be like when they got to the good stuff. She was combusting from the inside out as it was…

Gabe hadn't brought her there to make love with her. But now that she was showing herself amenable, he was just as hot and bothered as she was. Still kissing her ravenously, he took full possession of her lips, then moved to her ear, the nape of her neck. One hand found her breasts through the thinness of her cotton top and bra. Her nipples budded against his palms. Then she was pushing her hands under the waistband of his scrubs as his fingers slipped beneath the elastic edge of her panties to find her warm, wet heat. She arched against him, trembling, swaying slightly. Smiling at her responsiveness, he shifted her over onto the bed, lay down and stretched out beside her. Then bent his head to kiss her again, undressing her slowly, deliberately, letting his fingers and lips and tongue do their magic again. Driving her as crazy as she was driving him. Taking possession. Showing her just how potent and pleasurable a relationship between them could be. *Would* be. If they remained together in a way that suited them both.

Afterward, as they lay wrapped in each other's arms, he thought about what it would be like to do this every day…and every night. To no longer have to hide how much they wanted to be with each other.

"So," she said finally, cuddling close as he stroked a hand through her hair, "if you're serious—"

He shifted so they were both lying on their sides, facing each other. "Absolutely serious," he said in a low, gravelly tone.

Her blue eyes were alight with curiosity. And hope. "How would this work?"

Damn, she was gorgeous, with her hair all tousled, her cheeks pink and her lips damp and swollen from their kisses. His heart fuller than he had ever imagined it could be, Gabe held her close. "Well, the easiest thing to do would be to get married as soon as possible."

"Before you go back overseas," Susannah guessed.

He hadn't been thinking he would return to PWB after all if they got married, but he could also see that was the only way she expected this would work. And maybe she was right. Maybe they shouldn't try to change too much too soon.

Maybe it would be best to take things one step at a time. Get married. See the kids were safe and protected. Get used to each other. And then segue into a more normal existence.

"Yes," he said, watching her slip from his arms and then his bed, her expression sober now.

"I can't believe I'm saying this," she admitted, checking the time and beginning to dress. "But... okay." She turned to him with a shy smile and a quiet, determined manner. "I'll marry you, for the sake of the kids."

Gabe broke the news to his parents later that evening. To say they weren't exactly delighted was an understatement and a half. "For two people who've talked about nothing but getting all their kids married off with families of their own for the last decade, you really aren't showing a lot of enthusiasm," Gabe commented irritably, glad he had not brought Susannah along for this initial announcement. All the questions might have been enough to scare her away—or at least make her have second thoughts.

"We expected love to be a part of the equation," Carol said, refilling their glasses of iced tea.

Who said it wasn't? Gabe thought fiercely, taking one of the cookies his mom offered him. So maybe he and Susannah had sort of backed into this love affair they were in, but it *was* a love affair, complete with compassion and kindness and understanding, and sometimes, yeah, a whole lot of amazing sex, too.

Oblivious to the nature of Gabe's thoughts, his dad added sternly, "Along with a substantial dose of commitment."

Gabe resented the implication he could be so irresponsible. Hadn't he spent all his life, since age twelve, proving that was not the case? That although he might make a mistake, he would never do so deliberately. "I'm not going to abandon her."

His dad munched on a cookie, too. "You mean you're giving up your work with Physicians Without Borders?" Robert asked.

"No." That would be too much change, too soon. "Not initially," Gabe said firmly. "But I can see a day…" His voice trailed off.

His parents exchanged concerned glances. "Why not just get engaged first and then work it out when you're ready to resign and take a job here in Laramie? Or at least somewhere in the United States, where Susannah and the kids can reside with you?" his mom suggested gently.

"Because we want to get this taken care of now," Gabe insisted.

"As a matter of convenience," his dad guessed.

Gabe saw no reason to hide that he and Susannah were both being pragmatic. Keeping their emotions out of the arrangement was a plus as far as he was concerned. It would help him have the perspective he needed to protect her. Because the last thing he wanted was to ever be in a position again where his feelings about her in any way impacted his ability to think clearly. Or keep her—and the kids—safe.

"Yes. And importance. We consulted a family law attorney this afternoon over the phone, and she said the only way a court is liable to consider me an equal guardian—if I am working elsewhere—is if the two of us are legally married and I adopt the children. And so that is what we intend to do as soon as possible."

"If forming a family is the primary goal, then you need to make it a real marriage with a real wedding," his mother said quietly, looking him in the eye. "Susannah and the kids deserve that much, don't you think?"

An hour later, Susannah was getting ready for bed when her cell phone chimed to let her know a text message was coming in.

Gabe wrote, Are you still up?

Yes, she texted back, her heart racing with anticipation.

Can we talk?

Wondering if he was already having second thoughts, she texted back, Sure.

By the time she had donned a sleep cardigan over her thigh-length sleep shirt, he was on her front porch. She took him by the hand and led him inside, glad Mike and Millie weren't there to notice this midnight call. Or comment on it the next day. She led him over to the sofa, aware she'd been feeling all tied up in knots. Happy she was finally seeing so many of her dreams come true. And yet wary that something still might go wrong.

She sat down close beside him, turning slightly to face him, so her bare knee was pressed up against his jeans-covered thigh. "I presume you talked to your folks?"

"Yes." He went on to fill her in. She listened intently as he spoke. Surprised...and not...by their offer. "They want us to get married at their ranch?"

"Yes." His brows knit together in a frown, confirming her opinion this was dangerous territory. "In front of all our family and friends."

She jerked in a breath. "Does it have to be formal?"

He shrugged. "We can do it in jeans and T-shirts if you want."

Aware there was still so much she had yet to learn and understand about him, and that she didn't have a clue what he was thinking or feeling right now except mild annoyance at his folks, she raked her teeth across her lower lip, admitting ruefully, "Somehow, I think that would raise even more eyebrows than the fact of us getting hitched. Plus, we'd have to explain it to the kids."

He took her hand in his and turned it over, tracing the lifeline with his thumb. "Why we weren't getting dressed up."

Sensation swept through her, reminding her how very good it felt when they made love. Or when he just held her, or sat with her, talking, like right now. "They've seen a half dozen weddings the last year or so. All of them formal."

He propped his feet on her coffee table and stretched his long legs out in front of him, the action pressing his muscular leg even tighter against her knee. "Then a wedding dress and tux it is."

Susannah tried to make it as easy as she could on both of them. It wasn't as if this was going to be a real wedding, at least for the two of them, anyway. "You know, I could wear Belinda's dress."

He narrowed his whiskey-colored eyes at her. Objecting, as always, when he didn't think she was appropriately seeing to her own needs. "I think you should wear your own."

He was probably right about that. People would expect her to want to be the star on her wedding day, even if she and Gabe knew it was all mostly for show, as a bow to tradition. And that meant getting a fabulous dress. "I could probably pick one up pretty quickly if I went to the shop in town and just selected one of their samples."

Gabe smiled approvingly. "Ditto the tux. Although I figured I'd rent mine."

Susannah flashed a wry smile while mentally trying to figure out ways to save money on the celebration without diminishing it in any way. "I don't blame you, since there aren't a lot of places to wear either garment around here."

Gabe took his phone out of his pocket. On the screen, she could see he had already made a list. Which was something she usually did. "So…the next thing we need to do is set a date, time and place."

"What did you have in mind?"

"This weekend. Maybe Saturday afternoon."

Susannah did some rough calculations. "Five days from now?" Was he eager or what?

Not that she wasn't.

It would be nice to spend more time with him before he left again.

He shrugged off her initial concern that it might be all too soon. "We only need three days to get a license. My brother Cade can get us a DJ or musicians, whatever you want, to drive out from Dallas, no problem. And we could use flowers from my parents' ranch if you want to go native."

"It'd be great. We would just put them all in bell jars. But what about the food?"

His voice was gruff. "Maybe have a local restaurant, like the Wagon Wheel, cater, since we never did make it there for a date."

Sensing latent emotion in him, too, she agreed. "Invitations?"

"Mom and Dad said they'd send out emails and make phone calls and do that for us. As well as get the chairs and tables set up. And since the weather looks to be good and dry and not too terribly hot through the weekend…"

She gazed over at him, unable to help but think how handsome he looked in the soft light, how right it felt to be there with him like this, even so late at night. Although when they married, this would be an every-night occurrence. When he was in town, anyway. Her heart warming at the prospect, she studied him quietly, then asked, "You're really okay doing it this fast?"

His eyes lit up with the happiness she felt inside. "I really am."

Susannah squeezed his hand. "I am, too."

Now, all she had to do was tell Mike and Millie and enlist their help and approval, too.

"Is this because Millie and I were both in the hospital at the same time?" Mike asked later the next day, when they returned home and were relaxing in Susannah's living room while the children napped upstairs.

"No." Susannah disabused them of that notion, even though in a sense it was partially true. *It's because I realize how much I care about him and want him in my life. However we work that out*, she thought, wanting Gabe to be as happy and secure in their relationship as he wanted her to be in hers, with him.

"Do you love him?" Millie asked skeptically. "I mean, I know there is something really wonderful and exciting going on there. You can't help but notice the sparks whenever you two are within a fifty-foot radius of each other. But *marriage*. Honey, that's a lifelong commitment, and you two have been dating for how long now? Four weeks? Six?"

"He's been back for six. I guess we've been dating for four, maybe…"

"You don't know the actual date?" Mike asked, shocked.

Susannah hedged, "I could figure it out if I looked on my phone." *Maybe.* She skillfully changed the subject back to the older couple's own storybook romance. "And speaking of first dates, don't the two of you have an anniversary coming up?"

Mike and Millie beamed. "August first," Mike confirmed.

Susannah thought about the special plans Millie had made. How happy Mike was going to be when he found out his wife was recreating the date that had started it all for them.

She looked at Millie, knowing she needed her on her side. "Didn't you tell me once that love comes when you least expect it?"

Millie nodded.

"Well, Gabe and I didn't expect each other, and yet…like you said, there is something really wonderful and wildly exciting and fulfilling between us whenever we are together, and sometimes," she continued wistfully, telling them what was in her heart, "even when we're not."

Millie and Mike listened intently.

She paused, trying to find the words to make the case for their marriage. "I've waited a long time to feel this way about any man or have him feel this way about me."

So maybe it wasn't the kind of love that usually provided the foundation for a marriage. *Exactly.* But it was something unique that she hadn't felt for anyone else. The kids adored him. He adored her kids. And together they made a pretty great family unit. So it was enough. It was going to have to be.

"I want to do this," Susannah continued, surprising herself by getting a little choked up. "And I want both of you on my side."

"Honey, you know we're always there for you," Mike said, giving her a fatherly hug.

"We absolutely are," Millie echoed, getting a little emotional, too.

Susannah pulled herself together. "Do you think you'll have time to go wedding-dress shopping with me?"

The older woman teared up, abruptly looking as sentimental and approving as Susannah hoped she would be. Millie dabbed her eyes. "I wouldn't miss it."

Susannah turned to Mike. "What about you? Do you think you'll be up and about enough to walk me down the aisle on Saturday?"

"Try and stop me," he said gruffly, finally giving his full approval, too.

Relief flowed through Susannah. "I love you guys." Susannah hugged them both. She only hoped she and Gabe could be half as happy as the older couple.

"We love you, too." Millie and Mike hugged her back. Finally, Millie blew her nose and asked, "Have you told the kids yet?"

Another milestone. One they intended to tackle together. "Gabe and I are doing that tonight."

Mike tilted his head. "How do you think they are going to take it?"

Susannah shrugged, never one to predict when it came to the quintuplets. She knew how she wanted it to go, though. Splendidly. She smiled optimistically at Mike and Millie. "I guess we'll see."

Gabe had been wanting to borrow his parents' ice cream maker and show the kids how it used to be made in the good old days, so that was exactly what they did. And while he turned the crank and churned the cream and sugar and strawberries into a sweet treat, Susannah talked to the kids about their future together.

"So there's going to be a wedding?" Abigail asked finally.

Susannah looked at Gabe. Powerful emotion welled within her for this man and the children they now shared. She hadn't realized how much she longed to have a man around. Now, with Gabe in their life, she knew. Her world as a single mom had been good. But her world with Gabe in it was great. "Yes," she told her children, "there will be a wedding out at Gabe's family ranch."

The three girls jumped up and down, clapping their hands. "Can we all be in it?" Gretchen danced in excitement.

"I want to be a flower girl," Abigail declared.

"Me, too!" chimed the usually shy Rebecca.

"Yeah, and we want to carry the pillows." Connor did a somersault.

"With the rings!" Levi followed suit, then the girls.

Susannah looked at Gabe as the unbridled celebration continued among the little ones. "Told you they've seen a few weddings," she mouthed.

"Does this mean you'll be our daddy, instead of just our friend?" Abigail asked.

Susannah and Gabe exchanged looks again. "Yes," he told the kids. "I'll be your daddy then."

Another burst of spontaneous emotion rippled through the group. "Yay!" The kids danced around even more wildly.

"Yay!" Susannah whispered, too, tears of bliss filling her eyes. And for a second Gabe looked suspiciously misty, too. As if all his dreams were coming true as well. Finally, he cleared his throat. Whispered to her, "I guess we don't have to worry about them accepting me."

"Not at all," Susannah whispered back, joy flooding her once again.

Abigail walked over to watch Gabe churn the ice cream in the old-fashioned ice cream maker. Serious once again. "So are you going to live here with us every day and every night?" she asked.

That was a harder question to answer. Susannah and Gabe exchanged glances over the children's heads. With a nod, he indicated she should take the lead. Gently, Susannah explained, "Gabe's doctor job takes him far away, so he won't be here all the time, but when he's not being a doctor, he will come and live here in the house with us."

The children frowned, confused.

"Will he be gone a long time?" Connor asked.

Susannah looked at Gabe, leaving that to him. "I'll be doing six-week stints," he said, "then back here for two."

The kids looked at him blankly. Understanding they did not have a concept of time, he explained kindly, "So I'll be gone seventy-two days and then here for fourteen."

All their faces fell. That math they understood. "I want you to be here *all the time*, like you are now," Rebecca said, her lower lip quivering.

"I know," Susannah said gently, engulfing several of her children in a hug, while Gabe dished out the homemade strawberry ice cream into bowls. "But that's not how Gabe's job works. So we have to be supportive of him, and that means being happy when he is here and okay when he is not."

The kids stood motionless, bowls and spoons in hand, clearly still not able to grasp what their life would be like.

Gabe cleared his throat, suddenly looking as emotional as Susannah felt. "It's possible we could figure something better out…" he said gruffly.

But Susannah was unwilling to make promises

they couldn't keep or burden Gabe unnecessarily, to the point he would regret having come to their rescue and asking her to marry him in the first place. She gathered her children in for a consoling group hug, then walked them over to the picnic table out back, where they could all sit and enjoy their treats. She knelt down to their level, looking each one of them in the eye. "Listen to me, kiddos." She smiled reassuringly, knowing together she and the quints had faced much tougher things without Gabe's aid. "We'll work it out. It will be good for us. We will have time together. And time apart. And it'll all be fine. And you know why?"

The children shook their heads, listening intently now. Slowly, they began to eat their ice cream as Gabe joined them, two more bowls in hand. He handed one to Susannah and kept the other for himself.

Susannah sat opposite Gabe at the table. Their knees touched briefly beneath. The feel of his skin was warm and solid and enticing. Just like him.

Trying not to think how much she would miss Gabe when he left, Susannah continued, "Because Gabe likes working in far-off places, where they don't have doctors like they do here." She told the children proudly, "So if he didn't go to some of those faraway places and take care of the folks who live there, they might not have the medical care they need to get all better. And we like living here in our house and going to preschool, which will be starting again pretty soon, don't we?"

The quints nodded, enthused. "So this way, everybody gets to have what they want. So we're going to be fine," she emphasized firmly. Even if she would miss Gabe more than she had ever imagined possible.

Chapter Fifteen

"You look gorgeous," Millie said.

Certainly, Susannah thought, taking in the long white satin gown with the full skirt, portrait neckline and cap sleeves, prettier and more princess-like than she ever thought she could be. "You don't think it's too much?" she protested, feeling a little ridiculous— and a little majestic—all at once.

Millie dabbed her eyes, still looking as if nothing existed but this moment in time. "I think Gabe is going to be over the moon when he sees you walking down the aisle on Mike's arm."

Susannah teared up, too. She gathered the older woman in a heartfelt hug. "You've got to stop doing this!" She waved the air in front of her face in an effort to keep the sentimental tears away. "Because every time I see you get all weepy, it makes me completely emotional, too."

Millie gave her another hug, then stepped away. "You're supposed to be emotional. You're getting married."

"I know." Susannah released a dreamy sigh and turned back to the mirror. The whole process of planning their hasty wedding was so surreal. Magical, almost. Which made her not want to believe it could all be real. Or that it was actually going to happen.

"Now what's wrong?" Millie asked gently.

Susannah turned so the other woman could help her with the zipper. "I was just thinking about everything we have to do to get the kids ready for the ceremony." Which, thanks to the expedited schedule she and Gabe had readily agreed upon, was in a matter of days.

"Mike and Gabe are taking the boys to get fitted for their tuxes this afternoon, while we take the girls out to get their dresses," Millie said.

And thanks to the sample gown being available for purchase, she had her dress, Susannah thought.

"And they all already have dress shoes, right?"

"Yes." Susannah stepped out of her gown and handed it to the waiting clerk.

"So it will be fine," Millie reassured her.

Susannah knew Millie believed that because she assumed she and Gabe were marrying because they were madly in love, not out of convenience, to protect the quintuplets. And to give them the official legal father that they needed. And deserved.

So, Susannah promised herself, she would put aside her starry-eyed notions of happily-ever-after and find a way to make this work. After all, she and Gabe were good friends and lovers, too, as well as adults who realized romantic love wasn't always part of the equation. There were still other kinds of love that could be deeply satisfying, Susannah thought as she finished dressing, then checked the list on her phone.

Next item.

"We also have to order the flower wreaths for their hair."

"And yours," Millie added with a smile. "Don't forget you're wearing a crown of flowers instead of a tiara with your veil."

Susannah linked arms with her. "Maybe you should wear one, too. The kids would love it, as would I."

"You sure?" Millie hesitated. "Corsages are traditional for the mother of the bride." Which was what Millie was stepping in to be.

"Nothing about this wedding is traditional," Susannah murmured, stepping forward to pay for her dress.

A fact that was reiterated constantly over the next few days of preparation.

And never more so than at the rehearsal dinner the Lockharts insisted upon throwing for them at the ranch Friday evening.

The entire Lockhart family, including every one of Gabe's siblings, Millie and Mike, and the kids were all there with her and Gabe. The minister couldn't make it—he was officiating another ceremony that evening—but had prepared them for their traditional vows in a meeting at his study at the community church.

But outside, the wedding preparations for the next day were in full swing. An ornate dinner tent had been erected on the lawn, white chairs and a wedding arbor set up. A dance floor would also be put up when the reception DJ, and the flute and harp duo who had been hired to play for the ceremony, arrived the next day.

"Doing okay?" Gabe whispered in her ear.

He looked incredible in a yellow button-up that brought out the whiskey hue of his eyes, dark jeans and dress boots. He smelled good, too, like the brisk masculine cologne he favored.

Trying not to think how much she would secretly like to duck out of there and find somewhere to kiss and hold him until her prewedding jitters disappeared, Susannah nodded. "I can't believe how much trouble your parents have gone to. We're never going to be able to pay them back."

His manner as composed as hers was uneasy, Gabe inclined his head. "Sure we will. All we have to do is be happy."

Susannah checked on the quintuplets, who were playing lawn croquet with two of Gabe's sisters. "I meant all the money they're spending." For something that wasn't even real. Not the way they clearly assumed, anyway.

He tucked her in close to his side. "I don't think they mind, but if it will make you feel better, we can pitch in with the expenses."

Savoring his warmth and his strength, she rested her head on his shoulder. "It would."

He lifted her hand to his lips, kissed the back of it. Their glances met and held for several long beats. "Is that the only thing bothering you?"

How could she tell him she was suddenly getting cold feet without coming off as the most ungrateful woman on earth?

Gabe could see Susannah was overwhelmed by how fast everything was moving. But he had a feeling it was the only way to get her down the aisle. If she had too much time to think about it and/or worry about the untraditional aspects of their relationship, he knew she might just change her mind.

And he did not want her to do that.

Did not want to face a life without her.

Not after everything they had shared and found with each other since he'd returned to Texas.

"It's going to be okay," he said, privately vowing to do whatever he needed to do to gain her trust and faith in him. "Like we told the kids," he promised her softly, "we will work it all out."

Uncertainty came and went in her pretty sea-blue eyes, then she swallowed and took a deep breath. "This is the right thing for them," she said, all protective mom once again.

"And for us," he reiterated.

And for a while, anyway, from Gabe's perspective, it seemed to be that way as the meal progressed. It was only when the dinner wound down and the toasts began that things got awkward again.

Mike, representing the bride's side of the family, picked up his glass and went first, his voice as fond as the look on his face. "Susannah and the quintuplets came into our lives as the greatest blessing we had ever received. And though it wasn't a formal arrangement until recently, when she asked us to be official grandparents to the quintuplets, a mom and dad to her, we have held them that way in our hearts for years now. So—" he cleared his throat, beginning to get a little misty "—to see her so happy and content spending time with Gabe has been yet another godsend."

Mike turned to Millie, who nodded encouragingly, then back to the assembled family.

"And though it's all happened really quickly, we have seen them together enough to know they have the determination to make their family work on every level. So, let's all raise a glass to them and wish them our very best."

The crowd obliged. "Hear, hear," everyone said in unison.

Mike's words were sincere. But it still felt as if something was missing, and Susannah seemed to feel it, too, Gabe realized. Where, he wondered, were the mentions of love and destiny and happily-ever-after in the toast? Not that he and Susannah had ever dared talk that way to each other, for fear of upsetting their blossoming relationship. But it was certainly implied in their decision to marry, and it would have been nice on the eve of their wedding to hear someone else say something along those lines. He knew it would have reassured Susannah—who, beneath the polite smile, was becoming more and more tense.

Robert Lockhart went next, with his usual wry affability. "Everyone here knows how long Carol and I have waited for Gabe to decide to take the leap of faith required to commit to spending your life with someone else. Although we worried it might never happen with our *oldest son,*" Robert admitted, as the group chuckled in acknowledgment of Gabe's wanderlust, "because he has never been one to let any grass grow under his feet." He winked. "But maybe we should have known, because of his life of service to others, that he would eventually take up the mantle of responsibility and commitment required for marriage. And bring us grandchildren by way of the quintuplets. Who, by the way, Carol and I find completely delightful."

The quintuplets, knowing they were being talked about, grinned happily.

"So," Robert continued expansively, "we offer our heartiest congratulations and best wishes for this wonderful couple and their amazing new family."

"Hear, hear!" everyone said.

Smiling, Gabe and Susannah clinked their glasses along with everyone else. However, as he watched his bride-to-be nervously sip her champagne, he couldn't help wondering once again if she was having second thoughts about their impending union.

"You're awfully quiet tonight," Gabe said as he drove them back to town shortly after nine o'clock. He spoke in a low, hushed tone, mindful of the fact that the quints, tuckered out from the day's events, were snoozing in the rear seats.

Susannah knew she was in a mood. Guilt mixed with embarrassment. "Sorry. I've got a lot on my mind."

He frowned in obvious consternation. "The toasts bothered you."

Susannah drew in a jerky breath, wishing she knew how to quell the intractable emotion welling up inside her. "They seemed awkward," she admitted with no small trace of regret.

Apparently a lot more accepting of the pragmatic union they were about to enter into, he shrugged and said, "Probably because we sprang this on everyone pretty quickly, and they weren't sure what to say." He gave her a reassuring look as they waited at a stop sign at the edge of town. "But the well-wishes were there." Looking her in the eye with gentle persuasion, he reached over and squeezed her hand. "Everyone wants our relationship to work over the long haul."

His words were meant to be as comforting as his touch, but they fell short. "I know."

"But…" He frowned, upset by her wariness.

Susannah searched for a reason behind her melancholia. "I guess I'm missing Brett and Belinda," she admitted quietly, thinking how much family Gabe had at the party, compared to her much smaller group. She swallowed. "I always dreamed she would be my matron of honor."

Understanding, Gabe continued, "And instead our two witnesses are going to be Mike and my dad."

Susannah looked down at her hands, thinking, deliberating. The sentimentality edged back into her low tone. "I would really like to have Brett and Belinda be present in some way tomorrow for the ceremony."

"Do you want to carry a picture of them, or have one displayed there at the ceremony?"

Susannah shared the plans she'd made thus far. "Well, now that you bring it up…I've got a sapphire necklace of Belinda's that she wore on her wedding day, as something old. The flower garter she wore as something borrowed, and my own sapphire earrings as something blue. And, of course, my wedding dress as something new. But if we could have something of Brett's there representing him…"

Gabe grinned as the evening took on a more positive tone. "Obviously you've got something in mind?"

"I know he left you his collection of vinyl LPs from your college days. Some of the songs were played at their own wedding reception. So—" Susannah's mood lifted joyously "—if we could have the DJ spin a few of your and his old favorites?"

"It's a great idea," Gabe enthused. "They're in my storage locker. I'll go over there tonight."

"And I'll go with you, providing I can get someone to watch the kids."

* * *

Mike and Millie were instantly amenable when they found out what the mission was. So Susannah and Gabe left the older couple on the sofa, watching TV and relaxing, while the quints slept upstairs in their beds, and they headed off to the storage locker.

Gabe drove up to the entrance and punched in the security code. The gates opened, and he drove on around to the fourth building. He parked and used his electronic key fob to get into the building, and then another to open up the garage-style door that fronted the well-lit cement aisle.

The facility was deserted that late on a Friday night, and so it was quiet as he led the way into his fifteen-by-twenty-foot space. There in the center was the futon he and Brett'd had in their apartment in medical school. Towers of boxes, his bike and random athletic gear surrounded the only place to sit down.

"The vinyls are back here, I think, out of the way," Gabe said, already threading his way back there. "But feel free to look around to see if there is anything else belonging to Brett that would comfort you tomorrow. Maybe some wineglasses. Or…I don't know…"

"Thanks," Susannah said, spying a box with what appeared to be their med school yearbook on top.

Curious, and needing something concrete to remember her late brother-in-law by, she grabbed it and sat on the sofa. As she started to open it, a postcard fell out.

She didn't mean to pry. Honestly, she didn't, but when she saw the photo of the Hawaiian sunrise on

it, coupled with the postmark from six years ago…
she couldn't help but glance down at the writing. See
the message there. And what she read chilled her to
her very soul.

Gabe was moving around the stacks of boxes when
he saw Susannah standing there, postcard in hand,
her face a blotchy white and pink. He swore inwardly.
Realizing too late he should have remembered that
was here. And either hidden it or found out a way to
tell her that would've softened the blow. Panic tightened his gut. "I can explain."

She looked as numb as he felt. "That you promised to look after me before they left on their trip to
Hawaii?"

All along, Gabe had been telling himself it wasn't
love he wanted from Susannah, love he couldn't give
her in return. Seeing how dejected and disillusioned
she was, he realized how wrong that was. Because if
they'd already said they loved each other, or were at
the very least committed to each other in the usual
way of engaged couples, this wouldn't have been such
an issue. He edged closer, moving near enough to in-
hale the lingering scent of her wildflower perfume.
Taking her by the hand, he led her over to the futon
and sat down next to her. "They'd been worried about
you for a while."

She turned toward him, her knee accidentally
nudging his thigh.

She pulled back so their legs were no longer touching. "Why?"

Taking the hint, he let go of her hand, too. Shrugged. "You'd been wanting your own husband and family for as long as Belinda had and weren't any closer to achieving it."

Shock and hurt flared. "They thought I was jealous of them?"

"Depressed," he corrected, forcing himself to be completely honest, even as he tracked the moisture glimmering in her eyes. "Dejected about your own prospects."

Silence fell. He expected her to burst into tears and let loose the flood of emotion that had to be building up inside her. Instead, she regained her composure, her demeanor more distant than he had ever seen it. "And so you were to, what, exactly?" she asked.

"Find an excuse to see you while they were gone. Make sure you were okay. Let them know if you weren't so they could cut their second honeymoon short."

Her sadness and disillusionment palpable, she continued staring at him like he was a stranger. "Only they never made it that far."

"No." He made no effort to hide his grief. "Before I could get to Houston to drop in on you, the helicopter crash happened."

She dropped her head in her hands, sat there in silence for a few moments, then looked up again, eyes swimming. "So that's why you kept calling and texting and emailing me after they died, just checking in." Bitterness edged her tone.

What did she want from him? Gabe wondered

grimly. An apology for doing what the situation required? What any good person would do? He watched her get up from the futon and walk away. "I wanted to make sure you were okay."

Hands fisted at her sides, she swung back to face him. "For them."

The accusation in her eyes stung. "For me."

She smirked, a mixture of anger and disbelief in her expression. "So you wouldn't feel guilty," she guessed contemptuously.

Damned if she hadn't hit that nail right on the head. Gabe stood, too. He swallowed around the ache in his throat. "Yes."

"It's also why you were so negative about me trying to have the quints on my own."

Knowing she wasn't going to take this next part well—because it would take them back to a time when they hadn't gotten along well at all—he stayed where he was, legs braced apart, arms folded in front of him. "I worried the IVF wouldn't work out the way you hoped. And it'd be too much for you to handle if you lost all or even most of the embryos in what seemed to me at the time to be a fool's errand. Or conversely, that you would have multiples and you'd be overwhelmed as a single mother and unable to care for them. Or maybe even just too reminded of Brett and Belinda to finish grieving properly."

Exhaling roughly, he scrubbed a hand across his face. "Clearly, I was wrong about all of that. You were able to carry them all to term and bring them safely into this world and care for them afterward on your own, and you—*we*—are very lucky to have them."

She glared at him resentfully. "The quintuplets aren't a burden to you? Some responsibility you feel was thrust upon you, too?"

The situation was bad, given how betrayed and blindsided she clearly felt, but not unsalvageable, he reassured himself firmly.

"No," Gabe explained patiently. "I've cared about the kids from the very first day I met them."

Clearly, she didn't believe him.

"Which is why," he went on soberly, determined to give her concrete proof she needed, "I went to the trouble to set up college funds for all five of them weeks ago."

Susannah stared at him, hardly able to believe what she was hearing. "You did *what*?" she demanded incredulously.

"I knew how worried you were about depleting the trust before they ever got to college, so I went to Bing and I told him I wanted to take care of it for you."

Was there no end to the duplicity? "He never said anything!"

Gabe regarded her steadily and continued defending his actions, as if his high-handedness behind the scenes were the most natural thing in the world. "I asked him not to. This was between him and me."

Susannah paced back and forth, struggling with the depth of the betrayal. "So you weren't ever going to tell me?" she concluded unhappily.

Gabe shrugged his broad shoulders, correcting, "No, I was going to tell you. When the time was right."

"Which would have been...?"

Abruptly, he appeared to be caught in a trap of his own making. "When I thought you could accept it for the gift from the heart that it was."

Susannah wasn't sure whether he was being deliberately naive or stubbornly chauvinistic. "Gabe... I can't let you do something like this..." Not without feeling beholden. Which was the last thing she had ever wanted.

Gabe moved closer yet again. Then let out a long, frustrated breath and continued explaining, "It's not that much to start, Susannah, not spread out over five accounts, but I'm going to add to it every year. I've already put in some extra this summer from my earnings consulting at the hospital. And I'll add more from my PWB paychecks. Plus—" he lightly cupped her shoulders, holding her in front of him when she would have bolted "—and I know we haven't talked about this yet, but I also plan to pay my fair share of the daily living expenses for our family, too. In fact, knowing what you've generally budgeted, the fact you have no mortgage, I could probably handle everything."

"Right." Tears pushed behind her eyes. Susannah blinked, refusing to let them fall even as her heart filled with a mixture of bittersweet resignation and longing. She searched his handsome features. "And how long do you imagine it will be before your cash-strapped state has you feeling trapped by the burden of caring for all six of us?"

Gabe tensed. Irritation creased his brow. "I would *never* feel that way."

She stepped back and held up her arms to ward him off. "That's what my aunt Elda thought when Belinda and I moved in with her." Susannah drew a deep breath and spelled it out for him. "When she saw what raising two kids did to her budget, how we cramped her lifestyle, she couldn't wait to get rid of us."

Gabe jammed his hands on his waist. "I'm sorry she hurt and disappointed you, Susannah, but I am not your aunt."

Susannah shoved her hands through her hair. "I can't believe this," she muttered. How could she have been so blind?

Gabe grimaced. "So, what would make you happy?"

Defiantly, she held her ground. "For starters? You *telling* me the truth! You *consulting* me before deciding to go off on your own and do something like this."

Looking as offended as she felt, he warned, "I can't reverse the college funds, Susannah. Once they are set up, they're meant to stay in place."

"Then I'll have to find a way to pay you back for whatever you have already put in."

"Is this the way it's going to be?" he challenged back, clearly bent on having his own way. "Constantly keeping score over money? Me not able to do anything nice for you and the kids on the spur of the moment without you feeling obligated to do something in return?"

The reckless, romantic part of Susannah wanted to tell him to forget the whole argument. However, the part of her that had been devastated by not being wanted in the end knew better. "I thought I made it clear when I said yes to your proposal. I don't want the kids and me to be a burden to you."

"That's what marriage is. It's about taking care of each other, above all else."

Susannah would have agreed with that, had they said they loved each other. Or been more than friends and lovers. But they weren't…so…like it or not, she had to be practical. And force him to be so, too. "Until you can't do it anymore, and you want to end it or, I don't know, just stay away overseas, maybe for another *five whole years* again."

Gabe's brow furrowed. "I wouldn't do that to you or the kids."

Trying to be as gallant as he was at heart, Susannah returned miserably, "But don't you see that you should have the option if it turns out that is what you want?"

His jaw tautened. "What are you saying?"

She forced herself to be generous. "That maybe we're making a colossal mistake. I know you think you're doing the really noble thing here, Gabe, coming to my rescue and stepping up for the kids. And maybe it feels good in the moment, because of all the fun we've had and the hot sex that was thrown in. But if at the end of the day you're still just trying to work off this obligation that you were never really able to fulfill to my sister and brother-in-law…" An obligation she hadn't known anything about until now. And still wouldn't be aware of if she hadn't discovered it by accident.

Pretending her heart wasn't breaking, she took a deep, bolstering breath. "If all we really are is just a long-neglected duty to you, then you will end up resenting us and wanting your freedom back, and then where will we all be?"

Gabe, hurt and angry now, shook his head at her. "You really think that's all this is?" he countered disbelievingly. "Me making good on some long-ago promise?"

"It's not like we ever really loved each other, Gabe," Susannah admitted sadly. "Not like we should if we are going to be married for the rest of our lives."

"So, you're saying what, Susannah?" he demanded. "You want to call the whole thing off?"

Susannah handed him the postcard with the proof of the request that had started it all.

"I don't see that we have any choice," she said heavily, forcing herself to do the right thing, even as her heart shattered into a million pieces. "Do you?"

Chapter Sixteen

"Honey, what's wrong?" Millie said the moment Susannah walked in the front door.

Susannah burst into fresh tears. "Gabe and I broke up!"

The Smiths switched off the television and motioned for her to come and sit between them. Millie reached for a box of tissues and handed it to her. "It can't be that bad," she said.

"But it is." Susannah dabbed her eyes and blew her nose. Briefly, she explained about the postcard she'd found and the educational savings accounts Gabe had set up for the kids without her knowledge or consent. "I can't marry him knowing we're already such a burden to him."

"There are some responsibilities a man wants to take on," Mike said gruffly.

Millie nodded. "If I am sure of anything after watching you all this summer, it's that he loves you and the kids."

"As friends."

"As *more*," Millie insisted.

Silence fell. Susannah worried the tissue in her hand, tearing the damp strands apart. "I couldn't bear if he ever looked at me the way our aunt Elda used to," she admitted. "As if Belinda and I ruined her life, coming into it the way we did."

"So this is really your fears keeping the two of you apart," Millie surmised.

Susannah ignored the ache in her throat that usually presaged a fresh bout of tears. "I want him to have a good and happy life, too." Not the kind that was thrust upon him by some latent guilt and/or pre-death promise.

"And where do you think he will find that now, if he's not with you and the kids?" Millie asked gently.

Susannah shrugged, aware she hadn't ever felt this dejected or depressed. She still couldn't believe Gabe had kept all this from her. "He still has his work with Physicians Without Borders."

"Honey," Mike said, patting her hand, "I don't think that will begin to fulfill him, not after what he's had this summer with all of you. So the question you have to ask yourself is, who is really hurting who tonight—and why?"

* * *

Cade had his shirt off and was filling two large plastic bags with ice when Gabe walked in the door. Even from ten feet away, Gabe could see the swelling and bruising on the benched pitcher's shoulder. And he knew right then he'd been right to worry, that the reason Cade had stayed in Dallas had been to avoid Gabe's professional medical scrutiny. "Looks like you've been overdoing it," he said, figuring this was one more area of his life where he'd failed someone close to him.

Cade cut four lengths of tape, attaching them to the end of the kitchen counter as he went. "Perhaps you are mistaking me for one of the quints you are soon to be adopting," he joked, then added wryly, "But I don't need a manny."

Gabe exhaled, thinking about how it had all gone wrong. Earlier this evening, he'd had it all. Now… he had nothing. "I'm not going to be adopting them after all," he reported sadly.

Cade gave Gabe a long look, then taped the bags around his shoulder with the ease of an athlete who had done so many times. "Three hours ago you were."

Gabe paced. "Susannah called it off."

His brother did a double take. "Why would she do that?"

Briefly, Gabe explained about the postcard and the college funds he'd set up. "Although personally," he added grimly, "I think it's more than that."

Cade cast him a curious glance. "Like what?"

Gabe shrugged. "I don't know. Cold feet," he

guessed. "She's always been pretty independent. Maybe the idea of hitching her future to anyone else is more than she can tolerate." Hell, maybe it was just him. Maybe she'd changed her mind about the viability of their convenient marriage and had just been looking for a way out. Finding out what he had done in trying to protect her had given her that.

Cade pulled two beers out of the fridge, handed one to Gabe. "Mom and Dad are going to be so disappointed," Cade said sympathetically. "Me, too. I thought you really had it all together this time."

Gabe wanted to believe that. The proof said otherwise. "Did you hear their toasts tonight? Both Mike's and Dad's?" He paused to let his words sink in. "They were a little awkward, to say the least."

Cade sat down on a sofa in the main living area and waited for Gabe to join him. "The whole situation is awkward as hell, given how fast and unexpectedly it's come about," he said sagely. "That doesn't mean we all don't want to see you happy, though, which I still think means having you all together as the family you seem to have become. At least, if you and Susannah have the kind of love and commitment it takes to make a relationship last." He shrugged affably. "But maybe not, if you can't even make it from the rehearsal dinner to the ceremony without splitting up."

Gabe reflected on the time that had passed since he returned to Texas. "We do have that," he said before he could stop himself. "At least, I think we do."

Cade grinned. "All right, then. Want me to try and talk some sense into her?"

This was a first. Cade coming to *his* aid. Gabe felt the first glimmer of hope. "What would you say?"

"That you may be a responsible guy who has devoted his whole life to rescuing others. But there's a limit, even for you. And I think proposing marriage to someone just to fulfill a long-ago promise falls into that category." Cade paused to let his words sink in. "Or am I wrong?"

Gabe tensed. "I didn't propose marriage to her for that reason." Not even one that was convenient.

Cade nodded sagely. "Then maybe before anyone else gets in the middle of this, you should tell her the *real* reason you did."

After Mike and Millie left, Susannah washed the tears from her face, changed into her pajamas and sat staring at her cell phone, her heart awash in abject misery. It was nearly one o'clock in the morning.

It's not too late. He might still be up. Even if he's not, you could call and wake him up. Because it isn't over until it's over. And for her, despite the harsh words they had exchanged before the short, silent drive home, it did not feel over. Far from it.

Drawing a deep breath, she picked up her phone yet again. The screen flashed with an incoming text.

Gabe's ID appeared onscreen. You up? he wrote.

Her heart was in her throat. She forced herself to let go and trust. Not just in him. But that with love and effort, they would be able to work this all out. Yes, she typed back.

Can we talk? he texted in return.

Yes. *Heavens, yes!*

I'm outside.

Her heart skipped a beat. Be right there. Susannah quickly dressed and tiptoed down the stairs. Then, switching on the outside lamp, she eased out the front door, Daisy by her side. Gabe was standing on the porch, clad in his running clothes, hands braced on his hips, cell phone still in his hand. His whiskey-colored eyes were serious, intent. "Hey," he said softly.

Joy mixed with anxiety. "Hey." Tears threatened yet again. Though she yearned to just throw herself in his arms and let the physical side of their relationship make amends, she knew they couldn't just ignore their problems. They had to deal with them head-on as they came up. And first off, there was something she had to say. She took his hand in hers. "I'm so sorry, Gabe. I completely overreacted tonight."

He regarded her steadily, his eyes alight with kindness and another emotion she couldn't identify. "Why?" he asked, just as quietly.

With a deep breath, she continued, "For years now, ever since my parents died, I've been afraid to want or need anything from anyone, for fear that I would become a liability to them, the way Belinda and I were to our aunt Elda."

He nodded, acknowledging he knew this to be true.

She gripped his hand tightly, relying on his warmth and his strength. "So I've tried really hard not to ask anything of anyone, unless there was some way to repay them in return. I didn't want to burden anyone or be in their debt." Mike and Millie had understood that, as had the mothers in the Multiples Club, letting her repay every kindness with one of her own.

"And you succeeded," he said admiringly.

"With everyone but you," Susannah told him quietly, finally admitting to the guilt and uncertainty that had secretly been plaguing her.

She drew a deep breath and spoke from her heart. "But when you entered our lives this summer, everything started to change."

His eyes darkened. This, he hadn't known. "In what way?"

Susannah gulped. "As much as I wanted to, I couldn't seem to maintain the internal score keeping that has always kept me on an even keel." She held his gaze and forced herself to go on. "Even more alarming, I found myself wanting the kinds of things I had never allowed myself to yearn for, like a husband to love who would love me back and help me raise the kids. And a traditional marriage. And that in turn made me start to not just want but need you in my life."

"As your partner, in all things related to love and family."

Nodding, Susannah released a shuddering breath. "And I have to tell you that really scared me, because I knew you were leaving again at summer's end. And deep down, even though I said I was okay with that," she admitted, her lower lip quivering, "I wasn't sure I would be when it came time to say goodbye."

"And yet you agreed to the terms of our marriage of convenience."

Susannah nodded and confessed what was in her heart. "I wanted to give you what you wanted and needed, too, and I know how much your work means to you. So if that meant long absences… I was willing to abide by that and do whatever else was necessary to make our relationship work."

His face relaxed, and he moved closer still.

Basking in his nearness, Susannah continued, "So, you need to know, when you do go, the kids and I'll be right here, waiting for you. And the only thing we'll feel when you do return is happiness to see you."

He smiled, every inch of him resolute male. "Guaranteed?"

Susannah drew a stabilizing breath and forced herself to be completely honest. "Guaranteed."

The look in his eyes said he understood what a sacrifice that was for her. He wrapped an arm about her waist and held fast. "That means a lot to me," he told her gently.

She blinked back a mist of emotion. "Good."

"But it's not going to be necessary," he told her sternly. "Because I'm not going anywhere."

She waited, not sure she'd heard right.

He tightened his grip on her and confided, "You're not the only one who's been doing some soul-searching this summer. I've learned some things about myself, too."

A shiver swept through her. Aware how close she

was to surrendering to him on any terms, she asked, "Such as…?"

His lips curved into a sexy smile. "For a long time, I thought I had to go far away to be really of service as a physician, but my work at the local hospital and the medical crisis with Millie and Mike proved I could be of value here, too."

Ignoring the sudden wobbliness of her knees, Susannah tried to figure out where this was going. "Then why were you so set on going back to Physicians Without Borders?"

Sorrow mingled with the joy on his handsome face. "Because when it came to you and me and our relationship, and my concern for the kids, I was still all tied up in my own regrets and fears."

Opening up as never before, he went on, confessing soberly, "I tried to make up for past mistakes and the loss of my birth parents by devoting my life to helping others, but only those I was not overly close with. But when I started spending time with you and the quintuplets, my ability to stay emotionally remote went all to hell."

She thought about the way her children had plowed past all his defenses, with their never-ending questions and requests, and guessed it had. They had forced him to let down his guard, and she and he had done the same for each other, too. Forcing each other to change, like it or not.

He flashed a rueful grin. "You—and the quintuplets—made me take a good, hard look at myself and open up my heart."

Drawing her in against him, he kissed her temple. "The more time I spent here, the more I realized just how lonely I had been and how good it felt to be needed on a truly personal level." He drew back to gaze into her eyes. "And how much I longed to have you and the kids as my family."

"Why didn't you tell me about the request Belinda and Brett had made as we did get closer, then?" she asked cautiously, recalling how much it had hurt when she'd seen the note on that postcard and found out what else he had done behind her back. "Or let me know about the college funds?"

He inhaled sharply. "I knew how independent you were, and worried you'd reject my help on principle if you knew."

Sad to say, she probably would have.

"And I couldn't bear to lose you over that," he admitted in a voice that was thick with emotion. "And I didn't know how I would survive if that happened, because you've made me happier this summer than I ever imagined I could be."

She thought about all the times they'd spent as a family. How wonderful it had been when they had been able to steal a little time alone and make love. "You've made me really happy, too, Gabe," she whispered as happiness and relief welled up within her, too.

Gabe's eyes smiled first, then his mouth. "I love you, Susannah Alexander, with all my heart and soul."

"I love you, too, Gabe Lockhart," she murmured as he kissed her sweetly and cuddled her close.

He stroked a hand through her hair, another down her spine. "Glad to hear it," he said tenderly, kissing her yet again, "'cause I turned in my resignation letter to PWB a half an hour ago and wrote the head of the hospital here to let them know I would like the job on the diagnostic team. My life is here. With you. And the kids. And Daisy."

Who came over to be petted, her tail wagging.

"Speaking of our life together…" Or the one they'd had planned up until a few hours before.

Here was her chance. The opportunity to take that giant leap of faith.

Susannah looked into his eyes and continued with every ounce of courage and feeling in her heart. "Did you tell your parents the wedding was off?"

"No." He gave her a look that left no doubt about the depth of feelings he had for her, too. His breath sighed out, mirroring her relief. "Because in my mind, even though we had an argument, it was never really all the way off. Did you tell Millie and Mike?"

"I…tried. They weren't having any of it."

Understanding lit his expression.

"They swore I had a case of the bridal jitters and told me to sleep on it, that I would feel differently in the morning."

He grinned down at her, brows waggling, then nodded at his watch, which showed it was 1:30 a.m. "Well," he teased, "it is already morning…" He tightened his arms around her. "And that officially makes it our wedding day."

Her heart kicked against her rib cage. Joy swept

her soul. "You still want to get married as planned?" she asked hopefully.

"I do." He sealed the vow with another long and leisurely lip lock, then looked down at her, all the love and passion he felt for her reflected in his eyes. "But this time, for all the right reasons. Because we love each other and want a real marriage together, in all respects."

"For now. And forever," Susannah agreed, holding him close.

"So that's a yes to my proposal?" he said.

Susannah grinned, happier than she'd ever thought she could be. "Most definitely a yes!"

Epilogue

Movie night, ten and a half months later

"We'll help Mommy get the popcorn!" Gretchen and Rebecca said, taking on their usual chore.

"And we'll get the drinks!" Connor and Levi jumped into action.

"And Daddy," four and a half-year-old Abigail directed soberly, "you set up the movie."

Gabe didn't even have to ask which one. There was only one video the quints wanted to view on special occasions. And with their first Father's Day happening tomorrow, this evening promised to be a very special night. Both before and after the kids were asleep.

"Will do," he promised, catching Susannah's eye.

She smiled at him, looking gorgeous as ever in a spaghetti-strap sundress covered in wildflowers, reminiscent of the scent she wore. Her hair had been up all day. He itched to run his fingers through the sexy locks now tumbling down around her shoulders. And promised himself that and more would happen in due time. Meantime, he wanted to enjoy their family time with the quints.

A flurry of activity followed—snacks were arranged, seating discussed. Finally, all seven of them were settled on the sofa—Gabe and Susannah in the middle, Rebecca between them, Levi and Gretchen sprawled on their laps, Connor and Abigail cuddling close beside them. Daisy, as usual was curled up at their feet in front of the sofa, too. Gabe slanted another look at his wife. She had a look of such utter bliss on her face he couldn't help but smile. "Everybody ready?" he asked.

"Yes!" the kids chorused.

He and Susannah locked gazes as readily as they had already locked hearts. "Okay, then, here goes." Savoring the happiness that had inundated every corner of his life, Gabe hit the play button on the remote control.

His parents' ranch came into focus. The kids oohed and ahhed as Gabe took his place at the altar beside the minister.

"Here comes Daisy!" Abigail announced.

The golden retriever lifted her head and stared at the TV screen as if she too were remembering that very special summer day.

Onscreen, a decked-out Daisy could be seen trotting happily up the aisle in advance of the three beautifully dressed flower girls, who were busy strewing rose petals that matched the wreaths in their hair.

"Our dresses are so pretty," Rebecca sighed happily.

"It was a happy day." Gretchen beamed.

"Very happy indeed." Susannah gave Gabe a look that seemed to telegraph all the love in her heart. Aware she and the kids were the best thing to ever happen to him, he sent her one right back.

The strains of Pachelbel's "Canon in D" continued. "And here we come with the rings!" Levi and Connor said in unison.

They, too, looked adorable in their little tuxedos.

"And now Mommy," the girls breathed.

Susannah appeared onscreen in all her wedding finery. The videographer had done a split screen; Gabe was on one side, watching her come toward him, and she on the other, practically floating up the aisle, on Mike's arm, she was so happy.

When it came time to ask who gave her away, Mike and Millie and the kids stepped in and all said *they* did…

And from there, it was just Susannah and Gabe, pledging their love to one another and promising each other the future while their children beamed at their sides.

"And now they get to kiss!" Levi shouted when the vows had come to an end.

And kiss they did.

In a way that was both short and sweet but still worked up the crowd around them. Hearing the hoots and hollers and whistles, the kids echoed more of their own. When they finally quieted, the music started again jubilantly, and Gabe and Susannah marched back down the aisle, arm in arm, holding hands with all their children in the process.

The quints watched happily until the ceremony ended and then got up to dance in remembrance as the scene shifted to the reception. The music turned lively, and some of their favorite celebratory moments...including first dance, and cake cutting, and bouquet toss...ensued.

When all the popcorn was gone and the video ended, the kids clapped and cheered. "That was the best wedding ever!" Connor declared, and his siblings joyously concurred.

Gabe winked at Susannah. "Have to agree with you all there."

Bedtime followed. When the kids were all sound asleep, Susannah and Gabe met up outside on the back deck for a glass of wine while Daisy dozed nearby. "Think they'll ever get tired of their favorite movie?" she teased.

He wrapped his arm around her and pressed a kiss in her hair. "Doubtful. But it's okay. It's good to remember the official start of our life together as a couple and as a family."

"I think so, too." Susannah leaned in to kiss him. "And on that note, you know what tomorrow is..."

He squinted, pretending to think. "June fifteenth, maybe, or is it the fourteenth?"

She didn't buy his feigned confusion for one hot second. "Ha-ha. It's Father's Day."

"So it is," he murmured, his voice turning as tender as their feelings.

Susannah took his glass in hand with hers and put both aside. She turned back, splaying her delicate palms across his chest, provoking the accelerating beat of his heart. Sweet affection shimmered in her pretty sea-blue eyes. "And though the kids have lots planned for you tomorrow, starting with a picnic, I want to go ahead and wish you your first and best Father's Day ever right now."

Love flowed between them, fiercer than ever. He bent his head to hers, and they kissed deeply and tenderly, once again completely in sync with each other.

Knowing their lives were the way they were always meant to be, and that he could never say it often enough, he drew back and cupped her face in his hands. "Thank you for coming into my life and showing me just how happy I could be," he said gruffly.

"Right back at you, Doc," she whispered. "Because I never knew I could be as blissful as this, either." Encircling her arms around his neck, she leaned in close and kissed him again, tenderly at first and then with escalating passion.

When they came up for air, he threaded his hands through her hair and said, "I love you, Susannah Lockhart. So very much."

She laughed softly. "I love you, too, Gabriel Lockhart. So, what do you say we grab our wine and take this party upstairs?"

With a grin and a wink, he gave her his hand. "You bet!"

* * * * *

MILLS & BOON

Coming next month

A YEAR WITH THE MILLIONAIRE NEXT DOOR
Barbara Wallace

"Stella…" He breathed her name into her mouth like it was a prayer. She felt his fingers sliding along her cheeks until they cradled her face. He combed back her hair and pulled away.

"Stella," he repeated.

He was rejecting her.

"Well, isn't this humiliating," she said, backing away. "I…"

Linus backed away, too. The tenderness she imagined in his gaze had morphed into embarrassment. "I should go," he said.

"Yeah, I think that's a good idea."

She kept her attention glued to the coffee table while Linus got up and limped toward the front door. "I'm sorry," he said when he reached the landing. "But I don't think either of us wants to do something we'll regret."

Not trusting herself to speak, Stella only thanked God for that. She'd rambled on about her failings and made a fool out of herself, but at least she hadn't done something she'd regret.

*

Linus closed his front door and collapsed against it. That might have been one of most difficult things he had ever done. *Give yourself a pat on the back, old boy. You behaved like a gentleman.* Eighteen months ago, if a beautiful woman threw herself in his arms, he would have kissed the daylights out of her. Lips that soft and delicious? How could he resist?

But he did resist. Had to. It was clear his neighbor needed a friend far more than she needed sex.

I need to prove I'm not a disappointment.

How could the woman with whom he'd spent the evening disappoint anyone? It was inconceivable. She was funny. Beautiful. Smart.

His rejection probably hadn't helped her self-esteem issues. Still, he'd done the right thing. Maybe that meant he was evolving into a better person. Because for once he cared more about helping a woman than seducing her.

Now if he could only stop thinking about how amazing Stella's lips tasted, he'd be fine.

Continue reading
A YEAR WITH THE MILLIONAIRE NEXT DOOR
Barbara Wallace

Available next month
www.millsandboon.co.uk

COMING SOON!

We really hope you enjoyed reading this book.
If you're looking for more romance, be sure to
head to the shops when new books are
available on

Thursday 23rd July

To see which titles are coming soon, please visit
millsandboon.co.uk/nextmonth

MILLS & BOON
A ROMANCE FOR EVERY READER

- **FREE** delivery direct to your door

- **EXCLUSIVE** offers every month

- **SAVE** up to 25% on pre-paid subscriptions

SUBSCRIBE AND SAVE

millsandboon.co.uk/Subscribe

MILLS & BOON

THE HEART OF ROMANCE

A ROMANCE FOR EVERY KIND OF READER

MODERN

Prepare to be swept off your feet by sophisticated, sexy and seductive heroes, in some of the world's most glamourous and romantic locations, where power and passion collide.
8 stories per month.

HISTORICAL

Escape with historical heroes from time gone by. Whether you passion is for wicked Regency Rakes, muscled Vikings or rugg Highlanders, awaken the romance of the past.
6 stories per month.

MEDICAL

Set your pulse racing with dedicated, delectable doctors in the high-pressure world of medicine, where emotions run high an passion, comfort and love are the best medicine.
6 stories per month.

True Love

Celebrate true love with tender stories of heartfelt romance, f the rush of falling in love to the joy a new baby can bring, and focus on the emotional heart of a relationship.
8 stories per month.

Desire

Indulge in secrets and scandal, intense drama and plenty of s hot action with powerful and passionate heroes who have it al wealth, status, good looks...everything but the right woman.
6 stories per month.

HEROES

Experience all the excitement of a gripping thriller, with an ir romance at its heart. Resourceful, true-to-life women and stro fearless men face danger and desire - a killer combination!
8 stories per month.

DARE

Sensual love stories featuring smart, sassy heroines you'd want best friend, and compelling intense heroes who are worthy of
4 stories per month.

To see which titles are coming soon, please visit

millsandboon.co.uk/nextmonth

MILLS & BOON

HEROES

At Your Service

Experience all the excitement of a gripping thriller, with an intense romance at its heart. Resourceful, true-to-life women and strong, fearless men face danger and desire - a killer combination!

MILLS & BOON
MEDICAL
Pulse-Racing Passion

Set your pulse racing with dedicated, delectable doctors in the high-pressure world of medicine, where emotions run high and passion, comfort and love are the best medicine.

MILLS & BOON
Desire

Indulge in secrets and scandal, intense drama and plenty of sizzling hot action with powerful and passionate heroes who have it all: wealth, status, good looks… everything but the right woman.

MILLS & BOON

HISTORICAL

Awaken the romance of the past

Escape with historical heroes from time gone by. Whether your passion is for wicked Regency Rakes, muscled Viking warriors or rugged Highlanders, indulge your fantasies and awaken the romance of the past.

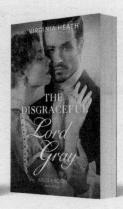